Falling for France

A Foreign Affair

Nancy L. Milby (signature)

Falling for France

A Foreign Affair

A Novel by

Nancy L. Milby

A Word with You Press
Publishers and Purveyors of Fine Stories
310 East A Street, Suite B, Moscow, Idaho 83843

www.awordwithyoupress.com

Milby, Nancy
Falling for France

ISBN-13: 9780988464643
ISBN-10: 0988464640

Falling for France is published by:
Word with You Press, A
310 East A Street, Suite B, Moscow, Idaho 83843

For information please direct emails to:
info@awordwithyoupress.com or visit our website:
www.awordwithyoupress.com

Book cover designed by Teri Rider from a photograph by Nancy Milby
Book interior design: Teri Rider

First Edition, February 2015

Printed in the United States of America

10 9 8 7 6 5 4 3 2 1   15 16 17 18 19 20 21 22 23 24

A Word with You Press˙
Publishers and Purveyors of Fine Stories
310 East A Street, Suite B, Moscow, Idaho 83843

Dedication

To my dear friend Tom dePaolo, for his inspiration and encouragement;
to my husband, Steve, for his unconditional support of yet another crazy
scheme; and to my closest friends who read the first drafts and cheered me
on—you know who you are.
A big thanks to you all—this one is for you.

Prologue

Yosemite National Park, Memorial Day Weekend, 1980

Their destination was Sierra Point, a wedge of granite jutting out into the mighty Merced River canyon, high above the water at the bend below Vernal Falls. Their path was a poorly marked trail of switchbacks up the north side of the canyon, a little-known, neglected spur off an otherwise popular trail.

Annie Shaw and Jack Campbell walked out of camp, hand in hand in the quiet pre-dawn, while the mist hung thick and sleepy over the river. The coming day was not yet in evidence—the narrow patch of sky visible between the canyon walls that soared high above them still black—but moonlight reflected off the granite cliffs, bathing the valley in an ethereal glow that lighted their path.

Morning alpenglow painted the stark peaks of the high Sierra a vibrant red gold, bestowing a brief, gloriously rare vision on the hikers as they crested their summit two hours later. They paused to catch their breath in the cold, thin air, standing together, watching, as it faded from the upper cliffs. As if in encore, the sky brightened to an almost painful blue, a blue that's possible only in the pristine air of high-altitude wilderness. And then the sun peeked over the far eastern horizon like a halo, drenching the silhouette of the distant peaks in ethereal light that blackened the inside of the near canyon walls for an instant while turning the sky white in its intensity. As the red-rimmed edge rose into a yellow ball above the landscape, the magic light evaporated and the day was born.

Their breath still ragged from the hike up the rough trail, they spooned together on a large rock facing the view. Annie was enveloped like a blanket in Jack's warmth, her back resting on his chest, his breath tickling the back of her neck, and his strong arms holding her under the girth of her expanded belly. They continued to watch the unfolding day as the morning dew on the tips of tree branches twinkled momentarily when the sunlight touched them, then blinked out like so many tiny camera flashes being swallowed up in a floodlight. When the edge of sunlight hit the rising mist above Nevada Falls, it was like a giant chandelier that sparkled for an instant before the light absorbed it all.

The natural sounds of the awakening canyon began to grow louder, or perhaps became more noticeable to them as their breath calmed. The trills of birds, the shuffle of small critters, and the roar of the majestic falls below combined like a symphony playing for their ears only.

Annie was suddenly hot. Sweat trickled down between her breasts under her shirt, and she started to lean forward, away from the human furnace behind her, when she felt the warm brush of his lips on the sensitive skin behind her earlobe.

She shivered, forgetting her plan, instead tilting her head to the side to allow him better access. His hand moved up from beneath her belly and rubbed the mound gently in a soothing motion. On cue, the baby started to roll around.

"I love you." A whisper in her ear as soft as a sigh. She exhaled and gave in to the sensation, forgetting her discomfort for a moment to revel in her husband's tender care.

Jack closed his eyes and drew Annie tighter to his chest, taking care not to squeeze her too tightly in the middle. He rested his hands on her belly as their child—their daughter—continued her gymnastics. The sensation never failed to disarm him.

Face buried in Annie's curly hair, he breathed deeply. She smelled faintly of campfire smoke, and he smiled, thankful that she took the lack of creature comforts with his family's camping holiday in stride. For a brief moment, he let his imagination wander into the future, where he pictured his precious girls laughing together next to a campfire with charred marshmallows at the end of sticks.

Annie shifted, turned around in his arms, and kissed him, her dark eyes full of love. Jack hugged her tighter, taking in the beauty of their perch and the radiance of her smile, knowing their privacy was limited. Before long, other ambitious hikers would invade their solitary moment.

"We should go, sweetheart," he whispered into her ear as he stroked back her curls. "I don't want to share this spot with anyone but you." He kissed her and inclined his head in the direction of the trail. "Are you ready?"

"Mhmm, and I'm hungry, too, but I confess I'm afraid of your mother. If we go straight to breakfast now, maybe she won't figure out that I've been hiking."

Jack cringed inwardly but only nodded. "If she asks, we'll say we went out for an early walk, which is true." He hoped that his mother would keep her mouth shut, but that wasn't her way. She may have grudgingly accepted the marriage to Annie, but she'd made it her mission to criticize every move his wife made. He buried that thought as he stood and reached his hand out to help Annie up.

The walk back down the mountain was unhurried, the narrow trail necessitating a single-file arrangement. And while the hike up had been more strenuous, it took less balance. In Annie's seven-months-pregnant state, she struggled on the uneven trail since she couldn't see where her feet landed.

Twenty minutes from the summit, they'd still not seen another hiker when the forest around them came to an abrupt silence. The silence came so fast, was so unnatural, that Annie and Jack both stopped and looked at each other. In the next moment, their world rocked. Literally. As they stood together on that precarious, narrow trail in the Yosemite wilderness, more than five hundred feet above the valley floor, the mountain started to shake.

They held frozen in horrified silence, clinging to each other as the violence of the tremors increased. There was nowhere to run, no place to take cover. The steep slope above and below was blanketed in pine and fir trees, nothing to offer any sort of protection, and the trail of switchbacks was all that stood between the drop-off of the river canyon behind them and the steep cut of a ravine in front. They were trapped.

The shaking became so intense, they had to stand with legs splayed, hugging each other to stay upright. Then the lurching stopped and the ground became still again, the only evidence of the earthquake in the creak and groan of the swaying trees around them and the soft rain of dust and pine needles dislodged from branches above. They stared, shocked, into each other's eyes.

"Whoa," Jack said, breathing a shaky sigh of relief. "Let's get out of here." He took her hand and turned to continue down the hill.

They had taken only a few steps when a loud *crack* ruptured the silence above them, followed by a low rumble that quickly turned into a crashing roar. The ground shook again, not from an aftershock but from a boulder the size of a delivery truck, shaken loose from the top of the ridge, that was now careering down the slope, taking a perfect but deadly track straight through the switchbacks of the Sierra Point trail.

Annie screamed, and Jack yelled, "*Run!*" as he grabbed her and hurled her ahead of him. They pounded down the trail, Jack pushing her from behind, but Annie's awkward bulk worked against her, and she tripped on a root, smacking facedown on the trail so hard, she bit her lip and felt a piercing pain in her abdomen.

Jack almost trampled her before he caught himself and sidestepped on the downhill slope, tripping himself and rolling a bit before being stopped by a tree.

"*Annie!*" he shouted as he quickly clambered back up, the crashing of the boulder shaking the ground as it bounced its way through trees and over rocks, pulling a growing avalanche of forest debris in its wake. Jack fought through the terror clouding his brain, realized they were near the north edge of the switchbacks, and prayed they could reach it in time.

In a desperate move, he grabbed Annie by the back of her jacket and the seat of her pants, and threw her forward toward the edge of the slope, just as the careering boulder came into view. She cried out, landing hard on her backside as he dove after her.

For an agonizing, slow-motion few seconds, Annie thought Jack would clear the crashing wreckage, but just as his body was arching toward her in the air, the protruding branch of a tree at the forward edge of the avalanche caught his hip and ripped him away down the mountain. Annie stared at him in frozen horror as his expression changed from grim determination, to shocked realization, to profound sadness … it all flashed across his face in an instant as his eyes locked with hers.

And then he was gone, swept away in a sickening wave of rocks, trees, pine needles, and dust.

"*Jaaack!*" She clutched her belly as she screamed his name.

The force of the passing boulder snapped centuries-old trees like toothpicks and uprooted any that dared to not break, causing an ever-growing cascade of tumbling mountainside. Annie felt the ground beneath her start to slide and pushed farther toward the edge, off the trail and out of the way of the avalanche, only to find herself toppling like a rag doll down the ravine at the edge of the slope. Before she could gather a breath to scream, she slammed to a stop, wedged against a tree.

She was so stunned that for a moment, she felt nothing as she struggled to breathe. The avalanche thundered in her ears, spraying her with dirt as it passed. Then, as quickly as it had begun, it ended. In the eerie quiet, she tried to open her eyes, her brain protesting the truth of what had just happened. And then the pain hit her like a hot poker stabbed straight into her gut. She opened her mouth to cry out, but the searing agony was so intense, she didn't utter a sound. Then everything went black.

One

San Francisco, July 1988

Annie Shaw tossed back the last of her vodka tonic, clutched the glass in front of her on the table, and surveyed the crowd in the grand ballroom of the St. Francis hotel. *So, here I am,* she told herself again. She had worked hard, put in long hours, played the game well, and got lucky breaks when she needed them. Two weeks ago, it had all paid off, and tonight's party celebrated her newly minted status and admission to that most coveted of private clubs, the partnership of Smith Cole Blakely. The largest accounting firm in the world.

Now what? The excitement of a goal achieved was already overshadowed by a floundering sense of dislodgement, like the floor was slipping out from underneath her. This is what she wanted, what she'd worked toward, relentlessly, for the past eight years. The brutal focus had kept the past in the past, the guilt closed away. But now? *No idea how to keep playing that game.*

She lifted her glass for another sip, realized it was empty, and set it back down. She tried to remember why she had wanted this so badly. *I'm more at risk now than ever,* she realized and wondered if every new partner went through this feeling of dismay or if hers was just a special case.

"Having second thoughts?"

Startled, Annie let go of her glass and looked up to see her boss, mentor, and friend pulling out the chair next to her.

She smiled weakly, shaking her head. "Just a slight case of buyers' remorse," she said. *Not to mention a horrible feeling that I've only delayed the inevitable.*

"Annie, don't let these guys worry you," John Franklin said, misreading her concern. "I know exactly what you're thinking because I thought it too, twenty years ago at my first partner meeting. But I guarantee you'll come to realize that not only are they a bright bunch of people, but they also have no balls at all, and that's to our benefit."

He smiled at her look of dismay. "Not one of them would risk their career by making a tough call for a client," he laughed, "without consulting a committee of the people who stand to lose the most. Why make a stand alone when you can make the senior partners take a stand for you?"

"Gee, that's comforting." *What would he say if he knew the real problem?*

"You should consider what *they* are probably thinking," he continued with a knowing smile while he surveyed the ballroom. "They're worried about *you*. They see a *younger* woman who is smarter and more confident than most of them. They've got a hell of a lot more to lose here than you do. Instead of thinking how *they* will cause *your* ruin, consider how *you* might convince *them* that you won't cause theirs."

Annie laughed. She hadn't thought of it that way, but yeah, it made sense. John was a true friend and had been since she joined the firm fourteen years ago. But she wished his wife was here now. Marie would understand, but spouses hadn't been invited to this meet-and-greet soirée.

John surreptitiously studied his new partner as she gazed out over the room. It was good to hear her laugh, even if it was in self-deprecation rather than joy. God knows she'd had little joy in the last eight years. Professional success to be sure, but nothing that could be called *joy*.

After that horrible accident in Yosemite, it had taken Annie a long time to recover. When she'd finally been pulled off the mountain, she was little more than a broken heap. But the multiple leg fractures, dislocated collarbone, cracked ribs, and concussion were physical hurts that could heal over time. Unlike the late-term miscarriage and the loss of her beloved husband.

Annie had not regained consciousness during the rescue effort and had remained in a coma for almost two weeks afterward. *Which was probably just as well,* John thought, given what she had to face when she finally woke up.

Her body had healed, but her heart continued to bleed. Not that she spoke to him about it; what John knew came from his wife. After the accident, Annie and Marie had become close. If it weren't for Marie's vigilance at her bedside, John doubted Annie would have found her way back. Studying her now, John could only admire her courage and fortitude. Once she'd been able to shake off the worst of her grief, she had pasted on a bland face, returned to work, and dived in.

John came out of his reverie and saw that Annie was frowning at him. Straightening and clearing his throat, he glanced at the empty glass on the table, nodded at it. "Can I get you another?"

"No, thanks. I think I'll take off. The social whirl is giving me a headache." She smiled again, this time small but genuine. She really was quite striking when she smiled. John wished, for her sake, she did it more often.

"All right." He leaned over and squeezed her hand. "I'll see you in a few weeks. Enjoy your time off. And congratulations again, Annie. You deserve this, and I'm proud to call you partner."

Annie nodded her thanks, left the ballroom, and walked through the main lobby out the front door to catch a cab home.

The next morning dawned bright and clear—a perfect day by the bay, and Annie didn't waste a minute of it. She bounced out of bed, threw on sweats and sneakers, shoved her wallet into a pocket, and ran down the stairs to the street. She walked toward the Embarcadero at a fast clip, dodging the random bum sprawled out on the sidewalk.

Her favorite café was warm and cheery. She snagged a section of the *Chronicle* from the community table, and scooted up to the counter. "Morning, Mac," she said to the kid at the counter. "Give it to me in a big bowl, please. I'll drink it here this morning."

"Sure thing, Annie," Mac replied, turning to pull a huge cup from the shelf. "Beautiful day out there. I hope you get to enjoy it—I'm stuck here till midafternoon."

She smiled at him. "I'm going to bask in it."

Mac handed her the coffee, took her money, and tossed the change in the tip jar when she waved her hand at it. "Thanks, Annie, enjoy."

Updated on the world news and filled with her morning quota of coffee, Annie headed out, an hour later, into the gorgeous San Francisco morning. It was still too early for the bookstore, but she headed toward downtown anyway, walking along the waterfront at a fast pace to get her heart pumping. As she walked, her mind went back to the party the night before and her conversation with John Franklin. There was no question she had been in an odd state of mind, and John had understood some of it—the professional angst—because that part stemmed from her change of status at the firm. The transition from being an employee to being a partner—an owner—had scary financial considerations. As crazy as it seemed, the most significant promotion of her life could in fact equate to a reduction in pay, at least initially, not to mention a significant exposure to liability.

To become a partner at the largest accounting firm in the world was as prestigious as it was financially challenging. In fact, it was the complete opposite of what most people thought. With the promotion her billing rate went from $375 to a whopping $500 per hour. Most assumed she was taking home a good portion of that, but it was an illusion. She saw very little of it personally.

But beyond the frightening financial implications—including the fact that she was now joint and severally liable for all mistakes in the firm—was the question of what came next. It was the goal of becoming partner that had her so focused for the past years. It had kept the gnawing guilt at bay, and it had given her purpose. But wasn't she beyond that now? Her drive had perhaps begun as a distraction, but now her pride and self-esteem were involved. Whatever her initial motivation, she'd achieved something remarkable. She was proud of her accomplishment—very proud.

As she walked, she thought as honestly and objectively as she could about where she was in her life. She was very good at her job. She'd created a lucrative niche for herself in the firm, not just locally but also nationally. As a partner she would now have complete autonomy with her clients—the kind of freedom a small practitioner had—yet she had the vast resources of a giant firm at her fingertips when she needed them. It was a heady, powerful place to be. She was young, smart, energized, and respected. She'd earned her place at the table, and she couldn't wait to make her mark.

A planner to the nth degree, she pondered her new status as she walked, sketching out the next years in her mind and formulating new goals. Down the Embarcadero to Pier 39, around Telegraph Hill, then back down Columbus to California, her circuit took her to the front stoop of the bookstore just as the door was being unlocked.

With a nod of thanks to the elderly lady who brandished the key, Annie stepped over to one of the stacks and took her bearings, inhaling deeply. She loved this bookstore—loved the tantalizing aromas of dust and ink as well as the barely contained clutter of the packed shelves—but she rarely indulged. But now, she had the perfect excuse: twelve hours on a plane and many lazy hours on a park bench somewhere in Paris.

She wandered around, perusing titles, pulling random books off the shelf to read the inside jacket, relishing the idea of burying herself in someone else's fantasy. Eventually she settled on a mystery, an action thriller, and an historical romance set in Paris before the revolution. Turning back down the aisle toward the cashier, Annie stopped dead in her tracks. Five feet in front of her, blocking the way, jaw clenched in an ugly sneer, stood her former mother-in-law.

Shit. Annie hadn't seen Sarah Campbell in eight years, not since she'd allowed the horrid woman to take Jack's stuff. It had been the end of a hellish affair, and she still had a hard time believing anyone could be so cruel. Sarah had buried her son while Annie was still in a coma, then came banging on the door to their apartment as soon as Annie was released from the hospital, demanding all of Jack's belongings. Annie ignored her, but a draining cycle of nasty-grams and threats of restraining orders ensued. Too weary to fight any longer, Annie packed up Jack's meager belongings and let Sarah come back to get it all. They hadn't spoken since.

Now, the woman looked worse than ever—meaner, if that was possible. Annie got her feet working again and moved toward her, intending to simply walk past. Sarah looked Annie up and down, then looked at the books in Annie's arms and smirked before she hissed, "Reading trash, I see. Like sticks with like."

Annie gritted her teeth, held her head up, and kept walking. She could feel Sarah's black gaze shooting daggers at her back. *God damn it, get over it. She's a cold bitch and she's not your problem,* she told herself. She forced her hand not to shake as she handed over her credit card, then took the bag and walked away calmly, but inside she was seething. *You did nothing wrong.* She repeated her old mantra as the familiar ache threatened to crack her open.

Suddenly exhausted and depressed, Annie walked back to her apartment with a heavy heart. She hadn't thought about Jack, their baby, or Sarah, for a long time. She had kept herself busy and moved on with her life, even if that meant working eighty-hour weeks. But it was *her* life, she'd made it what it was, and she was good with that. She cursed Sarah again. There was nothing wrong with her, nothing wrong with her decisions, and Sarah was nothing to her. She was at the top of her game and had just hit the goal most people in her profession only dream of achieving. Why then, did she let Sarah's derision get under her skin?

It was just past noon when she finally pushed her way into her apartment, nine o'clock in the evening in Paris. She picked up the phone, suddenly needing to talk to her friend.

"Annie? Hey!"

"Hey, Lori," she said, hearing the flatness of her own voice.

Lori Sheridan recognized it, too. "Oh no, no you don't. You are *not* canceling. I don't care what happened, you need this trip and I need you here, too."

"No, no, don't worry. God, I must sound as shaky as I feel." She let out a half laugh and took a deep breath. "I just saw Sarah Campbell."

"Oh, shit."

"You got that right. Her face is even more pinched, if you can believe that." Annie related the scene, and they laughed together at Sarah's trashy novel comment. Laughing with her friend eased the ache in Annie's heart and helped her dismiss the ugly encounter once they'd joked about how ridiculous it was.

"In just a few days, we'll be sipping French wine at a corner café," Lori said.

As Annie hung up the phone, she smiled, realizing her mood had swung back to happy. *Fuck you, Sarah. You can't touch me anymore.*

Two

Paris, France, July 1988

"Annie!"

Annie looked up over the sea of heads in front of her, then grinned and waved. She worked her way through the crowd swarming the baggage claim exit, dragging her suitcase and overstuffed carry-on bag behind her, then let go of the handles as Lori pulled her into a tight embrace.

"I can't believe I'm finally here!" Annie drew back and held her friend at arm's length. "Wow, you really look great!"

Lori grinned. "You too, girlfriend. It's been way too long. Come on, let's get out of here," she said, shouldering her friend's carry-on. "It's about a forty-five-minute train ride into Paris, and then you can relax."

Annie glanced down at her sleek, new, red roller bag, stuffed to capacity, as they headed for the train station across the terminal. "I hope I can haul this thing up and down stairs. It's pretty heavy."

Lori just laughed. At the Paris station, Annie schlepped her suitcase off the train, up, down, and around to the Metro station, then down more long corridors and another set of stairs until they found the right platform. Annie was sweating from the exertion but impressed at how easily her friend seemed to navigate the transit systems. She commented on it when they exited the final train at the station in Lori's neighborhood.

"I never go anywhere without my trusty Metro map," Lori said, holding it up. "You almost always have to transfer to get anywhere, but the stations are well-marked inside. So as long as you know the direction you're going, it's easy." She grinned as she started up the stairs from the station to the street. "Unless you're hauling a heavy suitcase."

"Yes, I can see that," Annie said as she struggled to drag her bag up the steps with both hands. At the top, she stopped and blew out her breath. *"Phew! I'll be in great shape at the end of this trip! Haven't the French heard of escalators?"* But she didn't hear the answer. She was too busy looking around her at all the motion and buzz of the city.

"Wow. *Wow.* I'm really here. It's awesome! Oh my God, is that the Opera House?" Both hands were still attached to her bag handle, but she pointed with her chin up the busy street to the elaborate white rectangular structure in the middle of the avenue, topped with winged creatures sculpted in gold on either side of an ornate cupola.

Lori nodded. "Pretty impressive, isn't it?"

"Wow" was all Annie could manage. They walked up the broad boulevard, crossed a couple of streets then turned right on Rue St. Augustine. Lori stopped in front of a huge wooden door, punched in a code, then stepped through a smaller cutout door, holding it open for Annie.

They emerged inside a large, cobblestone courtyard bisected by a row of mature trees in full foliage. The trees shaded the area without blocking out the light, giving the space an appealing atmosphere. Several Adirondack-style chairs were scattered around, suggesting the residents take advantage of the serenity here.

Beyond the trees, the entrance to the apartment building was marked by a stone archway. Lori opened the door to a narrow foyer and a massive flight of stairs. Annie groaned as she looked at them warily. Her friend burst into laughter.

"Fortunately for you, there's a lift. Barely big enough for the two of us plus your bag, but it works." They squeezed themselves and the huge suitcase into the tiny space, and the elevator lurched into motion.

Lori's apartment was more spacious than Annie had imagined it would be, with the elegant, classic lines of an earlier era. The tall windows in the sitting room stood open, revealing a narrow balcony that overlooked the courtyard below. The elaborate scrolled iron railing that adorned it was quintessentially

Parisian. Annie took a deep breath of the fresh breeze coming through, feeling like she could finally let go and relax.

Willi's Wine Bar on the Rue des Petits Champs was less than three blocks from the apartment and one of Lori's favorite haunts. The space was cramped, but the service was friendly and the homemade potato chips were delicious. It was a warm evening, and as they sipped a lovely dry, crisp rosé from Provence, Annie declared she was in heaven.

They talked about everything and nothing as girlfriends do, sliding into a comfortable familiarity as if it had been three weeks, not three years, since they'd last been together.

"You know," Annie said when there was a lull in the conversation, "that episode with Sarah made me realize that I need to move on."

Lori raised her eyebrows but said nothing.

"Jack will always have a special place in my heart. We didn't even get two years together, but I still love him. I always will, but ..." Annie trailed off, looking down at her hands gripping her wine glass. "I don't think he would have wanted me to be alone, to give up on love. I think he would have wanted me to find it again."

"I think you're right. It's been eight years, and you've grieved long enough. Finding love again is not disrespecting Jack."

Annie sighed. "I see that, I really do. And honestly, I stopped grieving for Jack years ago. I've let him go." *All but the guilt,* she didn't say. "It's just that I've been so focused at work, I haven't paid attention to anything else. Besides, I'm not exactly a magnet for men." She shook her head as if just figuring it out.

"Don't be ridiculous. You're a beautiful woman."

She felt her cheeks turn pink. "Thanks, but ... I realize I've had a 'do not disturb' sign stamped on my forehead all these years, and I'm not sure how to get rid of it. I doubt I'd recognize a man's interest unless he slapped me in the face."

"Let's hope it doesn't come to that," Lori said with a laugh. "And here's your perfect chance to start shedding that reserve. You've got two weeks in the

City of Love. Paris is a passionate place. What better place to let yourself open up? Don't look at your feet—look into people's eyes. You might be surprised."

The thought of putting herself out there, being vulnerable again, made Annie shudder, but as scary as it was, part of her wanted to give it a try. How bad could it be? It wasn't like she was going to fall in love with the first man she came across. This would be good practice, and if she made a fool of herself, she'd be gone in two weeks. No harm, no foul.

Conversation drifted back to work, and shop talk occupied them through another glass of wine until their table was ready. Once they got settled, Lori said, "I have a confession to make."

Annie leaned back in her chair and waited.

Lori gazed down at her lap. "I gave you grief when I thought you were canceling your trip, so you're entitled to get mad," she said then took a deep breath. "I have to go to London next week. I thought I could find a way around it, or postpone it, but one of my old clients has an acquisition pending, and they need someone for the due diligence. Since I'm here and I know the client, they've assigned it to me. I'm really sorry, Annie, but I have to go. I've convinced them to let me wait until Friday, so we have almost a whole week together."

She paused, but Annie said nothing. Lori rushed on. "You could come with me if you want. We can share my hotel room, and London is a great city. We could do the same thing there that we're doing here, just in a different place."

Annie took a sip of wine as she thought about it. Then she saw Lori's pained expression and smiled. "Geez, don't worry about me. I'm just happy you're here at all. I'm not sure about London, but I don't need to decide yet, do I?"

Lori shook her head.

"I was actually thinking, on the trip over, that I might try to convince you to leave town for a few days," Annie continued. "I mean, Paris is a great city and there's a lot to see, but I don't know when I'll get back here, to France, and I'd like to see a bit of the countryside.

"I have no specific plan or even an idea of where I might like to go, so let's just enjoy the time we have together, and I'll figure out if I want to stay here, go to London with you, or go somewhere else."

Lori looked relieved.

"Honestly, Lori, of all people, I do understand. It's not a big deal."

For the next week, while Lori worked, Annie explored Paris. She tried her best at being more open, but it wasn't easy. Parisians weren't terribly interested in making eye contact, but she smiled at strangers as much as she could and felt a small thrill when someone smiled back.

The girls went out to dinner every night, usually stopping for a glass of wine at Willi's before sampling the neighborhood restaurants that Lori had discovered. The food was fantastic, and Annie enjoyed discovering the French wines. Each night they asked their server to make a wine recommendation, and they were never disappointed. The whole idea of picking the wine to match the food, instead of just selecting a wine for its own merit, was a wonderful experience that Annie enjoyed immensely.

On Thursday, as she wandered through the main bookstore at the Louvre, Annie noticed a poster depicting a prehistoric cave drawing of a horse, and it piqued her interest. She'd seen the image before but couldn't recall where it was from. Looking around the bookstore, she found several books on the caves and other prehistoric sites, but they were all in French.

Determined, she dug through a pile of secondhand books on a table in the back of the store and finally found what she was looking for: an old travel guide, in English, for the Perigord Noir, a subregion of the Aquitaine Department of southwestern France where the prehistoric caves were located. The book also featured the medieval villages and castles that dotted the landscape along the region's main river—a river that, according to the book, was one of the most beautiful in all of France.

By the end of the day, Annie had read the entire book. She was intrigued with the medieval history, and fascinated by the mysterious cave paintings and the idea of seeing prehistoric sites. When Lori walked in the door that evening, Annie announced her decision.

She was heading south.

Three

La Roque Gageac, southwest France, Thursday afternoon

Kaden Macallister pulled into the gravel parking lot on the low bluff above the river and stopped to let his passengers exit the vehicle. He made sure they had all their personal belongings, accepted a few francs as tip, and bade them *au revoir.* Then he climbed back into the van, put it in gear, and executed a perfect arcing turn to position the trailer to back it down the boat ramp.

A tall, thin man with cropped, spiky hair and wire-rimmed glasses appeared from the back of the rental hut and jogged down the ramp. Cigarette dangling from his lips, he waved the "keep coming, keep coming" sign as the trailer rolled down the slope, then held up his hand and yelled, "Stop." Kaden put the van in park and pulled on the emergency break, then jumped out to help unload the canoes and kayaks.

"François," he said in a tone that made the man stop with a canoe halfway off the trailer and look up. "You have to get that seatbelt fixed. I had to tie it in a knot because the buckle doesn't stay locked. Not all your boys think like I do." He tapped his head for emphasis. "It's dangerous enough hauling this trailer up and down that road. If some idiot comes barreling around a corner too fast, this thing will end up in the ditch. Do you want to get one of us killed?"

"*Oui, oui, je sais,*" François grumbled. "I'll get it done. Relax. The season is almost over."

"The season has just started. And you know August is the worst on this road. If you want me to drive this piece of shit for you, get the belt fixed." Kaden pulled the last canoe off the rack, set it in the sandy gravel at the river's edge with the rest of them, then drove the trailer back up to the parking lot. He tossed the keys to François and glared at the man before turning and walking away.

François grunted that he got the message and went inside the hut to finish up the day's paperwork. He wasn't sure why his friend bothered to work for him; it wasn't like he needed the few extra francs. Shaking his head at the mystery, he picked up a stack of contracts and went back to work.

Kaden walked through the parking lot toward town, pausing to watch the sunlight bounce off the river like sparkling white diamonds. He stretched his long arms above his head and twisted to the right in a swift motion to crack his back. Letting his arms fall to his sides, he shook his head and let his shaggy hair fall where it would. Unconsciously, he brushed it out of his eyes as he continued to watch the water. He loved it here. There was a strange energy he always felt on this stretch of the river, and he enjoyed the simple labor of helping his old friend with the canoes, even if François was an idiot sometimes.

He squinted into the reflections coming off the water, watching one of the riverboats filled with tourists gracefully chug its way toward the dock. It was a replica of the historic flat-bottomed *gabarres* that had served on this river from Roman times up until the Revolution. The captain pulled the wheel and let the boat float effortlessly to the dock, just kissing the edge before a crewman jumped out and secured its lines.

As the passengers disembarked, he studied them, idly wondering who they were and what their story was. His musings were interrupted by the sound of a woman's voice calling his name. He turned to see François's wife skipping toward him across the parking lot.

"*Bonsoir, Juliette. Ça va?*" He leaned down to kiss both of her cheeks.

"*Bonsoir, ça va bien,*" said the petite redhead. *Kiss, kiss.* She was short and round where François was tall and lanky, and her long, silky auburn curls, falling in soft waves down her back, contrasted sharply with her husband's spiky, short-cropped hair.

"*Mais, j'ai un problème.*" She paused. "Gérard has disappeared again," she said with disgust, "and he was supposed to work at the booth tomorrow afternoon."

13

Kaden inwardly groaned, knowing what was coming. Gérard, his friends' seventeen-year-old son, was the definition of unreliable.

"Can I impose on you to sit there for me tomorrow afternoon?" Juliette asked. "It will just be for a few hours, from three to seven. It would really help me out."

Juliette worked more hours than anyone Kaden knew. She ran the local bar and the hotel above it, and received a small stipend to operate the small tourist information booth across the road from the hotel. Between the income from the canoe rentals, the bar and hotel management, and the tourist booth, Kaden figured that François and Juliette barely scraped by. Kaden knew the area well, he spoke fluent French and English, and his German and Italian were passable. And he was available. So really, he was a perfect substitute.

He sighed. It was better than getting killed on the damned river road. He had meant it when he told François he wouldn't drive the van until the seatbelt was fixed. "Okay, *petite*. For you, I will do it."

Juliette smiled with relief. "*Merci!* I promise to make it up to you. Stop by the bar tomorrow and I'll give you the key." She kissed his cheeks again then scurried back across the road.

He watched her cross the road and disappear into the bar before turning back to the river. It was just past seven, and though there were still several hours of light left at this time of year, the cliff cast the town in a soft shadow, with only the river and the wide parking lot still sparkling in the sun. The sight held him for a few more minutes as the light danced on the rippling water. He glanced over at the tourist booth and felt a tingle at the nape of his neck, coupled with a vague sense of anticipation. *Odd,* he thought, rubbing the spot as he headed to his car.

Four

Southwest France, Friday afternoon

Annie kept one eye on the red light in front of her as she studied the map in her lap, trying to decide what to do. From Brive-la-Gaillarde—a medium-sized city about five hours south of Paris by train—she'd driven her small rental car through some magnificent countryside en route to the medieval town of Sarlat, passing by fields and fields of sunflowers, tobacco, and wavy grains, with beautiful stone farmhouses and a handful of impressive castles along the way. With the radio blasting a French jazz station, she'd flown with the freedom and exhilaration of the open road.

And now she was stuck in Friday afternoon traffic in a medieval nightmare clearly designed for horses and not cars. She was hot and sweaty under a blinding sun, and after circling the town's perimeter twice, she still couldn't find a place to park. But as she sat contemplating the map while waiting at the same stoplight for the second time in thirty minutes, she noticed that the Dordogne River was not too far away. *Huh.* The towns along the river were much smaller than Sarlat. *Maybe they won't be as packed.* She looked again at the road sign up ahead and realized if she went straight instead of looping around the circle again, she'd cross the road that headed directly south to the river, toward a village called La Roque Gageac.

The light turned green. Annie dumped the map on the passenger seat, shifted into gear, and edged forward, veering right this time instead of left. The road went under a train bridge and south through a commercial section to another traffic circle. She made one full rotation, ignoring the irate honks of the car behind her. On the second go-around, she spotted the road she wanted and shot out of the circle.

The landscape transformed abruptly into a sleepy, tree-covered country road that made the air feel twenty degrees cooler. Without the sun blaring in her eyes, Annie pushed her sunglasses up onto her head to enjoy the scenery and the cooling breeze from her open window as she sped along. She passed a few dilapidated structures but there was not much else along the densely wooded byway.

Eventually the forest gave way to rolling hills then a wide valley, and Annie could see cliffs up ahead. More buildings stood along the roadside now—homes and the occasional barn. The river wasn't yet visible, but she knew it was close. She rounded a corner and gasped as she got her first view of La Roque Gageac. The cliffs above the town seemed to soar up to the sky, and the river sparkled in the sun below. But the sight that was so astounding was the town itself. Quite literally climbing up the cliff from the road, the buildings appeared to be built into the cliff itself, punctuated by a stately castle nestled in the trees at the far end of town. She slowed, then turned left into a parking area next to the river, alongside several large tour buses.

Annie took in her surroundings with the wide-eyed abandon of a rookie tourist. She grabbed her purse, locked the car, and walked toward the town. The entire scene was breathtaking. On the river, an open-air, wooden-hulled boat filled with people drifted toward her before turning in sharply. As she approached, she saw that it was destined for a dock just below the river wall. Behind her, laughter echoed off the water. Turning toward the sound, she saw several groups of people cavorting and splashing in canoes and kayaks. The river looked cool and incredibly inviting, and she envied them as they glided past her.

Just then the buses behind her roared to life, and she checked her watch. It was a quarter past six. Maybe they all leave town at night? *Wouldn't that be nice?* She looked around again and marveled at the amazing place she had found. It was so serene compared the chaos of Sarlat, and she couldn't help but congratulate herself for such a great find. Now all she had to do was get a room.

The town was very small, consisting of a quaint yet sturdy row of stone buildings rising up from the narrow road, and as she studied them, she was relieved to see a couple of hotels. She headed across the parking lot toward the closest one, a two-star according to the sign, then paused midstride as she studied it for a moment trying to find the entrance. So intent on her purpose, she failed to notice the man lounging on the porch of a small hut nearby, watching her with interest. Spotting the hotel's main door—tucked beyond a garden terrace on the second level, above the local bar—she headed for it with her usual purpose.

The door was open, and the moment she walked through it, she was hit by a blast of cool air from a fan. She paused, held out her arms, and let the air blow over her. A pretty redhead was hunched over the desk but looked up with a pleasant smile when she saw Annie. *"Bonsoir, madame, comment puis-je vous aider?"*

In her shaky French, Annie asked if there was a single room available with a private bath. The woman frowned slightly but replied in heavily accented English. "Let me check. We are normally fully booked at this time of year, but …" She shrugged as she pulled a large ledger book across the desk and opened it, flipping pages as she studied the entries.

Annie mentally crossed her fingers. She liked the feel of this place, she was tired, and the tariff board on the wall behind the desk told her the rooms were reasonably priced. While waiting, she looked around and saw a dining room just beyond the reception area that faced the river, floor-to-ceiling windows on two sides. *What a great place for breakfast,* she thought, imagining the sun streaming in through the windows.

"Ah, you are in luck." The woman said. "We have a single room on the third *étage*. It is small because it is in the roof," she gestured with her hands to indicate the slope of the gabled roof. "It has a private toilet and bath, and the rate is 250 francs per night. How long are you planning to stay?"

"Um, I'm not sure … I don't have any firm plans," Annie replied. "I have a week before I need to get back to Paris. How many nights is the room available?"

The woman studied Annie for a moment before looking back down at the book. "The room is available until next Saturday. I can reserve it for you for the week, but if you decide to leave early, please let me know two days in advance."

Annie nodded. "Fair enough, I'll take it." She handed over her passport and credit card, and while her booking was being processed, she walked into the dining room and admired the sun glinting off the rippling currents in the river. She couldn't wait to get back out there and feel the breeze on her face.

After being shown up the stairs to her room—three flights of stairs that were so steep, they could almost be considered a carpeted ladder—Annie took the key, dropped it into her purse, thanked the woman, and headed back outside. She stopped at the top of the terrace steps and took in a deep breath. *Yes!* She thought. *This is exactly what I wanted.*

Five

Annie crossed the road and headed straight for the low wall above the narrow quay where two of the wooden boats were secured. It was cooler here, with a refreshing breeze coming off the river. She sat on the wall and closed her eyes, feeling a strange but pleasant tingling in the air, and for several minutes she sat still and just absorbed it. No guidebook could even begin to describe the reality of this place.

Eventually she opened her eyes and took in the details around her. The sun was above the horizon, and the river sparkled in the early evening sunlight, but most of the town lay in the shadow of the cliff. Looking more closely at the buildings, she saw that many in the top row really were built into the cliff. And they looked like they'd been there for centuries. The wall she was sitting on ran along the edge of the riverbank for the entire length of the town, separated from the buildings by the road. Upstream from where she sat, the river curved away from the road to make room for a parking lot and a grassy expanse beyond. Café tables were set up under a large retractable awning at the edge of the parking lot, served by waiters who walked back and forth across the street between the bar and the tables, and it appeared they were doing a lively business. There was a ticket house for the riverboats, now closed, public toilets, and a covered area that was currently occupied by a few old men playing a game with silver balls. Then she noticed the small tourist information booth. To her surprise, the door was open. She checked her watch: it wasn't quite seven o'clock. *Perfect!*

While Annie studied the town, Kaden studied her. He stood, leaning against the back wall of the booth, watching her through the open door. She seemed drawn in by the atmosphere of La Roque Gageac, and it looked like she felt that weird sparkle in the air as the breeze blew off the river. Most of the people he watched didn't seem to notice it, but he could almost see the tension leave her body as her neck relaxed and a small smile played at her lips. Her dark curly hair, cut just above her jaw to expose her slender neck, was ruffling in the breeze, and he found himself mesmerized by the graceful motion of her hand that lifted occasionally to brush the curls off her face.

He had spotted her earlier as she walked alongside the river wall, surveying the town. Then she'd headed toward Hotel La Roque, paused as if studying it, then practically marched up the steps to the door. Something about the way she moved caught his attention. He couldn't exactly pinpoint it, but she had a confident, efficient gait that was surprisingly sexy. She appeared slender in her loose-fitting clothes, yet her posture exuded strength, not delicacy. His observations had been interrupted by someone asking him a question, and he'd had to turn away from the view of her disappearing into the hotel lobby.

As he watched her now, he wondered what she was doing here alone. Was she waiting for someone? When she looked around and suddenly stared directly at him, then stood up and started walking in his direction, he smiled. It then occurred to him, as she came closer, that she couldn't actually see him inside the hut, but was focused instead on the open door.

Annie stepped into the dim interior and almost tripped when she saw him. He was standing against the back wall, a tall man with broad shoulders tapering down to narrow hips, a thick mop of dark hair held away from his face by a pair of sunglasses perched on the top of his head. He was wearing a faded olive-green tee shirt that didn't hide his lean muscles, tucked neatly into equally faded khaki cargo pants, cropped just below his knees, and his feet were strapped into worn canvas sandals. He had the deep tan of someone who spent a great deal of time outside, and he was looking directly at her with an open and friendly smile. She couldn't see the color of his eyes in the dimness of the early evening, but she certainly felt their impact as he regarded her. He sported a day's worth of stubble on his sculpted jaw, and she could see the laugh lines etched in his tanned face. He must have been in his early forties, she guessed, before she realized she was staring.

"*Bonsoir, monsieur,*" she mumbled.

"*Bonsoir, mademoiselle.* How can I help you?"

Irritation spiked. "How is it that everyone knows I speak English?" She almost gasped, mortified by her outburst.

But the man didn't seem fazed at all, just amused. "Your accent," he said. She noticed that his accent was British, not French.

He had not stopped looking straight into her eyes since she walked in, and she suddenly felt a blush creeping up her face, so she shifted her gaze and nodded her understanding.

He waited a moment as she looked around at the displays of pamphlets before speaking again. "Can I help you find something?"

She looked at him but quickly averted her gaze again to the collection on the wall. "I was hoping to find a current guidebook for this area. The one I have is pretty old."

"Things haven't changed much here in the past hundred years or so," he said, eyes sparkling in the fading light.

She bristled again. "Very clever, but I imagine the hours of operation of some of the sites may have changed in the last decade."

If he took offense at her snappishness, he didn't show it. "Unfortunately, what we have here are mostly adverts and brochures, no guidebooks, per se. This little outpost is more promotional than educational. There's a tourist office in Sarlat that sells the kind of book you're looking for."

"I tried to stop in Sarlat today but unfortunately got swept away in the afternoon traffic. That's how I ended up here." *Why on earth did I just confess that?*

"Ah," he said. "You definitely made the right choice—that is, unless you're hoping for some night life." Her expression didn't change, so he shrugged. "Sarlat is definitely worth seeing, though. It was the first town in this area to be restored with funds from the Ministry of Culture. Tomorrow is the big market day there. Quite the experience."

She *was* interested in seeing a good market. "What do you mean, 'quite the experience'?"

"This time of year it's a madhouse, with people pushing and shoving their way through the streets. The Wednesday market there is good too, fewer vendors, but less crowded. How long are you staying?"

Annie wondered how he knew she *was* staying. "I don't know, maybe a couple of days. My plans aren't fixed."

"Well, you're welcome to anything we have here." He turned to the wall and plucked a few fat brochures from their holders, then handed over two of them. "These will give you an idea of the variety there is to see, for both the prehistoric sites and the medieval castles and such in the area." The edges of his lips curled up slightly. "Including the current hours of operation."

She nodded as she flipped through them. She might have smiled slightly, too, but she said nothing.

"Is there anything in particular you're interested in?"

"Medieval villages and prehistoric sights." She glanced at him, saw that he was trying not to laugh, then looked back at the brochures, feeling a blush coming on. "I imagine that's doable." *Duh,* she said to herself.

Kaden studied her for a moment as she fingered the brochures, then rattled off the sites he knew were the most popular for visitors. After a few minutes of commentary, he paused and waited for her to say something, but when she didn't, he handed over the third brochure. "This one will tell you about the sports available here, such as kayaking and canoeing, spelunking, hot air balloons, that sort of thing."

She fanned out the brochures in her hand, then looked up at him. He was friendly, genuinely so, but something about him just chafed her ever so slightly.

"Thanks," she said, holding up the brochures. "These will help. I appreciate it. I should go and let you close up."

He nodded. "My pleasure. *Bonsoir, mademoiselle.* Enjoy your stay."

"*Bonsoir,*" she said as she turned and walked out.

He pursed his lips as he watched her walk the length of the parking lot to her car, pop the trunk, and struggle to pull out an overstuffed suitcase. He smiled to himself, quickly locked up the hut, and hurried over to her. "Here, let me help you with that," he said as he reached for her bag.

She looked up in surprise. "Oh, no, no, please. I mean, thank you, but I can manage." The last thing she wanted was this local, who slightly irritated her for no good reason, to think she couldn't carry her own bag. Sure it was heavy, but she'd manage.

"I insist," he said with an infuriatingly attractive grin. "Besides, Juliette would have my hide is she knew I was out here and didn't help."

"Juliette?" Annie asked, confused. How did he know where she was staying?

Her question must have shown on her face because he gestured to the hotel and back at her. "You *are* staying at the hotel just there, aren't you?"

She nodded and narrowed her eyes at him a bit. "Do you work there, too?"

"Not exactly, no. I just help out occasionally. And if I know Juliette, I'll bet she's stuck you in that little room at the top? Three flights up?"

Annie had to laugh at that. "That's exactly where I am."

He tilted his head slightly, enjoying the sound of her laugh.

Oh, hell, she thought, then nodded gracefully and held up her hands. Something about him annoyed her, but she couldn't identify what it was. She might as well just give in and let him handle that stupidly heavy bag for her.

"Okay, I'll stop arguing. Those stairs are as steep as they are long."

She grabbed the smaller carry-on, and they walked together, back toward town and across the street. Kaden followed her up the stairs, glad he had insisted on carrying her bag. It weighed a damned ton. *What does she have in there, rocks? Jesus.*

Annie thanked him, bade him *bonsoir* once more, and waited until he had descended around the corner of the stairs before she unlocked her room and hauled her bags in. She locked the door behind her and looked around. *Well, that was interesting.*

Six

The rich, strong coffee and buttery croissant were perfect. Annie lingered over both in the hotel dining room as she flipped through the brochures again, the sun streaming in through the southeast window. The morning was warm already, and it would get downright hot before long. Her brochures were already dog-eared, marking places she wanted to see. Although she hadn't admitted it to him, the distracting man at the tourist booth had sparked her interest in many of them.

Saturday in late July was peak tourist season; it would be crowded wherever she went. She was tempted to check out the market in Sarlat, but after the frustrating experience she'd had there the day before, she preferred to explore that town when it was less crowded. And there were plenty of outdoor markets. There was one somewhere every day of the week, according to her brochure.

She looked at her map, then the brochures, and back to the map again. What on her list might be less interesting to hordes of tourists? The pictures of the Jardines de Marqueyssac caught her eye. According to the blurb, they were created in 1861 by Julien de Cerval after he inherited the château on the property. The extensive property was situated at the top of a cliff that overlooked the Dordogne River Valley. The gardens and the château had been restored and just recently opened to the public.

Maybe she should start there? She could soak up the beauty and stay out of the fray. The gardens were nearby and just across the river from Castelnaud-la-Chappelle, a medieval village with a large fortress that, according to the brochure, housed one of the most impressive displays of medieval weaponry in the country. Including those big siege catapults that she'd always wanted to see up close. She nodded to herself. She'd spend the morning at the Marqueyssac Gardens, and maybe the afternoon at Castelnaud.

The gardens were close and easy to find, and to her delight, the parking lot was fairly empty. It was early—just after nine. With luck, she'd be able to explore the place in relative solitude.

She walked up the main path from the gatehouse, through the manicured field of boxwood that could have been in the Mad Hatter's garden, as it swirled and wound around in curlicue shapes on top of the cliff with spectacular views all around. Following the path along the cliff, she headed into the wilder section of the property.

Annie wasn't sure how long she walked around the gardens. Once she left the formal area near the château, the wide trails wound back along the cliffs for what seemed like miles. From one lookout point, she found herself peering down on her village of La Roque Gageac. It was an interesting perspective from this height, the groups of canoes on the river looking as tiny as toy boats.

Even though it was hot, most of the trails were shaded by mature trees, and she was high enough up on the cliff that she caught a cooling breeze. When she checked her watch, she was surprised that it was close to noon. No wonder she was hungry—she'd been wandering around for almost three hours! She headed back to the entrance, thinking of the terrace café that she'd spotted at the back of the château.

The pretty wrought-iron trellis that graced the terrace gave no shade, so she picked a table with an umbrella. Situated on the western edge of the plateau, the table faced the valley downriver. Another medieval village lay tucked in the lee of the next bend, with a majestic castle resting high on the cliff above. She flipped through one of the brochures to read about it while she waited for her order.

The meal was deliciously French: a generous green salad with ripe tomatoes and a warm goat cheese crostini, along with a chilled glass of rosé. She took a big bite of the crostini and closed her eyes, loving the tangy flavor and the warm, gooey texture of the cheese. She felt a little bit trickle down her chin, and just as she reached for her napkin, she heard a loud *click-click-click* on the stones behind her. Spinning around with her napkin pressed against her mouth, she got an eyeful of a tall, lanky, very sweaty man in full cycling garb bearing down on her.

He pulled off his sunglasses as he reached her table. "*Bonjour, mademoiselle.* Are you enjoying your lunch?"

Shit. It was the man from the tourist booth, and here she was, stuffing her face. She ducked her head to finish chewing and swallow.

"Sorry," he said. "I didn't mean to catch you midbite. But I recognized you and just wanted to say hello."

Annie nodded while she finished swallowing. "No problem," she finally managed. "You just startled me." She eyed him curiously. "What are you doing here?"

Kaden grinned easily, looking very attractive despite the sweat that was dripping from his face. He hadn't shaved that morning, and the stubble on his jaw was even darker now. He absently wiped his face with his hand, but it didn't help.

"It's beautiful here, isn't it?" He nodded to the chair opposite her. "Mind if I join you? I need a bit of a rest. I just rode about forty kilometers." His grin widened. "Not much by most standards, but quite a push for me."

Annie stared at him for a moment then turned to the chair he indicated. She looked back at him. *Loosen up and give it a go,* she reminded herself. "Of course, please do. Do you come here often?" As soon as the cliché question left her lips, she flushed with embarrassment. *Gah, talk much?* She ducked her head to hide her heated cheeks, feeling beyond awkward. She had so little experience socializing with men. She hadn't flirted since she'd lost Jack. And now she felt like a complete dork.

He stepped over, pulled out the chair and sank down, then leaned back and stretching out his legs, seemingly unaware of her discomfort. He dwarfed the dainty bistro chair, and Annie couldn't help but notice that his tight cycling outfit showed off lots of lean, sinewy muscles. Muscles that practically rippled from his recent exertions. His bare arms and legs were tanned and glistened with sweat, which highlighted his impressive physique even more. She swallowed tightly, her mouth suddenly dry.

After a quick glance around, he plucked the paper napkin from a place setting at the next table, then, closing his eyes, wiped his face with it. Annie glanced around, too, and saw that there were plenty of empty tables. Why had he thought to join her? She turned her eyes back to him and waited. When he finished, he looked at her and smiled again, sliding his sunglasses back onto his head to restrain his wet mop of hair.

"I'm Kaden, by the way, Kaden Macallister." She saw now that his eyes were hazel green, and she felt like they were piercing right through her.

"Annie Shaw," she said, instinctively holding out her hand while thinking, *Macallister explains the British accent.*

"It's a pleasure to meet you, Annie Shaw. Are you sure you want to touch me?" He cocked an amused brow at her outstretched hand. "I'm quite sweaty."

She blushed again and pulled her hand back, the blunder fueling the awkwardness she was already feeling. "Good point. I guess not."

Kaden signaled to the waitress who had been openly watching him, and she practically tripped over herself as she scrambled to the table. They spoke quickly in French as Kaden ordered a cold beer and a glass of water. Annie rolled her eyes at the way the girl ogled him, but Kaden didn't react or return the interest. An act for her benefit, she decided, since she couldn't imagine a man not enjoying that sort of attention. She wasn't sure whether to be flattered or irritated. She got the feeling this wasn't the first time he'd arrived at the terrace café dripping with sweat, which made her remember her original question.

"This isn't your first time here," she said, deciding it was a fair observation.

"I've been here a few times. It opened just a few months ago. It's a good stopping point when I'm out riding, and so far, it's one of the few places not overrun with tourists." He eyed her appraisingly. "You managed to find one of the few peaceful spots in the valley."

The waitress returned with his beer and water, and a couple extra napkins as well, which Kaden immediately used to blot his still-sweating face. She asked something in French, but he responded with a shake of his head, which sent her reluctantly walking away.

"You aren't going to eat?"

"No, I just need something to get my throat wet. But please don't let me interrupt your lunch."

She looked at the half-eaten salad on her plate.

He grinned. "Any more than I already have, that is. *A votre santé.*" He raised his beer in salute.

She picked up her wine and nodded back, then took a sip. She felt awkward, not knowing what to say or how to start a real conversation. She simply didn't know how to chitchat. Even though she needed the practice—and this was certainly a good opportunity—she was apprehensive … swimming in unfamiliar territory. But she had invited him to sit down, albeit at his request, and she knew she needed to at least *try* to make conversation.

As it turned out, Kaden was happy to take the conversational lead. He told her about the bicycle routes in the area, asked her if she rode (no, she didn't), and opined about the hazards of riding a bicycle on the narrow roads when they were crowded with tourists. He did a goofy impression of a cyclist's experience riding in France. He had her laughing, and she had to admit he was entertaining and easy to listen to. And easy on the eyes.

He chattered on, just as he had yesterday, about this and that, sprinkling in questions that were probing in a friendly way but subtle enough that she was able to deflect them gracefully. Finally he asked her if she'd already walked through the gardens. She nodded, grateful for a nonpersonal topic, and told him her impressions.

"I haven't actually been beyond the swirly boxwood," he said. "I usually just come for a beer and the cool breeze."

"You pay the entrance fee just for a beer?"

"Well, not exactly. They know me here, friends of the family and all that. They don't charge me to come up here."

Annie was interested despite herself. "I can't tell if you're British speaking perfect French or a Frenchman speaking perfect English. How long have you been here?" He behaved like he was on vacation, yet he was working at the tourist booth yesterday, and he gave the impression that he did other odd jobs as well.

That made him grin. "Both, actually, French and Scot, but educated within an inch of my life in an English public school. The brogue was conditioned right out of me." He rolled the *r*'s and flattened the vowels, sounding exactly like a highlander.

"Ah," Annie said, smiling in spite of herself.

"My mother's ancestral home is not too far from here," he said, waiving his hand toward the valley. "Down river maybe thirty kilometers. It's a rather large wine estate. My father was from Inverness, and he met my mother at the end of the war, when the Allies were pushing back through here."

Annie's eyebrows pulled together. "It's hard to imagine being that close to such a horrible conflict," she said.

Kaden shrugged. "I suppose so. But for them, it was more about love than war, apparently. Part of the deal my French *grandpére* made with my father in granting permission to marry his daughter was that she had to come back every summer with the kiddies so he could know us and we could know our French heritage."

"Smart of him."

"So we did," Kaden continued. "Come here every year, I mean. We lived in London, but I spent every summer of my youth here. I have a handful of French cousins, and we were all of an age. We ran around together and spent most of our time at the river. Swimming, kayaking, fishing, and finding trouble. I do feel like I grew up here, even though it was just a few months each year."

"Wow," Annie said. She had been slowly working through her salad as he talked, but then she put her fork down and picked up her wine glass. "Your story makes my life sound so boring. What a great way to learn a second language. We don't get those opportunities in the US."

"There are advantages, I suppose," Kaden agreed. "But what about you? How did you end up here? And alone, I presume, since I haven't seen you with anyone else but me." He flashed that grin again.

But the question hit her like an invasion of her privacy, which was unfair, because he had just told her details about his childhood. "Just vacationing," she said vaguely. Sidestepping, she gestured with her wine glass. "How is it that rosé wine is so delicious and refreshing here? I'm from California, and I've always hated the stuff. It tastes nothing like this."

He frowned, looked away, and sipped his beer. Annie felt a stab of guilt.

"It's a tradition here in France," he said after a moment, masking whatever he may have felt by her non-answer. "On a hot summer day, there's nothing like it. Light, refreshing because it's always served chilled, and when it's made right, it can be the perfect accompaniment to a meal." He indicated her plate. "I imagine it was quite nice with your salad."

She looked down at her empty plate and nodded in agreement.

"The reason you probably don't like your California pink wine is because it's made with low-quality grapes and is typically sweet." His voice took on a condescending note. "Most Americans don't know anything about wine and tend to go for stuff that is either sweet or high in alcohol. The California producers are just giving you what they think you want."

It was insulting, being included in his universal *you*. But it was true she didn't know much about wine. She'd never spent any time in Napa, even though she lived close. Her experience with Lori in Paris had been a revelation.

"It's not our fault," she said a bit defensively. "We're just not exposed to it like you are here. I spent last week in Paris with a friend, eating out every night. Everywhere we went, we asked the waiters to recommend the wine. Their selections went great with the food every time. It added an extra dimension to the meal, something I've never experienced before."

He nodded, keeping his features bland, but inwardly frowned as he wondered who she'd been with in Paris, and then wondered why he cared. "That's what it's supposed to be like. In this country, we've been cultivating grapes and making wine for as long as we've been growing food. It's part of the fabric of the culture here, and a staple at every family meal. Anyone who grew up in rural France, or has family in rural France, has been involved in some way with the making of the family wine. Most of us don't make a big deal out of it. It just is what it is."

Annie watched him with growing unease. His speech was becoming more clipped, and he looked like he was getting tense. She swallowed hard.

"In America," he said, "and in the UK, too, I suppose, they make such a big deal about it, but very few people have actually dug in a vineyard or seen the grapes made into wine. They just don't get the connection with the land and the culture and the simplicity of it all. They get caught up in scores and prestige, and they lose sight of the whole point of enjoying a good bottle of wine with a good meal, around a table with good company." As he spoke, his voice had taken on an unpleasant edge.

Kaden finished his beer and stood up. "I'm glad you had that experience in Paris. It's common for us, the French, I mean, but not so much for others, I imagine."

"I, uh …" Annie stopped. She had no idea know what to say. He'd made her feel defensive with his condescending attitude toward Americans, and he'd made her nervous with whatever tension had gripped him, and now he'd just made her feel like *she* had insulted *him*. Geez!

"*Abientôt,*" he said as he tossed some francs on the table and gathered his helmet and gloves. "Thanks for the company. I imagine I'll see you around." And with that, he walked off, his shoes clicking on the stones.

Annie leaned back in her chair and shook her head. *What did I just do?*

$\mathcal{S}$even

Kaden cursed himself ten kinds of fool as he pumped his bicycle up the winding road home to Les Eyzies. *I'm a sodding idiot. Annie Shaw.* The name certainly suited her. Short and sweet, like the curls that framed her face. Smooth and efficient, like her enchanting gait. He imagined her entire life was organized and carefully planned, but something was off. *Who are you, Annie Shaw?* Kaden pondered the question as he shook the sweat off his face and pushed himself harder up the hill, punishing his already-screaming quads.

She guarded herself carefully, neatly sidestepping every question that was remotely personal, like she'd been doing it for years. She didn't look wary, exactly, just ... guarded. Ready to bolt at the first sign of trouble. Did she think he was trouble? *Probably,* he thought with a disgusted snort. *Especially after that stupid flash of temper.*

He'd practically barked at her, and he'd made her nervous. One minute he was having a normal conversation, and the next minute, he'd had an unwelcome vision of his ex-wife. How the hell had *that* surfaced? Felicia had been a wine snob, had never understood or liked his family's wines. He thought he was over it, he *knew* he was, damn it, except apparently she was still capable of throwing him into a rage with one random thought. At least he'd done them both a favor and gotten his arse out of there.

And damn it, but he couldn't stop thinking about Annie's friend in Paris. Who was he? Someone she would go out with every night ... was she sleeping with him? If so, why was she alone now? Did they fight? Was he the reason she was so guarded? *You're being an arse,* he told himself. She could have been visiting a girlfriend. She didn't want to give out any personal information, and he had to respect that, despite the fact that he wanted to know more about her. What was it about her that made him want to know more? He snorted again as he pushed up the hill. *Probably because she's not throwing herself at you.* But there was something else, too. She was vulnerable. She was cautious and careful. Something, or someone, had hurt her, and she protected herself with some very heavy emotional armor.

Somehow, he needed to apologize. After his performance this afternoon, he doubted she'd want anything to do with him, but he had to at least try to explain himself. Maybe if he opened up a little to her, she would let her guard down a bit. He exhaled heavily as he reached the top of the rise, took in a few big gulps of air, and felt the burn in his muscles ease as he coasted down the other side.

On Sunday morning, Annie took advantage of the empty roads and set out in her rental to explore the area, partly to figure out the lay of the land but mostly just to soak up the beauty. She discovered that the route through Sarlat was much easier to navigate when there was no traffic, and as she drove through the narrow streets, she found herself fascinated by the town that had frustrated her so completely just a few days earlier.

She retraced part of her route from the day before, this time heading north away from Sarlat, back up the road to the town of Montignac for a little reconnaissance, cruising through the main square before heading back south on a different road. This one followed the Vézère River and led to many of the famous prehistoric sites, and she admired the lush beauty of the countryside and the lovely old stone farmhouses that dotted the landscape.

As she approached Les Eyzies she hit a snarl of traffic and slowed to a crawl behind a long line of cars. The cause of the slowdown was a mystery until she spotted people walking away from the town center carrying baskets and plastic sacks. *A market!* She pulled into the first parking spot she found, grabbed her bag, jumped out of her car, and hurried toward the fray.

If she thought La Roque Gageac was built into a cliff, Les Eyzies was even more so. Although the cliffs here weren't as spectacular, the use of them certainly was. Above the main row of buildings, caves high up in the cliff wall were bricked up to frame windows that overlooked the town and the river.

The market stalls overtook a wide flat area at the river's edge, and people were crowded into the space between the stalls, causing a general air of pandemonium that everyone seemed to take in stride. She walked slowly through the gauntlet of vendors, admiring the goods on display. Fruits and vegetables were presented in an abundant kaleidoscope of shapes, colors, and textures—the vibrant red of radishes displayed in tight bouquets alongside perky heads of lettuce in shades of green from pale to dark, contrasting with the shiny purple of perfect *aubergines*—as if the vendors competed for the most appealing arrangement of their wares.

She could smell the earthy pungency of dry-aged cheese before she reached a table with large and small wheels of Comté, Beaufort, Cantal, Bleu d'Auvergne, and more, laid out in delicious enticement. A few stalls farther on, she found a stooped, white-haired man with a single enormous round of Bethmale, a traditional cheese from the Pyrenees, and as she tasted a proffered sample of the creamy, nutty, pleasantly sharp cheese she closed her eyes in ecstasy. She bought a small wedge and watched him wrap it with great ceremony in brown paper before handing it to her with a toothless smile.

The stalls of fresh produce, fish, and meat were interspersed with those selling the finely woven linens, fragrant oil-based soaps, and brightly painted ceramics of the region. Annie stopped to stare at a large truck that offered nothing but delicacies made from the local ducks and geese. In addition to the myriad of fresh cuts of who knew what parts, there was an array of tins in all shapes and sizes filled with foie gras, *rillette,* and *cassoulet;* she read the labels but couldn't sort out what most of it was. She ogled the variety of mouthwatering salamis that were spread out at one table and didn't resist when the man offered her a taste. It was divine, and she leaned over to read the sign, trying to decipher the French.

"*Sanglier* is wild boar." The deep voice from just beside her ear made her jump. Kaden was standing close, leaning over her shoulder, smiling. "*Bonjour,*

Annie Shaw. It's good, isn't it?" he asked, nodding to the sample board. "One of my favorites."

"Christ, you scared me," Annie said with more irritation than she intended, *again,* with her hand on her heart like it was going to jump out of her chest. *Damn it, don't be such a bitch.*

"Sorry," he said, looking contrite. She noticed he was freshly shaved and his thick mop of hair was combed back, still damp, like he'd stepped out of the shower not too long ago. She wondered if he lived nearby.

"Do you ever walk up to people so they can see you coming, or do you just enjoy giving everyone a fright?" she asked, trying for a friendlier voice while waiting for her heart to slow, afraid that the rapid beat may not just be the result of being startled.

"Actually, I figured if you saw me first, you'd bolt. I wanted to apologize for yesterday. I wasn't angry at you, but I'm afraid it appeared that way." His expression was sincere, and his eyes were warm.

Her irritation melted, replaced by a small dose of regret. She looked at her toes, remembering how she'd rudely shut off his questions. "Apology accepted. I probably could have been nicer myself." She looked around and noticed the *saucisson* vender was watching them curiously. She motioned to the one she'd just tasted and nodded.

"Can I buy you a coffee?" Kaden asked as she paid for her purchase.

She sighed. She didn't have any place she needed to be, but … she looked at him and shook her head. "Thanks, but I don't think so."

"Okay, maybe another time," he said, ignoring the pinch of disappointment as he forced a smile. "And I promise not to sneak up on you again. *Bonne journée.*"

She watched him walk away and hoped she hadn't hurt his feelings. *Crap. I suck at anything to do with men.* She continued on her way through the market, letting the swirl of humanity around her lift her spirits: women with baby carriages, grannies pulling grocery carts and haggling with the vendors, men gesturing in the air with cigarettes as they argued good-naturedly among themselves, young girls giggling together. She soon forgot about the handsome semi-stranger as she let herself get lost in the pulsing liveliness around her.

From his stool in a nearby bar, Kaden tracked Annie's progress through the throng of market-goers, trying to figure out what it was about her that captured his attention, and wondered again what she was doing here alone. He couldn't think of one woman he knew who would willingly travel to a foreign country alone. He thought about her friend in Paris, irritated at the flash of emotion he could only describe as jealousy. *Fuck.*

Eight

Annie's plan for Monday was to see the famous cave paintings of Lascaux—the image that had inspired her sojourn to this area. She reread the description in the brochure over breakfast before setting out. The site that one visited now was, in fact, a replica of the original cave that was estimated to have been painted some eighteen *thousand* years ago. Discovered in 1940 by four teenagers and a dog, it was opened to the public in 1948, but soon afterward, the paintings began to show visible damage caused by the carbon dioxide produced by the volume of daily visitors. The cave was closed in 1963 in order to preserve the art. Lascaux II opened some twenty years later, in a bunker set into the hillside a mere two hundred meters from the original. It was said that the replica itself was an incredible achievement and a precisely exact copy. Painted with the same methods, materials, and light sources that had been used thousands of years ago, it had taken ten years to complete. Annie couldn't wait to see it.

Confident that she knew her route, she dawdled at breakfast. Once on the road, she discovered that Sunday morning was the *only* traffic reprieve in Sarlat. She simmered impatiently in the crawling line of cars that nudged their way through the town. Stuck behind a truck that spewed out enough diesel fumes to make her gag, she had a pounding headache by the time the knot of traffic loosened and the truck veered off in a different direction.

She sped along for a few kilometers only to be pulled up short behind a slow-moving vehicle that was so ancient and dilapidated, it made her laugh, even though it was going at a snail's pace. The miniature, three-wheeled ... antique ... looked like a cross between a motorcycle and a truck. It was comical as it teetered down the road, rusted out and rattling along like it could fly apart at any moment.

Okay, it was only comical for about a minute. Oncoming traffic was a steady stream, and the driver of the little rattle trap didn't pull over, so Annie stewed as she crawled along at the head of a long line behind him. When the oncoming traffic finally broke, she sped up to pass and chuckled again at the grizzled old man who was hunched over the wheel, hands gripped tightly at ten and two, with a chewed up cigar sticking out of his mouth.

Annie finally arrived at Montignac and pulled into the parking lot she'd scouted the day before, but she had to bite her lip to keep from screaming when she encountered a group of elderly men hovering around the single parking ticket machine, talking and gesturing, clueless about how it worked. She gritted her teeth and waited while they eventually figured it out and purchased their ticket. She quickly dropped a coin into the machine, rushed back to her car to drop the ticket on the dash, and then headed toward the tour office.

Her heart sank when she saw the line. Frustrated but determined to stick with her plan, she took a deep breath and settled in for a long wait, willing herself to relax.

When she eventually got to the front of the line, she learned the next English tour was scheduled to start in thirty minutes. Relieved, she bought her ticket, walked back to her car, jumped in, and drove out of town, following the signs for the cave.

Just as she turned onto the main road, she had to slam on her breaks as an enormous bus pulled out of a side street in front of her. She swore and gritted her teeth for the third time that day—or was that the fourth?—as the bus lumbered out into the main road. Her headache resurfaced with a vengeance as she followed the slow-moving vehicle up the curvy road to the caves. Annie took a deep breath and checked her watch. There was plenty of time, and she reminded herself she was on vacation. *Relax, damn it!* Yeah, that helped. She squeezed her shoulder blades together and back, then rotated her head in a wide circle on her neck to release the tension.

She finally swung around the bus as it lurched slowly into the front entrance, and then she drove farther up the road, and pulled into the main parking lot. The place was packed. She found a half spot to wedge in her little car, French style, grabbed her purse, and jumped out.

Down the endless row of parked cars she marched, the visitor's center in her sights, only to be waylaid by the bus she'd been following, which was now parked so that it blocked the pedestrian path to the entrance. She stepped around the front of it and stopped dead in her tracks. A horde of Japanese tourists—a whole damned bus full—milled around in front of the building, blocking the way entirely. "Oh for God's sake," Annie muttered as she started elbowing her way through the crowd. She wasn't tall, but she had half a head or more on these people. She must have looked comical shoving her way through the crowd like an aggressive bull, but her patience had snapped.

Couldn't anyone just get the hell out of her way today? She felt like she was slogging through an ocean tide, with the people churning and swirling in a disorganized milieu, hindering her forward movement. She took a deep breath and swore. *Christ, get a hold of yourself and calm down. You're on vacation.* She finally nudged her way out of the throng and looked around to see where she needed to go to catch her tour.

And there, leaning casually against the wall of the gift shop, watching her, was Kaden Macallister. *Oh, crap.* Was the guy stalking her? What the hell was he doing *here?*

"A little testy with our visitors, aren't you?" he asked in a teasing voice.

What? She wanted to smack him. Instead she just stared.

"You obviously haven't had the pleasure of rearing children. They make you learn patience."

A knife to the heart could not have struck more true, as a painfully clear vision of a child that never was flashed through her mind.

"*What?*" she finally said, feeling so lost that her own voice sounded far away. Instinct took over, and she threw back her shoulders, poking a finger, hard, into his chest. "What the hell is wrong with you? You don't know anything about me! Can't you just leave me alone?"

She spun around, spotted the restroom, and dashed for it, where she slammed herself into an empty stall. The door banged closed, and she leaned

39

up against it, breathing hard. Then she brought her hands to her face and burst into tears.

How had that happened? That door had been shut a long time ago, and she never, *ever,* let it open. Hell, she hadn't even thought about her lost baby since … well, since that bitch Sarah stepped into her path a couple weeks ago. What was it about Kaden Macallister that dug under her skin?

Outside, Kaden stood stock still, stunned by Annie's reaction. He'd spotted her pushing her way through the throng of tourists, and the impatient look on her lovely face had been so comical, he couldn't help but laugh. *Bugger me,* he thought now. *Nice job, you wanker. Really well done.* He groaned at the damage done by his pathetic attempt at humor. God, the look on her face when he'd tried to tease her—she'd gone from irritated to … distraught. *She's right: you don't know a damn thing about her.*

A fierce desire to fix his blunder washed through him, and he steeled himself to face her again. She'd try to sneak out and avoid him, but he wouldn't let her get away with it, not until he at least *tried* to explain himself. But what could he say, other than he was sorry for being such a stupid sod? What was it about Annie that made him jab at her?

Annie blew her nose, took a few deep breaths, and wiped the smeared makeup from underneath her eyes. She glanced at her watch. *Shit.* Her tour was going to start in ten minutes. Surprisingly, she felt better—the burst of tears had helped her forget the stupid frustrations of the morning. Leaning her head back against the stall door, she laughed at herself. What a jerk she was. Here she was on vacation, with an attractive guy trying to be friendly, and she kept acting like a bitch. Maybe Sarah had rubbed off on her, after all. With that horrifying thought, Annie stepped out of the stall, cringed at her reflection in the mirror, repaired what she could of her makeup, and walked back outside.

Kaden was waiting for her, looking adorably remorseful, she thought, as she eyed him cautiously. She felt like a fool for getting so emotional over his teasing comment, and she felt the blush creep into her cheeks as he slowly came toward her.

She had a hard time meeting his eyes, but she did her best. He kept his eyes on hers, pulling her in with a serious, intense, yet warm look. He looked genuinely agonized as he reached out and gently touched her arm. "I'm so sorry, Annie. I didn't mean to upset you. You're right—I don't know anything about you, and I had no right to tease you. Please forgive me."

His hazel-green gaze was just too intense, like he could count the scars on her soul, and she dropped her gaze, shaking her head as she studied his toes. "Don't worry about it. It's not your fault. I had a challenging morning, and your comment … conjured up some bad memories. I guess I just let the frustration of this morning get to me." She let out a little snort of a laugh and shook her head again. "I probably deserved it." Then she looked up at him with curiosity. "But honestly, why are you here? I'm beginning to think you're stalking me."

He let out the breath he was holding, relieved that she hadn't kneed him in the groin like he deserved. "I ferried some visitors up here from Hotel La Roque … you know, playing a bit of the tour guide."

"Let me guess, filling in for someone?" She managed a small smile, something in her softening. "Why do I get the feeling you do a lot of that?"

His face lit up into a gorgeous smile, and he laughed. "Yes, I suppose I do. Juliette is a good friend, and I try to help her out when she needs it. I don't mind. The people are usually nice, and sometimes they're even interesting." He looked like he wanted to say more.

Annie caught herself staring at him, then got her brain back in action and looked at her watch again. "Listen, I need to get down to the cave entrance or I'll miss my tour." She hesitated, too, wanting to say more, but not sure what. Instead, she said, "I'll see you around."

She turned to go, but Kaden put his hand on her arm again to stop her. "Wait."

She did. It was a moment before he finally spoke.

"Annie, can we start over? I'm not usually such a bloody arse, truly."

The edges of her mouth curved up. "What did you have in mind?"

"Would you care to take a canoe ride with me this afternoon? The river is lovely in the afternoon light, and I promise I won't tip you over." He flashed that irresistible grin. "You haven't been on the river yet, have you?"

"No, I haven't," she said softly. She watched him, struck by the sincerity of his request and the hint of vulnerability in his eyes. Such beautiful eyes! He was a perfect male specimen who had women tripping over themselves just to get a look at him. Why was he bothering with her? She'd done nothing to encourage him, had done just about everything in her power to shut him down, in fact, including biting his head off only minutes earlier.

Annie's instinct was to turn him down, but for once, her instinct didn't feel right, and she wondered at the incongruity. Whatever his motivation, his desire to spend time with her appeared genuine, and now, after her outburst, was oddly heartening, making her feel … cared for. When was the last time she'd been on a date with a man? *Too long.* Not since Jack. A shadow crossed over her heart briefly, but she mentally chased it away.

Could she trust him? Everyone else apparently did, she thought ruefully. Could she trust herself? It wasn't like she was planning to dive into the sack with him, just enjoy a pleasant afternoon on a beautiful river. Would it really be so terrible to enjoy the attention of a handsome man? What was the risk in that? That she'd remember how sweet it felt to be admired, to be valued as a woman? *Take a chance, Annie,* a small voice echoed in her head.

"I haven't," she repeated, "but I would like to." She nodded to convince herself as much as to give her answer. "All right, this afternoon sounds great."

Annie joined her group at the entrance to the bunker just as the tour began.

Nine

Kaden was ready when Annie walked down to the canoe hut later that afternoon. He introduced her to François, who dealt with her paperwork while Kaden found the least grungy life jacket in her size. After she buckled and adjusted it, she accepted his outstretched hand, and he walked her down the dirt ramp to the canoe waiting at the river's edge.

He was pleased to see she had on waterproof sandals, sunglasses, and a good hat. "You put on sunscreen, *oui?*" he asked as he stuffed her bag into a watertight container.

"*Oui.*" Annie smiled.

"Did you bring a sweater?"

"No, should I have? It's so warm out."

"No problem, I have one in the office. Let me just run up and grab it for you." He was off like a shot. While she waited for him, she surveyed the river. It was a different perspective from down here at the water's edge. While the air was warm, the cool breeze off the river was refreshing and soothing.

Kaden returned and stuffed the sweater into her canister, secured it in the little craft next to another one, buckled his own life jacket, and hauled the canoe into the water. Before he shoved it off shore, he motioned for her to step in. "Sit in the front."

She gingerly climbed in, shuffled forward ungracefully, and settled on the front seat before turning back to look at him, almost losing her balance in the bargain as he simultaneously shoved the canoe into the river and stepped in to take his seat in the rear. She grabbed on to the sides as the boat shot forward into the river, catching the current as it moved downstream. Laughing, she reached for the paddle that was wedged under her seat.

"Have you ever been in a canoe?" Kaden asked as he steered them into the center of the river.

"A few times, but never on a river," Annie called back from the front. "I've paddled before, but not in a canoe. In college my friends were into backpacking and river rafting, so I did a lot of both in the California high country. But the only time I've been in a canoe was on a perfectly still lake."

"Just paddle as you are, then," Kaden said, taking in her form. "You're doing fine for keeping us moving. I'll steer from back here." He saw that she held the paddle properly, appearing relaxed as she dipped, pulled and lifted it without splashing. She had a very nice form, he decided, as he watched her from behind.

As they silently sluiced down the river, Annie felt an unexpected desire to keep talking. "My mom was into canoeing. She grew up in Kentucky, near a lake, and it was a big deal there. When I was a kid, we vacationed on a lake in northern California, and we would haul a canoe up with us every year. She loved that canoe. Tried to teach me, but I never got it." Annie laughed, thinking how stupid that must sound. "I could never figure out what the J-stroke was. Back then, I guess I was more interested in getting a suntan."

Kaden smiled to himself. *Finally,* she was volunteering personal information, and he was pleased with what he heard. She liked the outdoors enough to go backpacking and river rafting. Her mother sounded interesting, but Annie had used the past tense. No sense in spoiling the mood by talking about deceased parents.

They floated downstream at an easy pace, and Annie became lost in the beauty of her surroundings. Passing through La Roque Gageac at river level made the village look even more endearing. It stood above them, solid and proud, merging gracefully with the cliffs. They paddled on around the bend, leaving the quaint village behind. The river was wide, with enough current to make it just a little chore to keep the canoe moving as they passed fishermen standing midstream.

A comfortable rhythm developed between them, where Annie paddled on one side until she got tired then switched to the other side, and Kaden paddled with the majority of the strength and also steered.

"Look up to your left," he said after a while, breaking the silence. Annie swung her head around and inhaled sharply. Perched high up on a limestone cliff that seemed to form its foundation sat an imposing fortress built of blond stone darkened with age yet still glowing in the sunlight. Brilliant red-and-blue banners with golden fleurs-de-lis flew from its parapets, giving the otherwise somber castle a regal air.

"It's magnificent," Annie sighed.

"Yes, it is. I never tire of seeing it. Castelnaud is one of the most important historic sites in this area. Just around this bend, you'll be able to see its rival, Château de Beynac. The lords of Castelnaud and Beynac were enemies during the Hundred Years' War."

"What was that war about, exactly?"

Kaden loved the topic and welcomed the question. "It's in the history books as a war between the French and the English, which was absolutely true, but it was more like a nasty family quarrel that spiraled out of control."

"How is that?" And how had she not noticed what a wonderful, deep voice he had?

"A century or more before the conflict started, Henry Plantagenet II married Eleanor of Aquitaine. Eleanor's lands, this entire section of France"—he spread an arm wide, indicating the surrounding area—"known as the Aquitaine, came under Henry's control, and he became duke of Aquitaine. Not look after their marriage, he ascended to the English throne. Despite the fact that Henry was king of England, in his capacity of duke of Aquitaine, he was obligated to swear homage to the king of France."

"Huh? How did that work out?"

"It was fine at first, because Henry II and Louis VII, the French king, were friends and cousins; in fact, Louis VII was Eleanor's previous husband. Several generations later, however, it became much more political, and the manner in which the then-French king demanded homage to be given by the duke of Aquitaine became untenable to the then-English king, who continued to hold the title."

Annie had stopped paddling to listen, with her head slightly cocked.

Kaden grinned. "It was a chore to sort out who was who back then, and that was one of the issues. There was a small point of whether that English king—Edward III—had a more defensible claim to the French throne than the one current sitting on it did."

She laughed. "I guess that could get tricky."

"It undoubtedly did. Anyway, during the war, or series of wars, Castelnaud went back and forth between factions, but Beynac held firm in loyalty to the House of Valois—the French side. Many pivotal battles took place between these two castles. Have you been to either site yet?"

"Not yet, but I want to see both." She wasn't sure whether to be more awed by the history or the man reciting it.

They paddled on, passing under a graceful six-arch bridge built with the same stone as the castle. As they rounded the next bend, true to Kaden's word, the monolith of Beynac loomed high on the cliff top in front of them. Kaden steered the canoe over to the south shore of the river to a narrow beach. "Let's pull ashore here for a bit. We'll have a nice view, and I brought a snack."

"A snack?" Annie hadn't noticed she was hungry until he mentioned it.

Kaden powered the canoe straight into the beach, allowing Annie to jump out without getting her feet wet. He then stepped out of the canoe and dragged it out of the water.

While Annie gawked at the castle, Kaden pulled a few items from the canoe. By the time she turned around, he had a blanket spread on the ground and a lovely picnic arranged. She looked at him in surprise.

"I put my foot so deep in it today, I figured I needed to pull out all the stops to come close to redemption."

Annie smiled, slightly embarrassed. She wanted nothing more than to forget the whole episode of Annie-turned-psycho-bitch. Whatever it was about him that had bothered her before—and she still couldn't pinpoint what it was—was gone now. He was charming, handsome as could be, and he was trying to win her favor. A terribly tempting combination, but she still didn't understand why he made the effort. What could possibly be in it for him? She was leaving in a few days, and they'd never see each other again. She felt a twinge of regret that this … date … couldn't be the beginning of anything. She'd never see him again after she left France.

Well, she conceded to herself as she dropped her life jacket onto the blanket, *just because there's no tomorrow for us doesn't mean I can't enjoy today.* As she settled herself on her life jacket–turned-pillow, she studied the fare. *Wow. This guy has moves.*

Reading her thoughts, Kaden settled down on his own life jacket, picked up her hand and kissed it chastely, looking deep into her eyes. "I may look like and act like an Englishman," he said, *"mais dans mon coeur, je suis français."*

Without waiting for a reply, he popped the cork on a bottle of rosé wrapped in an ice pack and poured it out into two plastic cups. He handed her one, touched her cup with his, said, *"Santé,"* and took a sip.

Cheeks warm from his courtly gesture, she nodded and took a sip, too. Then she closed her eyes and took another sip. *Good Lord, this is delicious.* She opened her eyes to find Kaden looking directly at her. "What do you think?"

"I think I'm in love with French rosé."

"That's a start. I told you it was different here." He pulled the bottle out of its chilly cover and showed her the label. "This is from Bergerac," he said, like that explained everything.

When she didn't look impressed, he elaborated. "Pink wine, what we call rosé, is made all over France. It's made from black grapes that normally would be used to make red wine, except they're harvested earlier to ensure high acidity, then crushed and pressed off the skin within just a few hours to avoid the color and tannins from the skin of the grapes. There are many styles of rosé, but in my opinion, this is the best."

"I could agree with that," she said, closing her eyes and simply enjoying the moment.

Kaden watched as she leaned back on an outstretched arm, looking relaxed. He hoped she was finally letting down her guard with him.

They nibbled on the snacks—bread, a couple of different cheeses, *saucisson,* an apple that he sliced into wedges—and he let her ask the questions, content to tell her what she wanted to know without prying into her life. At her request, he talked about the summers he had spent as a boy at his grandparents' estate, running through the vineyards with his cousins, helping his uncles with the never-ending work of tending the vines, being drafted to pick grapes when harvest started, and learning about how to make wine.

He told her about the hours and hours they spent at the river, swimming, fishing, paddling, and exploring the ruins and the caves. "There are so many caves in this area," he said, "you could spend a lifetime exploring them and never find them all. Most of them aren't accessible by road, but there are trails all over the place."

Kaden was sprawled out on the blanket, propped up on his elbows, staring at the river as he spoke. Annie drank in his profile: strong jaw with a shadow of whiskers, straight, Gallic nose, and long, thick eyelashes. How could she have not noticed those lashes before?

He abruptly turned to her. "How did you like Lascaux?"

"I liked it very much. Do you think it really looks like the original?"

"It does indeed. I saw the original. My mother took our gang to see it when I was thirteen. Lucky for us, since it closed the next year. The images in the replica are more vivid than what I remembered, probably because the black mold had already darkened the originals when I saw them. They've since been restored, but now only scientists and others doing special research are allowed into the original cave."

"It's too bad they had to close it. I think it's pretty amazing how they made the replica, though, and how many people still come to see it."

Kaden nodded. They were relaxed and comfortable in the moment, and he hated to leave, but they needed to get moving down the river before the late-afternoon wind made paddling too much of a chore. In minutes, everything was packed up and he shoved the craft back into the river.

Beyond Beynac, they passed under another bridge, and then the river was shrouded by broad trees on either side, blocking the view of anything else. With the wind blowing straight at them, they had to put some muscle into it to keep the canoe moving.

They paddled in companionable silence for a while, but when the river made a turn to the right, Kaden steered the canoe to the south bank, into a deep section that was protected from the wind by the trees. "Time for your canoe lesson," he said.

Annie turned around and looked at him, eyebrows arched.

"Everyone should know how to pilot a canoe."

She was game and caught on quickly. "I'm not sure why I had such a hard time with this." She laughed as Kaden called out "*á droite*" or "*á gauche*" and she executed them with ease … once she translated the direction in her head.

"Probably didn't have the right incentive to impress your teacher."

"Probably not," she grinned.

By the time they reached the take-out point, Annie was tired and chilled. Kaden saw the goose bumps on her arms and pulled out the sweater he'd brought for her. "Here, put this on."

It was cashmere soft and warm from being inside the container. "Thanks. Ooh, this is cozy." It was way too big for her and fell past her hips. She pushed the sleeves up to her wrists and hugged herself inside it to get warm. The sweater had a delicious scent of something woodsy and masculine, and she felt like purring.

Annie wasn't the only one affected by the sweater. Kaden thought she looked adorable and had an urge to wrap himself around her while she wore it. Instead, he secured the canoe to a chain that was looped around a tree, grabbed their gear and the paddles, and headed up the dirt track. "Come on, my car is just up here."

If she was alarmed by the sudden huskiness of his voice, she didn't show it. "How did you manage that?" she asked as she followed him.

"François. We shuttle his clients and the canoes back up from here. I followed him down when he made an earlier pickup, and left my car here. They'll get the canoe tomorrow when they make the morning pickup."

"We?" Annie was curious about Kaden's work, or lack thereof, and she'd meant to ask him about it, but he'd distracted her with his stories of childhood escapades.

A sporty silver Peugeot waited in the shade. He stowed everything in the trunk then held the passenger door open for her. "I work for him occasionally during the summer."

"You seem to work for everyone occasionally during the summer."

He laughed. "I suppose I do." He closed her door then came around and got in the driver's side. He buckled his seat belt but didn't start the car. He looked at her, hesitated, and then said, "I'll tell you all about it if you have dinner with me tonight."

Ten

As Kaden helped Annie out of his car a few hours later at the restaurant La Belle Nicole, Annie felt a tingle of anticipation along with a healthy dose of uncertainty. The afternoon had been delightful, and she'd been pleased and flattered when he invited her to dinner. He was easy to be with, playful and entertaining, no hint of prickliness … well, other than that day at the garden. But today—after the episode at the caves—he had respected her boundaries, giving not the smallest hint that he wanted something from her that she wasn't prepared to give. She suspected he had depths to his personality that she had only just begun to discover. And she *did* want to discover more. *But to what possible end?* How ironic that her first foray into the dating world in eight years found her an engaging, handsome, and interested man with whom it would be geographically impossible to have any sort of relationship. She sighed inwardly and reminded herself to just enjoy the moment and try not to overthink it.

He escorted her to the entrance, one hand lightly pressed to the small of her back, and Annie regarded him surreptitiously out of the corner of her eye. It was the first time she'd seen him in anything other than faded cargo shorts or his skin-tight cycling outfit, and he looked fantastic. The cuffs of his dark slacks broke perfectly over polished black loafers, and a celadon silk shirt that complemented his eyes hung beautifully from his wide shoulders. He'd tamed his hair into a stylish comb-back; it was a little long and curled up at the ends, making him look sexy as hell. And for the first time, she noticed that he smelled nice, too. Something woodsy and masculine, like the sweater she'd reluctantly given up earlier.

The restaurant was small, tucked into a commercial street in the village of St. Cyprien. No touristy pretensions here, but she suspected that she would not be disappointed. The place was full, the many conversations humming with the pleasing cadence of the French language and the occasional tinkle of laughter, yet the intimacy of it was warm and inviting.

Inside the door, they were met by a beautiful woman dressed in a simple black dress that conveyed graceful professionalism. She greeted Kaden warmly with a double-kiss, and Annie heard him say, *"Bonsoir, chére,"* before the woman turned to Annie with curious eyes.

Annie felt like a bug under a microscope for a moment and was glad she had made an effort to look her best, wearing a sleeveless silk tunic the color of freshly roasted coffee beans and a matching skirt that flared in soft waves just above her knees. The ensemble was belted loosely at the waist and highlighted by a beautiful yet simple beaded necklace that she'd found in Paris the week before.

Kaden made the introductions. "Annie, this is Nicole Bouvier, my cousin's wife. He's the chef here. Nicole, meet Annie Shaw." He grinned at Nicole's attempt to hide her astonishment.

The women smiled and nodded at each other. *"Enchanté,"* Nicole said. "Will you please come with me?" She showed them to a table in the back corner. *Private and cozy,* Annie thought.

Nicole left them to fetch their aperitif, indicating that Jean Claude would be out shortly to discuss the meal. After she'd gone, Kaden said, "Jean Claude doesn't confine himself to a menu. He picks up whatever looks best at the market in the morning and creates the basis for a few dishes, but then he likes to discuss the final dish with his customers individually so he can make any changes they may want. Everything is market fresh, mostly locally grown, and he only uses what's in season. The customer-choice thing is a little unorthodox, but he is a master. People come from all over the area to eat here." He indicated the crowded room. "Most of these people are regulars."

Nicole returned with a *kir* for each of them, a glass of dry white wine with a touch of *crème de cassis* to give it a pink hue and a bit of sweetness. "Mmm, delicious," Annie said after tasting it.

"I'm glad you like it." Kaden sat back and regarded her. "I wasn't sure you would, since you don't like sweet wine, but this"—he held up the glass—"is different."

Surprised he had remembered her comment, she was about to reply when Jean Claude appeared at the table.

"*Et tu voilà! Ça va, mon vieux?*" The chef smiled broadly at Kaden, but his eyes strayed with obvious interest to Annie.

Kaden chuckled and responded in kind as he stood up and they slapped each other on the back in a manly version of a hug. Jean Claude then turned to Annie and said in perfect, accented English, "Ah, you must be Annie." He held out his hand and leaned over hers in an elegant gesture. "It is a pleasure to meet you, *mademoiselle*. A great pleasure indeed, as this big oaf has never once brought a lady to dine here with him, even though we are family." He winked at her as Kaden groaned.

Annie's brows rose at this admission as her gaze darted to Kaden, but she attempted to hide her confusion by smiling at the chef. "Thank you. It's a pleasure to meet you, too. I understand I'm in for a treat tonight." *How can he have never brought a woman here before?*

"*Bien sûr*, you are." Jean Claude said without a trace of conceit. Giving no indication that he noticed the effect his previous words had had on Annie, he proceeded to explain their choices for the night. After much discussion between the men about preparations, sauces, and other details, including the best wine to go with their selections, Jean Claude performed a little bow, glanced knowingly at his cousin, and left the table.

Kaden and Annie stared at each other for a moment in awkward silence before Kaden sighed and cleared his throat.

"The downside of introducing you to my friends," he said, "is that I put myself at their mercy. I wasn't ready to confess to you that small detail, but since he brought it up ..." He reached for her hand, tugged it to the center of the table, and covered it with his own, looking into her eyes in that intense way of his. "I will admit to you that I've not been interested in a woman for a long time. But I am very interested in you."

His words warmed her but made her nervous at the same time. She turned her hand under his and curled her fingers around his. The small contact felt … good. "Thank you," she said, "but I'm not sure I understand why."

Kaden eyed her with something akin to disbelief. Was she truly unaware of her appeal? "Will you tell me about yourself, Annie Shaw?"

It was her turn to sigh. "I will, but there's not really much to tell. Your history has to be more interesting. And besides"—she cocked an eyebrow at him—"weren't you supposed to be explaining how it is that you work for everyone here during the summer?" *And perhaps I'll be able to figure out why you are unattached when you seem so perfect. Or are you just playing me?*

He laughed. "You're right. That was brilliant, wasn't it, because here you are. I will talk first, then, but you're not off the hook."

She nodded, hoping to discover if his open charm was part of the real man or just a shiny veneer. She liked him, and her heart told her to trust him, but her heart was rusty, to say the least. But why introduce her to his family if he was being insincere?

"Okay, let's see," he said somewhat briskly, sitting back in his chair. "You already know that I was raised in England and spend my summers here. For the rest, the short version is that after university, I worked in London, rose up to the top in business, married, went through a nasty divorce, emotionally crashed and burned, got fired, then went crawling to my uncle Henri, who helped me revive my soul working with him on his land." He paused to gauge her reaction before continuing more slowly. "I now spend my summers here again, with my cousin, but I live in Provence with my uncle during the rest of the year, working with him in the vineyards and the cellar." He shrugged. "That's about it. Your turn."

Annie tilted her head. "Do I get to ask questions first? I promise to stay away from the personal stuff. I don't have any business asking you about that." *Nasty divorce? Ouch.*

He gave her a steady look. "It's an integral part of the story, and I won't shy away from it. Ask what you will."

"What kind of business?"

As the first of several delicious courses arrived, along with the wine, Kaden started the story, hoping the pain of it would stay in the past.

"I graduated Cambridge with a master's degree in international finance and was lucky enough to land a rather coveted position with Wilson Marks Ltd., quite the most exclusive investment bank in London. That was the first summer I missed the trip to France, since they wanted me to start right away."

Annie laughed. "The moment you realized you're an adult."

"No doubt," he said with a smile. "But it was a unique opportunity—Wilson Marks rarely took associates right out of school, even grad school—and I wasn't about to argue about summer vacation. I loved it from the first minute. Crazy hours, of course, but complex, fascinating deals with world-wide impact, and the work consumed me. After a few years of hard work and some lucky calls, not to mention a string of wildly successful public offerings that I can hardly take sole credit for, they made me a partner."

Annie's eyes widened. Kaden saw her reaction and tried to judge her thoughts. Did she understand what it meant? He had no idea, since he still knew nothing about her. He glanced down at her plate and frowned.

"Don't you like it?"

She'd been listening intently and hadn't taken more than one bite of the delicate squash blossoms that Kaden had selected for their appetizer. "Of course!" she said quickly as she took another bite. "This really is delicious. The texture is perfect." She took a sip of wine, closed her eyes to savor the flavors, the wine and the dish seeming to elevate the other. "How many years into it did they make you partner? You can't have been that old."

"I was twenty-eight." He felt himself blush at the admiration in her eyes and tried to shrug it off. "They appreciated my work ethic. Even though I grew up in a privileged environment, my parents always seemed to keep us grounded. The summers in France allowed me see a simpler side of life that re-volved around the family as a solid unit and, well, family values. That sounds trite, but it's true."

Annie nodded her understanding.

"But despite that, I got caught up in the game, and in the trappings of wealth. Most of my clients came from old money, aristocrats and old nobility for the most part. I'd been raised in their environment, went to the same schools, so I was comfortable with them and they were comfortable with me. They trusted me because in many respects, I was one of them. And I had some good ideas on market timing for large-scale deals, so I was in demand."

Their first course had been cleared, and now Nicole brought their main plate—a beautiful pan-seared rack of lamb with a dark, rich sauce that smelled divine. A waiter followed with a bottle of wine, which she took from him and opened with great ceremony for Kaden's approval. Annie watched with amusement as Kaden swirled the garnet-colored liquid in his glass and sniffed it, considering it for a minute before winking at Nicole, who smirked and shook her head before she poured Annie's glass, set the bottle down, and left them alone.

"*Bon appétit,*" Kaden said as he tilted his glass toward her. "I'm not boring you, am I?"

Annie took a sip of the wine and moaned in appreciation. "Not at all. Everything is fantastic ... the wine, the food, and listening to you. But, what you said at first doesn't make sense. If you were so successful, how is it that you got fired?"

He sipped his own wine then cleared his throat. "Ah, well, that would have to do with my divorce."

"You don't have to tell me if you don't want to, Kaden. I know it's none of my business." She gave him an apologetic look. "Especially after my own behavior."

"Can I ask you a question?"

"Of course," she said, bracing herself.

"Are you seeing someone? In San Francisco, I mean? Is there a special man in your life?"

A fraction of hesitation, then, "No." She pushed a bite of lamb around with her fork then raised her eyes back up to his. "I wouldn't be having dinner with you if there was. I ... I haven't dated anyone in ... a long time."

He reached across the table and took her hand again. "Then I want you to know who I really am, Annie—and my divorce, the mess I made of my career, it's all part of it. But I'm afraid it's not terribly flattering."

She squeezed his hand and surprised herself with her next words. "I want to know who you are, warts and all. We are none of us perfect, me especially. But I respect your boundaries, just as you've respected mine." The notion that he had some serious imperfections—even if his challenges were in the past— was actually a relief to Annie.

Kaden pulled his hand away and nodded, taking a bite of his lamb and considering what he wanted to say as he chewed and swallowed. He cleared his throat. "The senior partner of the firm had a beautiful daughter. Felicia was high society all the way, classy and elegant, but with a wild streak. It was a deadly combination. She was also a self-absorbed snob, but I didn't figure that out until it was too late." He paused, took a sip of wine, and closed his eyes briefly. "I look back on that period in London and wonder where the hell my senses were. Most particularly, my sense of self-preservation."

Felicia had set her sights on him, and her father encouraged it. Why not marry off his uncontrollable daughter to his most promising young partner? With her father whispering in his ear about his future, the unspoken implication that Kaden would be the heir apparent when the old man stepped down, he let himself get pushed into a big-society wedding.

"I hadn't thought it through—what it would actually mean to be married—just went along with it all." Kaden was looking off in the distance as he said this, his expression full of regret, and Annie felt a wave of compassion for him. Her own marriage had been a dash to the altar for an altogether different reason, but there had certainly been love. Kaden had not yet mentioned the word as pertained to the captivating Felicia.

"I bought her a big flat in a fashionable part of town, and she spent outrageous amounts of my money decorating it and filling it with art. She threw lavish society parties, sparing no expense to make hers the most desired invitation in the city." He tossed back a gulp of wine, the movement betraying the agitation he was feeling as the story unfolded.

"Kaden …" Annie tried to stop him, guessing where this was heading and not wanting him to have to relive it on her account. Jesus, they barely knew each other! Why was he doing this? *I want you to know who I really am.* His words echoed in her mind.

Her soft plea went unheeded, and the story tumbled on. While his wife had London society eating out of her hand, Kaden's work consumed him. There seemed no end to the choice projects rolling his way, all of which were intense and time-consuming, requiring armies of professionals working for weeks at a frenzied pace. The pressure was immense, yet so were the rewards.

Kaden paused in his tale as Nicole appeared tableside to refill their glasses. Annie didn't miss the concerned look she directed at Kaden as she inquired about the meal, or his nod of assurance. After a sip of wine, he continued.

"I loved the job, but was frankly bewildered by my wife. At first she whined about my hours, complained to her father, threw childish tantrums … but then … after a short while, once she got involved in her parties, she didn't seem bothered at all that we barely saw each other, seemed almost put out when I did accompany her to some function or other. I was too caught up in my work to think about why." To Annie's relief, the calm was back in his voice and the strain of tension gone from his features.

Light glinted off the dark wine as he swirled it around and around in his glass, lost in thought, as if his past created a similar pattern in his memory. Annie waited.

"I came home early one afternoon and found her shagging some … kid, maybe not even twenty years old."

"Oh, God," Annie breathed, thinking how wretched that must have been.

"I kicked him out. The poor kid was terrified." He slowly shook his head, looking disgusted. "Felicia was furious; no explanation, no apology. I remember her ranting on about … about me, her father, her friends … I saw her clearly for the first time, I suppose, and finally, *finally,* understood that I'd been played for a fool. I was a vehicle for her, a means to an end, nothing more. She didn't love me, never had, and I … I didn't care, because I hadn't loved her, either. I'd just been along for the ride, doing what seemed to be expected of me. I told her it was over, that her game was up. That sent her fury into the orbit."

"Kaden," Annie said softly, "as painful as it was, it's not that unusual. I don't think any less of you for it."

Kaden scoffed. "I haven't even gotten to the bad part yet."

Annie swallowed. *Uh oh.*

"Our divorce was even more sensational than our wedding," he said, the disgust evident in his voice. "We'd been married for less than a year. Felicia spread vicious lies about me and our life together to anyone who would listen, which was just about everyone, since she was society's darling. I was made into a brute. It was all so much bullshit, and anyone who knew me knew it was, but that didn't help in the eyes of the public. I was hounded by the press. Worse, the firm was hounded, and naturally, there were some who relished the idea of a public hanging, so to speak, and they were more than willing to offer up more lies."

He took a bite of lamb, then a sip of wine, looking ruefully at the glass before setting it down. "I started drinking to escape the fray. It was nearly six months before some other scandal lured the attention away from us. Her demands were so absurd, I fought everything at first. She had her own trust fund, it had been my money that had paid for the flat and all the crap that filled it, but she dug in with her claws and fought me over every little thing. My drinking increased in proportion to the size of checks I wrote to my solicitor, and at one point I was so out of it that I made an ass out of myself by insulting a client. We lost the client, and I recognized that I was losing it myself. I finally gave up fighting her and agreed to whatever she demanded. I just wanted out." He shook his head. "It took longer to unravel the damn thing than the marriage itself lasted."

Annie clung with both hands to her wine glass. She understood only too well the despair he must have felt, his life spiraling out of control with no way to rein it in. He'd handled it differently, but it was still the same—the suffering was still the same. It was a strange realization for someone who'd always been sure she was the ultimate victim.

"Just as the divorce was finalized, Felicia's father came to see me. It was clear I couldn't continue with the firm, because by that point I was a disgraceful mess. He did me a favor by firing me.

"I left London two days later, without a backward glance. I packed one small bag, with a few tee shirts, jeans, a couple of sweaters, a warm coat. I left all my Armani suits, Hermes ties, and Cartier cufflinks for Felicia to sell, give away, or toss out the window."

Annie's instincts screamed at her to reach out and make a connection. Ditching her fear of intimacy, her uncertainty of his motivation, and the knowledge that she'd never see him again after her vacation ended, she stretched her hand across the table and lightly touched the one he had wrapped around his wine glass. He turned his wrist and grasped her fingers in his. He looked into her eyes with such a haunted expression that it made her heart lurch. *Jesus,* she thought. *Why did I let him open this can of worms? How long ago did this happen?*

"It was six years ago," Kaden said, as if reading her mind. "I showed up on Henri's doorstep unannounced, a total basket case. I hadn't stopped drinking and was soused by the time I arrived—it was a miracle that I even made it. God bless Henri, he took one look at me, hugged me like a long lost son, and dragged me inside. He shoved me down into a chair at the kitchen table, pulled out a bottle of Cognac, and poured us both a glass."

Annie almost spit out her wine. "He gave you *more* to drink? I thought you said Henri helped you!"

"I told him everything. Why not? My life was ruined, and I was planning on drinking myself into an early grave. I had nothing more to lose. Henri listened without comment, just kept refilling my glass."

He had that far-off look in his eyes again, but instead of regret, his expression held affection.

"I'm sure I passed out in the chair, but I woke up on a cot in the pantry. Henri was banging on the door, yelling for me to get up. I was disoriented and still drunk, but he dragged me out of bed, threw a ratty sweatshirt at me, handed me a cup of coffee, and pushed me out the door. It was dark, the dawn just a faint glow on the horizon, and I felt like my head was going to split open. I followed him in a stupor to the barn, where he gathered some tools then marched me out to the vineyards."

"Oh, that sounds helpful," Annie muttered, not liking Henri one bit.

"It was mid-May. The rains and the winds had gone, and it was time to do the first real work in the vineyard since winter pruning. He pointed at a vine, then turned his back and set himself to work. So I did the same."

Annie's agitation cooled as she allowed that Henri was perhaps more savior than sadist, although she wasn't prepared to completely dismiss the latter.

"Henri did help me, by simply being there. He didn't push me to talk, and he didn't coddle me. He just worked. And he expected the same from me. So I followed his lead. It took me awhile to remember what the bloody hell I was supposed to do, but it eventually came back to me, and Henri and I worked side-by-side in those vineyards all season long. When it came time for harvest, I was fit and sober and eager. We put in long days, as long as I had done in London, but the difference was that I was working the land with my blood uncle, who had a passion and respect for the land that bespoke generations."

Kaden looked around and saw that most of the patrons had gone. He looked at his watch. *"Merde,"* he cursed. "I've talked you to death … are you still awake?" He gently touched her cheek.

She smiled. "Hmm, barely." In truth, her heart was breaking for this beautiful, sensitive man who had been so hurt by lies and deception and then slowly healed with time, perspective, and the unconditional love of family. No one would make up a story like that—it was too … revealing. She didn't understand why he'd chosen to disclose such a personal story, but she believed him. *I want you to know who I really am.* He'd given her a gift of trust. Her heart was breaking a little for herself, too, since any relationship with him would be impossible, despite her desire to explore it.

Kaden suddenly looked embarrassed. "So, that's it, really. Now you know all my dark secrets. I live most of the year at Henri's estate in a small village in northern Provence called Rasteau, and I come back down here in the summer to stay connected with my family here, and my friends. François was one of our gang during my summers here as a boy. He and Juliette let me feel useful. They love to take advantage of my goodwill, and I love for them to do so."

Annie's warm look of understanding chased some of the chill from his heart. "Jean Claude and Nicole bought an old farm property several years ago. I helped them renovate it. There was an old dilapidated barn on the property, and I claimed it, fixed it up. That's where I live when I'm here. It's just outside of Les Eyzies."

"No wonder you looked like you just got out of the shower," Annie said. He gave her a questioning look, and she smiled shyly. "Yesterday morning, when you scared the wits out of me at the *saucisson* vender, you were clean shaven and your hair was wet."

Pleasure washed over him at the thought that she had noticed. "The farmhouse is just outside of the town. We usually go in on Sunday for market day. When I saw you walking through the stalls, I thought I was hallucinating. I'd been thinking of nothing but you since we met in the gardens." He caressed her hand. "You owe me your story, but we should probably leave. Jean Claude is giving me dirty looks."

They said their farewells to his cousins, and he drove her back to La Roque Gageac.

He parked, stepped around and helped her out, then just stood there, holding her hands in the moonlight under the cliffs. He seemed troubled, and Annie yearned to soothe him.

"Kaden," she said tentatively, not quite sure of her words. She reached one hand up and touched his cheek. He looked at her with his honest eyes, and it gave her courage. "What you shared with me tonight … I know it was difficult. I doubt you expected to let all that out."

He started to reply, but she held up her hand to stop him. "The Kaden Macallister I'm beginning to know is a thoughtful, loving, complete soul who cares for his family and friends. The journey to get to a good place is always rocky. I'm impressed that you made it to *this* place, that you are who you are now after all you went through. I will never judge your past. Thank you for a lovely evening."

Before she could overthink it, she leaned in to him, let go of one hand and snaked it around the back of his neck, tilted her head up, stood on her toes, and kissed him. He responded immediately, wrapping his free hand around her waist and pulling her toward him, deepening the kiss. It was heady … potent. It had been so long since she'd been kissed by a man, and she never wanted it to end.

Eventually, she pulled back. "I still owe you a story," she said, a little breathless, looking into his eyes.

"You do, indeed. What are you doing tomorrow?" His melancholy mood gone, he was looking at Annie like he wanted to devour her.

"I haven't decided. Do you have a suggestion?" Her dark eyes sparkled in the moonlight as she smiled up at him.

"I have many suggestions for you, *mademoiselle*. What time will be convenient to begin?"

"You'll be my guide, then?" she asked, one hand still wrapped securely around his neck. "What about everyone else who depends on you?"

"I would be honored to escort you." He lifted her hand and kissed her fingers softly. "And as to everyone else …" He gave a Gallic shrug. "They'll just have to do without me." He held her gaze as he brought one hand up to cup her cheek. "Will nine o'clock suit?"

"I'll be ready, but are you sure?" She stared at his lips as she said this, then watched them quirk and turn up in a sensual smile.

"I promise to make it worth your while," he murmured as he leaned in close to her ear, settling a whisper-soft kiss there.

After a few more kisses, he forced common sense to the fore and walked her up the long stairs to her room, where he leaned her against the door and kissed her again thoroughly. She had to suck in her breath to keep from swooning when he finally pulled away.

"*Au demain, chérie,*" he whispered, and then he was gone.

Eleven

"Uncle Kaden!" The small voice cut through the quiet morning mist as its owner raced down the back steps of the main house and came barreling toward him.

Kaden grinned and set down his coffee cup, bracing himself for the impact. His four-year-old cousin Alex launched into his lap and hugged him. "You're up early, *mon petit homme*. Where's your mum?"

"Still sleeping," Jean Claude said as he stepped out his back door with his own cup in hand. He remained standing on the stoop as he watched his young son squirming on Kaden's lap.

"*Pouvons-nous aller pêcher aujourd'hui?*" Alex asked in the hopeful way of children anticipating a treat. "Misha and I caught a frog in the creek yesterday, but Mama made us let it go."

Kaden laughed and ruffled the boy's hair. "What? She didn't let you keep it?"

Alex slanted a glance at his father and, in a stage whisper, said, "Mama said Papa would fry it up for breakfast if we didn't let it go." His big round eyes indicated that he had believed her.

Kaden grinned and whispered back, "Better for the frog, then." He tapped his finger on the tip of Alex's nose. "But I'm afraid I can't take you fishing today. We can go on Saturday," he added quickly as the boy's face fell. He had every intention of spending the next few days with Annie, if she let him, but she was leaving Saturday morning.

"Alex, go see if your brother is up," Jean Claude said, "and you both can go with me to get the croissants."

Fishing disappointment forgotten, Alex scrambled off his cousin's lap and ran back across the lawn into the house.

Jean Claude chuckled as he shut the door behind him and walked over to join his best friend and cousin. He took a seat at the small bistro table where Kaden was sitting and looked at him intently. "Do I detect a change in the routine?"

"For a couple of days, anyway," Kaden said noncommittally.

"She's a lovely woman …"

"Don't start. I know how bloody stupid it is. I just can't bloody help myself. I feel like I've been hit over the head with a brick."

"Nicole was worried about you last night. She—"

"I'm fine." He took a sip of his coffee and looked at Jean Claude, who was watching him closely. "I, ah, told her everything."

Jean Claude almost spit out his coffee. "*Ce qui? Pourquoi?*"

Kaden shrugged. "I'm not entirely certain, but … I don't have a lot of time here, and I wanted to get it all out there. She's … there's something about her. She's special."

"That was an American accent I heard."

"San Francisco."

"Convenient. What does she do there?"

"Hell if I know." At his cousin's amused look, Kaden shook his head in affectionate frustration. "Getting personal information out of her is like trying to pry open a stubborn oyster. Hard as hell, one slip and you're bleeding. She's pretty guarded, but I think I made some progress last night. She's definitely softening toward me."

"*Oui,* bleeding your heart out all over my restaurant could do that." But Jean Claude's voice held compassion behind the teasing words. "So what is your plan?"

They stood together on the Promenade in the bastide village of Domme, at the stone wall of the old ramparts, looking out over the Dordogne River. Yet another perspective of the sweeping valley, and there was a lot to see from up here. Annie hadn't realized how many fields were under cultivation until she saw it from this vantage point.

Kaden knew the area well and had given her interesting facts about the town as they'd made the short drive to the top of the hill. Now, he named the villages and other landmarks as they looked out over the expansive view.

"Domme also played a minor role in the demise of the Templars," he said.

"The Templars? I read something about them in that old guidebook. Soldiers from the Crusades or something like that, right?"

"The 'Poor Fellow-Soldiers of Christ and the Temple of Solomon' is what they called themselves. They were a religious-military order, the first and most powerful of its kind." Kaden started into the story as he motioned her toward the square that led down to the main commercial street.

"The Order was formed in the early years of the twelfth century by a French knight who had been a veteran of the First Crusade. Its purpose was to protect the pilgrims who journeyed to the Holy Land. They were considered to be warriors of God, and they were officially endorsed by the pope himself to fight for Christianity in the Holy Lands."

"Wow," Annie said, enjoying the professorial tone he'd adopted.

"There are any number of conspiracy theories about how they actually garnered the pope's favor," Kaden continued, "but once they had it, their accumulation of wealth was as swift as their rise to power.

"By the end of the thirteenth century, the Templars had amassed a fortune in lands and other property throughout Western Europe and the Near East, but by this time the tide had turned in the Holy Land. The Order was a convenient scapegoat for the loss of Jerusalem back to the Muslims, and there began a wave of dissatisfaction and suspicion about the Templars among the public, which was fueled as much as possible by the king of France, Philip IV. The king was deeply indebted to the Templars and had no intention or means of repaying them."

"The king borrowed money from them?"

"Just about everyone did. Because of their wealth and their far-reaching properties across the continent and the British Isles, the Order acted as bankers, of sorts, to all the monarchies of the day. It was an important element of their power, but a dangerous one.

"By far," he said, "the Order's largest holdings were in France, including a significant amount of property here in the Aquitaine.

"In a ploy to gain access to the Templar treasure, the king played on the increasing public dissatisfaction with the Templars and was able to get the pope to agree to his plan. Philip lured the Order's grand master, Jacques de Molay, and his personal guard of knights to Paris on some pretext. Then on the morning of Friday, October 13, 1307, a secretly organized, countrywide mass arrest was executed, and most all of the Templars in France, including the grand master and his Paris entourage, were imprisoned."

"That's incredible—and hard to imagine something like that was even possible!"

"It is, I agree. Those who were rounded up in this area were brought here and held in these towers." They emerged from a narrow lane, and Kaden gestured to the twin towers of the Porte des Tours that loomed up in front of them. "If you peek through those slots in the stone, you can see some symbols and words that they carved into the stone while they were imprisoned."

"What happened to them?" Annie asked, intrigued, as she craned her neck to see through the narrow gaps in the stone.

"They were eventually all executed. Most were burned at the stake for a whole list of fabricated charges, from heresy to sodomy to obscene rituals. Most everyone knew the charges were false, but no one was willing to go against the king. Plus, there was resentment for the wealth the Templars had amassed, and some felt their downfall was justified. There are two interesting footnotes to the story."

"And they are?"

"The reason why Friday the thirteenth is considered unlucky."

Annie laughed in disbelief. "No way, you're kidding!"

"Not at all," he said smugly, enjoying her reaction. "Can you think of any other reason?"

She watched him, unsure if he was pulling her leg or not. When she sensed he was serious, she shook her head. "I guess not. I suppose that's how superstitions get started, with some basis in fact. What else?"

"Their treasure is said to have never been found. Some people think it never existed; others think it's still hidden somewhere here in France." He laughed at Annie's expression. "We get people coming through here all the time looking for clues as to its whereabouts."

"You seem to know everything about this area," she said with admiration as they walked back up the street to the main square.

"Probably no more than anyone else who lives here with an interest in the past. And you must agree the history *is* fascinating. I've no doubt that you could tell me quite a lot about the history of California."

"Well, sure, but that's about two hundred years of history, not a thousand."

"Even so, you know what history there is, I'd wager. And now …" He steered her over to a café on the square that had small tables set out on the patio. "It's your turn to talk."

"You want to hear about California history?" she asked, pretending not to understand. They took a seat at a table in the shade of an awning.

"No, I want to hear the history of Annie Shaw." Kaden leaned back in his chair and waited.

She sighed, trying to decide what she should tell him. She wanted to reciprocate his openness, but she wasn't prepared to tell him about Jack or her miscarriage. Tales of death and destruction tended to put a damper on the day, and besides, she didn't want his sympathy. Ever cautious, she started with the present.

"Given your previous career, I'm sure you know what this means to me—last month I made partner at the San Francisco office of Smith Cole Blakely." She raised her eyebrows at him in challenge. It was an international firm, and she knew he would recognize the name.

The look on his face confirmed his surprise, but it was all admiration. He whistled softly. "My, my, aren't we full of surprises. I do understand what a milestone that achievement is, and it is quite impressive. Congratulations."

The waiter chose that moment to stop by the table, and Kaden ordered coffee for them both. When they were alone again, he said, "When I was in the business, the accounting side was an old-boys club, no women at all. I can't imagine it was easy."

"It wasn't, but like you ... when you were in London, I mean ... I love the work. And I've had a good mentor—my boss, actually. It's essentially consumed my life, but it's been exciting. John says I thrive on the challenge."

Kaden frowned. "John?"

"John Franklin—my boss." Annie saw his frown deepen. "His wife is my best friend."

"Ah," he said, relaxing. They were silent as the waiter brought their coffee.

"The deals are the most fun," Annie said. "My specialty is real estate. There's so much exciting redevelopment going on in San Francisco right now, and the new tax laws have made everything that much more complex and challenging. I've had lots of opportunities to be creative and really help my clients. On the tax side, we're dealing with real money, not just financial statement presentation. I've created a niche for myself in a couple of key tax code sections dealing with rehab and investment tax credits as well as the entity structures for holding real estate."

"Partnerships and REITS?" Kaden asked, even more impressed.

"Mhmm," she answered, taking a sip of her coffee. She wasn't surprised he got it after what he'd revealed the night before.

"I almost envy you," he said. "I loved doing deals. There's an incredible adrenaline rush when a big project finishes well."

"Exactly." Annie said with a smile. "Of course for me, once the transaction is finished, there's all the ongoing compliance—tax returns and the like—to keep us busy, and keep our billings up."

She talked about her clients and her work, warming up as he encouraged her and asked her questions now and then, but mostly he just listened. He listened like he was truly interested, and she loved that he really understood what she was talking about. Not many people did. And none of the swirl of humanity around them distracted him. They were sitting at an outdoor café in the middle of a busy square, but he kept his eyes and his focus on her alone. It felt nice. Very nice.

Over the rim of her cup she studied him. So relaxed, so confident, and so gorgeous. And so very interested in *her*. She wanted to tell him something about what drove her, without revealing the heartbreaking stuff. After a moment she said, "I was in a bad accident once."

"What kind of accident?" His immediate look of concern made her feel warm.

"I was caught in an avalanche in Yosemite."

"Good God, Annie, what happened?"

"I was hiking on a steep trail above the valley floor, there was an earthquake, and a big boulder dislodged at the top of the ridge and came crashing down." Her voice went soft, and her eyes cast down at her hands holding the coffee cup. "I suppose I was lucky, because people died that day."

For no specific reason—just something about the tone of her voice—Kaden knew that she was holding something back, but he stayed silent.

"I don't remember much about it, really. I must have hit my head pretty hard, because I was in a coma for ten days. One minute I was in Yosemite with the ground shaking under my feet, and the next thing I knew, I was waking up in a hospital bed in Modesto. I had some broken bones and lots of bruises, not to mention a whopper of a concussion. It took me a while to get back on my feet. John's wife, Marie, was my … she was a good friend, and helped me pull through. After that, I was just totally focused on my work. I didn't have time to dwell on the accident, and that suited me just fine."

Kaden wasn't fooled by her nonchalance. There was definitely something she was leaving out. His heart squeezed at how she seemed to draw inward, and he guessed there were memories about the accident more painful that just her physical injuries. He hoped she would eventually trust him enough to reveal it.

She abruptly pulled herself back to the present. "After years of all work and no play, I decided to reward myself by taking a real vacation." She smiled at him. "So here I am." She took a sip of coffee. "Actually, I wasn't really intending to come down here at all. I went to Paris to visit an old friend and planned to spend my whole vacation there."

Kaden's stomach lurched, and his jaw tightened. *I don't want to hear about the guy in Paris.* Annie didn't notice his sudden tensing.

"But our plans went sour when she got called unexpectedly to London. Lori and I have been friends since college, and we both work for Smith Cole, just in different cities."

The breath he didn't realize he'd been holding whooshed out of him as his gut unclenched. "I'm glad to hear that, because I was afraid I was going to have to go to Paris and punch some poor sod in the nose."

"Huh?" Annie looked at him quizzically.

"Your friend in Paris."

"Lori?" She was confused.

Kaden fidgeted with a packet of sugar and actually blushed. "That day I met you at the gardens, you said you had been in Paris the week before with a friend, going out to dinner every night. The way you said it, I assumed you were with a man, and that you were down here alone because you'd fought." He winced at how pathetic that must have sounded. "I have a very vivid imagination. I've been working out how to get his name so I could go up there and smack him around for hurting you."

Her eyes widened. "No kidding."

He shrugged, fidgeted some more. "No excuses. Sorry."

"I'm sure Lori will be happy to know she's safe from you." Annie laughed and shook her head.

Twelve

For the next three days, Kaden ferried Annie around the area, taking her to all the places she wanted to see, and some she hadn't known about. He played the charming tour guide and made her laugh. They enjoyed lazy lunches together, and intimate dinners. Kaden certainly knew the restaurants in the area. She never dreamed food—and wine—could be so good.

They talked of many things—almost everything, really, except what was happening between them. She told him about growing up in California, about her family, and about San Francisco, but she couldn't bring herself to spoil the mood by bringing up Jack. He told her about his uncle Henri, and Annie revised her initial impression of him, realizing how much Kaden loved and respected him. He talked at length about the vineyards in Rasteau and painted a vivid verbal picture of the Rhône Valley and Provence. It was so clear that he truly loved the place. She wished she could see him there, in his element, but she kept that to herself.

The conversations were not limited to stories of their individual lives. They talked about current events and debated viewpoints and ideas, finding they had more in common than not on many topics. Annie confessed she rarely indulged in reading anything beyond technical journals, whereas Kaden did a great deal of reading for pleasure. He told her about recent books he'd liked and why, giving her some enjoyment of them as well.

The attraction between them practically sparkled. They held hands and touched affectionately throughout the day, and enjoyed delicious kisses as they said *bonne nuit* at her door each night. Annie was tempted to invite more intimacy with Kaden, but her good sense prevailed. She was leaving soon, she rationalized, and as much as it pained her, she knew it was unlikely that their life paths would ever cross again. And for his part, Kaden remained playful and affectionate but respected her boundaries and didn't push for more.

She eventually learned how he managed to live like he was on vacation all the time. It turned out that Kaden Macallister had never stopped being a financial wizard. In addition to managing his own portfolio—other than the flat and its contents, he had succeeded in extracting himself from his marriage with the bulk of his assets—he owned Macallister Enterprises, Ltd., a private investment company that funded emerging technologies.

"But how do you stay connected to the markets and information on a real-time basis from rural France?" Annie asked as they strolled through a street market.

"Ah, an excellent question, and something I'm excited to tell you about." She looked at him expectantly, but he just smiled and shook his head. "But not just now. Right now, I want to shop for our dinner."

"Shop for our dinner?" Annie asked, looking up at him. Kaden drew her hand he'd been holding to his lips, which he brushed across her knuckles.

"*Oui, ma chérie,* I want to cook for you on our last night together." He looked at her intently. "You wouldn't want to leave me disappointed, would you?"

Butterflies took flight in her stomach. This could get dangerous, but how could she possibly refuse? He had been the perfect gentleman all week, and she *was* curious to see the restored barn that he lived in. "I didn't know you cooked. I'd be honored," she said.

He turned her hand and kissed her palm, giving her a delicious grin.

The hunt for ingredients became an undertaking that he took quite seriously. She continued to be amazed at the variety of food and other goods available at the street markets, even the smaller ones. It was a way of life here, and she knew she would embrace it if she was a local.

They selected beautiful summer squash and fingerling potatoes, a crisp head of lettuce and a couple of ripe tomatoes, and Kaden insisted on buying a bagful of perfect little purple plums that came from the orchards near Agen. She asked what he was planning to do with them, but he just kissed the tip of her nose and said it was a surprise. They decided on *magret de canard,* duck breast, for the main dish. On their way out of the market, Annie stopped at a flower stall and bought a large bouquet of sunflowers.

"Let's drop all this off at the house, then go to La Roque Sainte Christophe," Kaden said as they put their bags in the trunk. The impressive stone shelter that Annie had seen on her exploratory drive the previous Sunday was the final place they were planning to visit. Kaden had saved it for last, since it was his favorite.

He sped up the road, hung a right just before Les Eyzies, and after a few moments, he slowed to make a right turn onto a small lane. They rolled along beneath a tunnel of tall trees with full leafy canopies before the lane ended at a big expanse of lawn in front of a beautiful two-story stone farmhouse with neatly painted berry-red shutters and blooming flowerboxes at every window. Annie recognized the same creamy, gold-blond stone with which every old building in the area was constructed. The roof was gray-black slate. There were lots of mature trees on the property that appeared perfectly situated to provide shade to the house without making it feel crowded.

"My place is around the back," he said as he drove the track around the main house. Set against the edge of the forest that loomed up behind was a charming barn-like structure. It was smaller than Annie had pictured, but it was beautiful in its rustic simplicity, with sloped roof and a largish dormer window upstairs toward the back. A simple rectangle, it was made from a combination of weathered blond stone and wood timbers, with a pair of old-fashioned rolling doors dominating one end, painted the same shade of red as the shutters on the main house. Along the wall adjacent to the rolling doors, modern windows framed a small porch where the main entrance was located. The porch was draped with a trellis of wisteria in full bloom that hung over the top to frame the Dutch door. There was a gravel path that led from the driveway to the porch.

"It's adorable!" Annie jumped out of the car before Kaden could open her door.

They carried the grocery bags up to the door, and he opened it, motioning for her to go in. She stepped inside and looked around. It was essentially one big open room, half of which was open all the way to the rafters, the roof canting in near the top. A loft was accessed by an open wood-framed staircase that disappeared up the wall across from the front door. The room upstairs was blocked from view by a half-height wall. His bedroom, she assumed. Under the loft, centered against the back wall, was a beautiful fieldstone fireplace that dominated the space, flanked by book-laden shelves. An overstuffed couch faced the fireplace. Rough, exposed beams held up the loft. There was a small door beneath the stairs that hid a powder room.

The combined kitchen-and-dining area was situated at the opposite end. It was open and airy under the tall ceiling, consisting of an L-shaped counter tucked into one corner, with an aged butcher block in the center doubling as both a workspace and a casual bar. High above the block dangled an antique iron rack with gleaming copper pots. There was a bay window over the sink that held pots of fresh herbs. A charming old wood table took up the other corner, presently covered with an array of computer equipment that frankly astonished Annie. It was more impressive than the computer room at her firm. *Who had that kind of equipment at home?*

The main feature on that end of the house was the pair of rolling doors that Annie had seen from the outside. From the inside, it looked like there was a glass wall against the doors, but looking closer, she could see that it was a series of glass panels that could slide back, out of the way.

Kaden had been standing in the doorway, watching her as she took in his space. Seeing what held her attention, he set his groceries on the butcher block then turned to the glass doors, fiddled with the latch and slid them open. They silently retracted, tucking neatly into slots in the wall on each side. Then he unlatched the wood doors and rolled them open. The effect was stunning. The morning light came streaming in, and the view through the doors looked straight across a wide expanse of fields gently sloping down the hill. On the horizon, she could see more of the same dense forest that circled the back of the barn. Annie stepped out onto the flagstone patio, outfitted with a charming bistro table and chairs. Since the doors faced west, they allowed a breeze into the room without the glare of sun until late in the afternoon.

Annie was enchanted. "Did you design it?"

He nodded. "It's small, but it's all I need. I'm here only in the summer, but I put the fireplace in, just in case, and eventually if Jean Claude ever sells the property, this can be rented out year-round as a separate unit."

He stowed the duck breasts in his tiny fridge, dumped all the produce into a large basket that sat atop the butcher block, then took the flowers Annie was still holding and leaned them in the sink with the base of their stems in water. Then he grabbed a couple apples from another basket and tossed her one. "Let's go. You'll have plenty of time to admire my barn tonight."

Annie laughed and bit into her apple. Juice dripped down her chin, and she casually wiped it with the back of her hand. He winked at her and led the way back out.

Kaden dropped her at the hotel in the early afternoon after they'd spent an enjoyable few hours exploring the stone shelters. She didn't know how late she would be out tonight, and she wanted to be ready to leave early the next morning to catch her train. She spent the afternoon packing, trying hard to reflect on the wonderful experience she'd had with Kaden rather than dwell on the fact that tonight would be their last night together. And the fact that she'd probably never see him again.

Thirteen

For their last night, Annie strived for casual but flirty, wearing a light summery dress with a flared skirt and low-heeled sandals. The evening air was warm and balmy, and she debated whether to bring a sweater; she would probably need it if they sat out on the patio, but the thought of wrapping herself in Kaden's sweater again was tempting. In the end, she brought one of her own.

When they arrived back at his home, the barn doors were wide open and the evening sunlight washed the barn in a soft glow. Mozart filled the air. She caught a whiff of something delicious and looked over to the kitchen, spying a small pot simmering on the stove. She smiled when she saw arrangements of sunflowers set around on the butcher block, on the table outside, and on the low table in front of the couch.

Behind her, Kaden put his hand on the small of her back, leaned in to kiss the top of her ear, and whispered, "You look lovely, *chérie.*" He kissed her ear again. "Sit here." He nudged her gently toward a stool at the butcher block. "I have a few more things to do."

"Let me know if I can do anything. It smells wonderful." *What could be better,* Annie thought, *than having a sweet, handsome man cook for you?* He wore a soft cotton long-sleeved tee shirt tucked into faded jeans. The shirt hugged his form, and she wasn't sure if it was the delicious aroma or his sexy physique that was making her mouth water.

He pulled a bottle of chilled rosé from the fridge, popped the cork, and poured them both a glass. He handed one to her, picked up the other, and gently clinked them together while holding her gaze.

"To a *very* enjoyable week with you." His voice was husky. She met his gaze and saw something there behind the smile … sadness?

She cleared her throat, feeling a bit sad herself. "And with you," she replied, then took a sip and closed her eyes. How was she ever going to get her head back into her own world? He was still watching her when she looked again, and she blushed.

"You've spoiled me," she said with a little laugh. "I never thought I could enjoy something so much."

"You'll just have to come back for more, then." She stilled, knowing they weren't talking about the wine. The room suddenly got warmer as their eyes held.

Kaden shifted back, returned the bottle to the fridge, pulled out the duck breasts, laid them on a plate, and expertly scored the fat side. He set the duck aside then quickly sliced the squash into perfect circles. Then he sliced the potatoes. As he worked, he explained what he was doing. Apparently, he had learned a trick or two hanging out with Jean Claude.

Next he worked on the salad, washing the lettuce, slicing the tomatoes. He minced up a shallot and tossed it in a bowl, pulled some Dijon mustard from the fridge and with a small whisk scooped some out and dropped it into to shallots. From a rack on the counter, he plucked bottles of white wine vinegar and extra virgin olive oil. He poured a bit of the vinegar into the bowl, sprinkled in some salt and pepper, and whisked it all together. Then, whisking with one hand and holding the bottle of oil with the other, he slowly poured it into the mixture, emulsifying it to perfection right before her eyes. Finally, he cut a lemon in half, squeezed a bit of juice into his hand to catch any seeds, dribbled a few drops into the mixture, then whisked it again.

When he was finished, he held the bowl out to her. "Care to taste it? You can tell me if I need to make any adjustments."

"You think so?" she laughed as she dipped her little finger into the mixture. She brought it to her lips and sucked the dressing off the tip. "Hmm," she mumbled around her finger. "Perfect."

Yes, you are, Kaden thought, wishing it was his finger in her mouth. *Jesus, get a grip.*

He cleared his throat. "Good, okay, that's done. Now the duck." Selecting a patinated copper sauté pan from the rack above the block, he set it down on the stove, then moved back to the fridge and snagged the wine, refilling their glasses. Back to the stove, he tossed salt and pepper on the duck breasts. "The trick with duck is to get the pan hot, then sear the breasts fat-side down, letting the fat render and get nice and crispy. I'll pour it off as it melts to use with the potatoes."

The sizzling, searing duck made a loud, splattering mess. After a couple times pouring off the fat, he flipped the breasts, let them sear a few more minutes on the meat side, then transferred them to a small sheet pan and popped it into the oven. She noticed he occasionally stirred the contents of the small pot that was sitting on a back burner.

After pouring some of the duck fat back into the pan, he added olive oil and let it heat up, explaining that by mixing the oil with the fat, the potatoes could be cooked at a higher temperature than in just the fat alone. "The duck fat gives great flavor, but it burns easily."

He added the potatoes to the pan, shook it to coat them in the fat, then added salt and pepper. He played around with them a bit before turning down the heat and letting them alone.

"That should do it," he said as he reached into a cupboard and brought down two plates. Lettuce and tomatoes were arranged onto them just so, and then he whisked up the salad dressing again before drizzling it over the top. He finished them with a flourish of fresh cracked pepper and said, "*Voilà!*"

Annie smiled.

"If you take the plates out to the table, I'll grab the wine. Just leave your glass here—we're switching wines and I have fresh glasses on the table." She did as instructed, and Kaden grabbed another bottle from the fridge before following her out to the table.

The new wine was from Graves, a district of Bordeaux known for white wine that was tartly crisp and lemony with an interesting earthy, wet-stone quality. It was perfect with the salad. In fact, it made the salad taste even better.

As they lingered over the first course, Annie asked about the farmhouse renovation project.

"Historic restoration and the modernization of old properties is a serious matter here, as you can imagine," he said. "Everyone has an opinion, and it was a bit of a circus. In the end, Jean Claude and Nicole got what they wanted, but the process was a killer. Then we tackled the barn, but that was mostly me. The restaurant was busy, and neither of them had any more time to help. After I showed them my drawings, they let me alone with it."

"Are there any other buildings on the property?" She had the impression the property itself was more extensive than what she'd seen.

"There's an old stable down the hill on the other side of the main house, plus a few smaller outbuildings, mainly stone huts that were once used for storing the farm equipment. Nicole wants us to remodel the stable, turn it into a playhouse for the boys."

"They have children?" A little pang went through her.

"Two wild boys. Michel is six, and Alex is four. I'm surprised they haven't come out to meet you yet. They're very inquisitive." He grinned. "They remind me of us when we were that age. They're the main reason Jean Claude bought this place—to give them plenty of room to run around." He paused, as if caught in a memory. "I love those boys, love spending time with them. I take them fishing at least once a week when I'm here."

Annie thought he sounded wistful. She understood the feeling.

They cleared the plates, and Annie washed them while Kaden went back to work at the stove, pulling the duck out and setting it on the counter to rest.

"That smells incredible!" Annie said, and Kaden just smiled, turning to the stove then back to kiss her quickly. "Just you wait."

He stirred up the potatoes then put the pan in the oven. He pulled another pan from the rack, poured in some olive oil and a tiny bit of duck fat. As it heated up, he tossed the squash with salt, pepper, and some sort of dried herbs he pulled from a little ceramic jar on his spice rack.

"What's that?" Annie pointed to the jar.

"*Herbs de Provence:* a mixture of thyme, fennel, basil, and savory. It's a staple in a French kitchen. I use it mostly with vegetables, but it's good on lots of things."

She watched, fascinated, as he dropped the squash slices into the hot pan, tossed them around, waited, watched them sizzle a bit, tossed them around some more. He then drew a knife from the block and sliced the duck breasts into perfectly even pieces. The potatoes came out of the oven, and he dumped them into the pan with the squash, tossed it all together, added a dash more of salt, then divided the contents between two plates. Next he fanned the sliced duck along the edge of the veggies. Finally, he reached for the small pan that had been sitting on the back burner and poured a dark, dense, silky-looking sauce over the duck. He finished with a twist of cracked pepper and a sprig of fresh thyme for garnish.

He winked at her. "Ready for round two?"

She grinned as she took the plates out while he reached for a bottle of red wine from the rack under the stairs.

Annie had never had anything so delicious. And he made it look so simple! The wine was from his uncle's estate in Pécharmant—a blend of Merlot, Cabernet Sauvignon, and Malbec, which he explained were the typical grapes of the region. He showed her the label. "The 1982 vintage was one of the best in a long time. At six years old, it's still pretty young, but it's tasting good, I think."

"The wine is perfect, again," she said after she'd tasted the food and a sip of wine. "How do you know what to pick?"

"It's not hard, but you have to know the wine's structure and flavor characteristics as well as the food. Most of us know what to expect with the food, but not everyone knows what to expect from a certain wine. When in doubt, pair the wine of a region with the food of the same region, and you'll never be disappointed."

She nodded, thinking she had a lot to learn if she wanted to keep up with him in this area. And she *did* want to. But how? How would they have any sort of a relationship, living half a world apart? She fought back the sadness that threatened to swamp her. Her rusty heart felt full to bursting. Where a week ago she didn't think she'd ever feel desire or romantic longing again, now she ached with the impossible situation that was forcing her to let it go.

They finished their meal and lingered over the wine with a selection of local cheeses. Annie sighed as she leaned back and looked out into the night. It was ten o'clock, and the sky was finally fading to black. The air was still, with just the *cigales* chirping out their steady rhythm, and the main house was dark. *The boys must be in bed,* she thought.

The silence between them was comfortable, but then Annie felt a soft brush on the nape of her neck and turned her head to find Kaden leaned toward her, his wrist resting on the back of her chair to stroke her curls. He was looking at her intently. "Annie," he spoke softly, with so much feeling, she felt her heart lurch. "We need to talk."

She looked into his eyes. "I know." She leaned into his caress, closed her eyes. "But I'm a little chilly. Can we go inside?"

They brought the dishes in from the patio, and Kaden rolled the barn doors together and pulled the glass panels shut. She started to wash the dishes, but he stopped her.

"I'll do that later. Come with me." He took her hand and guided her to the couch, then sat and pulled her down next to him. A wall sconce cast a soft light across the room.

Still holding her hand, he regarded her tenderly. "I would prefer to take you up to my bed and make love to you all night long, but I'm not going to do that."

She felt a stab of disappointment, though she wouldn't have let it happen either. She nodded slightly, eyes captured by his mesmerizing gaze.

"If I did …" His was voice husky, as his free hand lightly caressed her cheek. "I wouldn't be able to let you go in the morning."

She swallowed.

He looked down at their clasped hands, lightly ran his fingers over hers. "Annie, I know it's been only a few days, but I … I've come to care for you. Very much. There's something about you … something that draws me in. I know you have to leave, and that your life is somewhere else, but I can't accept that you'll walk out of my life forever tomorrow."

His words mirrored her feelings exactly. She'd been struggling with it all day. She lifted her free hand to his face, touched his cheek. "I feel the same way. I … I feel like my heart is about to be ripped from my chest. But I don't know what I can do."

He leaned his face into her caress, closing his eyes. "I was hoping you would say that." He opened his eyes and captured hers. "And I have an idea." He smiled slightly when her expression turned hopeful.

"Really? What are you thinking?"

He shifted, settled back onto the couch, and pulled her close, wrapping his arm around her shoulders. "Let me just hold you, and I'll explain." She snuggled into him and laced her fingers through his.

"We need to stay connected, and we can do it the same way that I tie in to the financial centers in London and New York. It's no secret, really. It would have been impossible five years ago, but now, it's very possible. I assume you've heard of the internet."

She frowned. "We have what they call an *intranet* at the firm," she said, describing the network they used to electronically transmit information between offices. "But I think that's just internal," she said.

"It probably is, but it works the same way." He explained that by using regular phone lines connected to a personal computer, the computer could then dial up a service center and link in to the internet.

"In a big city, with a big company, the lines are larger and more powerful, usually dedicated to handle nothing but electronic data. The individual computers at your firm are likely connected to that line through a mainframe or server system, which is a more powerful machine that controls access to stored data and outside links for all the computers in your office.

"There are internet service providers, or centers that you can connect to, in every major city in Europe and America. More are popping up all over. Using residential lines, the phone connection can be slow, especially during peak hours. I usually do my work very early in the morning or late at night."

He inclined his head and waved his hand back toward the table with the array of computer equipment. "As long as I have my stuff hooked up, for the price of a phone call to Bordeaux, I can access financial databases all over the world. And I can send and receive messages to or from anyone. Anywhere."

"Send and receive messages?" Annie glanced over her shoulder at the equipment. She wasn't exactly sure where all this was going.

"If you have access to your company's internal communications on the computer at your desk, then you have an email address. That means you can send and receive messages electronically."

Kaden studied her as she looked thoughtful. "I suppose I do. I wonder what it is."

"Do you have a computer at home?"

"No, but I've been thinking about getting one. I'm to the point where I use my computer at work for virtually every project. I do a lot of spreadsheets and a lot of writing. If I could work at home in the evening, I could actually get out of the office, which would be nice. I don't mind working the hours, but I don't like having to be at the office so late. I would be much more comfortable working at home."

Kaden agreed. He didn't like the idea of her crossing town in the middle of the night, even in a cab.

"I think you should buy one," he said. "You have two platform choices, Macintosh or PC. I have a PC, made by IBM, which works well for my business, but there are others that make a competitive product. New software for the PC is being developed all the time, and each version outstrips previous capacity and functionality. In other words, it just keeps getting better and better. I do my best to keep what I have updated, since software becomes obsolete very quickly. At this stage in the game, every new version of just about anything is exponentially better and more powerful than the last."

She was listening intently, thinking.

He watched her for a moment and then continued. "There's a company in America called Quantum Computer Services that offers a dial-up email service to consumers. It's an inexpensive monthly subscription, and you just pay for the local phone call when you go online."

Annie was leaned back against his arm, looking up at him. "So if I buy a computer and sign up for this email service, then we can communicate over the internet?"

"Exactly." He leaned down and kissed her forehead. "We don't have to be in the same time zone, and we don't have to run up long-distance phone bills. We just need to be able to write. We can carry on a slow conversation by email. You don't have to write a long letter, just a line or two. Tell me about your day. Vent your frustrations. Tell me that it's raining. Tell me that you miss me." He kissed her again. "And I'll do the same.

"As close as I feel to you now, we still don't know each other very well," Kaden said softly, "and it will give us time to become better acquainted. I know there are no guarantees, Annie, and I'm not asking for one. But I want to try. We'll know if it's not right. If we have to struggle with it … we'll know. I'm willing to take that risk."

"How quickly do the messages go through?" Annie asked.

"It depends on the speed of the transmission at each end, but theoretically, it's instantaneous. If you email me at midnight, your message should arrive in my inbox almost immediately—nine in the morning here. I'll see it the next time I open my email.

"If I send you a message early in the morning, my time, it will be in your inbox when you check your email at midnight, before you go to bed." He brought her fingers to his lips and pressed kisses along her knuckles. "I could give you something to dream about."

He was a hand holder and a knuckle kisser, and she loved it. "What makes you think I'll check my email at midnight?" She had to smile, though, because that's probably when she'd end up doing it.

"That's when I would be, if I still worked like you do." God, how was he going to let go of her? Kaden knew it was late and she needed to get back to her hotel. He planned to be there in the morning to help her drag that heavy bag down to her car. But he wasn't done with her yet tonight.

She laughed. "You know me better than I thought." For the first time, she felt like maybe there was a chance, and the weight of pending gloom lifted.

Kaden unwrapped himself from her and stood up. "Wait right here, I'll bring the dessert."

"You made dessert, too?" She watched him pull the lid off a covered cake dish, and gasped. "The plums! Holy crap, you made a plum tart?!" She laughed out loud and clapped her hands. "Bring it on!"

It was well past midnight when Kaden finally walked her up to her door. She wanted to ask him in—he wanted her to ask him in—but they both knew how that would end up. They had something special, and they wanted to make sure it would live across the distance before they sealed their relationship with that level of intimacy.

But that didn't stop him from molding himself to her and giving her a soul-searing kiss to let her know what she was missing.

Fourteen

When Lori Sheridan opened her apartment door to Annie the next day, they hugged like the old friends they were. Then Lori held her at arm's length, looked at her critically, and said, "Tell me."

Annie wasn't sure whether to laugh or cry, but over a bottle of wine, a baguette, and some deliciously stinky cheese, she spilled the whole story.

"So now what?" Lori asked.

Annie took a deep breath. "I'm going to buy a computer the minute I get home."

Lori gave her a you-can't-be-serious look, and Annie frowned. "You're the one who encouraged me. I know I just met him, but we have this ... connection. It's hard to describe, but I just can't ignore it."

"I don't want you to get hurt, Annie. What do you really know about this guy?"

"I know enough, and I have nothing to lose. And don't look at me like that—he was a perfect gentleman the entire time. We may never be more than long-distance friends, which is what we are now. If the romance part fizzles out, well then, at least I'll have a computer that I can work on at home."

"But you just made partner! You can't just throw that away and move to France!"

Annie looked around the room in exasperation. "What conversation are you in? Who said anything about moving to France? I'm not stupid. You know how hard I've worked to get where I am at the firm, and I have no intention of giving that up. I love what I do, I love the power of my position, and I have a real opportunity to make my mark. I know what I've got ahead of me, and I know coming back here is not an option any time soon. Kaden's not destitute. If this goes anywhere, he can come visit me, or move to San Francisco, for that matter. Who says the woman has to make the move?"

Lori rolled her eyes, and they both started laughing.

Two weeks later, Annie watched a pimple-faced kid connect the multitude of wires that snaked all over her desk to the new toys sitting on top of it. She had laid down a tidy sum of money on the computer, modem, and printer—not to mention all the software to run the new system. She had no clue about the setup, but she hoped it would be finished soon.

Upon her return to San Francisco, she'd thrown herself back into the fray of work. Her job gave her a sense of purpose and pride, and she loved the challenge every client threw at her. And it took her mind off Kaden … sort of. He was never out of her head completely, but she was able to set thoughts of him aside when she was buried in client issues.

She had picked out the computer setup as soon as she could steal a few minutes away from the office, and today was the first day a technician was available to come set it up. She was anxious to try out the modem to see if she could really send a message to Kaden from her home. It made her almost giddy thinking about it.

Although it was a poor substitute for the real thing, the idea of reaching out to him from her home made her happy. In their time together, they had talked about a lot of things, big and small, but there was so much more to know and to share. *We have all the time in the world at this point,* she thought wryly. If nothing else, they would get to know each other. Would they continue to like what they learned? *I guess we'll find out.*

She was yanked out of her reverie when the kid suddenly sat up and said, "Okay, let's fire it up and see if it works."

After another torturous three hours of watching him load all the software and set up her email account, he finally showed her how to connect to the internet and log on to her internet service provider.

Once she was alone, Annie sat at the desk staring at the array of equipment. *Okay, here we go.* She pulled out the paper Kaden had given her with all his personal information—two mailing addresses, three phone numbers, his email address, and his birth date.

She found the dial-up screen, went through the access steps, entered her login name and password, and after a short delay she heard the faint sound of a dial tone, then the sound of a number being dialed, then a pause, then faint ringing, followed by a crackling that the kid had told her was the sound of the connection being made. She looked at the screen, and sure enough, up popped the service graphics. She pointed her cursor at the New Message button and clicked. A simple message form appeared. She entered Kaden's email address on the first line, then sat back and stared at the subject line.

What to say? *Greetings from San Francisco.* No, too stiff. *I'm here!* Too stupid. *Are you really out there?* Annie considered that a moment. Why not?

She typed it in the subject line and looked at her watch—four in the afternoon here, which meant one in the morning there. Perfect. She composed her message.

To: Kaden@meltd.com
Date: August 13, 1988
Subject: Are you really out there?
Hi Kaden,
(Kiss-on-both-cheeks)

You probably thought I wouldn't do it, but here I am, sitting at my brand-new computer with wires and cords going everywhere. Is it always like this? Geez. The kid who set it up couldn't have been out of high school yet, but he seemed to know what he was doing.

Before I write you a long message that may get lost in … ah, wherever these messages end up, email me back to let me know I found you.

A nice wet kiss on the mouth,
Annie
PS: I miss you.

Kaden slumped on a stool at Juliette's bar, nursing a beer and staring out at the river.

"You look like a pouty puppy who got left behind when everyone went out to play," Juliette said to him as she cleaned a table nearby. It was mid afternoon, but the bar was empty.

He looked at her and scowled. "A puppy? Please."

"Okay, an old dog."

Kaden nodded and took a swig of his beer. "More like it. That's how I feel. Like a mangy old mutt with gray whiskers. And fleas. And a limp. So pathetic that no one wants him around."

"I take it you haven't heard from her yet."

He looked at the floor as he shook his head.

"Give her time, *cher*. You can't expect her to run right out the minute she gets home and buy a computer. It's a big investment, and it takes time. Even if she *did* run out and buy one, which she probably did because she is crazy about you, it takes time to get it all set up. Not everyone understands those computers like you do. Give her time."

Kaden knew she was right, but it didn't make him feel any better. It had only been two weeks. Two weeks since he'd held her in his arms and kissed her goodbye. If he closed his eyes and concentrated, he could still feel her enticing body pressed into his.

She had promised to be in contact as soon as she could. He could just call her, but he really needed for her to make the first contact, as they had agreed. She would email him as soon as she got set up. And if she couldn't get set up for any reason, she would call him. That's what they'd agreed.

He watched a group of middle-aged Brits coming up from the quay where they had just disembarked from one of the *gabarres*. They headed across the parking lot, straight toward the bar, talking and laughing. Kaden sighed. He didn't feel like playing the cheery local. He dropped some money onto the counter, waved to Juliette, and left.

Not interested in sitting by himself at La Belle Nicole, he stopped at the market on his way home to pick up supplies for dinner. Maybe he just needed to sweat out his grumpy mood in a good workout. He stowed his groceries, donned his cycling gear, retrieved his bike from the garage, and headed out for a punishing ride.

Hours later, Kaden sat at the table on his patio, drinking a bottle of Henri's wine, brooding. After his ride he'd showered, then sat at his desk and fired up his computer to check his email. A couple of interesting messages from various business contacts, but nothing from Annie. He'd poured himself a glass of rosé—he couldn't drink it now without thinking of her, as if he needed one more thing to remind him—and made an effort to focus on some financial reports.

He'd got caught up in one particular report on a company he was keen to invest in, and when he'd finally lifted his head to stretch his neck out, it was dark outside. Surprised to see it was almost eleven, he'd shut the computer down, made himself dinner, and poured himself some more wine. He knew he needed to be careful with the wine. He was not going to let himself get caught in that vicious spiral again. Especially not over a woman he'd only known for a week and hadn't even slept with.

He was brooding over that little detail now, fantasizing about what it would have been like to take Annie to bed. She had a lean but curvy body and generous round breasts. She had looked fresh and lovely in that dress she'd worn the last night and he'd wanted to peel it off her. And she had fit so perfectly snuggled up against him. As much as it killed him, he knew he had done the right thing by not going beyond kisses. He doubted she would have resisted for long if he pressed, but that didn't help him now. Would it have made it harder to think about her now if they had made love? Probably, if the experience was anything like he expected it to be. She had a passionate nature, and he could only image how responsive she'd be.

He pondered what her secrets might be. There was something she had left out of her story, something about that avalanche when she'd been injured. He wished he could find out more about it. An avalanche in Yosemite would have made the news somewhere, probably even San Francisco. Perhaps ... was it possible he could find something on the internet that could tell him what had happened?

Suddenly with a purpose, he tossed his dishes in the sink and sat down at his computer. While he waited for the modem to connect, he thought about the best way to find what he was looking for. 1988 was still a nascent period for the internet, but daily, more and more data was being made available online. The trick was figuring out how to find it. He'd worked with it more than anyone he knew, but even for him it could be a challenge.

He accessed a website that listed major newspapers around the world and found two in San Francisco. He picked the *Chronicle* first, connected to that website, and saw that he could use a keyword search to find archived articles that had been digitized. He stared at the screen for a moment, thinking about what he was looking for, then typed in *Yosemite, avalanche,* and *injuries.* He was surprised when his search pulled up over a hundred documents. *A lot of people get injured in avalanches in Yosemite.*

As he started scanning the articles one by one, he noticed a common theme that didn't jive with what he knew. These articles were all dealing with avalanches involving snow. Annie didn't mention snow—she said she'd been hiking on an unmaintained trail *There had been an earthquake! Of course!* He reentered his search terms, adding the word *earthquake* with the others.

Better—there were only ten articles. He scanned them and quickly found what he was looking for. Not much detail, but this had to be it. Memorial Day weekend 1980, an earthquake of magnitude 6.9 on the Richter scale hit in someplace called Mammoth Lakes. There was some damage in that town, but no injuries. The earthquake apparently caused a boulder in Yosemite to dislodge and topple down a trail, injuring several hikers and killing a man. The man's pregnant wife was also critically injured. *Pregnant wife? Bloody hell.*

He scanned the other articles, but none of them seemed relevant to a woman being injured. He read the article again. There were no names mentioned. He noted the date of 1980, and thought back. That fit. And he remembered she'd mentioned something about a boulder. It had to be her. She'd thrown herself into her work once she recovered and had just made partner at the tender age of thirty-four. Impressive. Bloody impressive. Eight years of self-punishment and, he guessed, agonizing guilt. And amazing courage. No wonder she didn't tell him. He felt an irrational stab of jealousy and wondered what her husband had been like. Had she been in love with him? *Of course she had, you stupid sod. She was carrying his baby.*

At that moment he heard a soft *ping* and saw that a new email had come in. He switched over to his email account. *From: annieshaw@qcs.com, Subject: Are you really out there?*

"You better bloody believe it," he said to the empty room. He clicked on the message and smiled as he read it. "I miss you, too, Annie, and I think you just saved me."

Fifteen

Annie checked out all the cool stuff on her computer, trying to figure out what would be useful and what wouldn't. She had purchased a whole suite of software to duplicate what she had on her office computer, and she'd brought home a couple of floppy disks with work projects to try out.

She was startled by a soft *ping* coming from the computer. She stared at the screen trying to figure out what she'd done wrong and eventually noticed the little flashing icon of an envelope at the bottom of the screen. She pointed her cursor at it and clicked.

It was her email. She had a message. And it was from Kaden. She nearly fainted. *So soon?* She clicked and opened it.

From: kaden@meltd.uk
Subject: Believe it, I'm here
Bonsoir, chérie. And a really long kiss back at you, coupled with a crushing hug. Welcome to the internet. I told you I went online at odd hours, it's the only time these crazy French aren't tying up the phone lines. That little ping when your message arrived made by heart leap.

Juliette said to tell you *salut* when we finally connected. She'll be happy to know the moping old dog I've become since you left has a reason to smile again. I've missed you so much, it's embarrassing.

I'm leaving shortly to go back to Rasteau. Henri thinks harvest will come early this year, and I want to be there with him when it starts. Besides, I need to throw myself into long days of backbreaking labor to keep my mind off a certain lady.

Je t'adore.

Kaden

Annie smiled so wide, her cheeks hurt. Thank God she was at home. *Note to self: Never email Kaden from the office.*

———————◆◆———————

Over the next months, they kept up a constant chatter through email. Sometimes they caught each other online, like they had the first time, but mostly they sent a message, finding a reply the next time they logged in.

Kaden went back to Rasteau and dove into the exhausting harvest and crush. His emails brought it to life for Annie, and she was fascinated by how deeply he connected with the land there and how much he loved and respected his uncle Henri.

For her part, Annie wrote about her work. With client projects completed for the year, she spent much of her time doing training sessions for Smith Cole offices around the country. She admitted to Kaden that she loved to teach, especially when she could tell that the people actually followed and understood what she was telling them.

As they grew comfortable with their private correspondence, the details they revealed became more intimate. Not as any sort of big reveal, but in small confidences. Annie found herself opening up as she'd never done before. Except she never mentioned Jack or her miscarriage. It wasn't like she was holding it back, but now it was just too awkward. What was she supposed to say? *Oh, and by the way, in that avalanche I told you about? I forgot to mention that I was pregnant at the time, lost the baby, and it was my husband who was killed.* Right. But she actually *wanted* him to know, just so they could move on from it, and she now regretted that she hadn't told him in France. It was like a dark cloud hanging over their growing intimacy.

She pictured him in her mind when she wrote and wished she had a photograph. How could she have not taken even one photo of him? In truth, she had no photos at all from that week in the Dordogne, which was ridiculous.

The holidays were coming up, and she wanted to give him something personal and special. What fun little San Francisco memento could she send? She thought about her wish for a photo of him and wondered if he felt the same. Well, at least she could send him one. He could toss it in the trash if he didn't want it.

She roped Marie and John into helping her, took extra care in applying her makeup, and then headed out to the Presidio where her friends took turns snapping pictures from different locations in the park. They didn't stop until they had a whole roll of film of her in various poses and positions with the Golden Gate Bridge as a backdrop.

When the film was developed, she was pleased to find one perfect shot of her looking happy and carefree with the beautiful bridge behind her. She had it made into a 5" x 7" print, found a touristy frame for it, and packed it into a box with a miniature replica of the bridge. At the last minute, she tossed a Giants baseball cap on top. She shipped it off, crossing her fingers that it would arrive in time.

A week before Christmas, Annie received a package from France. Her fingers shook as she cut away the thick postal wrapping. The box was heavy. When she opened it, she almost swooned. Packed on top of a two-bottle wine shipper was something carefully packed in bubble wrap. When she pulled the wrapping off, she held in her hands a beautifully framed photo of Kaden in what had to be his uncle's vineyard. He was sweaty and slightly unkempt, his thick hair pulled away from his face by the sunglasses on his head, and he had several days' stubble on his jaw. But the look of happiness on his face, his eyes shining into the camera, brought her to tears.

She held the frame up and touched the image of his face. *The man truly is a mind reader.* She couldn't have wished for anything more from him, and she hoped that he was equally as pleased with her gift.

The wine was from Henri's estate, and Kaden had included a recipe for a Provençal roast leg of lamb that would make the wine shine. She laughed and hugged the framed photo to her chest.

On Christmas Eve each year, Annie usually joined John and Marie for their family celebration. This year, Annie invited them to her apartment. Marie teased her about it, but Annie simply said, "You just wait and see."

She recreated the simple salad and vinaigrette that Kaden had made for her that night in his barn, even going to the trouble of searching for a white wine from Graves to serve with it. For the main course, she made the lamb recipe, which she had practiced once to make sure she did it right. She felt a surge of affection for him as she proudly sliced it and arranged it on the plates for her friends. Kaden had also included a few ideas for sides to go with it, not sure what was available in San Francisco during the winter. She used his ideas and turned out an amazingly delicious meal.

Although Annie had mac and cheese at the ready for the Franklins' two boys, Marie insisted they would be happy with the lamb. The couple glanced at each other over the boys' heads as Annie smilingly presented the main plates with a flourish. She sat down at the table, still smiling, poured out the wine, and lifted her glass to them for a toast. Then she frowned.

"What?" She looked back and forth between them, trying to figure out what she was missing. Marie looked like she was about to cry.

"What's wrong?" Annie asked, glancing around the table to see what she'd screwed up. Marie just shook her head, and John simply smiled. Then Marie got up, stepped over to Annie and bent down to hug her.

"Do you know how long we've waited to see you smile like this again?"

Annie was stunned, and a little confused. "Ah … hmm," she stammered. Then she smiled, raised her glass, and said, "Here's to living in the present, and looking forward to the future."

They all clinked glasses. The boys laughed and toasted with their sodas, which eased some of the awkward tension.

She hadn't had the confidence to attempt a fancy fruit tart, but the local French bakery provided an excellent alternative. When her friends finally left for the evening, Annie was so happy, she hugged herself. Then she sat down at her desk and fired up the computer.

Sixteen

Kaden returned to the house in the early evening of Christmas Eve, weary from spending the day in the cellar, racking barrels and testing samples. He was pleased with the quality and progress of the current vintage. It was all in barrels now, midway through malolactic fermentation, which was a critical step in the evolution of the wine. It was a naturally occurring process they never interfered with, just monitored closely.

As he stepped into the kitchen, the rich fragrance of Henri's legendary roast leg of lamb wafted from the oven. It smelled fantastic, as always. Several of the neighbors were coming that evening for dinner, an annual tradition, and he needed to get himself cleaned up and presentable.

He swung his tired body toward the hallway that led to his wing of the house—and stopped in his tracks. Sitting on the kitchen table was a smallish package wrapped in brown shipping paper. From where he stood, he could see an array of colorful postage stamps. He stepped toward it, his heart suddenly thumping in his chest. It was addressed to him. From Annie.

He reached for the package, touched it with his fingertips. His heart swelled. Annie had told him last week that she'd loved his gift, that she had parked the photo on her desk where she could look at him as she wrote to him, and that she was planning to make the lamb and serve the wine for dinner with the Franklins for Christmas Eve. Tonight, he realized.

He picked up the package and took it to his bedroom, closing the door behind him. He tore the paper off and opened the box. On top, there was a card featuring Santa and his sleigh being pulled by reindeer over the San Francisco skyline. He opened the card and read it.

Dear Kaden,

As I pondered an appropriate gift for you, I found that I missed seeing your smiling face, and hoped you might miss mine. I've never been good with gifts, so forgive me if this is silly. Close your eyes and imagine me scattering little kisses across your jaw, ending with a long, lingering kiss on your lips.

Joyeux Noël,

Annie

P.S. The answer to your question is John and Marie.

He frowned at the postscript and set the card aside. Next was a San Francisco Giants baseball cap. Kaden tried it on, pleased that it fit.

Looking back inside the box, he took out the first wrapped gift and laughed when he pulled off the paper to reveal a perfect miniature imitation of the Golden Gate Bridge. He set it aside then reached for the flat rectangle at the bottom of the box, hoping it was what he thought it was.

Carefully peeling away the paper, he discovered a campy frame covered with San Francisco icons surrounding a beautiful image of Annie in front of the Golden Gate Bridge. He just stared at it, his heart tightening. *Is she really that beautiful? God, I miss her.* He touched the image of her face and admired her curls blowing in the wind. She looked so vibrant and alive, like her smile was just for him, with the magnificent orange structure of the bridge in the background. He did as she bid, closing his eyes and imagining her kisses, then looked at the image again and wondered who took the picture. He read the card again and smiled.

As a Christmas gift to himself, Kaden called Annie the next day. He couldn't help it—he needed to hear her voice. They talked for almost an hour, an outrageous extravagance if he was paying attention to such things, but he wasn't. He held her picture in his hand for the entire conversation, rubbing his finger against her cheek in the image, wishing it was the real thing.

She lay on her bed, cradling the phone against her pillow, staring at his image as they talked. She had emailed him an abbreviated version of her dinner party success, but now she gave him the blow-by-blow of how perfect it had turned out.

He smiled through her entire narrative, loving how passionate she was about her success. "I'm glad I could inspire you, *chérie*. I only wish I could have been there to see it. And I love your gifts, too."

"How could we have not taken a picture together last summer?"

"I was distracted," he said truthfully. "What's your excuse?"

"I'm thinking the same thing. But next time, let's not forget." She was about to say more when she heard some sort of commotion on the other end of the line. A female voice. She frowned.

"Oh, Christ. Annie, hold on a second," he said. Though he spoke away from the phone, Annie heard the conversation just the same, as if he hadn't made an attempt to muffle the receiver. Kaden spoke in rapid French, and she didn't catch it all, but she shamelessly struggled to understand nonetheless. She thought he'd asked whoever had interrupted something like "What are you doing here?" but she wasn't sure.

A breathy female voice responded. Annie caught the words *Joyeux Noël* and her stomach dropped. They'd never specifically said they would be exclusive … but she'd assumed … *shit*. Her dreamy mood evaporated as humiliation took over. Had he been playing her for a fool all this time? What did she really know about him, other than what he'd told her? A sick feeling erupted in her belly.

Kaden's voice sounded angry; the female voice sounded whiny. Then she heard the slamming of a door and Kaden cursing.

It took a moment before Kaden returned to the phone. "Annie? Are you still there, *chérie*?" He sounded tentative and … frustrated.

Annie swallowed. "Yeah, I'm here, but I think I'd better—"

Her voice sounded so dejected that Kaden cursed again. "Annie, it's not what it seems. Our neighbors were here for dinner again. Henri is very close with them—well, with Sophia. She's a widow about Henri's age. Her daughter is another story, but he can hardly invite the mother without including the daughter … but Monique has a hard time understanding boundaries."

"Listen, don't worry about it. We were about finished anyway, right? Don't let me keep you. Thanks for the call. It was great talking to you." Annie tried to keep her voice light but missed the mark.

"Annie! Do not hang up. Not like this. Bloody hell, do you think I'm fooling around with someone here? Give me a break."

She could hear his frustration. "I ... I don't know what to think ... but then, it's really none of my business. I just thought ... just assumed ... oh, never mind." *This is too much,* she thought desperately.

"No, I will mind. It is your business, and for your information, you are the only woman in my thoughts and in my life, and have been since we met. Let me be clear. I consider you to be my girl. To me, that means exclusive, regardless of the distance."

"Kaden ..." Annie wanted to believe him, but the niggling doubt wouldn't recede. He was such a gorgeous man! How could she expect him to stay celibate for a woman he barely knew who lived six thousand miles away?

"Listen, Annie." His voice was gentle and sincere. "I'm no saint. I won't deny there have been women since I left London. But I can honestly say there's been no one special, no one who's ... stirred me like you do. And there's been no one at all since I met you. There won't be, not as long as we can keep building what we have, and I can hope that I might be able to see you again someday."

But neither of them knew when that would be.

The new year brought new business and exciting challenges for Annie, and she dove into busy season with gusto. As a partner now, she shouldered a level of responsibility that was new to her, but she took tremendous pride in her new role. She'd already been running the jobs and managing the clients, but this was the first time that the buck stopped at her. And she loved it.

If people noticed the difference in her bearing or the extra bounce in her step since summer, they credited the extra energy to her promotion. Which was certainly true, but there was more to it than that. Only John Franklin knew what kind of epiphany Annie had experienced on her trip, and he chuckled to himself when he caught a slight smile on her face—one that had not ever been there before.

Annie was glad she hadn't hung up on Kaden on Christmas, and had listened to what he said. She told herself there was no reason for him to lie and besides, why bother to keep up some pretense with her if he wasn't sincere about it? It wasn't like she was an easy mark. If he met someone else, she had to believe he'd be honest with her. As she would be, in the same situation. And the fact that he had a breathy young neighbor who wanted to distract him shouldn't bother her, damn it!

Kaden, too, had opportunities that kept him busy when he wasn't working on winter pruning. In February, one of the technology companies he had staked went public, and he was engrossed in monitoring the lengthy pre-offering process, albeit from a distance. He was tempted to travel to London to assist with the deal, but resisted. He knew the guys running it, and trusted them, and in the end it all went very well.

Despite their busy lives, Annie and Kaden emailed back and forth every day. Annie's replies were a little strained for a while after Christmas, and Kaden made a concerted effort to push past what had clearly been a setback in her trust. But he could tell when she began to relax with him again. Their messages were sometimes short and sweet reminders of affection; other times they were longer dissertations on what was going on with their respective businesses.

They'd fallen into the habit of sharing technical issues—over the months they'd been emailing, they realized that they understood much about the other's business and could often provide an informed opinion from an outside perspective. They usually incorporated these tidbits of questions and discussions into their regular emails, and Annie thought nothing of the consequences.

However at one point, she revealed sensitive information about a deal that was pending with one of her clients. She asked Kaden for his reaction on how a particular part of the transaction was about to play out, which prompted him to pick up the phone and call her.

Annie was asleep when the phone rang, and it took her a minute to register that it was Kaden.

"What's wrong?" she asked worriedly as soon as she was lucid.

"Nothing is wrong, *chérie,* but I longed to hear your voice, and I thought it would be better to talk to you about your recent inquiry over a more private medium."

"Huh?" she asked, still slightly groggy.

"You need to be more careful, love, about what you put in your emails," he said gently, then explained that with the growing popularity and usage of the internet, the security around email communication had not kept pace. He told her that when she revealed sensitive information that could affect a public company, it triggered his internal alarms.

"Do you mean others are reading our private emails?" Annie was horrified.

Kaden hated to discourage her, but he had to be honest. "It's a distinct possibility, so you must be careful not to tell me anything commercially sensitive over email. Hacking into personal databases has become a fashionable pastime for bright kids who don't have any respect for what they are hacking into."

"Oh."

"Annie, I'm honored that you ask for my opinion. You work with interesting clients and you are incredibly creative, and I'm flattered that you care to know what I think. Your mind works in a fascinating way, and I don't want you to stop telling me about what you're doing. I'm just concerned about the security of our communications."

"I had no idea." She suddenly felt a little sick.

Kaden heard the trepidation in her voice. "Not many people do, but the damage could be extreme. I would hate to see you compromised in any way."

"I understand," came the soft response.

Hating that he had worried her, he tried to reassure her. "The telecommunications industry will eventually catch up with security software, but until then, love, just call me. Reverse the charges if you want—you know I don't care about that. I want to help if I can, and I would prefer to hear your voice, even if it's just a business call."

"Thank you for telling me," Annie whispered over the phone. Then, since he had already called and she was sitting propped up in her bed, she asked him about Rasteau.

She could hear his smile over the phone as he told her what was going on in his world. It was early May, and the worst of the rains were finally behind them.

"We're in the middle of a mistral," he said with a laugh, describing the crazy powerful wind that whipped down from the cold northern plains and screamed through the northern Rhône River gorge before raging across Provence. "But I think it might be over in a day or two. Then we can start working the vines again."

"What are you going to do for your birthday?" Annie asked.

"My birthday?"

"Yes, according to my notes, your birthday is next week—May 15."

"How do you know that?"

She chuckled. "My notes. Don't you remember? You gave me everything except your social security number, probably because you don't have one."

At his uncle's house in Rasteau, leaned back in his desk chair, Kaden closed his eyes and groaned. "I must have been delirious. Sorry."

"Actually, I'm the one who should apologize. I haven't sent you a gift." Annie sounded remorseful. What she didn't tell him was that she was afraid to appear too clingy.

"Just hearing your voice is gift enough." Kaden knew he had woken her up and wanted to ask what she was wearing, whether she was naked in bed, but he wasn't sure he was prepared to hear the answer. Phone sex might be interesting, but he wanted their first time to be in person.

Then he ventured the question that had been top in his mind. "Will you be able to take some time off this summer?" He tried to sound nonchalant about it but knew his voice strained a bit.

She hesitated. *Not good,* he thought.

"I, ah ... I don't think so. I have a new client that I just talked into giving me several big projects, all with September deadlines. It's going to be a busy summer. Plus I have a big conference to prepare for." She sounded unhappy, at least.

"A conference?" he asked.

"Mhmm, I just found out about it. It's a big real estate conference in Washington, DC, in October. I've been invited to give a talk and to participate in a panel discussion. It's a pretty big deal, very high profile. It will be my first national speaking engagement since making partner." The pride in her voice made him smile.

"Washington in October? How long will you be there?" He might just have to find a reason to be there at the same time.

"I'm not sure yet. The conference goes for three days, but my part is just the first day. My talk is in the morning, and the panel is in the afternoon. It's a Wednesday, I think. I haven't decided whether I want to stay for the whole time or not."

"What if I gave you a reason to stay, say, through the following weekend?" Kaden held his breath.

"Are you saying you could meet me there?" Annie jumped up in bed, the excitement evident in her voice.

Kaden breathed a sigh of relief at her reaction. "I think I could, yes. It's good timing for me, since the crush should be over by then. Henri and the crew can handle the ongoing work by themselves for a few days. And besides, I have an idea that I've been toying with, a business idea that would require my presence on occasion in America, at least on the East Coast."

"Oh, Kaden, could you really come to Washington? I love that city, and I would love to show you around to my favorite places. I'm sure I could swing a few days off, especially after the grind I'm going to be in up until then. It's a great time of year there, usually clear and beautiful, unless it snows, of course." She laughed, her mind already racing, picturing them snuggled in warm coats walking arm in arm around town.

If it were up to Kaden, he would jump on a plane in a heartbeat and come to San Francisco to see her, but he knew that wouldn't work. Not only had she not invited him, but he had nothing to do there. The last thing he wanted was to be a hanger-on, in limbo while she worked, accepting what little time she could spare to focus on him.

Washington is perfect, he thought as they phone-kissed goodbye and hung up. It was neutral territory, they would have four full days together—and four nights, he reminded himself with a smile—and she would be in a good mood after acing her presentation. He had no doubt that she would, it was just her style.

Annie lay in bed after the call ended, cradling the phone in her arms. Her heart pounded at the prospect of seeing Kaden again, touching him and kissing him and, yes, making love to him. How had she let this happen? Because she couldn't resist him, she admitted to herself, and she was afraid she was already hopelessly in love with him. How ridiculous was that? She'd spend five days with him. But in those five days, they'd touched each other's spirit—connected—in a way that was unforgettable. And then over the internet—the internet, for God's sake!—they'd nurtured a small matchstick-size flicker of desire to a roaring fire.

The impossibility of the situation made her eyes sting, but she forced herself to be rational. Fantasy had no place in her world. She could no more leave her career that he could leave his beloved land. But that cool recitation of facts didn't stop her from wishing October here *now,* nor did it keep her heart from cracking with the knowledge that the one person she could love again in her life was someone she could never truly have.

Seventeen

The summer was indeed a grind for Annie, but she thrived on the work, loving the challenges and loving the successes even more. She had more projects going than ever, but she had a good team under her who worked well together, which freed her up to spend more time interacting with her clients and getting even more business out of them.

But in the back of her mind, she clung to her memories of that magical week last summer with Kaden. She allowed those memories to take center stage every night as she sat with his picture and emailed him. When she finally closed her eyes and fell asleep, she dreamed of him. As exciting as Annie's career was, for the first time since she'd sealed off her psyche to anything but work all those years ago, she felt like she was missing something in her life.

While Annie's summer flew by with complex projects and challenging clients, Kaden did what he did every summer. During the day, he helped out François and Juliette where he could and faithfully took his small nephews fishing, but most mornings and evenings, he sat at his wooden table with the barn doors flung open, computer humming, as he studied new technology and internet security developments.

His main project, however, was the one that would give him a reason—or an excuse—to travel to America: an import company that could bring his family's wines to a broader market. He'd floated the idea past Henri when Annie had first mentioned Washington, and his uncle had embraced the prospect of having access to the American market. It was no secret that the demand for French wine was declining in their traditional markets—France, the UK, and northern Europe—and not just from overseas competition. The French themselves were drinking less.

Kaden's research showed that the American demand for premium wine, especially French wine, was growing. While the wines of Rasteau were not well-known, their quality was high, and their similarity to the prestigious wines of Chateauneuf du Pape, right down the road, made them an interesting and affordable alternative for people who enjoyed those wines.

When Kaden had arrived back in the Dordogne in July, he'd gone to see his other uncle, Maurice, who owned the Pécharmant property, and pitched the idea to him. Maurice was enthusiastic about the project as well. Both Henri and Maurice had gathered interest from their neighbors whose wines they respected, and Kaden now had a portfolio of a dozen producers with a lineup of more than forty wines, including white, red, and rosé. Together, his portfolio represented seven distinct appellations in the Rhône Valley and the southwest of France. Kaden was glad that, with help from his cousin Jean Claude, who had many contacts in the French culinary community in America, Kaden had an impressive lineup of restaurants to call on once he arrived.

He worked on another project during the summer, as well, this one for Nicole, who was desperate to have the old stable converted to a playhouse for the boys. Kaden spent a few days down at that end of the property, thinking through design options. The goal was to make the space functional without destroying the character of the original structure. They also needed to keep one stall intact for the sweet old mare Belle, a retired draft horse that had come with the property.

After a few days of weighing the possibilities and sketching out ideas, he came up with a design and presented it to his cousins. With their support he began the process of getting the approval of the local building authorities. That proved to be tricky and tedious, but he prevailed. The permit was granted just as it was time for him to return to Rasteau.

Kaden felt good about what he had accomplished as he packed his equipment and files into his Peugeot for the long drive back to Rasteau. The permit was good for a year, and even better, in less than two months, he would see Annie.

Eighteen

Washington, DC, October 1989

Annie walked up the Jetway at Washington National Airport wheeling her roller bag, the other hand gripped tightly to her briefcase. Her heart was pounding in anticipation of finally seeing Kaden after more than a year of nothing but emails and phone calls.

She looked down to make sure her blouse wasn't gaping open. Having opted for comfort, she wore jeans and black half boots, with a silk blouse, scarf, and her favorite black jacket for a casual but pulled-together look. During the entire flight, she'd concentrated on her presentation, knowing that once she landed, there'd be no looking at it again until she was standing at the podium.

With a deep breath, she stepped into the terminal and looked around. Then she saw him, and her heart pounded even harder.

He stood beyond the crowd milling around the gate, casually leaning against the far wall, eyes glued to the Jetway door. When she spotted him, his handsome face broke into the most gorgeous smile, and he pushed away from the wall and started toward her, hands in his trouser pockets. She shook her head to clear it and did a double take. She'd never seen him dressed so beautifully. He was wearing a well-cut dark gray double-breasted suit, a crisp white shirt, and a perfectly knotted garnet silk tie. His long black overcoat hung elegantly from his shoulders. Even his hair was stylishly cut and neatly combed back. He was a vision to her, and she prayed she wasn't hallucinating.

She stopped just beyond the doorway, out of the stream of deplaning passengers, and waited, never breaking eye contact. He walked toward her slowly, stopping less than a foot away so they could simply take in the sight of each other. They were so focused on each other that they became oblivious to the travelers swirling around them. Kaden moved first, pulling his hands out of his pockets and raising them slowly to cup her face, and without breaking eye contact, he leaned in and gently pressed his lips to hers.

"Hi," he whispered hoarsely as he pulled back.

"Hi," she breathed. He leaned in and kissed her again, flashed that special little smile she remembered, then moved closer and touched his forehead to hers. Just then, someone bumped Annie's roller bag, jerking the handle in her hand and breaking the spell.

They grinned at each other, and Kaden tugged the heavy briefcase away from her, took hold of her hand, and said, "Let's get out of here."

They were too distracted with each other to notice anything on the drive downtown until the cab pulled up in front of the hotel. Kaden hovered while Annie checked in. They took the elevator up to her floor, and taking the card key from her, he opened her door and held it wide as she rolled her bag in past him. She flipped on the light switch and stopped dead in her tracks.

"What ..." she trailed off as she took in the suite. "I think there's been some mistake." Confused, she turned to Kaden, who had a boyish grin plastered to his face.

"I took the liberty of upgrading your accommodations," he said smoothly. "Since I'm planning on spending some time here myself, I thought we should at least be comfortable."

He stepped into the suite and let the door shut behind him. "Unless, of course, you object, in which case I'll do my best to convince you to spend time in *my* suite."

"You have a suite, too?"

"Mhmm ..." He came toward her, leaned her briefcase against the wall, gently tugged the handle of her roller bag out of her hand, and set it aside before taking her into his arms. He kissed her thoroughly, squeezing her tight, then held her head against his shoulder and reveled in the clean scent of her hair. "*Ma belle chérie,* it's so good to have you in my arms at last."

Her arms had come up around his waist at the same moment he'd wrapped his around her, and they stood in the dim light of the suite's foyer, letting the warmth surround them. *Now I feel complete,* Annie thought.

After a few moments of just holding each other, Kaden sighed and moved back a little. "I imagine you must be hungry?"

She nodded. "I didn't eat on the plane."

"Good. I made reservations for us at one of the restaurants I called on yesterday. It's in Georgetown. Does that sound okay?"

Her brown eyes shined up at him. "It sounds perfect." She stood on her toes to kiss him, then stepped away to her retrieve her bag. "Let me just hang up my clothes, shake myself out a bit, and I'll be ready to go."

As she pulled her bag into the bedroom, she stopped and turned back to him. "I'll be just a few minutes. Since you plan on spending time here, why not start by making yourself at home?" She gave him a cheeky look, then pulled her bag into the bedroom and shut the door.

Kaden felt a satisfied smile tug at his mouth as he walked around the sitting room of her suite. He hadn't been sure how his upgrade would go over, but he was pleased that she'd taken it in stride. He had been honest about his reason—he *did* want to spend time with her—and figured she would be more comfortable in her space rather than his. And having a bed in the room was just awkward, at least until they'd actually shared it.

And Kaden certainly wanted to share a bed with her. Hell, he could barely keep his hands off her. She had looked incredible when she stepped into the terminal. A perfect blend of cool professionalism and warm sensuality. His heart hadn't stopped pounding since he'd first laid eyes on her at the airport. He wanted her more than he'd ever wanted any woman. But he knew he had to be patient. He'd become a master at patience, but this was becoming a sore test of his reserve.

When Annie opened the bedroom door ten minutes later, Kaden sucked in a breath. She still wore the tailored black jacket with the soft silk blouse and scarf underneath, but she had traded her jeans and boots for the jacket's matching skirt, super-sheer black hose, and a pair of sexy black pumps. The skirt was slim and tapered, hitting her shapely legs about two inches above the knee. He almost fell to the ground.

She caught the admiration in his eyes and halted a step out from the doorway, blushing. He crossed the room to her in three strides, took her hands in his, and brought them to his lips. "*Tu es très belle,*" he whispered.

He must approve, she thought, as a giddy thrill went through her. It was her most flattering suit, and she had hoped to make an impression. *Mission accomplished.*

They made an extremely attractive couple as they strolled through the hotel lobby—Kaden tall, lean, and expensively dressed in what could only be a European ensemble, long cashmere overcoat brushing the back of his calves, his elbow angled for her, and she in the exquisite simplicity of her expertly tailored black suit. It hadn't occurred to Annie that some of her colleagues would be at the hotel tonight, and she didn't notice them now as she and Kaden headed for the front doors to catch a cab. But they certainly noticed her.

The restaurant was a tiny establishment squeezed into the bustle of fashionable M Street in Georgetown. The French menu was limited but mouthwatering. It was a similar culinary experience to the one they had shared at La Belle Nicole, absent the heavy conversation.

With no effort at all, they fell into the intimate banter they'd shared for the last fifteen months over the internet. There was no awkwardness between then, only simmering desire as they held hands across the table. He told her about his recent meetings in New York and DC, sharing his optimism that the import company would gain traction, and she told him about the hours of research and preparation she'd put into her talk and the panel discussion to follow. She confessed she was nervous, and he assured her that her fears were unwarranted.

"I can't imagine anyone coming to the podium more prepared than you, *chérie.*" When she looked skeptical, he shrugged his shoulders. "We'll discuss it tomorrow, after it's over. What time do you go on?"

She appreciated his confidence in her, and it helped her relax. After she finished her meal with a cup of decaffeinated coffee—an American aberration, according to Kaden, who refused to even try it—they returned to the hotel.

As he opened the door to her suite and stepped aside for her to enter, Annie asked, "Where is your room?"

"Just down the hall," he said, dropping her card key on the table by the door. At her raised eyebrows, he smiled sheepishly. "Next door, actually. I wanted to be close to you."

She reached her arms out for him, and in an instant, he was wrapped in her embrace, and she in his.

Eventually, Annie pulled back enough to look up into his eyes. They were dark with desire, as were hers, she was certain. Arms wrapped around his waist, she took a deep breath. "Kaden," she said, "I want, more than anything, to take you to my bed and make love with you. But when we do, I won't want to leave it for a day or two, or ten, and I have a big presentation in the morning. Will you be terribly disappointed if we wait until tomorrow night?"

"*Non, ma chérie, je comprends.* But I need a souvenir to get me through the night."

She arched her eyebrow at him. "What did you have in mind?"

He kept his eyes locked on hers and, with a sly smile, drew a hand up to caress her jaw, then let it slide back to her ear, and drop slowly down the line of her neck. She felt him tug at her scarf, felt it pull free from under her blouse as he drew it out, bunching it slowly in his hand. "This," he whispered as he bent over to caress the tip of her ear with his lips, "has been against your skin all day and has your scent. It will have to be enough." He made an exaggerated show of preparing to endure the most severe punishment, and she couldn't keep herself from laughing as she pushed him out the door.

Nineteen

Annie was brilliant. Her talk was complex and highly technical, but rather than sticking to the jargon of the trade, she used layman's terms whenever possible to make her points. The topic—a highly anticipated set of tax regulations that had been released earlier that year—had far-reaching implications for thousands of transactions across the country. Her audience followed closely, interrupting her to ask pointed and detailed questions, which she fielded with finesse. It was a superb performance.

Kaden made his way into the back of the large room before she began, hiding himself from her view among the last rows behind a few other tall men. Now, watching her in her element, he was seriously impressed. As lead investor in many companies, he understood the implications, but not the details, of what she presented. She was as passionate about this complicated topic as she was with anything else that was important to her, and he was proud to witness a side of her that he'd known existed but had not seen firsthand. *She really is bloody damn good at what she does.*

He had been aware of the subject matter and also knew she had worked with the tricky new rules closely in the last year as they pertained to her clients. But he was stunned to see how acutely she understood their ramifications on entities at every stage of their life: beginning, middle, and those that were near their end point as assets were divested, and profits were allocated and distributed. *I need to hire her myself,* he mused.

Annie finished her presentation with twenty minutes left for questions. The clamor for her attention continued beyond the allotted time until one of the conference officials finally asked the audience to disperse so they could prepare the room for the next speaker.

After loud and lengthy applause, the audience started to file out. But a number of people from the crowd surged up to the podium to try to get a private word with her and some free advice, and Kaden felt a jolt of concern and protectiveness as she appeared to be overrun.

Just as he was about to launch himself through the crowd and kick everyone away, she stepped back and held up a hand to the crowd. *"Please,"* he heard her say in a forcefully direct tone. "I appreciate your interest, but I really need to leave now. My contact information is in the materials."

And with that, she calmly gathered her papers, gracefully stepped off the platform, and headed for the doors, straight toward Kaden, whom she noticed the moment her foot hit the aisle. But his expression and the barely perceptible tilt of his head prompted her to walk straight past him. He spun around, took a quick moment to admire anew her sexy stride, and then walked out behind her, blocking anyone obtuse enough to misunderstand her dismissal.

"You were bloody brilliant."

"Thank you. And thank you for the bodyguard treatment." She glanced back at him but continued walking. "What the hell is wrong with these people? And what are you doing here?"

"Winning my bet."

"I wasn't aware we had a bet."

"Not precisely, in a manner of speaking, but you were worried you'd make a poor showing, and I was sure you would be brilliant. Which you were. So I decided I won, as it were."

"That all sounds very British. Do you often bet against yourself?" They were beyond the fray, still in the conference center but well past the milling crowd, so she slowed to look back at him and saw he was still trailing behind like a bodyguard, eyes suspiciously on her *derrière*.

"Only when I'm certain of the outcome." He smiled wolfishly, reached for her hand, and twined his fingers with hers. "How much time do we have?"

In the afternoon panel discussion, Annie sat with three other Smith Cole Blakely partners. The heady topic was "Structuring Real Estate Transactions under the New Regulations." After a brief statement by each panelist with respect to his or her specific area of expertise, the audience largely dictated the discussion by throwing questions at the panel.

Kaden leaned against the back wall in the standing-room-only chamber. Not surprisingly, most questions were directed to Annie. In deference to her more senior partners, she engaged them in the discussion, but they didn't know the rules nearly as well as she did, and it made them look incompetent when they answered in vague equivocations. Eventually, Annie just answered the questions then turned to the other panelists for their views, mostly just getting their nods. She was comfortable and in control but appeared to be scoring no points with the big boys in her firm. It made him angry to see her put in that position, although she didn't appear concerned.

Afterward, as he walked her back to the lobby of the hotel, Annie shrugged it off. "Honestly, Kaden, they were glad I was there to pull out the heavy guns. The only reason it was a 'panel' was to have a firm-sponsored forum. Every one of those guys depends on me to handle these issues for their clients." She smiled widely at him. "They wouldn't know what do to without me, which is why they made me a partner." She looked at him a moment, then said seriously, "I told you I was good at what I do."

Kaden laughed, having no intention to argue with that.

It was six thirty, and Annie was done for the day. She looked at him thoughtfully. "Have you ever worn that baseball cap I sent you?"

"Every day in the vineyard … despite the ribbing I take from the crew." He grinned when she grimaced.

"Well, as it turns out, the Giants are in the World Series. There's a game tonight in San Francisco. Let's get changed out of these clothes then go to the bar in the lobby and watch a few innings. It's probably as exciting as your cricket. I'll be fascinated to see how quickly you become comatose." She laughed at her own joke.

Kaden raised his brows at her. It wasn't his first choice of evening entertainment, but she was pumped up on adrenaline from her success, and he didn't want to be a downer. She needed to blow off some energy, and he'd go along with whatever she needed.

"Let's do it," he said, taking her arm.

They waited in a considerable crowd for the elevator, which forced her to chat with colleagues. When they finally made it to their floor, Kaden escorted her to her door, kissed her forehead, then went to his own room to change.

Thirty minutes later, they were back in the lobby, comfortable in jeans and sweaters. They found a vacant table in the bar facing one of the big television sets that was set to broadcast the game.

"Since we're watching baseball, we have to drink beer," Annie declared, wiggling back and forth on her stool as she watched Kaden frowning at the drink menu.

"Good thing," he said, tossing down the menu. "I'd rather drink hemlock than any of the wines here."

They ordered a local microbrew and some cheesy fries, at which Kaden looked supremely skeptical. Annie plucked one out of the gooey mass, popped it into her mouth with relish, leaned into him, and kissed his jaw, leaving a little grease spot. "American comfort food," she teased as she wiped off his chin with her thumb.

Beer in hand and greasy potatoes on the table, they turned their attention to the television. The game had not yet started, and the sound was muted. Annie asked if he knew anything about the game.

"Not really." He eyed the cheesy fries, then pulled one from the melted stringy mess and studied it. Against his better judgment he popped it in his mouth and chewed. He made a face and took another sip of his beer.

Annie watched, laughing at him. "Pretty awful, aren't they?"

"Why exactly did we order these?"

"I wanted to prove to myself that I wasn't the only one who thought they were disgusting."

"Thank you for your confidence in my culinary acumen. Can we order something else?" He reached for the bar menu.

Annie ate another fry and gave him the basic structure and rules of the game, concluding with, "In essence, it's a lot of waiting around, with a few moments of cracking action. I don't understand why it's considered to be America's pastime, unless it's because it just gives us all an excuse to take a nap." She chuckled and took a sip of her beer.

Kaden didn't care what the game was as long as she was sitting there with him to watch it. He set the menu aside, found her hand under the table, and tugged it into his lap just as the bartender turned up the volume of the television. They both turned toward it to listen.

Someone was talking about the Giants' batting lineup when it looked like the camera started to shake—the reporter got really blurry, and the background was moving up and down. Annie frowned and put her beer down. The commentator's eyes got wide. "I think we're having an earthquake!" Then the screen went blank.

Annie experienced a jolt of fear and felt a chill go up her spine. She turned to Kaden, who shrugged as he took a draw from his beer. "They must be having technical difficulties."

"He said … he said they were having an earthquake," she stammered, telling herself it was probably just a small tremor.

"Well if they are, I'm sure they'll get the transmission back up shortly." Kaden had no experience with earthquakes and therefore registered no concern.

But Annie's heart had started to pound. Something wasn't right. Now, instead of a blank screen, there was a graphic that said, *Special Report.* And at that moment, an audio feed came on that said, "The San Francisco Bay Area has just experienced a major earthquake. Please stay tuned."

"Oh my God!" Annie cried, grabbing on to Kaden's arm. "Did you hear that?"

Kaden nodded. "That's what that bloke seemed to think … Annie?" Her panic finally registered. He looked around the bar and realized no one else seemed even remotely interested or concerned. He looked at the *Special Report* graphic on the TV, then back at Annie, who was trembling and had gone pale. *Bloody hell, of course she's scared.*

He pulled out his wallet and tossed some money on the table, grabbed her arm and pulled her off the stool. "Come on, let's go to your room. CNN will have coverage on what's happening out there."

Kaden opened the door to her suite, walked her to the couch, sat her down, and turned on the TV. He quickly found CNN, just in time for a dramatic aerial shot of the Bay Bridge with a big chunk of the upper level tilted down, resting on the lower span. *Shit.*

"Oh my God," Annie whispered, eyes huge.

The next shot was worse. As the aerial camera panned the now-flattened double-deck Nimitz Freeway in Oakland, showing huge slabs of freeway sections piled on the ground at unnatural angles with flattened cars poking out the sides, Annie let out a sob.

Kaden looked over, saw tears streaming down her face, and immediately wrapped his arms around her, pulling her close to his chest. "Shh, Annie. You're okay, you're fine." And then he suddenly realized she had no idea if her friends were.

"Who can you call?" he asked.

"John and Marie!" Annie scrambled out of Kaden's arms and lurched for the phone. She called the office but got the exchange recording: "We're sorry, your call cannot be completed at this time due to heavy volume. Please try again later."

She cursed, tried their home number. They lived in the Oakland Hills, and she prayed it wasn't as bad there, although with the Nimitz collapsed, she didn't hold much hope. The call went through, but she got the answering machine.

"Marie, it's Annie!" she practically yelled into the phone. "I'm in DC, and we're watching footage of the earthquake damage on CNN. It looks horrible! Please call me and let me know you're safe ... here's the number ..." As she rattled off the hotel phone number, her hands were shaking, she gripped the receiver so hard. When she hung up, she just stared at the phone.

"My brother will want to know I'm not in that mess," she said as she reached for the phone again. She dialed his home number in Los Angeles and the call went through. Adam answered on the first ring.

"Adam! It's Annie."

"Thank God. Where are you?"

"I'm in DC, I'm here for a conference. We were about to watch the game when the quake hit. We're just now watching CNN, and I can't believe the devastation. Oh Adam, people got trapped in those cars on the freeway—they can't have survived." She started to sob again into the phone. She felt warmth as Kaden began to gently rub her back.

She glanced up to watch the news again, and this time the cameras were above the Marina District of San Francisco, showing homes toppled into the streets and others on fire amid the chaos of smoke and fire trucks and flashing hoses. "Oh God, there's a neighborhood on fire in the city—it must have ruptured the gas lines." She held on to the phone in silence with her brother, watching the TV.

Then she got a grip on herself. "I'm okay here, Adam, I just needed to let you know. I'm with Kaden so we'll keep watching the news. I'm here through the weekend. I'll call you when I get home. I love you."

"Love you too, Annie. Call me again if you, you know … need to talk."

Annie closed her eyes. "I will. Bye."

As she slowly placed the receiver back on the cradle, she turned to look at Kaden. He sat next to her, not crowding her but supportive, his eyes gentle but intense. She needed to tell him. She needed to tell him why she was freaking out so badly, about the horrifying memories from another earthquake that had surfaced. But she had waited too long, and she was scared he'd be angry that she hadn't trusted him before. It was too little too late, but he deserved to know.

Annie took a deep breath and looked at him. In the shadow of the soft lamplight, she could see the silhouette of the day-old stubble on his jaw, which made him look almost rakish. Except for his eyes, which were gentle. His eyes told her that he understood. Would he still when he learned she hadn't been completely honest?

Kaden waited, willing her to trust him. The anguished look in her beautiful brown eyes spoke of the unbearable pain that haunted her. He had sensed a shadow of it before, but now it was plain in her face. Stark pain and sorrow, memories of tears shed long ago, and the massive earthquake in San Francisco had just brought it all boiling to the surface. He hoped, *prayed* she trusted him enough to tell him.

She shifted on the couch, grabbed a pillow from beside her, curled her legs up underneath her, and hugged the pillow to her chest. In an unsteady voice, she said, "I need to tell you something that I should have told you already. I wanted to, but ... it was never the right time, and I didn't want to ... spoil our time together. And now ... now I'm scared."

Her last words were barely a whisper as she looked at him, her eyes brimming with more tears. She reached for his hand, and he grasped hers tightly. She locked her eyes on his and saw the gentleness, the caring ... the love?

"Never be afraid of me," he whispered and gave her hand a reassuring squeeze.

"What I didn't tell you before was that ... was that I was married once, for a short time, and ... and pregnant ..." she began softly, looking down at the floor. She glanced back up at him, heavy with hesitation, expecting to see shock, disappointment, anger—God knew she deserved it after he'd been so open with her. Would he forgive her for withholding something so important? How could he ever trust her again? But she saw none of those things in his beautiful, intense eyes. She saw nothing but concern, so she took a deep breath and continued.

"I met Jack just before my twenty-fifth birthday, at one of those big music festivals in Golden Gate Park. He was a musician. His band was playing there and ... well ... he was handsome and had a beautiful voice and when he sang on stage, he made me feel like he was singing just for me." Annie pulled her courage together, determined to be honest no matter what it cost her. "We fell in love, very quickly. Before I knew it he was moving into my tiny apartment. It was ridiculous but ..."

"Love is never ridiculous, Annie, unless it's false." Kaden spoke from his own painful experience, made more acute by the truth in Annie's eyes.

She shook her head. "That's the thing—it was real. For both of us." She laughed, but the sound came out a little hysterical. "So when I found myself pregnant—at twenty-five, on the ascent of a demanding career—it was scary joyful, not just ... scary." She wiped her runny nose on her sleeve. "Jack was ecstatic.

He insisted that we get married right away. So we did. But his parents didn't like me. His mother, mostly." She blew out a breath. "Actually, she hated me."

Kaden frowned. He'd known about the husband and the pregnancy and did his best to ignore the dagger piercing his heart from her admission of love, but he hadn't considered in-laws. He squeezed the hand he still held, willing her to understand he was solidly with her. Kaden sensed that this was cathartic for Annie—getting the story out now was as much about her own cleansing as it was about being honest with him.

"We married at City Hall then presented the marriage and the coming baby as a *fait-accompli* to his parents." She shook her head. "It was a disaster. I wasn't good enough—would never be good enough—for Sarah's precious Jack. She was angry. She had only tolerated me, she said, because she knew Jack would come to his senses."

Annie shook her head at the painful memory. "And she had the nerve to say it in front of me like I wasn't standing right there, like I wasn't his new wife carrying his first child. But Jack stood solidly beside me. He told his mother she had a choice: accept me or lose her only son."

Kaden clenched his jaw to keep from spewing his outrage while struggling to keep it off of his face. It would do no good now. This was all past history— ten years past history. Annie had already suffered the unimaginable pain of it all. But his heart broke at the injustice of his beautiful, amazing Annie being so maligned. So unfairly maligned. And the last thing he wanted was for her to think he was angry with *her*.

"The Yosemite camping trip was supposed to be a truce of sorts. Sarah pretended she accepted me as a daughter, and I pretended her bad acting didn't hurt me. It was her pending grandmother status, I'm sure, that finally swayed her to relent."

After a moment's pause, she said, "I told you I got caught in an avalanche, and that I was seriously injured." She'd been staring at their clasped hands, but now she looked at him to see his reaction. He nodded, trying his best to convey understanding without judgment.

"Jack and I got up early that morning to have some private time. He'd been up to Sierra Point before and wanted me to see it. It was a rough hike, but I was in good shape despite being seven months pregnant." Another pause. "It was on the way back down that we got in trouble. I was terrified when the earthquake hit—we both were. There was no cover, nowhere to run." Tears had started tracking their way down her cheeks again, and Kaden gently, silently, reached over to wipe them away with his thumb.

"I don't remember much else. We ran, but …" She shrugged her shoulders like she was remembering the helplessness of the moment. "By the time the boulder reached us, it was pushing an avalanche ahead of it. The only reason I made it at all was because Jack picked me up and literally threw me out of the way. I saw him get pulled down with the hillside just before I fell into a ravine."

She was quiet for a moment, staring at their hands, breathing carefully through her nose, whether reliving that awful moment or pulling herself back out of it, Kaden didn't know. He said nothing, not letting go of her hand but also not interfering with her private thoughts.

"I told you I was in a coma for ten days," Annie continued in a robotic voice. "But what I didn't tell you is that … when I came out of it, I learned I had lost my baby as well as my husband."

Kaden closed his eyes against the image, unable to fathom the strength it must have taken, the emotional fortitude, to move on. How the hell had she survived? He'd had the basic facts, yet hearing it in her own words … Jesus, the pain of it pierced his soul. Her friend Marie had done more than he could ever imagine anyone doing for a friend.

The phone rang, startling them both. Annie grabbed the receiver and was relieved to hear Marie's voice. "Oh my God, have you seen the news? It's so awful! Are you okay? Where's John?" Annie sniffled and wiped her nose again on the sleeve of her sweater, willing her wits back into place as she tried to pull herself together.

"We're both fine," Marie told her. "A little shaken, excuse the pun, but no permanent damage. Everything is chaotic here … you probably know more than we do because our TV stations are out. John was already out of the city, thank God. He had a meeting in Berkeley and was just getting into his car when it hit. I was picking up the kids from school. We're all fine," she said again. "Everyone here is fine."

"I couldn't get through to the office," Annie said. "What's it going to be like getting into the city tomorrow? Will the trains be running?"

Kaden stayed where he was as he watched Annie talk to her friend, and he marveled again at her strength and resilience. She'd just relived her worst nightmare, not only feeling it but also *explaining* it to him, and now she was asking about trains? He was in awe of her and … maybe even feeling a little unworthy. Not that that would stop him. He'd make himself worthy. He heard Annie tell her friend that he was with her, that she had talked to Adam, and she promised to check in tomorrow.

Annie hung up the phone and looked at Kaden. She expected the weight of all she had just revealed to him to be hanging in the air between them, but it wasn't.

"They're both fine, and their kids, too," she said in a small voice.

Kaden finally moved. He reached his hand across the couch and touched her cheek, a touch so gentle and loving that it released another stream of tears. He moved closer, wrapped an arm around her and pulled her to his chest. Annie came to him willingly, relieved that he wasn't angry, but she still didn't understand why. He scooped her up and pulled her into his lap. "Shh, *chérie*, don't cry. I'm so sorry. I can't begin to tell you how sorry I am."

She clung to him as he held her in his lap, one arm wrapped securely around her waist, the other cradling her head against his shoulder. He kissed her on the top of her head and buried his face in her curls. "Annie," he whispered, "you're so brave. I can't believe your courage. So brave, so beautiful, and so strong."

"I'm so sorry I didn't tell you before," she whispered. "I didn't want to hide it from you, but … I didn't want to spoil our time together. I didn't tell you at first because, well, I didn't know where this would go, but then … then I felt … stuck. I didn't want you thinking about me like that. I *wanted* you to know, but I didn't want to tell you."

He hugged her tighter, kissed her hair again, then eased her back and tilted her chin up so their eyes could meet. In his beautiful eyes, she saw nothing but love and understanding. Then she frowned.

"You knew."

Eyes still locked, judging her reaction, he nodded slightly.

"How?" she asked, puzzled.

He let out a shaky breath and kissed the tip of her nose, keeping his eyes on hers. "It was when I was waiting for your first email." He looked away, apprehensive. "I was in agony waiting. I was missing you so much, feeling sorry for myself, imagining the worst. I knew you had held something back when you told me about your accident. I thought if I could figure out what it was, I might be able to understand ... well, as I said ... I was in agony waiting."

Annie brought her hand to his cheek. "I was trying my hardest to get my computer set up so I could contact you."

He turned his head and kissed the palm that rested on his cheek. "I knew that, but the wait was killing me. And your timing, by the way, was perfect. I had been searching online for an old newspaper article about your avalanche and had just found it and learned that it had killed a man and left his pregnant wife in critical condition. I put two and two together and figured the woman had to be you, as no other story fit. So when your first email popped up, I was feeling completely wretched. Not just for your terrible loss but also because I felt like I'd invaded your privacy, learned something you hadn't wanted me to know. But then your message arrived, and it was so sweet and so tentative." He reached up and took her hand, pressed her fingertips to his lips. "It pulled me back."

Annie stroked his lips, then pulled her hand away and used it to cover her eyes. "God, I can't imagine what you must have thought. I'm sorry you had to find out that way. I'm sorry I didn't have the courage to tell you myself."

"You just did," he said gently.

"I mean ... before."

"Annie," Kaden said softly, tilted her chin up again so she had to look at him. "It's an intensely personal and difficult story. I didn't blame you. I was just amazed that you got through it and moved on. Don't ever think you don't have courage. Not many people could have gone through what you did and survived emotionally. You told me once that the journey to get to a good place is often rocky and that you'd never judge my past. I would say the same to you. That journey is part of what makes you the incredible woman you are today. The woman I'm in love with."

Annie's eyes widened.

"Let me make love to you, *chérie.* Let me make you feel my love."

Annie buried her face in his shoulder. "Kaden, I haven't, um, I mean … you know … not since, um … not since I was married."

"It may be very selfish of me, but I'm glad," he said, kissing the top of her head. "I promise you won't have anything to worry about."

She pulled back to look at him. "But … what if I …"

"Shh," he whispered. "We'll take it very slow … which is what I wanted to do anyway. I've waited so long for you, Annie, I want to savor every inch of you."

Twenty

Kaden led her into the bedroom, then stopped at the end of the bed. He gently pulled her sweater up over her head and openly admired the sight of her lacy bra cupping her soft, round breasts. *"Lovely."* He sighed, brushing his fingertips over the lace before reaching down and pulling his own sweater off. Then it was her turn to sigh as she reached up to touch the broad expanse of his chest, running her fingers through the sprinkling of dark hair that adorned his skin and made a little pattern around the flat discs of his nipples.

He wrapped his hands around hers, drew them down around behind his back and held them there, pulling her to his chest as he leaned in to kiss her deeply, plundering her mouth with his tongue. Easing back, he maneuvered her onto the end of the bed. He toed off his own shoes, then knelt in front of her and tugged off her boots and socks. Then he wickedly ran a finger up the sole of one foot, which caused her to squeal.

"Ticklish, are you?" He grinned and, still kneeling, picked up her foot to kiss the tips of her toes. She giggled and tried to pull her foot away, but he held on to it and tortured her for another minute before releasing her foot and running both hands up her legs to her knees, which he gently pushed apart as he moved in between them. He ran his hands up the length of her thighs to the top of her jeans as he leaned his body into her and wrapped his arms around her waist. He kissed the soft skin just below her ear before slowly dragging his lips lower, sprinkling kisses down her neck and across her shoulders.

Kaden was a generous lover. He took his time, touching, kissing, and nibbling all over her body as he slowly awakened the need that had been dormant in her for so long. And awaken it, he did. She responded to his touch and his whispers of encouragement as he had known she would—with passion and sensual abandon.

They were loving and open and playful with each other, experimenting with touches and kisses and learning what drove the other wild. It felt so right to be together this way, and they reveled in it, neither wanting it to end.

Eventually, they lay naked and sated, with the covers pulled up around them. Annie was tucked against his side, head resting on his shoulder, leg thrown over his, her hand resting on his chest while her fingers brushed through the soft hair there. Kaden had his arm wrapped around her back and was holding her securely to him with his large palm cupping her bottom while his thumb drew lazy circles on her flesh.

The room was dark, but the glow from the streetlights below their window provided soft illumination. Kaden lifted his free hand to gently smooth the curls from her forehead, leaning his head down to lay featherlight kisses along her brow. "*Ma chérie, je t'adore,*" he whispered against her skin.

Annie snuggled closer, wound her leg tighter around his, and virtually purred. She had never felt so loved, so worshipped, so adored. She hadn't known it was possible to feel so complete, so perfectly sated. Her body was boneless, like a limp doll. Her heartbeat had slowed but still thudded in her chest as she breathed in his scent and felt the hair of his chest tickle her nose. "I adore you, too," she whispered back, burying her face in his chest.

They slept, awoke in the wee hours of morning and made love again, then slept some more.

As the morning sky brightened, the light coming through the open curtains eventually woke Kaden, and he found himself wrapped around his Annie, with her back to his chest and her bottom tucked snuggly against him. He groaned, pulled her closer, and inhaled the sweet scent of her hair on the pillow beside him. Then he rolled her onto her back and gave her a good-morning kiss as she groggily opened her eyes. He smiled devilishly as he slid between her legs. She moaned and welcomed him in, and he moved slowly and deliberately, with his intense eyes locked on hers. His actions reflected the assured pace of a man who knew how to please his woman.

Never letting their gaze break, he brought her to another shattering climax, then closed his eyes and followed her into ecstasy.

I could wake up like this every day for the rest of my life, Kaden thought as he brushed his mouth over Annie's kiss-swollen lips one last time before rolling off of her. She curled up like a kitten as he climbed out of bed and walked to the bathroom.

Not too many minutes later, fully dressed, he sat down on the edge of the bed where Annie was still snuggled under the covers. He stroked her cheek lightly. "Come on, sleepyhead, let's go get some air."

"What time is it?" she mumbled while squinting out the window.

"Six thirty. The sunrise is less than an hour away, and it's a beautiful clear morning. Let's go catch it."

She regarded him with sleepy eyes. "Really?"

"Do you mean is it really clear, really six thirty, or do I really want to see the sunrise? All true, actually." He grinned then yanked down the covers.

She yelped and tried to grab them, but he just laughed and reached over to tickle her in the places he had discovered last night. She dissolved into a fit of squirmy giggles, but he didn't relent until she agreed to get up. "Okay, *okay! Stop!* I'm getting up!" She wiggled away from him and raced naked to the bathroom.

The capital city was already bustling as they stepped out of the hotel and headed down 14th Street toward the National Mall, hand in hand. It was clear but cold, and Annie was bundled in a warm anorak jacket while Kaden wore his elegant overcoat.

Annie felt alive, her blood singing in her veins like electricity pulsing through power lines. Is this what she'd been missing all these years? She couldn't remember ever feeling this way with Jack. For a moment, reality crashed in on her happy revelry, reminding her that this was only temporary. She shoved that thought aside and vowed to simply enjoy being with Kaden in the here and now.

They crossed Independence Avenue and walked out onto the mall, the grime of the city falling away as they were surrounded by beautiful expanses of lawn, mature trees, and manicured walkways. To the west, the Washington Monument stood tall and proud; to the east, the cupola of the Capitol building rose above everything else. The buildings of the Smithsonian Institute lined the mall on either side, half-hidden by trees that had not yet lost their foliage. Walking toward the Capitol, they found a bench facing east. The sunrise was coming, and the first golden rays touched the statue at the top of the Capitol building as they huddled close, their breath causing small puffs of condensation in the cold air.

It was a breathtaking sight as the white stones of the Capitol began to glow. It reminded Annie of the sunrise she'd witnessed all those years ago, but now, perhaps because of her confessions last night, the thought didn't give her the emotional jolt she expected. She leaned her head against Kaden's shoulder.

"The last sunrise I intentionally watched," she said, "was the morning of the avalanche. It was so beautiful, with the alpenglow on the canyon walls … followed by the sunlight flashing on the morning dew."

He pulled her closer, shut his eyes briefly as he rested his cheek on the side of her head, his fingers interlaced with hers. He didn't want to hear about Jack right now, not after they'd made such sweet love last night, but if she needed to talk about him, he would listen. She'd bottled up his memory for a long time, and she'd finally trusted him with the story. Perhaps talking about it would help her let him go for good.

Kaden was embarrassed to realize that he was jealous of a man who had been dead for almost a decade, and he forced himself to set it aside. Annie was *his* now, and that's all that mattered. He would eventually find the right moment to explore her past feelings, but it wasn't now.

He lifted her fingers to his lips, skimmed her fingertips, and kissed her cold knuckles. "In Rasteau, we're often out in the vineyards before dawn. Henri's property is near the top of a slope, and you can see for miles around. I love watching the sun come up over the mountains and chase the shadows from the valley. I never get tired of it. It's part of what gets me out of bed so early," he said, giving her hand another little squeeze. "I would love to show it to you."

Annie turned in his arms, stretched up to kiss his jaw, and he leaned down to capture her lips in a gentle kiss. "I want to see it," she said. "I can *feel* it, from everything you've told me, but I can't picture it in my head."

They sat in silence, watching the day come alive around them. After a time, she sat up and stretched, then turned her head toward Kaden and gifted him with a beautiful smile. "Let's get some breakfast," she said with a surge of playful energy. "I'm starving!" She grabbed his hand to pull him up. "I know of an awesome little place on Dupont Circle that has great big gooey omelets and home fries. It's a good walk from here, so we'll earn our big breakfast!"

The omelets were as enormous and delicious as Annie had promised, and an hour later, she pushed her unfinished plate away and groaned. "Now I'm stuffed." She looked up at Kaden and eyed him speculatively. "Are you finished with your meetings here?"

"I am," he answered as he shoveled the last of his omelet into his mouth. "This was amazing. What about you? Do you need to make an appearance at the conference?"

Annie's eyes sparkled as she shook her head. "I'm taking time off for good behavior."

"You've certainly earned it."

She smiled at the warmth in his words. "Have you ever seen Embassy Row? From where we are now, we're really close to some beautiful mansions."

After paying their bill in the upstairs café, they wandered through the bookstore on the ground floor. Annie cried, *"Aha!"* and held up a pocket-size book on walking tours of Washington, DC. She purchased the book, and they headed up Massachusetts Avenue to the start of the Embassy Row walk.

Several hours were devoted to following the routes suggested in the book. They read aloud the narrative about the people for whom the mansions were originally built, and those who occupied them now. They laughed, speculated about the foreign diplomats who now lived and worked behind the elegant façades, and generally enjoyed a clear and beautiful autumn day together in the nation's capital.

It was late afternoon when they finally found their way back to the Marriott. They had walked for miles through the city and were both exhausted, wanting nothing more than a shower and a rest.

Their timing was terrible. As they entered the lobby, Annie realized the conference had just wrapped up for the day. People were milling about chatting, and there was a long queue at the elevator. To her dismay, she noticed several people from her firm—at the same time they noticed her.

She pulled her hand from Kaden's and held it out to greet her colleagues. They surrounded her, offering congratulations on yesterday's performances. Despite the outpouring of goodwill, she got the feeling they were more interested in the tall, handsome man positioned a half step behind her.

In particular, there was a woman from San Francisco who Annie did not like. Her name was Diana Butler, a tall, curvy, voluptuous blonde who never failed to have perfect hair and lipstick. Diana was older than Annie but hadn't worked hard enough to advance in the firm; nevertheless, she had openly disparaged Annie's promotion the year before.

Blunt as ever, Diana pushed for an introduction. "So Annie, are you going to tell us who your friend is? I noticed you two together the other night." She spoke to Annie but stared at Kaden like he was her next meal.

Annie turned to her, forcefully resisting the urge to slap her face. In a cool voice, she said, "Of course." She then turned and connected her gaze briefly with Kaden, who got the silent message and smiled blandly.

"This is Kaden Macallister, managing partner of Macallister Enterprises, Ltd., a boutique investment firm in France specializing in high-tech ventures. He's interested in expanding the reach of his company, utilizing the new structures now available for foreign investment in the US, and he's here to investigate potential opportunities to invest in emerging American companies as well as to find channels for American investment in his European funds."

It was not entirely a crock of bullshit, but Annie's spin made it sound like Kaden was a powerful and influential member of the European investment community. That part was true, despite his low profile, but it implied that her connection to him meant potential opportunities for the firm. And his goals, as she stated them, fit specifically into her area of expertise. She smiled inwardly as the crowd in front of her blanched.

Then she turned to Kaden and waved her hand at the crowd. "Let me introduce my colleagues ..." and she rattled off their names and where they were from.

Kaden bowed slightly and, in his best aristocratic British accent, said, "Pleasure, I'm sure."

That should do nicely, Annie thought as the group in front of her struggled to find something to say. Even Diana Butler seemed tongue-tied.

Annie took advantage of the stunned silence before any of them could insinuate themselves into her private plans for the evening. She turned to Kaden and, in complete dismissal of everyone in the crowd, said, "Shall we?" He nodded, inclined his head again to the group, took her elbow in perfect British style, and they moved on.

Rather than wait in the queue at the elevator, Annie and Kaden ascended the wide stairway to the mezzanine level, then calmly walked along the corridor to the internal stairwell. Neither looked back or said a word until the stairwell door had closed behind them. Then Kaden grabbed her, pushed her up against the wall, and captured her mouth in a hungry kiss.

"That was bloody well done," he said with an appreciative smile after he released her mouth.

She laughed. "I considered introducing you as a vineyard worker from the south of France, but then I probably would have had to pry Diana off of you with a crowbar. She was that close to flinging herself at you." She made a face. "Yuck. Does that happen often?"

He groaned and closed his eyes, then leaned in to kiss her again. "Not terribly often."

She chuckled, snaked her arms up around his neck, and pulled him to her. "Poor baby," she murmured as she went for another kiss.

Twenty-One

The first order of business was decampment to more private quarters. Annie had no desire to run into any more people she knew, and Kaden had no interest in acting the role of the British snob she had set him up for. As soon as they had left her gape-mouthed colleagues behind, they had quickly packed their bags, exited the Marriott through the back door, and removed to a single cozy suite in the elegant Four Seasons Hotel on M Street in Georgetown.

That night, they opted for room service in their new suite so Annie could get an update on the news from San Francisco. It was grim. People had been killed when the bridge and freeway spur had collapsed, and many buildings had been damaged or destroyed throughout the city. Annie talked to John, who had checked her loft.

"I'm sorry, Annie, the kitchen is a real mess. It looks like everything was flung out of the cupboards." John said, sympathetically.

"Did you see my computer?" Annie asked. "Was it still on the desk?" She didn't care about the dishes, but her computer was her lifeline to Kaden.

"It was there on the desk, no apparent damage."

Annie whispered a prayer of thanks. "Okay, good. Nothing else there matters. I'll see you Monday."

Kaden availed himself of the Four Seasons hospitality, ordering a bottle of Dom Pérignon and the hotel's famous caviar service, complete with three different types of Caspian Sea caviar, house-cured salmon, buckwheat blinis, and all the accoutrements.

Wrapped up in the euphoria of their newfound intimacy, they got a bit carried away. Annie giggled and admitted that she'd never had anyone sip

Champagne from her belly button but allowed that there was a first time for everything.

The next morning dawned clear and cold again, and Annie announced that they would rent bicycles, declaring, "It's the best way to see the city."

Their bikes were clunkers, but that didn't stop them from racing around town like a couple of kids. Annie played tour guide, leading the way along the river path to the Lincoln Memorial at the west end of the National Mall, then on to the Vietnam Veteran's Memorial Wall where they dismounted and walked the length of the provocative monument, then around the Tidal Basin to the Jefferson Memorial. From there, they rode down the long triangular peninsula of East Potomac Park, which ran south from the Tidal Basin between the Potomac River and the Washington Channel, DC's fishing harbor and waterfront district, and ended at Hains Point at the confluence of the Potomac and Anacostia Rivers. It was a large, beautiful park, mostly empty on a Friday morning.

The best part was at the very end, at the point itself, where the sci-fi sculpture, *The Awakening*, depicted a giant in midscream struggling to emerge from the earth. The sculpture consisted of five separate pieces planted into the ground, the biggest of which was the giant's right arm that towered overhead. They leaned into the open palm of his left hand, protruding at ground level, and made out like teenagers until a group of Girl Scouts arrived in a bus and overran them.

Kaden enjoyed the city, but he was more enchanted than ever by Annie. She was a unique combination of confident, seasoned professional, and playful, enthusiastic youngster. He was deeply in love her; he had recognized it at some point over their long separation, and he confessed it to her repeatedly as they made love each night. He felt certain she loved him, too, though she hadn't given him the words.

After the night of the earthquake when they had finally made love and, he supposed, her coming clean with what happened in Yosemite, something had changed between them. In truth, there were no secrets now, just honesty and trust. Her smile was brighter and more open now, and her eyes held a sparkle he hadn't seen before. Previously she had always seemed to hold something back; now she was spontaneous, playful and sparkly.

On Saturday Kaden rented a sports car, and they drove out to Annapolis. As they walked around the picturesque town that fronted the Chesapeake Bay, Annie commented that as one of the oldest cities in America, it was still not quite three hundred years old. "Our history isn't nearly as interesting as yours," she lamented.

But he wouldn't let her dismiss it quite so easily. "The American colonies were settled on principles of freedom, by people who wanted to live without fear of religious persecution and the crushing constraints of a social class system. Never discount the significance of that kind of dedication—and sacrifice—regardless of how recently it may have happened."

She nodded. "Well, when you put it like that … I guess I see your point. But I still love the really old stone castles of the Dordogne."

He grinned at her and left it at that.

Annie insisted he try the typical food of the region. Kaden was skeptical when she dragged him inside a grungy restaurant on the main waterfront, but the fact that the place was packed gave him hope.

Seated on a hard bench at a beat-up wooden table covered by newspapers, Kaden had his first experience with Maryland crabs. He felt like a character in a bad movie wearing a plastic bib, their only utensils consisting of wooden mallets and tiny forks—just like everyone else in the restaurant—but he had to admit that the bucket full of steaming crabs, which had been unceremoniously dropped on their table, smelled enticing. Plastic cups of melted butter, a paper plate of corn on the cob, and big frosty mugs of beer completed the spread.

Annie's demonstration of how to crack open a crab and remove the yucky guts brought Kaden's skepticism roaring back, until she fed him a piece of succulent meat dipped in the drawn butter. He closed his eyes as it melted on his tongue. The messy meal was delicious, the ice-cold brewpub beer a perfect pairing with the crab, and Kaden had to admit it was a unique and enjoyable culinary experience, although he drew the line at the corn. "That's duck fodder where I come from," he quipped. Once they were finished, the waitress simply dumped the mallets and plates into the now-empty crab bucket, rolled up the newspapers with all the crab shells and guts, shoved in the bucket, too, and carried it away.

"What else would you like to see?" Annie asked as they drove back toward Washington. It was midafternoon, but this night would be their last together.

Kaden took his hand from the gearshift and reached over to squeeze her knee, then took one of her hands in his. "You, naked in bed, flushed with the passion of our love." He brought her hand to his lips and kissed it, a habitual gesture that she never tired of. She blushed, bit her lower lip, and looked at him from underneath her lashes. It was what she wanted, too.

They left the car with the hotel valet to return and went straight to their suite, leaving only the *Do Not Disturb* sign in their wake.

Twenty-Two

The rest of the day was devoted to much touching, kissing, playing, and exploring; memorizing every curve, every muscle, every inch of flesh, every sensitive or ticklish spot, every reaction, every feeling. They made love slowly, with their souls bared, then lounged together in the huge Jacuzzi tub, napped, and made love again. Early evening found them propped up by pillows on the floor in front of the gas fireplace, limbs wrapped together, sipping wine, staring into the flames. They spoke little, but the communication they shared with their eyes and their touch could have filled volumes.

They eventually dressed in jeans and warm jackets and, hand in hand, strolled in the fading evening light, finding their way to the newly completed Washington Harbour development by the river, where they sat on a low wall near the floodgate and watched the last bit of daylight disappear from the water.

A new Italian restaurant at the Harbour was convenient, and they were pleased to discover that the food was authentic and delicious. Sensing the mood was becoming a bit melancholy, Kaden lightened it by entertaining her with a story about how he and Jean Claude had traveled through Italy one summer, sampling the food, the wine, and anything else they came across.

"It was the summer before my final year at Cambridge," Kaden told her. "Jean Claude had just graduated from culinary school but felt the need for a broader perspective. He convinced me to join him on a tour of Italy." He shook his head at the folly of it. "The point of the trip was for Jean Claude to learn more about the food, but it ended up being quite an adventure."

"How do you mean?"

"Jean Claude was without shame, and could talk himself—us—into the most unbelievable invitations. We were nothing but tourists, but being a chef gave him a certain cachet, I suppose."

"I can only image the invitations two handsome young men could garner."

"At one point, we found ourselves in this tiny, ancient village just south of Orvieto, permanent population around fifteen souls," he said, warming up to the subject. "It was a dying town, surviving only by its touristic charm, built on a high, narrow plateau that had once been connected to the lowlands around it by a land bridge that had collapsed a few decades earlier. God only knows where Jean Claude had heard of the place, but he swore there was culinary gold to be mined there if we were patient enough to find it. We hiked up the ridge to the town and found a fossil of a woman, toothless and all, peddling the most sublime olive oil I have ever tasted."

Annie listened in amusement as he described the details of the strange encounter.

"We ended up dining that night at the old woman's home, then sleeping in her barn."

"She invited you to her home? To stay with her?" It didn't sound safe, even in the backwaters of rural Italy.

Kaden nodded, a small smile playing at his lips as he remembered it. "Dinner was a surprising array of courses of the most exquisite Umbrian peasant food you could possibly imagine. Jean Claude hovered by her elbow the entire time in her kitchen. God only knows how she knew she'd be feeding two hungry men.

"Her son, who was eighty years old if he was a day, was there to protect her honor." Kaden seemed amused by the memory. "While his mother turned out magically delicious fare, he told us stories about defending the town and the olive orchards during the conflicts."

"The conflicts?"

"World Wars I and II," Kaden said as he sipped his wine, grinning.

"Oh."

"We drank in her hospitality—literally—then slept it off in the rafters of her old barn, along with her son. Apparently she had a fondness for inviting traveling chefs to dine with her."

Annie was grateful for the opportunity to laugh with him, and to avoid thinking about tomorrow, as Kaden told more about their antics in Italy.

"It was the last time he and I did anything like that," Kaden said. "Even though we lived most of every year apart, we were, and still are, like brothers. Truth be told, I'm closer to Jean Claude than I am to my *own* brothers."

"I wondered about that," Annie replied. She was glad that he stayed so connected to his childhood friend. It spoke of a sense of loyalty and commitment throughout life's trials that comforted her.

Later that evening, cuddled together on the couch in front of the fire, they finally allowed themselves to talk about tomorrow, about saying goodbye, and most importantly, how and when they could be together again. Kaden was holding both of her hands, which were resting in her lap. Drawing circles with his thumbs on the backs of her hands, he was direct as usual.

"Annie, I can't go another year without seeing you again. Being with you now, this week, has proved to me beyond any doubt that I want you in my life. I love you; it's that simple."

Annie felt the truth of his words, but she wasn't sure how to respond. She didn't know how she felt. *No, that's not accurate,* she corrected herself. She was sure she was in love with him, too. The problem was that she didn't know how she felt about being in love with Kaden. She had changed, and it was because of him. With his patient and unconditional love, he had broken through all her barriers, allowed her to start living again. With him, she was completely open and unreserved.

Over the past year of getting to know Kaden and revealing herself to him at the same time, the change had taken hold slowly, but it had happened. Although it took seeing him here, and the shocking, emotional experience of the earthquake, to recognize it. The truth was, not only did she love him, but she also trusted him—more than she had ever trusted anyone in her life, even Jack. She trusted him with her heart, and she believed he would never hurt her.

When she'd arrived in Washington, she'd been excited to see him and had known they would take their relationship to physical intimacy, but she had not been prepared for the emotional intensity between them or the searing passion that he had awakened in her. And with that awakening, she had acknowledged her faith in this man and had given him her heart as a result. Frankly, it scared her. It was easier to live behind barriers than with this unspeakable vulnerability. And none of it solved the fundamental problem that a lasting relationship with him was impossible. Her career was in San Francisco, and his life was in France.

"Talk to me, love," Kaden said, and she realized he misunderstood her silence as uncertainty, so she disengaged a hand to reach up and touch her fingers to his lips and silence him.

"I don't hesitate because I'm uncertain," she said softly. "I hesitate because I can't find the words to express my feelings, and I don't want to do them an injustice by speaking too quickly."

He grasped her hand and held her fingers to his lips, eyes questioning, waiting.

Honesty had to go both ways, she knew this. He'd been honest with her, and now it was her turn, even if it meant admitting her fear. "You've slain me, Kaden. You did it so slowly over the last year, so honestly and openly that I forgot to be wary about letting you in. It happened gradually, and I didn't see it until … until the other night, I guess, when I knew I had to tell you the truth about the avalanche. And just when I believed you'd be angry that I'd held the truth back, you embraced me and loved me. You've stripped away my barriers, and you've taken my heart. I'm feeling very vulnerable, and I'm frightened."

"Annie," Kaden sighed as he pulled her up on his lap and hugged her to his chest. He kissed her hair, her forehead, her eyelids, and every part of her face he could reach. "Your heart is safe with me. I will cherish it, and I will never, ever, intentionally hurt you. I've a confession to make to you, too. I've never felt like this before. My heart has never beat so hard for anyone, and I'm also scared. You've captured my heart and my soul as well, and no matter how long it takes for you to understand and accept my love, I will be here for you." His voice dropped to a whisper. *"Ma chérie, tu es la plus belle femme que j'ai jamais rencontré, tu as touché mon âme et l'amour apporté à la vie pour moi et je ne veux plus jamais vivre sans toi."*

She didn't understand all the words, but she felt the meaning to the depth of her soul as he whispered them in that beautiful language of love. And that made it all the worse. "But how will this ever work? We live six thousand miles apart. And my career … my career is all I've got. I don't know anything else."

Eventually he released his snug grip, tilted her back, and tipped her chin so she had to look at him. He smiled softly, and in an attempt to be light-hearted, he said, "That's a detail, love, and details can be overcome. My question is, now that we both know how fragile our hearts are, will you come to Rasteau in the spring?"

She laughed and wrapped her arms around his neck, snuggled her face in his hair, and kissed his ear. She had to trust him on this—there was no other choice, and she didn't have the heart to argue. *"Oui, mon coeur,* I'll come to see you in the spring."

Kaden let out the breath he'd been holding in. *This woman will kill me,* he thought, *and I'll die with a smile.*

Twenty-Three

"Crap," Annie cursed as she surveyed the damage to her apartment. The kitchen looked like a bomb had gone off. The remains of shattered glasses and ceramic dishes covered the floor. There was water on the floor, too, but she wasn't sure where it had come from. At least her refrigerator door had held. She pulled it open only to have half the contents spill out onto the floor. *Argh!*

She glanced at her watch. Past eight thirty. It was three hours later on the East Coast, but Kaden would expect her call and wait up for it. She hauled her roller bag up the stairs to her bedroom loft, peeled off her traveling clothes, and changed into her flannel pajamas.

"Annie?" he asked as he picked up the phone on the first ring, slightly softening her crappy mood.

"Yeah, it's me. My kitchen is a total disaster. There's nothing left in the cupboards—it's all shattered on the floor in the kitchen. And then, to top it off, when I opened the refrigerator door, a half-empty carton of orange juice, a jar of mustard, and a flat of eggs came spilling out and shattered all over the floor. It's a God damned mess."

On the phone in his room in New York, Kaden tried desperately to keep from laughing out loud. He could totally picture her standing there frustrated and pissed off, and the image made him … laugh.

She didn't appreciate the humor in the situation, and said so.

"Annie, please, I'm sorry. I know it's bad. If I could be there, I'd clean it up for you. But you have to admit, from my end, it *is* kind of funny."

She blanched, ready to pummel him verbally, but then burst into laughter. "God, you are so right. I'm alive and my friends are fine. Who am I to complain, really?"

Kaden laughed with her but quickly sobered at the sentiment. "Have you talked to any neighbors?" he asked, curious about the earthquake damage in her area.

"No, but the security guard told me most everyone in the building had some amount of property damage. I assume he meant the kind of breakage that I have. He didn't say anything about structural damage. Everything seems fine, though. The elevator worked." She glanced up at the wall of windows. "My windows are fine." She glanced over at her desk, where her computer sat just where she'd left it. "My computer is fine, so I can still email you. Nothing else matters. The rest is just stuff that can be replaced."

———————————————◆———————————————

For Christmas, Kaden sent Annie a beautiful, finely woven cashmere shawl that he had purchased for her in Paris on his way back home, along with more of Henri's wine and another recipe. She sent him a little sculpture of a crab, ingeniously crafted by a local San Francisco artist from pieces of silver flatware.

They talked for more than an hour on Christmas Day.

"How's the import business going? Do you know when your first container will land in the US?" Annie was impressed with how quickly Kaden had been able to move things along.

All the chefs he'd met in both New York and Washington had expressed interest in trying the wines. When he returned home, Kaden had organized boxes of samples for each restaurant, and with the help of his Washington attorney, managed to get them approved through customs and delivered to the chefs. The samples had arrived in mid December, and most of the restaurants had placed orders. Now he just needed to get the product on US soil.

"It's coming along well. I have label approval for all but three of the wines, and those should be finalized shortly." The US Department of Treasury was very strict on labeling requirements for alcohol sold in the country, and every label, front and back, had to be approved before the product was allowed to be released. It was a process that Kaden had started back in the summer when he first developed his plan, anticipating the immense amount of time it would require. Now he was glad that he'd thought ahead. The last thing he needed was for wine shipments to be held up in some administrative process.

"In fact," he said, "last week I was able to secure space in a container scheduled to leave Bordeaux in mid-January, so even with inevitable delays, it should arrive at the New York docks by the first week of February. I was hoping you might be able to sneak away to meet me. I need to be there to take possession of the wine and get it to the bonded warehouse I've hired to handle my distribution. I'm trying to time it so the wine can be delivered to my customers by Valentine's Day."

Annie hoped this might happen. A quick trip to the East Coast was much easier than hauling herself to France.

"I think I can manage that," she said happily. "As a matter of fact, I might be able to manage more than just a weekend, if you don't mind me working during the day. One of my partners in Manhattan has been bugging me to come out there to meet with a client and do a training session for his staff. If I can set that up to coincide with your container arriving ... hmm, this might just work!"

She bounced off her couch, pulled her calendar out of her briefcase, and flipped to February. "I'll try to set up the meetings for the Thursday and Friday of the second week of February so I have an excuse to be there, and we can have the whole weekend. Will that work?"

Kaden relished the excitement in her voice. "That will definitely work. I'll do my best to let you out of bed in the morning to make your appointments," he teased and was rewarded with her sexy bedroom laugh.

Annie spent the first day of 1990 with her best friends, watching college football, munching on snacks, and drinking beer. While John and his boys cheered and cavorted, she sat with Marie at the kitchen bar counter on the other side of the room. Annie had filled her in on the big picture after she'd returned from DC, but they hadn't had time to have a real girls' talk about the details.

Marie could see the glow as Annie spoke about that night of the earthquake and how caring and understanding Kaden had been. "He actually knew about what really happened. He had figured it out somehow, so he understood why I was freaking out so badly. I didn't know he knew, and he didn't ask any questions, just helped me to calm down, encouraged me to call you and Adam, and was like an anchor in my storm of emotions.

"I knew I had to tell him about it. God, I felt so guilty that I hadn't already, since we'd shared so much personal stuff, but I don't know, there never seemed to be a good time. I didn't want to just throw out some heavy, 'Here's what really happened that day.' But that night, I had to make him understand why I was so upset. I was so scared about what he would say. I thought he would be hurt that I'd held it back, but when I finally let it out, he was just so ... so *gentle* and caring."

Annie pointed her beer bottle at her friend. "You called right at the perfect time, just after I let the bomb drop. But then after we hung up, he took me in his arms and made me feel so protected. And suddenly I understood that he had known all along. He confessed and was actually a little embarrassed; he told me he'd felt like he had invaded my privacy by learning about it online."

"Online? What does that mean?" Marie asked.

"On the internet. The man is a wizard with computers. He's been using the internet to access financial databases in London and New York for years. He stays up with all the latest hardware and software developments—even invests in them."

She glanced over at John and lowered her voice. "He's a serious player in the industry. I mean, he's led start-up funding for a bunch of incubator technology companies in France and the UK." Annie hadn't been exaggerating when she had introduced Kaden to her colleagues in Washington.

"Okay, so the man is a computer wizard. Then what happened?"

"He told me that he loved me, and we had amazing sex all night long." Annie laughed and shrugged at Marie's shocked expression. "Why are you so surprised? You knew it was inevitable."

Marie waived her hand dismissively. "Never mind the sex part, I expected that. He actually told you that he loved you?"

"Mhmm," Annie replied with a nod while taking a sip from her beer. "It was really sweet. I was nervous because, well, you know, I hadn't been with a man since Jack. And hoo-boy," she grinned and fanned herself. "The man has moves. But ... I believed him. I *do* believe him, and ..." She paused and looked down at her hands. "I love him, too."

Marie looked closely at her friend.

Annie caught the look and smiled. "Something happened, Marie. After that night, I was different. It was like a film had been removed from my eyes and everything was suddenly in focus. I know that sounds silly, but I don't know how else to explain it. In his patient, gentle, caring way, he totally captured my heart and my soul. It's scary as hell. But I won't deny it." Annie shook her head. "I *can't* deny it."

Marie reached over and squeezed her hand. "I can tell. You actually *look* different. Honestly, you've looked different for a while. But now you look comfortable with it."

Annie nodded. "I know, I can see it too. I can feel it here." She pointed at her heart. "The connection between us is strong. But you know, it's not just physical. Don't get me wrong, I had the most incredible sex of my life, but we connected—really connected—on so many levels long before Washington." Annie took a sip of her beer and let out an audible sigh.

"And the problem is?" Her friend wasn't fooled.

"The problem is that my life is here—I've worked my ass off to get where I am at the firm. People are depending on me. That DC conference was huge for me, and business is coming out of the woodwork, and ..."

"And?"

Annie ran a frustrated hand through her hair. "I love my job. I get incredible satisfaction out of being good at what I do. I have national respect—and not just within the firm. People in the industry know who I am and seek me out. It's ... powerful. I'm not ready to walk away from it. But now, now I feel like I need to think about doing just that if I want to keep Kaden."

Marie frowned. "But who's to say he can't move here? If he loves you and wants to be with you ..."

"I don't know. I get the sense ... I get the feeling that would be a mistake. We're still pretty new, you know. Even though we've known each other for a year and a half, we've hardly spent any time together, I mean, physically. We haven't talked about the long term, logistics, anything, but ..."

Marie waited as she watched Annie struggle through her thoughts.

"I'll be spending two weeks with him at his home—his real home—in May. When I'm there, I'll get a better sense of what I'm really up against. Until then, I have to just enjoy it. If I overthink it, I'll miss out on the fun of having a boyfriend for the first time in almost a decade!"

When Annie finally kissed her friends goodbye and headed home, she felt energized. As she drove, she thought about the wonderful connection with Kaden that she had described to Marie, and she marveled at it. They were thousands of miles apart, yet their bond was growing stronger. She missed him terribly, couldn't wait to see him and touch him again. Was she crazy? The geography was hopeless, yet she felt oddly satisfied with their relationship nonetheless.

Despite their separation, it was as if she was wrapped in a cocoon of their shared emotion. Their relationship had evolved *because* of their distance and the dynamics of their separate lives. The distance had forced them to work at communicating, and they had shared an emotional intimacy long before a physical one.

She wished there was an easy solution for them to be together permanently, but she knew what that would involve, and she couldn't think about it. For all the reasons she'd cited to Marie, she wasn't ready to make that sacrifice. As easy as it might be for Kaden to relocate to San Francisco, she knew he wouldn't. And she wasn't sure she would want him to—it would make him a different person. She could never ask him to leave Rasteau. He'd made his decision years ago, and his love for his uncle Henri and the visceral connection he had with the land there were part of his DNA. It was part of what made him Kaden.

If anyone moved, it would have to be her. She would have to be the one to uproot her life, give up her world, change who she was. She resented it, and besides, would he even like her then? The thought of becoming a grasping, dependent, insecure woman made her shudder. The woman he fell in love with was a confident, independent, original-thinking professional. By giving in, she'd turn into someone he would never be able to respect. She could never do that to him, or to herself.

But in the back of her mind, she visualized what it would be like to be free of her corporate yoke, living in rural France. The image did not discourage her as much as she thought it might, and that surprised her, but the fear of losing his respect pushed that bucolic image away.

Twenty-Four

New York City, February 1990

Kaden had been in New York for a week, haggling with US Customs to release his wine from their dockside warehouses, by the time Annie arrived. As she joined him in the hotel suite, she couldn't help but notice the desk covered in an array of equipment, including a printer, fax machine, and the smallest computer she'd ever seen. At least, she thought it was a computer. It was thin, no more than two inches thick, with a flat screen that stood up from the back of a hinged base that had a keyboard imbedded right in it. If the screen was pushed down, it would be no bigger than a large book.

"Good Lord, is that a computer?" she asked.

He grinned and nodded. "They call it a laptop."

"You brought all this over with you?"

"No, I bought it all here. I've hired an agent to represent the company here, and I'll leave the printer and fax machine with him. I've been watching the development of these laptops closely over the last couple of years, and huge strides are being made. This new design hit the market just a few months ago. It's portable enough to go home with me, and it has more power and memory capacity than my current system does. Plus it has an internal modem. I won't have to haul my bulky equipment back and forth between Rasteau and Les Eyzies anymore."

Annie had been staring at the desk while Kaden spoke, and now he took her by surprise when he wrapped his arms around her from behind. She hugged him close, then leaned back and closed her eyes as he sprinkled her temple with kisses. The equipment on the desk, and nearly everything else, was forgotten as her body reacted to his touch.

"I made us a late dinner reservation," he whispered as he traced her ear with the tip of his tongue then blew on it, making her shiver.

"How late?" Annie sighed as he unbuttoned her jacket. She let it drop to the floor before turning around in his arms.

"Late enough."

They had just settled into a cozy booth at one of Kaden's new accounts when the chef, who had worked with Jean Claude in Paris, came out to greet them. He insisted on creating a special tasting menu for them, and they enjoyed the fine fare almost as much as they enjoyed being together again.

By the time they left the restaurant, the temperature was below freezing and snow was in the forecast. Annie was shivering and chilled to the bone when they finally arrived back at the hotel. Her overcoat was more of a lined raincoat, appropriate for San Francisco but not nearly heavy enough for winter in the northeast. Kaden noticed her shivering and frowned, but said nothing.

For the next two days, they woke early and went their separate ways to attend to their business, but they had the nights all to themselves, which they enjoyed to full advantage. On Friday evening when Annie arrived back at the hotel, she was exhausted and cold. The thought of leaving the warm hotel suite made her groan, even though she was hungry. Kaden held her close and rubbed her back to warm her up.

"I suppose we could order Chinese take-out," he said. "But before you decide, I have something for you." She gave him a questioning look, but he just grinned. "I had some free time today, so I went shopping."

He took her hand and guided her into the bedroom where, laid out on the bed, was a beautiful dark-gray overcoat, a feminine version of the one Kaden wore. Annie gasped. She stepped over to it and lightly ran her fingertips down the fine fabric. It was cashmere, incredibly soft, and the cut was stunning. Generous but not bulky, with elegant lines that she knew would look fabulous as it fell from her shoulders, whether she paired it with her dressy business suits or simply wore it over jeans. She looked at him, stunned.

"We can't have you freezing to death, my love. Will you try it on?"

She scrambled out of her raincoat and tossed it in a chair, then reverently picked up the new garment and held it to her cheek. "It's so soft! Oh, Kaden, I don't know what to say."

"Here, let me help you." He took the coat from her hands and kissed her cheek where she had held the coat. "Turn around." She did, and he held it while she slipped her arms into the sleeves. He settled it lightly on her shoulders, smoothed it out, then reached around under her arms and enclosed her in the soft folds, buttoning it from behind. Then he stepped back and spun her gently around to face him.

"Well, how does it fit?" He smiled as he took another step back. It looked beautiful on her. The stunned expression remained on her face, but her hands were clutched in the lapels, holding the coat to her with eyes shining. She spun around in a circle and stepped over to the mirror to delight in her appearance. Catching his eyes in the mirror, she sent him a glorious smile.

"Thank you," she said softly. "It's perfect. Beautiful. And warm!" She laughed and spun around again, then stepped up to him and pressed herself against his solid form to kiss him with abandon.

When they finally broke from the kiss, Kaden kept his arms around her, kissed the tip of her nose, and asked, "Still feel like Chinese take-out?"

Twenty-Five

The snow finally made its appearance in the wee hours of the next morning. Kaden and Annie woke to the muted gray light of a dawn shrouded in softly falling snowflakes. With no commitments, they lingered in the warm cavern of their bed, then lazed their Saturday away at the Met, which was an easy walk from their hotel on shoveled sidewalks and was blissfully uncrowded due to the weather.

The storm blew through overnight, and Sunday morning dawned shockingly bright and clear, but the temperatures hadn't climbed at all. Bundled up in their matching cashmere coats, they took a cab downtown to the Empire State Building. The view from the top was breathtaking—breathtakingly beautiful and breathtakingly cold, but they lingered up there for as long as they could stand it, admiring the view.

Walking back up Fifth Avenue, they passed a movie theater featuring the blockbuster film *Hunt for Red October*.

"I love Sean Connery!" Annie said. "Have you seen this movie yet?"

"No, but I liked the book." He looked at the posted showtimes. "It looks like a show is about to start. Shall we?"

The movie was all exciting, fast-paced suspense, and they cuddled up in a dark corner at the back of the theater with a big bucket of popcorn, reveling in their cloaked privacy as they enjoyed the on-screen action.

In the early evening they were lounging in their sitting room, stretched out together on the couch, wrapped in the soft, thick robes provided by the hotel, when there was a knock at the door. Annie jolted up with surprise, but Kaden was apparently expecting it. She pulled her robe more tightly around her, curled up on the couch with her feet tucked in, and watched him saunter up to the door.

She heard, *"Bonsoir, monsieur,"* then a brief exchange in French, and watched in surprise as a white-jacketed waiter wheel a large cart laden with silver dome–covered dishes across the room. In the middle of the cart was a crystal bud vase with a single red rose. Other than a brief nod and *"Bonsoir, madame,"* the waiter ignored her.

Kaden winked at her, then directed the man to the small table in the corner of the sitting room. Out came snowy-white linen, crystal stemware, and silver flatware from some hidden place in the cart, and within moments, the table was set. Once he had everything just so, and two bottles of wine were opened and tasted, Kaden nodded, satisfied. The waiter then bowed slightly, bade them *bon appétit,* and exited.

"He looked familiar," Annie said as she drew her brows together.

Kaden grinned and walked toward her with his hand outstretched, which she accepted and let him pull her to her feet. "He waited on us at Chez Robert on Wednesday night. Since you enjoyed the meal there so much, I asked the chef to make us a special Valentine dinner that we could enjoy here by ourselves. Come, *chérie,* you must be hungry."

He sat her down with a flourish, and she laughed as he unfurled a pristine white linen napkin and laid it across her lap over the bathrobe. He then plucked the rose from the vase, knelt down by the side of her chair, and kissed her cheek as he handed it to her. "Happy Valentine's Day, Annie."

She accepted the rose and the kiss with a misty smile.

The meal started with heart-shaped lobster ravioli in a sinfully delicious broth, served with a crisp Chardonnay that Kaden explained came from the village of Puligny-Montrachet in Burgundy. "Lobster and the best white Burgundy," he expounded with a wink, "is a culinary match made in heaven." He was clearly enjoying himself.

The next covered plate revealed a petit filet mignon with a heart-shaped pat of herbed butter on top, melting decadently over the meat. New potatoes and glossy baby green beans completed the elegantly simple plate. Everything was delicious, including the wine that turned out to be from his uncle's vineyards in Pécharmant.

"The wine was finally delivered to the restaurants on Friday," he said in answer to the surprised look on Annie's face.

For dessert, there were two small molten chocolate cakes. Rather than remain at the table, they brought their dessert back to the couch and curled up there to enjoy it.

Annie put her empty plate on the coffee table, relieved Kaden of his, and before he could move, she gathered the hem of her robe up around her thighs and straddled his lap. She pushed his shoulders back against the cushions and leaned in for a long, deep kiss. They both tasted like chocolate, and she smiled when she finally pulled back.

"Wow," he said, slightly breathless, holding her waist so she wouldn't move too far.

"Wow is right," she said. "You floor me," she whispered just before she plundered his mouth again. She felt his muscles tense as she began to move her hips sensuously in his lap. They were both naked under their robes. As he snaked one hand up to untie the sash of her robe and slide it open, Annie sighed and relished the feeling of being so adored. *I will never get enough of him,* she thought, just before he sent her reeling.

And she sent him reeling too, provocatively loving him with a wanton abandon that surprised and delighted him. Eventually, when their hearts had stopped pounding and their breathing was back to normal, Kaden skittered light kisses across her temple. "I guess that means you liked my surprise," he murmured into her curls with a smile.

She moved against him, snuggling closer to his chest. "You think?"

Kaden chuckled softly, lifted her from him, and bent down to retrieve her robe. "Put this back on, *chérie,* I don't want you to catch cold."

"I think my blood's too heated for that," she replied with a secret little smile, but she took the robe and wrapped herself back in it.

Kaden took her hands and held them flat against his chest. "I'm not sure my heart can handle another reaction like that, but I do have one more small surprise for you."

"Kaden," she said in exasperation. "You're spoiling me. Are you sure this is a good idea?"

"This is just a little thing," he said softly as he reached into his robe pocket. "I thought you might have put your knee through it, but it seems okay." He drew out a small, flat little box in that robin-egg blue that screamed Tiffany's, tied with a thin white satin ribbon, and held it out to her. "Please, Annie. It would make me happy."

She bit her lower lip as she reached for the box, tugged the ribbon, and let it fall away. Then she slowly lifted the lid. Nestled in dark-blue velvet was a small silver Tiffany heart on a slim silver chain. She timidly touched the heart then looked up at him with an aching tenderness in her luminous brown eyes.

"*Ma chérie,* you already hold my heart in your hands, but will you wear it around your neck as well? It would make me happy to know you have this small token of my love against your skin." He tenderly touched her cheek.

Eyes brimming with emotion, she smiled at him and shook her head in wonder. "You truly do floor me. I'll wear it always," she promised as she pulled the chain from beneath the velvet. He took it from her, opened the clasp, and as she leaned forward, he fastened it around her neck.

"Thank you," he whispered, as he drew her back to him for a gentle kiss.

The next morning came way too quickly, but at least Annie didn't have time to be sad as she scrambled around getting ready. Kaden accompanied her to the airport in the hotel's limo. It was a bittersweet parting as they shared a final kiss at the gate, but at least they knew they would see each other in three months.

Twenty-Six

A typical Saturday morning in the middle of tax season, Annie was sitting in her office, plowing her way through the pile of files awaiting her review when her phone rang. "Annie Shaw," she answered on the first ring.

"Annie! Thank God you're there!" It was Marie, and she sounded hysterical. There was background noise, like she was calling from a payphone in a crowded location.

"Marie? Are you okay? Where are you?" Annie pushed down the panic that immediately swamped her.

"John's had a heart attack!" Marie barely got the words out on a sob.

Annie sucked in a gasp, jumped out of her chair, and gripped the phone tighter. She closed her eyes. *Oh God, please no.* "Is he ... is he ..."

"He's alive." Marie let out an anguished sob. "But ... he's critical."

"When did it happen? Where are you?" Annie forced calm authority into her voice, needing to break through her own panic and her friend's hysterics.

"I'm at Alta Bates." Marie's voice was so shaky, she could barely get the words out. "We just got here a few minutes ago." Sniffle, cough. "They got him out of the car and onto a gurney, then rushed him inside. They're working on him now."

"You drove him?" Annie was flabbergasted.

"Hell, yes, I drove him! If I'd waited for the fucking ambulance, he would've died!"

"Jesus Christ, okay, okay. You did the right thing." Marie had been a nurse before she'd given up her career to raise her boys. Annie had a thousand questions, but they could wait. "I'm on my way. I'm leaving right now. I should be there in twenty minutes."

"Hurry, Annie, I'm losing it." She sobbed into the phone.

No shit, Annie thought as she dropped the phone into its cradle, grabbing up her coat and purse. *So I'd better not.* Her door was blocked by several colleagues who had heard her loud voice and stepped out of their own offices to find out what was going on, but they jumped aside as she sprinted past them.

"John Franklin just had a heart attack," she called back over her shoulder. "He's alive." And she was gone, racing for the elevators.

Annie's heart was pounding as she paced in front of the elevators waiting for one to reach her. She was tempted to just take the stairs, but she was twenty floors up, so even with a wait for the lift, the elevator was quicker. Besides, she wasn't sure her legs would carry her down twenty flights of steps … she was already shaking badly.

The ping of the elevator made her jump, and she bolted for the door as it opened. Less than a minute later, she was on the ground floor racing for her car. She peeled out of the garage and tore through the deserted streets of the financial district toward the on-ramp for the Bay Bridge.

As she sped across the bridge, she took some deep breaths to calm her racing heart. She had no idea about survival rates for heart attack victims. Surely, if he had survived the initial attack, and what had no doubt been *Mr. Toad's Wild Ride* to the hospital, that was something. But what were the odds of permanent damage?

Life is so fragile; it can change in a heartbeat. Literally, in John's case. And in hers, too, she reminded herself. As she dashed to get to her friend, she thought back to her own accident and about how much her life had changed in an instant. With a curious out-of-body sensation, Annie looked back on it without emotion. One minute she had been married and pregnant and happy, with all the time in the world to love her husband and raise their daughter, and in the space of a few moments, it was all gone.

And how had she dealt with it? She had survived, yes, but what had it cost her? She'd worked like a machine and achieved an impressive goal, but in the process she'd gone eight long years without allowing herself to love— or allowing anyone to love her. She had boxed up her heart to keep it from being ripped away again, and she had let a part of herself die for a while. She survived, but she hadn't lived.

It had taken Kaden's tenacious determination to snap her out of it, to remind her of the simple pleasure of affection. She had changed over the course of their long-distance courtship, and she liked the new Annie. The feeling of being loved and cherished by him was exhilarating, and she treasured the liberating feeling of loving him back.

She fingered the little silver heart that hung around her neck as she raced to reach Marie. Her friend—her dearest friend—sat quaking in a puddle of misery and pain while her husband, her lover, her friend, lay in critical condition in a sterile hospital room. What was more tragic, having a great love and losing it, or never having the love at all? Annie certainly knew how the first felt. But would she have passed on Jack if she knew how quickly it would end? No, she admitted to herself, she would have taken the love. However much it hurt, the heartache was worth it.

And that gave her a sobering thought: if she had succeeded in shutting Kaden out when he'd come on to her … if he had let her … she would never have known the purity of the love they shared. For that's what it was. There was a purity and honesty to their shared emotions that she had never experienced before. It was so right, so uniquely *them,* and it made their souls touch, even though they were so far apart. How sad that would have been, she realized, to have missed it.

She and Kaden were half a world apart, but Annie's emotional connection with him was so strong. And so different from what she'd had with Jack. More mature, certainly deeper. Their physical intimacy was so steamy hot, it made her warm just thinking about it, but the foundation of their love was based on friendship and respect. Did she love Kaden more than she had loved Jack? *What the hell does that matter?* she scolded herself. *The point is, Kaden is in my life now, and I love him.*

She was saved from further self-examination when she pulled into the Alta Bates Hospital parking lot in Oakland. She jumped from the car and ran for the ER as she checked her watch, relieved that she'd made it in less than twenty minutes.

Annie found Marie huddled in a ratty plastic chair in the waiting area, her thin shoulders hunched forward and a Kleenex clutched in her hand. She looked up as Annie strode toward her, and a fresh batch of tears came spilling down her cheeks. *She looks so fragile and broken,* Annie thought as she knelt down to embrace her friend.

"How is he?" Annie asked as she held Marie's shaking shoulders.

"They've stabilized him. They're putting in a stent, but they can't tell yet about any permanent damage."

Annie let out the breath she didn't realize she was holding. "Thank God." Marie cried against Annie's shoulder, and she held her, stroking her back.

It was hours before they were able to see John. He was awake but groggy, pumped up with drugs. They'd moved him to a private room, and he was already grumbling. *A good sign,* Annie thought. After what seemed like just a few minutes, though, the nurse kicked them out. John was weak and needed to sleep, so Annie quieted her friend's protests and took her home.

Back at the house, Annie poured them both a glass of wine while they waited for the boys, who had been off on an all-day school excursion, mercifully spared the terror of seeing their father at his most critical point. Annie shuddered at the thought of having to explain to two preteen boys that their father wasn't coming back.

When they arrived, the kids seemed to take the news in stride, which was a relief. Once the story of how their mom had pushed their dad ass over elbows into the car and driven like a crazy woman to the hospital had been retold for them several times, Annie suggested they get ready for bed, a hint they actually took. Next she gave Marie some Tylenol PM and helped her to bed.

When Annie finally stumbled into her apartment late Sunday afternoon, she was exhausted. She appreciated anew the endless, tender care that Marie had shown her during her own recovery. For now, John had dodged a bullet, and Nurse Marie had straightened her spine to take charge.

It was late, or rather, very early morning in France, but Annie needed to talk to Kaden. She'd made a quick call to him Saturday night from the

Franklins' house to let him know what was going on, but now she needed to hear his voice … needed the irrational assurance that he was there.

She fired up her computer as she pondered making the call, uncertain whether she should wake him up to basically say nothing, well nothing other than "I miss you and need to hear your voice." *He wants you to,* Annie reminded herself.

She opened her email and smiled when she found two messages from him. She clicked on the most recent, sent just a few hours ago. She read it and smiled wider.

Call me as soon as you get home, whatever the time. Love, K

Twenty-Seven

Paris, France, May 1990

Annie spotted Kaden over the crowd at the baggage claim area at the Charles de Gaulle Airport—the same exit she had come through almost two years ago on the trip that had changed her life. When she reached him, he swept her up into his arms and hugged her tight, making her squeak. He laughed and set her down, kissed her softly, touched his fingertip to her little silver heart, and kissed her again. *"Bonjour, chérie. Bienvenue à Paris."*

She kissed him back. *"Bonjour à toi."*

Still smiling, he relieved her of her carry-on and commandeered her roller bag with the same hand, setting one on top of the other, then locked his free hand with hers. As he steered her toward the exit, he asked her about the flight.

"You know it was fine," she said, rolling her eyes—he'd gifted her with a first-class ticket. "But I can't believe you came all the way to Paris to meet me."

"I would never pass up a chance to dine with you in Paris, even if I do have to share you with your friend."

Her friend, Lori Sheridan, was still living in Paris, and Annie had asked Kaden to include her in their dinner plans. He'd hedged until she pointed out that if it hadn't been for Lori, they never would have met. She would forever tease him about his early concern that her Parisian friend had been some man who'd dumped her.

Their car pulled to the curb at the Hotel du Vieux Paris, a tastefully converted nineteenth-century mansion on the left bank near Notre Dame, and Annie squeezed his hand. "I'm beginning to recognize your style," she whispered as the driver stepped out to open her door.

He chuckled as they climbed out, then gestured to the door that the bellman held open, and she preceded him in. The foyer was small but inviting, with an old-world ambiance. The gentleman at the reception desk greeted them and handed Kaden his key.

The moment the door to their third-floor room swung closed behind them, they were in each other's arms, holding on tight. She clung to him, suddenly desperate to feel his embrace. When she let out a little sob against his chest, Kaden tipped her chin up to look into her face and was alarmed to see she was crying. "What is it, *chérie?* Is something wrong?"

She sniffled and wiped her eyes, feeling foolish. "Nothing's wrong, I just … um, I guess I've been thinking too much about how fragile life is, how tenuous. I'm just really, really glad to be here, to touch you and feel your embrace again."

Kaden studied her face, alarm bells going off in his head. His chest tightened, and his heart started pounding as he imagined the worst. "Annie," he persisted, trying to keep his voice steady. "Are you sure you're all right? Please, sweetheart, tell me what's wrong."

Annie heard the panic in his voice and realized he'd jumped to the wrong conclusion. She put her hands on his face, held his eyes to hers, and tried to smile. "Nothing is wrong with me. I'm sorry if I scared you. It's just that … John's heart attack affected me more than I imagined. It made me think of what I would do if something happened to you, and I wasn't here." She tried to get a little laugh out to lighten the air. "But here you are, very real and very fine, and I'm just extremely grateful that you are, that's all."

"Me too," he whispered in her hair as he hugged her tightly.

They took advantage of the balmy afternoon and strolled along the bank of the Seine, walking slowly, aimlessly, with heads leaned together, enjoying the fresh air, the beautiful city, and being together again. Their meandering took them up the left bank of the river, across the Pont des Arts, then down the other side, eventually back to their hotel.

As he watched Annie napping later, laying snug in his arms, Kaden turned his mind to his most pressing challenge—how he was going to convince her to marry him, give up her career, and move to France for good. He knew it wouldn't be this visit, but he planned to pull out all the stops to show her how much she needed to be here with him. *He* needed her here—there was no doubt of that. He'd promised her he would wait as long as it took, but he needed to nudge her along. She had unwittingly given him a signal that she might be receptive to a little encouraging when she had revealed her fears about his well-being after John's heart attack. That was to his advantage. *After all, all's fair ...*

Annie pressed the call button at the entrance to Lori's building. When the buzzer sounded, Kaden pulled it open and she walked in. They crossed the courtyard then took the teeny lift up to the fourth floor. Her friend's door was open when they stepped out of the lift, and she popped her head out before they reached it. The girls embraced, and then Lori looked beyond Annie's shoulder to the tall, striking figure of Kaden and gasped.

"Good Lord, are you Kaden?"

"Close your mouth. I told you he was gorgeous. Didn't you believe me?" Annie smirked then introduced a suddenly blushing Lori to an even more flushed Kaden.

Lori led them into her sitting room and popped a bottle of Champagne to toast Annie's arrival in Paris. Kaden listened with amusement as the friends chatted and caught up but had to swallow the sudden lump in his throat when Annie relayed the news about John.

Eventually, he signaled that it was time to go, and the ladies tittered with anticipation. He'd made the dinner reservation but had declined to tell them where, only insisting that they dress up.

When their cab pulled up in front of Taillevent, one of the few three-star Michelin restaurants in Paris, Lori nearly fainted, as the famous restaurant was so far beyond her means, she'd never dreamed of eating there. But Annie, by now accustomed to Kaden's taste in dining, just shrugged and winked at her friend. As it turned out, the current *chef de cuisine* was a close friend of Jean Claude, and they were not only treated to the sort of food and service one expects in a three-star restaurant in Paris but VIP status on top of that.

Throughout the exquisite meal, Kaden entertained them with stories of life in rural France, some of which Annie had heard, but many of the tales were new to her as well. She was very curious about the beloved uncle she was going to meet very soon, and Kaden was full of humorous and touching stories about him. He was apparently quite a character in his adopted town of Rasteau.

Lori wanted to know why Henri had left the Pécharmant estate to branch out on his own. "Was there a disagreement among the family?" she asked.

"Not at all," Kaden answered. "But he would always have been a minority owner in the business. My other uncle inherited the controlling interest, as had been my grandfather's plan. While the French inheritance laws prevent legal heirs from being disinherited, one can still be favored over another."

At the time of his death, Kaden's French grandfather had three surviving children: Kaden's mother, Marianna; and his uncles, Maurice and Henri. Maurice, being the oldest son, was expected to carry on the family business and was thus gifted the maximum allowed under the inheritance laws, which was fifty percent. The remaining half was split between Marianna and Henri.

"Henri preferred to run his own operation rather than work under his brother." He shrugged. "Maurice bought out his portion in an amicable arrangement, and Henri used the money to purchase a large but neglected property in Rasteau."

"Why there?" Annie asked. "Why not stay closer to home?"

"My aunt Hélène, Henri's late wife, was born and raised in the area, and it's a far more prestigious wine region than Pécharmant." Kaden paused for a moment as if considering. "Henri has never said in so many words, but I suspect he wanted to be away from an overbearing older brother. He was certainly shrewd in his choice of property. At the time it was nothing but a rundown estate, but Henri saw the potential, and they were able to buy it with his limited means because of its condition. He's spent the last twenty-five years making it what it is today."

"What about the Pécharmant property?" Lori wanted to know. "Does your mother still own her share?"

"She held on to it but contractually agreed to let Maurice manage it. It's a common enough arrangement among siblings and cousins who inherit vineyards in France, where she became a silent partner of sorts. Maurice does a fine job and she had no interest in interfering, but she wanted to save the legacy for her children—myself and my brothers."

"So do you own a piece of it now?" Annie asked. It had never occurred to her that he might have some interest in either of his uncles' properties.

Kaden nodded. "I do. Actually she left it to the three of us, but my brothers weren't interested in their shares, so I bought them out. I own the original 25 percent she inherited. Of course, I've continued to honor the management arrangement that she set in place."

Annie was intrigued and gave voice to what she'd just figured out. "Jean Claude will inherit a portion of the estate when Maurice dies. Does he plan on taking an active role in the business?"

"No," Kaden said unequivocally. "He has the wines at La Belle Nicole, of course, and helps with marketing in his area and with chefs he knows, but his only interest in wine is in how it accompanies his cuisine. His brother Fernand will eventually take over. Fernand studied at the Institut d'Oenologie at Bordeaux University, and he's done stints at a number of châteaux in Bordeaux under the tutelage of well-respected *vignerons*. He's only just recently returned home to work with Maurice."

"Does Fernand follow the same wine-making philosophy as Maurice?" Annie asked.

Kaden flashed an intimate smile her way. "An interesting question, Annie. What makes you ask?"

She blushed, more from the smile than the comment. "I'm just trying to understand the world I'm about to step into. I've heard you talk about the traditional versus modern styles of wine making, and I get the impression that both Maurice and Henri would be considered traditionalists, but I think you would call yourself a modernist."

"Go on," Kaden said with a nod when she paused.

"Well, I'm curious about Fernand, since he would be representing the younger generation—your generation—and I wondered if the people he worked with in Bordeaux take a different view on things than Maurice."

Lori watched the exchange between the two of them, feeling like an outsider but not minding it—much. Their casual dialogue belied the intense focus they had on each other. When one spoke, the other truly listened.

God, I love this woman, Kaden thought. "As a matter of fact, Fernand *has* been trying to make changes, in vineyard management primarily, but Maurice is resisting. Fernand is pushing ahead despite the resistance, and he's been making progress, but the biggest challenge for him, and a serious bone of contention with Maurice, is ridding the vineyards of synthetic treatments for mildew and other rot issues."

Annie thought for a moment. "Does that mean he wants to go organic?"

"Yes, exactly." Kaden said, pleased that she understood. "In point of fact, he wants to take it a step further, to what is called *biodynamic* farming, but he'll never accomplish that while Maurice is still running the show."

"Sounds complicated," Lori chimed in.

"Sounds fascinating," Annie modified.

"It can be both—complicated and fascinating," Kaden acknowledged, taking care to include both of them in his response. "But it's way too boring to go into now, in the middle of this incredible meal."

He reached across the table and put his hand over Annie's. "I'm glad you find it interesting, *chérie,* because I've been looking forward to explaining it to you in Rasteau. Henri and I have been working on making these same changes for the past several years—it wasn't hard to convince him it's the right thing to do. We're finally beginning to see the results. This is going to be a very interesting year for us, if it works."

Lori glanced away from them as the cheese trolley rolled to a stop in front of their table. The intensity between the couple was practically combustible. She was happy for her friend but just hoped it didn't all blow up in her face.

Twenty-Eight

Paris was drizzly and gray the next morning when Annie and Kaden left for the train station, but as they made their way south through the French countryside, the clouds gradually gave way to sunshine. However, when they stepped out onto the high platform at the Avignon TGV station, they were blasted by a fierce, cold wind.

"Bloody hell," Kaden grumbled as he squinted against flying particles of grit and steered Annie into the protection of the station. "Welcome to Provence, and the mistral."

"Mistral? Is this the wild wind you told me about?"

He nodded. "The wind from the north. In France, all the winds have names, and ours is the mistral. It beats the rains, I suppose, which is all we've had for the last two weeks. And Henri will be happy—the wind will dry out the vineyards. We have lots of work to do. Hopefully this one won't last more than a few days."

Annie followed as he strode quickly through the station with their bags, out the south door, and down the steps into the parking lot. She recognized his silver Peugeot as they walked toward it, and she felt a giddy thrill. He stowed the bags in the trunk and opened the door for her. As she climbed in, she couldn't keep a smile from her face. *I'm really here!*

Kaden seemed to realize the same thing as he put the car into gear, then hesitated. He took his hand off the gearshift, squeezed her knee, and turned his sparkling eyes on her. "I can hardly believe you're finally here. There's so much I want to show you. As much as I love the Dordogne, this is my home."

She put her hand over his and stroked his knuckles with her thumb, no words needed.

The station was just south of the old walled city of Avignon, a beautifully preserved example of an ancient edifice, sitting proudly on the banks of the mighty Rhône River. It had survived, even thrived, through the millennium. Kaden drove along the narrow road between the imposing old walls and the river while Annie craned her neck to see the full scope of the ramparts.

The road continued north along the river, and Kaden navigated them through the ebb and flow of midday traffic. After a few miles, they left the highway for a rural road that wound through orchards, vineyards, and a few small villages. Annie spotted more villages set on hilltops all around them.

Kaden swept his hand to the horizon, indicating the surrounding landscape. "This is the heart of the Vaucluse, known to the wine world as the Southern Rhône Valley. It's one of the oldest wine regions in the country."

"Really?" Annie was staring out the window, trying to take it all in.

There wasn't any single main road out here, just a network of small roads connecting one village to the next in a haphazard sort of way. It appeared they were heading toward a village on the conical-shaped hill ahead of them, with a church tower rising from the highest point. She gave him a questioning look.

"Rasteau," Kaden confirmed with a nod. "But we won't go into the village just yet. Henri's estate is on the slopes just to the east, over there." He pointed to the vine-covered slopes in the near distance as he drove into the traffic circle at the base of the village, then veered toward the right. In what seemed like less than a heartbeat, he turned off onto a small, single-lane road. They bumped along, winding through vineyards that seemed to be planted down to the very edge of the pavement, following the contours of the hillside as they gradually gained elevation.

He stopped the car in front of a gravel lane marked by a pair of weathered stone pillars. "Welcome to Domaine de la Terre des Roches, 'Land of the Rocks.'"

Annie twisted around in her seat. "Are all these vineyards yours?"

Kaden waved toward the area uphill from the entrance. "All the land from here up to that ridge is ours, and everything around the manor house. The vines across the road"— he tilted his head to the side as he drove down the gravel lane—"they belong to neighbors. Henri also has a very old vineyard at the top of the village near the church and a few more in other villages in the area."

Kaden parked in front of a lovely sprawling farmhouse made of cream-colored stone with periwinkle shutters framing every window and door. "Here we are." The lines of the house were simple yet elegant as it stood tall among the vineyards. The second level was set back, with shuttered doors opening onto a long balcony that traversed the front of the structure, hacienda style. Window boxes with a profusion of red geraniums, currently dancing in the wind, accented each of the windows. At the far end of the house, the branches of a wide, majestic willow tree were also cavorting wildly. Little whirls of dust rose up off the gravel driveway only to go skittering out into the vineyards.

Kaden watched Annie's reaction as she took in the house, and she felt a surge of pride and relief as a little smile played at the corners of her lips. He leaned over and kissed her cheek. "Welcome home, *chérie.*"

With her heart thumping, Annie slowly climbed out of the car, then stopped and stared as a tall, barrel-chested man with a deeply lined face and a thick mop of wavy gray hair stepped out of the front door. He was dressed in faded-green dungarees, a thick flannel shirt, and well-worn boots. She would have been frightened if he hadn't immediately broken into a big grin that changed the look on his face from menace to delight.

He marched forward, clapped Kaden on the back without taking his eyes off of Annie, and held out both hands to her, beaming. "*Bienvenue, bienvenue, ma petite.* You are Annie, *mais oui.*" He leaned in to kiss her on both cheeks then pulled back, still holding on to her hands. "*Enchanté,* you are more beautiful than he described." His heavily accented English was perfect.

"*Merci, monsieur—*"

"*Non, chérie,*" he gently cut her off. "You must call me Henri, *j'insiste.*"

Annie was taken aback by the obvious warmth in his eyes. "*D'accord, Henri.*" She smiled and bent her head slightly to the side in acquiescence. "*Enchanté.*"

Henri threw Kaden a triumphant smile. "*Tu ne m'as dit pas qu'elle parlait français.*" *You didn't tell me she speaks French.*

"She doesn't, not much at any rate; she's just trying to be polite." Kaden sighed as he came over with a slow smile and took one of her hands from Henri. "But I hope that between you and me, she will learn more while she's here."

The house was larger than Annie had imagined, and Kaden had an entire wing to himself that was accessible from a private entrance on the side of the house as well as down a hallway from the kitchen. The downstairs portion included an office and a cozy sitting room with a fireplace and a stone terrace situated just beyond French doors, shaded by that cavorting willow tree. Kaden's enormous bedroom, complete with a bathroom featuring both a modern shower and an old-fashioned tub, was just upstairs from the living space. There was also a small balcony off the bedroom that faced south down the valley with a dramatic view of the Dentelles and Mont Ventoux to the east.

Once she got herself settled, she was given a grand tour of the property. The wind was fierce and cold, but she was bundled up in her warm anorak jacket with a little wool cap pulled down over her head. Neither of the men seemed bothered by the wind.

With no awkwardness at all, Henri treated her like family. As they walked the vineyards, he told her about how he and Hélène had fallen in love with the property all those years ago, and though it was run down and needed plenty of work, they saw the potential.

"The house was a wreck when we bought it," Henri said with a twinkle in his eye, "but we were so much in love that we didn't care."

They stood on the rise looking down at the beautiful old house with pristine trim and gleaming windows, and Annie struggled to imagine it any other way.

"Our first winter here, we huddled together on a small cot in the kitchen to stay warm." He got a faraway look in his eyes, and a smile played on his lips. "We would stoke the old wood-burning stove just before going to bed then snuggle together under the blankets, trying not to roll off the cot. Ha! Fortunately, we were young."

Annie glanced at Kaden, who was watching Henri with an odd expression.

"That was quite a winter," Henri continued with a chuckle. "We shuttered all the windows, but that didn't do much good when some parts of the house had no roof at all! I'd planned to wait until spring to work on it, but Hélène put her foot down when a ragondin got in."

"A what?" Annie asked as Kaden laughed out loud.

"A mischievous, mean little critter, not unlike a marmot, and he was intent on getting into the pantry. We had so little money back then, I think Hélène was more upset about losing the food than having the thing in her house." Henri shook his head with the fond memory. "I almost killed myself getting up on the roof in the snow to patch the hole, but Hélène threatened to lock me out if I didn't."

The vineyards had been in desperate need of work, too, but the vines were producing, so for the first several years, they did just enough in the fields to keep the production going. They sold the grapes to the local cooperative, using the money to repair the house and build a barn that would eventually become the cellar.

She looked around, seeing nothing but the vines dancing in the wind, a neat line of trees in the distance, and the house down the hill. "Where is the cellar?"

"Just beyond that rise, on the other side of the house," Kaden answered, gesturing down the hill. "There's another access from the main road that the tractors take. It keeps the dust away from the house. We can walk down to see it—there's a path from the other side of this vineyard."

Annie took a deep breath as she gazed out across the valley. It was late afternoon, and the whole scene appeared to ripple in the haze caused by the strong wind. Kaden had often described the view from the top of the vineyards. She remembered him telling her about watching the sunrise from here, but until she witnessed the view firsthand, she hadn't understood how moving it could be. Something stirred in her soul, giving her a fleeting notion that there was a presence here bigger than the view. Just then, Kaden tugged on her hand to continue their tour through the vineyard and down the path to the cellar.

None of them noticed the slender woman watching through the trees beyond edge of the vineyard.

Twenty-Nine

Dinner that night was a simple affair, but Annie caught on that Henri liked to cook. He had a pot of what smelled like lamb stew simmering on the stove and was putting a pan of sliced herbed potatoes into the oven as she walked into the kitchen. He implored her to make herself at home. "We are very informal here, *ma petite*. If you want something, just ask, or better yet, help yourself."

"Okay, then can I help with something?"

"Can you make a salad?"

"*Je pence qu'oui.*" She laughed and looked in the fridge to see what was available. She found a big beautiful head of lettuce, a bunch of green onions, and a little pot of mustard. Henri watched with approval as she poked around the cupboards, pulling out olive oil and vinegar, then purloined a shallot, tomatoes, and a lemon from a bowl sitting on the massive wooden island that stood in the middle of the kitchen.

She turned to survey the long counters that wrapped around the large kitchen and, tracking her thoughts, Henri reached into a low cupboard to pull out a cutting board for her and then unsheathed a large knife from the block.

By the time Kaden joined them, freshly shaved and hair still wet from his shower, Annie and Henri were chatting like old friends while they worked side-by-side in the kitchen. A stab of pleasure pierced his heart at the sight of her looking so comfortable. At that moment she noticed him, and her face lit up with a wide smile. He was dumbstruck, almost staggering at the intensity of his feelings. He wanted her here always, just like this, and he promised himself he would make it happen, no matter what.

He came around to hug her from behind and kiss her hair. "Henri has already put you to work, I see."

"I'm beginning to suspect you didn't learn all your culinary tricks from Jean Claude," Annie teased.

Henri guffawed. "Is that what he told you?"

She laughed. "Not exactly, but he didn't correct me when I made the assumption."

Kaden smiled sheepishly and confessed he had learned from them both. Jean Claude had taught him many useful techniques, but it was Henri who had taught him about country staples and living from the land. "The garden is still too young to get much other than herbs now," he told her, "but in the summer, we rarely buy vegetables at the market."

Henri explained that his wife, like most women raised in rural France, had a knack for growing vegetables and, of course, for cooking. "They're born to it, French women—it's in their blood. I learned from her, and now Kaden learns from me."

"Well, hopefully I can learn from both of you," Annie said and told Henri how inspired she had become with the recipes Kaden had sent her for the past two Christmases.

"Aha!" Henri laughed. "That is good, *petite*. We will add you to the rotation. You see, as a couple of poor bachelors, we take turns cooking."

Annie looked at Kaden in near panic. "Truly?"

He shrugged. "It's either that or eat out, but fortunately we both have simple tastes, and when the mistral is not howling around our ears, we use the grill on the terrace. But don't worry, *chérie*, I'm looking forward to playing with you in the kitchen." He gave her a lecherous wink, and she laughed.

They lingered at the end of the meal over a plate of cheese and a glass of Rasteau Vin Doux Naturel, the dessert wine for which the town was known. It was fortified like port but fruitier and sweeter. As Kaden listened to Henri entertain Annie with more stories of the early days at the farm, he was heartened by their rapport. He'd spoken at length to each about the other, so perhaps it made sense that they'd feel comfortable together.

For his part, Henri took great delight in entertaining Kaden's lady and looked forward to the next two weeks. He had witnessed Kaden's worst hours, had seen him broken from his own self-indulgence and self-destruction. He'd also seen him struggle back. When his beloved nephew had returned from his summer sojourn two years ago and confided that he'd met his soul mate, Henri had suffered conflicting emotions. At once, he was thrilled and relieved that Kaden had met a woman who was worthy of his attention, but the circumstances concerned him.

Underneath all that confidence and keen intelligence, Kaden had a vulnerable heart, although Henri was probably the only one who recognized it. He had witnessed the development of their unique relationship—albeit secondhand—and he'd wondered at how such a thing was even possible with the crushing challenge of the physical distance. Yet Kaden was nothing if not patient and determined, and it was clear from just a short time in Annie's company that she was worthy of his boy's affection.

But Henri continued to worry. Despite the depth of their love, Annie was tied to her high-stakes career in America. She wasn't ready to give up that life, and he dreaded the possibility that Kaden's love for her would draw him away from the land—a recipe for disaster for his brilliant but sensitive nephew.

Now, with Annie finally sitting at their table, Henri resolved to play his part well. He knew how important this time would be for them, how desperate Kaden was to get Annie out there, working in the vineyard and feeling the land, to share his connection with it. They had timed her visit to coincide with the first real work with the vines since winter pruning. The rains had ceased, allowing for work to commence in a few days' time. Henri was pleased with the wind, as Kaden had predicted—it would dry things out and make it easier to start working.

Because the fields would be too muddy for at least another day, Kaden suggested they use the time to orient Annie to the area by visiting the neighboring wine-producing villages, and to do some tasting so she could begin to understand the subtle differences of the *terroir* from each place. Annie thought it was a fine idea.

Kaden didn't waste any time standing around. They bid an amused Henri *bonne nuit* as he grasped Annie's hand and pulled her toward his rooms. His heart was pounding with the promise of finally having her in his bed, but as he shut the bedroom door behind them, he forced himself to take a deep breath and slow down. He'd been waiting for this for nearly two years. Surely he could find his patience for another few minutes.

Annie had a different plan. She spun around the instant the door closed and threw herself into his arms. He caught her, and without hesitation joined their lips in a searing, searching kiss.

"Annie," he whispered, breaking only to come up for air.

"Please." She took another kiss. "Take me to bed before I wake up and realize this is just a dream."

Kaden all but growled. He pulled her sweater up over her head, divested her of her bra, and dragged her over to his bed. He stopped only to pull off his own clothes as she shimmied out of her jeans, and they fell into his soft bed with limbs wrapped together.

Thirty

Annie was relieved to learn there was some domestic help for the two bachelors, but she wasn't thrilled with the manner in which that knowledge came to her.

She and Kaden were lying entwined in his bed in the not-too-early hours of the morning, caressing and kissing their way awake, when there was the sound of footsteps on the stairs. The door burst open to a singsong female voice. *"Bonjour, Kaden!"*

Kaden whipped the blankets up to cover them as a pretty young woman came waltzing into the room, then stopped dead in her tracks. *"Oh, mon Dieu! Je suis désolé!"* Despite her wide-eyed apology and a delicate hand over her mouth, she continued to stand there looking at the bed. Annie stared, horrified, but not too stunned to miss that the woman's hand didn't quite cover the smirk on her face.

"Sortez, Monique!" Kaden barked.

After thoroughly surveying the scene for another moment, Monique spun around and left, slamming the door behind her.

Annie jumped out of the bed in one great leap, her mind racing to the worst conclusion in her half-awake state. "Jesus Christ, *that* was Monique?" Shaking with equal parts mortification and rage, Annie quickly swiped up her clothes from the floor.

"Annie, wait! Christ, calm down." Kaden jumped out after her.

"Calm down? *Calm down?*" Annie was practically hyperventilating, and tears were pooling in her eyes as she held a bundle of clothes to her chest. "That woman just waltzed in here like she owned the place! Like she owned *you!" What the fuck just happened?*

Kaden grabbed her by the shoulders, gently but firmly, and held on while she continued to take in gulping breaths. "Annie, look at me. *Look at me!*" He was standing naked in front of her, calm yet impossible to ignore. She wanted to disappear into the floor, but she stood her ground at looked into his eyes.

"Annie, I have *never* slept with that woman. I have never touched her, never encouraged her, and she has *never* invaded my privacy like that before. I have no idea what that was about." *But I can guess.*

Annie stared at him, unable to move or speak. She took another deep breath and forced down the panic.

Kaden rubbed a hand over his face in frustration, keeping the other hand on her shoulder. "That was Monique," he confirmed. "The daughter of our neighbor—the one I told you about. Her mother is Henri's friend and takes care of our housekeeping, and occasionally—*occasionally*—Monique helps her, but I swear to you Annie, there is *nothing,* and *has never* been anything, between us. I was just as shocked as you when she came into the room."

Annie remained still, expressionless. "Please believe me," Kaden said softly, fighting back his rising nausea.

After another frozen moment, she just deflated, feeling like the worst kind of idiot. The tears she had been holding back rolled down her cheeks, and she started to shake again. Kaden took it as a good sign and pulled her to him, wrapping his strong arms around her, cupping her head to his shoulder and kissing her hair. "God, Annie, I'm so sorry. I don't know what the hell that was about, but I can guarantee you it will never happen again. That little slut will never make that mistake again." He was seething, gritting his teeth so hard, his jaw hurt, but he needed to get Annie calmed down first before he dealt with Monique.

She sobbed against his shoulder and wrapped her arms around him. *I've never been this insecure in my life … this vulnerable.* God, why did she ever open herself up to love? She felt like a stupid, moronic, idiotic fool.

After an undignified sniff, she lifted her face to look at him. His eyes burned with anger that was not directed at her. She reached up to touch his face, and his expression went soft.

"Please believe me," he whispered. His eyes held such torment.

"I do. God, I'm such an idiot. I'm sorry … I'm so sorry for thinking the worst." She closed her eyes and lowered her head, murmured so softly against his chest that he barely caught it. "I've never experienced such a raging fit of jealously in my entire life."

As disgusted as he was with the incident, his heart swelled. *She's jealous!* But he shelved that thought and murmured soothing words into her hair until she relaxed against him.

Twenty minutes later Kaden was fuming as he stalked downstairs to find Monique humming while she dusted the main parlor. She started at his stomping feet, then smiled sweetly at him.

In ragged, colloquial French, Kaden spat his words at her. "Do not *ever* do that again, you conniving little whore." She flinched at the biting words. Glad that he had her attention, at least, he continued, "I'm tempted to kick your skinny ass back to the *gendarmes* and tell them exactly why they should throw you to the wolves." She paled, and Kaden pushed harder.

"You have grossly overstepped your bounds here, *mademoiselle,* and I am tired of your games. If you ever so much as *look* at my woman, or if you ever again interfere with my personal life in *any way whatsoever,* I will make damn sure that you are charged with the crimes you have committed." Kaden's tone was so deadly, Monique shuddered uncontrollably.

"I-I-I am truly sorry, *monsieur.* I was only jesting—"

"Bullshit, Monique, that was no *jest.* It was intentionally hurtful. And there are no second chances. Now get the hell out. I don't ever want to see you here again."

Kaden waited, unmoving, until Monique dropped her duster and left through the front door. Only then did he take a deep breath. *Bloody hell.*

He turned back toward the kitchen, still seething, but stopped short when he saw Henri casually leaning against the counter, a steaming cup of coffee in his hand. The raised brows indicated he had heard the exchange but didn't understand the context. In measured tones, Kaden filled him in.

Henri swore an oath under his breath. "I will inform Sophia." He sighed. "She will not be pleased."

"Henri, she insulted Annie in an unconscionable way. I cannot overlook it."

"*Non, mon fils,* I do not expect you too. I feel the same way," Henri said with a heavy sigh. "Let me handle Sophia, and the *gendarmes,* if it comes to that."

Kaden had not been off the mark with his vulgar, yet apt address to Monique. She was a pretty young woman of some twenty-six years, but stupid and lazy. She'd been arrested the previous summer for prostitution in the seaside city of St. Tropez, treating her mother to an unwelcome dose of worry, expense, and inconvenience to bail her out.

If that wasn't bad enough, Kaden discovered afterward that turning tricks had been a guise to case the homes of the men who bought her services. There'd been a rash of break-ins among the posh homes in the St. Tropez area during the summer, with thefts of antiques and other valuables, but no one had been caught.

It was pure happenstance that Kaden had been in Vaison la Romaine, a village not ten kilometers from Rasteau but some two hundred kilometers from St. Tropez, during the Saturday morning antique market last September. He had spied Monique with a greasy-looking man twice her age at a table with an impressive array of items. As he approached her, she panicked and her companion took off. Unable to hold up under Kaden's scalding inquiries, and reinforced by his threat to report her to the St. Tropez *gendarmarie,* she confessed through excessive tears how she'd obtained the goods. He forced her to pack it all up and drove her and the illicit booty back to Rasteau.

Sophia had been horrified, Monique sullen, and Kaden disgusted. Henri took pity on Sophia and convinced Kaden to let it go, provided the stuff was returned. Sophia somehow managed to return it all anonymously to the St. Tropez authorities. Whether any of it was reunited with its owners, he had no idea.

"I think we're making a mistake by keeping quiet about her," Kaden told Henri now. "I'll continue to abide by your decision for Sophia's sake, but I don't want her near me, and absolutely nowhere near Annie. Sophia will have to find someone else to help her in this house."

Ignoring the unfortunate start to the day, the three of them piled into Henri's battered old truck and headed out to tour the Côtes du Rhône Villages. They spent the morning driving around the area, letting Annie get her bearings along with an education. As Kaden drove, Henri maintained a running commentary of the region, starting with the geological history including the deposits of limestone and the unique river rocks, or *galets roulés,* that blanketed much of the land.

They made a large circuit, visiting Carainne, Vinsobres, Seguret, Sablet, Gigondas, and Vacqueyras, pulling off to the side of the road at each place to walk the vineyards so Annie could see the differences in the soil. She noticed that it varied in color, from gray to brown to even red, and that some of the soil had lots of rocks while other areas had less, and that the rocks themselves differed from place to place. Henri nodded as she commented on it, and he explained how such differences, along with elevation and aspect to the sun, served to create the distinct wines that each village was known for.

A large flock of birds swooped over them as they stood at the edge of one vineyard. "Are birds a problem for the vines?" she asked.

"Not at this time of year," Kaden said. "But they can be a right pain in the arse at harvest—or just before harvest."

"The birds are attracted to the sugar in the fruit. They don't bother with the plants until the fruit is ripe," Henri explained. "But they can do extensive damage if left alone."

"What kind of damage?"

Henri frowned. "They peck at the ripe berries and suck out the pulp, leaving a shriveled skin sack with the seeds rattling around. Losing a few berries is not a big deal, but birds are filthy creatures, and they can carry bacteria or worse. A bird-damaged berry can cause unwanted bacteria to grow in the must during the fermentation process, giving off flavors to the wine."

Annie looked at the birds cavorting overhead then at Kaden. "What do you do to keep them out of the vineyard?"

Kaden grinned. "Henri's a pretty good shot."

"What?" Her eyes flew open wide.

Henri chuckled. "We tie metallic strips on stakes throughout the vineyard. They flutter in the wind, catching sparks of light from the sun, and it spooks the birds enough to mostly keep them away. Occasionally, I get out my shotgun to let them know I'm serious."

Annie wasn't sure if they were pulling her leg or not, but she let it go.

Henri had called a few *vignerons* in advance, and the group was greeted warmly and invited to taste wherever they stopped. They tasted wine from bottle, tank, and barrel. Most of the conversation with the *vignerons* was conducted in French, but either Kaden or Henri translated what Annie didn't understand. They also taught her how to swish the wine around in her mouth to get the character and flavor then spit it out so her brain didn't get clouded with the alcohol.

By early afternoon they were ready for a break. Kaden took them to lunch in the most famous wine village in the region.

"Chateauneuf-du-Pape," Henri said as Kaden drove through a narrow stone archway onto a high plateau surrounded by vineyards but dominated by an ancient, ruined edifice. "It was so named because it was the site that Pope Jean XXII chose to build his summer palace in the fourteenth century—apparently the stench and congestion of Avignon were offensive to his sensibilities during the summer. But he appreciated good wine, and he is credited with doing much to improve the quality, and thus the reputation, of the wines from these vineyards during his reign."

"What happened to the palace?" Annie asked as she stared up at the remaining corner of what must have once been a grand structure.

"It was sacked after the last Avignon pope died. Two centuries later it was set upon by the Protestants at the beginning of the Wars of Religion. What was left was finally and utterly destroyed by the Germans in 1944 as they made their retreat from French soil."

Annie glanced at Kaden, a little embarrassed at her ignorance. "I'm not Catholic, and I don't have any clue about the popes, but I thought they all lived in Rome."

Kaden grinned. "They did, and do, except for a period of about seventy years—most of the fourteenth century—where there was a, um … schism … in the church, and the seat of the papacy was temporarily moved to Avignon. It's why the walls there are so impressive—they were terrified the city would be attacked and so ordered the walls to be built high and reinforced."

"Ah" was all she said, distracted by the view. It was spectacular from the old palace, with the broad Rhône River winding off into the distance and the valley bearing its name spread out below them. On a clear day, like the one they were enjoying thanks to the wind, the low coastal range that flanked the Mediterranean Sea to the south was clearly visible.

An ancient stone stairway led from the ruins down into the town. Not twenty steps down, a beautiful terrace opened up on the left to reveal a restaurant that appeared to be built into the foundation of the palace. They had a wonderful lunch there, chatting with *le propriétaire* about the wines of the village—and tasting them—and the styles of various producers, particularly what made them special compared to the other villages they'd visited that morning.

By the time they rolled back up the lane to la Terre des Roches, Annie's head felt like it was going to explode from trying to cram in so much information. She was grateful for the education, though, and fascinated by the historic significance of wine production in the area.

———————◆◆———————

Across the valley, in a dark corner of a seedy bar in Vaison la Romaine, Monique rolled her eyes as she was berated for her morning's folly. "*Stupide pute,* what the fuck did you do? I need access to that house!"

"Relax, Georges, we'll think of something. It's not the end of the world. I can always sneak in when they're all out working in the vineyards." She sipped her drink, feigning nonchalance. Georges scared her when he was like this.

"And risk Macallister making good on his threat? It would serve you right, but you're so fucking stupid, you'd probably get caught and finger me, too. He knows you didn't work alone." Georges sucked in a deep draw on his cigarette and blew out the smoke in disgust. "Stay away from that place. You'll just screw it up more than you already have. I'll think of something else."

Beyond his dubious talents as a petty thief and pimp, Georges had another skill. He was extremely adept with computers ... and hacking into computer systems. Unlike Monique, he *wasn't* stupid, although he preferred taking money rather than earning it. Through the sincere if misguided efforts of the socialist French government, he'd been "rehabilitated" out of a drug program and trained as a computer programmer—little did they know, they were training him to be a better crook.

Since then he'd paid close attention to advancements in computer technology, and kept himself in good practice, hacking into just about anything he could find just for the entertainment of it and, sometimes, profit. If anyone saw his tiny apartment, they would be amazed at the equipment he had. He made sure that no one ever did. So far, his electronic thieving had remained low level, but he bided his time, knowing that he could make a killing if he could find the right opportunity.

When he had hooked up with Monique the year before, it annoyed him that she couldn't stop talking about some dickwad named Kaden Macallister, her mother's neighbor. Georges had eventually done a bit of checking, and his interest was immediately piqued when he learned that Macallister's low-key rural persona was a clever cover, as his name was listed in many places as a heavy hitter in London financial circles.

This guy has serious money, Georges had realized, and from that moment he was determined to get some of it. Hacking into bank accounts was challenging but not beyond his skills. All he needed was an account number to relieve this neighborhood paragon of a few million francs. *He wouldn't miss it—he hardly ever spends any money. He doesn't even drive a nice car!* But Monique hadn't found anything in his office ... no bank statements or any other financial information, and nothing resembling a password of any sort. The only thing he had to show for his patience with her was a credit card statement. He'd make use of it, of course, but he needed access to the man's hard drive for the real payoff, and he had mistakenly assumed that the lovely but brainless Monique would be able to get him inside. Now he was back to square one.

Thirty-One

As the sun rose over Mont Ventoux, the wind was still blowing, but it wasn't as cold, or as strong. Kaden, Henri, and Edouard, the cellar master, were strung out across the upper vineyard, commencing the laborious first pass through the vineyards. This entailed cleaning up the green shoots and suckers that sprouted out of the vines in places they weren't desired. Annie followed Kaden as he hunched beside a thick, gnarly vine with four fat, twisted arms. Bright-green shoots sporting newly unfurled leaves and nascent seed clusters sprouted out of the top of each arm. Several leafy shoots poked out of the trunk down lower. This old vineyard of Grenache boasted plants in excess of sixty years old, and Kaden explained that the pruning method they used here was called spur pruned bush vine, because after harvest, the vine was pruned down to spurs, or small points at the tip of each arm of the mature wood, beneath which the next year's canes would grow. As a result, the vine would resemble a loose bush when grown out for the season, without the support of a trellising system.

He pointed to the green shoots sprouting out of the trunk, down low. "These are suckers; you can just knock them off." He demonstrated as he talked, breaking them off with a flick of his finger at their base. They were small and tender, and they easily snapped off. Kaden let them lie where they fell amid the wild grass and other ground cover that surrounded the base of the vines.

"Now up here"—he moved his hand to the top of the vine—"it gets a little trickier because most of what you see here are the main spurs that will turn into this year's producing canes." He indicated the spurs, which were wooden points sticking up from the top of each gnarly arm, and ran his fingers over one of the green shoots growing out of the base of a spur, already a foot or more in length and covered with new leaves and tiny green clusters that would eventually become grapes.

"Up here, there are two things you need to look for. First, you need to identify the main shoot from each spur—there will be only one—then pinch away any interlopers trying to crowd in on the main shoot." Again, he demonstrated by gently holding the main shoot from one spur back and flicking off a smaller shoot that had sprouted right next to it.

Annie was watching his hands closely as they moved over the vine, trying to make sure she understood what he was doing. His hands were large, confident, and sure, tanned from the constant exposure to sun and wind, with long graceful fingers whose gentleness belied their underlying strength. She shivered, not from the cold but from remembering those same strong hands gently stroking her body that very morning.

"Are you cold?" Kaden stopped what he was doing to scrutinize her.

She shook her head and bit her lower lip, trying to suppress a smile.

"Are you sure? You were shivering."

"Nothing to do with the cold." She felt her face warming. "Please, continue." She waved at the vine.

But Kaden just studied her, momentarily enchanted by the vision she presented in her faded jeans and beat-up hiking boots paired with a worn fleece vest over a long-sleeved tee shirt. The bright red bandana tied around her neck and the little cap pulled down around her ears so just the tips of her curls danced in the wind gave her a jaunty look that was charming. Under his scrutiny her cheeks became flushed.

When he continued to study her and made no move to continue, she laughed and rolled her eyes. "Okay, so I was just a little mesmerized while watching your hands, but I'm over it, so please, continue." She gestured again at the vine.

Kaden gave her a half grin and turned back to what he was doing. He cleared his throat. "The second thing you need to do is evaluate the direction that the main shoots are heading." He indicated an arm with three shoots where two were poised to grow outward, away from the center of the vine, but one was pointed inward. He touched the inward-facing shoot. "This is a potential for removal because it will grow toward the center of the vine, making it difficult for bunches that develop on its cane to get enough sunlight." He glanced at Annie, and she nodded.

"But you have to evaluate all the new canes together to decide if you need to remove one or more." He touched the tops of the other three arms. "In this case, each of the other arms has only two canes, all poised away from the center, so it's unlikely one cane pointed toward the middle will be a problem. In addition, all together, this vine has only nine canes. We're okay with up to ten per plant. If there were more, say twelve, I'd pull this one off, but I'll leave it for now. We can always remove it on the next pass through the vineyard, at the end of June after fruit set. It may make a difference when the fruit starts to ripen during the summer."

He stood up and brushed his hands on his jeans. "That's it, really. You just need to clean up the suckers from the base or any other part of the wood that isn't a top spur, pinch off any shoot that is not the primary from each spur, then evaluate for shoot position and total numbers of shoots per plant. Use your judgment, and if you're not sure, leave it. Like I said, we'll make another pass after fruit set."

"That's it?" She asked with a laugh. "Are you sure you trust me with this? What if I knock off the wrong shoots?" She was a bit nervous about making what seemed like life-or-death decisions for the plants.

"Then we'll end up with a little less fruit at harvest." Kaden said, unconcerned. "Come on. Let's move to the next plant, and I'll watch you do it."

They did, and she was surprised at how much it actually made sense once she had her hands on the plant. She didn't make her decisions nearly as fast as the others. She had noticed Henri and Edouard moving rapidly down their rows; but then, they'd been doing it for years, not minutes.

Kaden nodded with satisfaction as he watched her work on one, then another plant, and declared her ready to work on her own. She smiled as he quickly leaned down to kiss her cheek. He squeezed her shoulder and headed for another row.

Annie turned back to her row and fell into a pattern of work that was as calming as it was interesting. It was also backbreaking. *Jesus Christ,* she thought as she stood up and stretched out her back before she'd completed half a row. She watched how the others worked and realized that she'd been bending over the vine, rather than kneeling at its base to work. She adjusted her stance at each vine, alternately going down on one knee then the other, concentrating on keeping her back straight, and it helped.

In the early-morning chill, her body stayed warm from the exercise of standing up and kneeling down, but her hands were freezing. She noticed that Edouard had wool gloves with the top half of the fingers cut off, and she decided she needed to find a pair of those for herself.

As she worked, she thought about the bygone generations of people who had performed this identical task before her, about the comforting repetition of following the cycles of the seasons and working the land for a living, and about the inherent risks and dangers in doing so. This new experience was a revelation to her, and it was one she had never even considered until she'd met Kaden.

She glanced around and spied him a few rows down, his back to her as he hunched down, focusing on the vine in front of him. He looked so natural here, like he truly belonged on this hillside, working in this vineyard. She let herself admire the broad span of his shoulders encased in a faded tee shirt that hugged his form, revealing the shifting muscles beneath as he worked, tapering down to narrow hips and his deliciously firm ass. She sighed. He wore the Giants baseball cap she had sent him the year before, and his thick hair was sticking out beneath it, some clinging to his neck, damp with sweat.

He's a conundrum, she mused. His life firmly straddled the modern world and the ancient, yet he took it in stride like it was no big deal and had worked out a comfortable balance between the two. When he wasn't doing manual labor in a family vineyard that was older than the millennium, he was plugged in to the high-powered world of international finance and emerging technologies, making decisions that affected the futures and fortunes of millions of people.

Kaden enjoyed the honest labors of working the vineyard, hauling canoes for his friends, and chatting with tourists about the sites to see in the Dordogne, yet his personal net worth had to be in the tens of millions pounds sterling. You would never suspect it, though, meeting him here in his rural element. He was so earthbound. Heck, she hadn't suspected it until that dinner at La Belle Nicole, and even then she'd had no notion of the extent of his wealth.

Although she'd come to realize more and more over that first year of email communication that Kaden had considerable financial means, she hadn't had her first true view of the modern-world Kaden until she'd met him in America, where he'd revealed his aristocratic upbringing and shown impeccable taste in clothing and a penchant for private dinners and roomy hotel suites. And then there was his generosity. She didn't want to think about what he must have paid for her gorgeous cashmere overcoat, and she *didn't* actually think about it, because he so clearly didn't care. She had needed a coat; he had delighted in giving her one.

She sighed again and went back to her vine. This was good, she admitted to herself, very good. Being out here in the vineyard, doing such honest work, finally experiencing the land as he had described it to her so often, and she wistfully wished she could see the entire cycle of these beautiful vines. What incredible satisfaction Henri and Kaden must have felt when they finally tasted the wine made from the grapes they had lovingly cared for and found it to be as good as they'd hoped. So simple, and so honest and pure.

The crew broke at noon, and Kaden motioned for Annie to follow as he headed toward a copse of trees at the far end of the vineyard. There, shaded from the sun and blocked from the wind, was a weathered picnic table with a couple of large baskets set on top. Henri was unpacking them, pulling out bread, cheese, fruit, roasted chicken, some *saucisson,* and of course, chilled bottles of rosé.

Kaden draped his arm over her shoulder and pulled her against his side, kissing her temple. "Hungry?" he inquired with a grin.

She leaned into him. "Starving." She hadn't noticed it until her mouth started watering at the sight of the food. "I'm beginning to think this is standard French fare for lunch."

"It is. Sometimes we bring leftovers, or Sophia packs something else for us." He opened the wine and poured it into the glasses that Henri set out. Handing her one, he took one for himself and touched it to hers, smiling gently into her eyes. "*Santé, chérie.*"

Henri watched the exchange as he finished laying out the food, then picked up a glass and waved it in their direction. "*Santé!*" Eyes sparkling, he turned to Annie. "Well, *petite,* what do you think of the life of a vineyard laborer?"

"I'm certainly getting the labor part of it," she laughed as she stretched out her back again. "I'm afraid I've used some muscles that have been dormant for some time. Remind me to pop a few aspirin tonight so I don't wake up stiff."

"*Oui,* it can be taxing to the body if you aren't used to it. But don't worry, by the end of the week you will feel much stronger."

She didn't doubt it. Turning to Kaden, she said, "Perhaps I'll have to beg for a massage tonight."

He tightened his hold on her shoulders, and his eyes sparkled just like Henri's. "No begging will be required, but perhaps reciprocity."

As they rested and enjoyed the simple meal, they discussed their initial progress and the work still to be done. They had worked through about a quarter of the top vineyard. There were three smaller vineyards directly adjacent to the estate, plus the small one at the top of the town near the church, and another larger vineyard a few kilometers away. Henri estimated that at their current pace, it would take them the rest of the week to finish this first pass.

Kaden watched Annie's reaction as she heard the news, gauging whether she looked horrified or game. He was pleased to see she took it in stride, but he still made sure she understood she was not required to work with them the entire time.

She was shocked at his suggestion that she bail out. "Whatever else do you think I would do? Of course I want to help. I can handle hard work, especially if you feed me like this ... and massage my stiff muscles at night."

"*Bien sûr,* I would have it no other way."

Their days and nights fell into a pattern: up before dawn to head into the vineyard, work for a few hours, then break for enough time to walk back to the house for coffee and croissants delivered from the local *boulangerie* by Sophia. Then they'd head back into the vineyard and work until lunch. Annie discovered there were picnic tables set at various locations among the trees at the edge of the fields, ensuring that they never had to walk far to find a place in the shade.

With just a short midafternoon break, they would call it a day around five o'clock. While the crew toiled in the fields, Sophia kept their kitchen stocked with food so there was always something to make for dinner. True to Henri's pronouncement, they took turns cooking, though Kaden and Annie shared their duties.

Annie got the flutters at the simple domestic pleasure of working with him in the kitchen. He was a much more experienced cook, and she loved to watch him and take direction for whatever needed to be done. She also learned quite a lot. Their meals were not elaborate, but the flavors of the local produce seemed to make everything more vibrant.

With the long hours in the vineyards, everyone was exhausted by the end of the day, and no one lingered over the table. That didn't prevent Kaden and Annie from loving each other passionately each night and most mornings, too. The feeling of waking up with Kaden's big body wrapped around hers was a delicious bonus to this very rural and domestic experience.

Kaden fit in time each day to monitor his financial data and respond to email and phone inquiries, and to initiate funds transfers as required to participate in the deals he evaluated and approved. He was a bit uneasy being able to direct the movement of vast amounts of money from his nondescript country outpost in the middle of rural France, but he couldn't fault the convenience.

It was precisely that convenience and the accompanying discomfort that drove him to ensure his computer system was protected by the latest, most powerful software for encryption and security. Kaden was obsessed with computer security and sought out companies to invest in that were developing new software and systems for that purpose.

Since he had been involved in the internet expansion from its infancy, he had heard many horror stories about companies and individuals who had been wiped clean—from viruses or piracy. He utilized every viable security measure and kept everything updated with changing passwords, locks, and interlocks—whatever it took. He also took a very simple precaution—since the house was unlocked most of the time with people coming and going—by unplugging the equipment when he was away from it.

Kaden had an uncanny memory for numbers and strings of data and, as a result, none of his account numbers or passwords were recorded anywhere other than on documents locked inside a floor safe that was embedded in a block of cement in his office, covered by carpet. The combination lock code was committed to his memory, but he also had it written down, hidden in an innocuous location in the event that someone else needed to open it. No one, not even Henri, knew the safe existed. He'd installed it on a rare occasion three years ago when Henri had gone to Paris to visit some friends. *Better that he doesn't know,* Kaden rationalized. With the amount of money at stake, Henri would understand if he ever learned of Kaden's paranoia in regards to security.

Thirty-Two

To celebrate the completion of the vineyard work, the cessation of the mistral, and Kaden's fortieth birthday, Henri hosted a dinner party, to which he invited a few of his neighbors—excluding Monique, of course. Annie found herself immensely enjoying the noise of the convivial group in Henri's large dining room.

Kaden sat at one end of the long table, comfortable in the setting, while Henri sat tall and proud at the other end with their friends spread out between them. Annie sat on Kaden's right, frequently holding his hand under the table. While the crew had finished up the work in the vineyard, Sophia had outdone herself in the kitchen, presenting an array of delicious dishes, all served family style on large colorful platters. The party drank heartily, too—there were many open bottles of wine on the table for everyone to enjoy.

The conversation and jokes swirling around them were all in French, most of which went over Annie's head, but she didn't mind. She sat back and enjoyed the lively, happy intercourse. *Such a simple and honest life,* she thought for the umpteenth time since she'd arrived. His neighbors were farmers like Henri, most living on land that had been in their family for generations. And while they never grew rich, they took pride in carrying on the tradition and finding pleasure in the daily toil. The deep affection and respect among them was evident. *The simpler the life, the richer the experience,* Annie realized, and suddenly understood that Kaden had figured that out years ago.

After the cheese board had been passed around the table and everyone's glass was refilled, Henri stood up and waited for the table to quiet. With that customary sparkle in his old eyes, he smiled fondly down the table at Kaden and lifted his glass. "To my nephew and dearest friend: *bon anniversaire, mon fils.* May you have many more years, filled with much happiness."

Kaden bowed his head slightly in thanks, embarrassed but not surprised by Henri's open affection. As the guests around the table all raised their glasses and added their voices to the toast, he reached for Annie's hand under the table and squeezed. When the crowd quieted again to take a sip of wine, Kaden held his glass up in the silence. "And here's to Annie, *mon coeur.*" He spoke to the room, but his eyes held hers. "Thank you, *ma belle chérie,* for working alongside us in our vineyards. You are part of our land now, and your presence here is, for me, a dream that has come true."

He repeated it in French for the group and, as one, the guests sighed at the love in his words. Annie blushed brightly, but she held his gaze, and their mutual adoration was clear to all.

Later that evening, after the guests had departed and the kitchen had been cleaned, Kaden kissed Sophia's cheeks and thanked her.

As Kaden pulled away from her, Sophia stopped him with a hand on his arm, a pleading look in her lovely gray eyes. "Please forgive Monique for her behavior. She is a troubled girl and doesn't understand the harm she causes." Kaden held her gaze and kept his expression blank. Monique was a conniving bitch and knew exactly the harm she caused, and Kaden suspected it was more than simply making Annie uncomfortable. But he didn't want to add to Sophia's pain, so instead of saying anything, he nodded, squeezed the hand that still held his arm, and stepped away.

Sometime during the kitchen cleanup, with Henri's help, Annie had snuck a bottle of Champagne in an ice bucket and a couple of glass flutes to Kaden's sitting room and lit a fire in the fireplace. When Kaden pulled her into the room and closed the door, he looked around in surprise.

"I hope you don't mind, but I wanted a private celebration with you."

Before Kaden could respond, she swung around to a side table and fished the Champagne bottle out of the ice water, preparing to open it.

He intercepted the bottle with a grin. "Let me do that, *cherie.* I don't want you to put your eye out—or mine." She laughed and acquiesced.

The cork eased out with a sigh, and he poured the bubbly liquid into the flutes. She handed him one, took one herself, and gently touched the rims together.

"Happy Birthday, *mon amour*," she said softly as her luminous brown eyes held his. They each took a small sip, and then Kaden gently removed the glass from her hand, set them both down, and gathered her into his arms.

He'd understated his feelings at the table—having Annie here with him this past week had been far better than he had dreamed it would be. She eased so comfortably into the routine of the estate, took every quirky French oddity in stride, never complained, and was delighted with every new thing she saw or experienced. She laughed readily with him and Henri, asked intelligent questions about what she learned, and took a genuine interest in his rural world.

As good as she felt in his arms, he had to shut his eyes against the painful need in his heart. He had no fucking idea how he was going to let her go this time, not after the last week. He kissed her hair and breathed in its fresh scent. "*Mon coeur, ma chérie,* thank you for being here. *Je t'aime.*"

Annie snuggled in his embrace and sighed contentedly. If he held her a little too tightly, she didn't mind. She cherished his need to express his emotions, and she loved him even more for it. "There's nowhere else I would rather be," she whispered into his chest. Then she looked up at him with a shy smile. "I do have a couple of small gifts for you, but they're kind of private."

"You are gift enough, *chérie,* but I will endure the torture of opening gifts if you insist." He sighed dramatically, and she laughed.

She pushed him into one of the cozy chairs in front of the fire, brought their Champagne over to the small table beside it, and settled on his lap. There were two small wrapped packages sitting on the table. She reached for the larger one and handed it to him. "This is more for your business, but it's connected to the second one."

He raised his eyebrows as he unwrapped the small paperback book, *Zagat's Restaurant Guide for San Francisco.* "In case you wanted to expand your import business to the West Coast, San Francisco is the logical place to start." She bit her lip, watching him.

A slow smile spread across his face as he flipped through the book. "This is wonderful, and very thoughtful. Thank you," he said with a kiss. "I was wondering how you would feel if I needed to travel there for my business."

Annie smacked him on the shoulder. "Of course I want you to travel there." She reached for the second, much smaller package and handed it to him. "In fact, this should prove it."

This time he looked truly perplexed, but when he opened the small box, he stilled. He held his breath as he slowly lifted the campy metal disk embossed with an image of the Golden Gate Bridge and studied the two keys dangling from it. He looked at her, a question in his eyes, daring to hope but not wanting to presume. But one look at her as she held her bottom lip in her teeth, almost as unsure of herself as he was, and he knew.

He let out his breath and closed his eyes, pulling her to him in a fierce hug. "I'm honored," he whispered into her hair. "Annie, I love you so much. Thank you. Thank you for trusting me."

"My home is your home, Kaden. Please come and stay with me, even if it's only for a few days." She swiveled around on his lap so she was straddling him, cradled his face in her hands and tenderly planted a kiss on his brow. He set the box and keychain on the table and put his hands on her waist, holding her so she couldn't squirm away. She pulled back, smiling sensuously as their eyes held in a smoldering gaze.

"I have just one more little thing for you," she whispered, as she slowly reached up to the top of her shirt and started undoing the buttons. Heat flared in his eyes as he tracked the movement of her hands, but he kept hold of her waist as she slowly and seductively worked her way down the placket. When she had enough buttons undone, she reached up and slowly pulled the shirt apart, and Kaden again let out a breath, this one he hadn't realized he'd been holding. Under the prim, white, button-down shirt, Annie revealed a skimpy, sexy, lacy pink demi-bra that seemed at once to hold her breasts up high while barely covering them at all.

"*Mon Dieu*," he breathed and leaned his head forward to snuggle in the deep valley she displayed for him. He closed his eyes and gently rubbed his cheek against her delicate curves. "If the bottom half of this lingerie is anything like the top, I'm a dead man."

Thirty-Three

Annie had another full week to spend in France, and Kaden wanted to show her more of the area. They started out at the *marché* in Vaison la Romaine, a nearby town named for the ruins of an ancient Roman village that marked the center of the modern town.

As they wandered through the stalls, Annie bought a few gifts for her staff, a beautiful Provencal tablecloth for herself and one for Marie, and some of the local soap, which she'd discovered in Kaden's shower. She also purchased a couple of campy pot holders for Henri, as she had noticed the few he had in their kitchen were stained and threadbare.

When she was finished shopping, they enjoyed a coffee and croissant at Kaden's favorite *boulangerie* in the town, and Annie had to roll her eyes at the flirty female clerk. He just shrugged when she ribbed him about it. "You know I don't pay any attention, *chérie*. And now that she sees me with you ..." He leaned over, wrapped his arm around her shoulder and pulled her close for a sweet kiss. "... she'll leave me alone."

Annie laughed. She had no doubt that the clerk had witnessed his affectionate display since they were sitting in front of the shop's window, but she doubted it would discourage her.

After enjoying the coffee, Kaden took the rare opportunity of a clear day without the wind to drive to the top of Mont Ventoux. It was the equivalent of the top of the world in Provence, and the view did not disappoint, even though it was too early in the season to appreciate the full effect of the lavender fields at the base of the mountain.

Thus they spent the next several days leisurely exploring the region, going farther and farther, even as far as the coast, to the delightful fishing village of

Cassis, known for its crisp white wine and exquisite seafood. They explored the Roman ruins in Orange and Nîmes, the interior of the walled city of Avignon, and the quaint hilltop villages in the nearby Luberon Valley, including Lacoste, known mostly for its infamous eighteenth-century resident, the Marquis de Sade.

They didn't talk about the future, and they didn't talk about the past—they just enjoyed the present. Kaden gave her a brief history lesson for each place they visited, and they enjoyed the very specific local wine and food in each village. Annie couldn't help but notice the pride the locals took in their wine, their food, and their heritage. *The simpler life is, the richer the experience.* These people were clearly onto something.

Annie's last night in Rasteau was a farewell party, and Henri made his famous roasted leg of lamb. In addition to Edouard and Sophia, a few of the neighbors from Kaden's birthday party were invited, too. They all brought bottles of their own wine, and it was another festive atmosphere.

Annie was praised for her unfailing work with the vines, toasted, and declared an honorary local. Henri presented her with a shiny new pair of clippers as well as a bright red pair of fingerless gloves, which he instructed her to leave at the farm so she would have them the next time she came to visit. It was such a sweet gesture that she had a hard time keeping back tears as she hugged him in thanks. She was sad to go—shockingly so—but at least Kaden was coming back to Paris with her, where they would spend one last private night together.

As they lingered around the table at the end of the meal with cheese and sweet Rasteau dessert wine, laughing and telling stories, Annie looked around and felt like family. These people had welcomed her into their midst like a daughter. Other than that unfortunate incident with Monique, who had not shown her face since, these people were genuinely glad to have her among them. They hadn't judged her or questioned her motives. They hadn't asked her about her life outside of the present. Kaden was one of them, flesh-and-blood family as tied to the land as they were, and he loved her, so that made Annie one of them, too. It was unconditional, and it was something she had never experienced before. *Simple and honest.* Annie had a lot to think about.

Thirty-Four

The return to San Francisco was far worse than Annie expected. Her apartment was stark and lonely; it felt cold and bland after the warm vibrance of Domaine de la Terre des Roches. She looked around her space and wondered why she'd never bothered to decorate. The industrial look and feel of the place had attracted her so, with one entire wall of windows and the air ducts and plumbing pipes exposed beneath the metal beams of the ceiling. Now, it just left her cold.

Her office was even more dismal, with stacks of files and reports that needed her immediate attention, projects that her team had completed while she was away that were now ready for her final review. There was a one-inch stack of phone messages held together with a binder clip that her assistant had thoughtfully arranged in order of priority—of which client was screaming the loudest. She'd known her re-entry would be a challenge, but it seemed that every project they'd worked on in her absence was screwed up in some way. It was like her team had stopped using their brains. What the hell had happened while she was away?

She spent hours meeting with her staff, showing them the mistakes and talking them through the correct analysis, calculation, or report conclusions. Because much of the work needed to be redone, a couple of projects were delayed beyond the promised date to clients. Annie was normally adept at talking her clients into accepting inevitable delays, but this time they'd all become inexplicably impatient, and she was unsuccessful in that effort as well. One of her biggest clients even had the audacity to call John Franklin to complain.

Annie dragged herself home in exhaustion each night, drained from the long hours and the pressure of trying to get the projects straightened out, and twice over the first two weeks after her return, she had fallen asleep without sending Kaden an email. The first time it happened, he overlooked it, knowing the pressure she was under to catch up. He made some mild quip on his next email about trying not to work so hard that she forgot about him, but he got the impression from her response that Annie didn't appreciate his attempt at levity.

The second time it happened, he became concerned. As he sat at his desk in Rasteau, staring at his inbox that was bereft of any new message from Annie, he forced himself to be rational. Forced himself to think back on his years in London, when he had worked around the clock and had no time for anything but the project he was tackling. He closed his eyes and pinched the bridge of his nose. *She's going to kill herself working this hard.* He recognized the downward spiral but didn't know what to do.

The sharp *ring-ring* of her phone woke Annie with a start. She blinked her eyes and looked around. *What the hell?* She was laid out on her couch, still in her sweats, papers scattered on the floor. The phone pealed *ring-ring* again and she looked around, trying to orient herself. She leaned over and grabbed the receiver from the table. "Hello?"

"Good morning, *chérie*," came Kaden's soft voice. "I'm sorry if I woke you, but I just needed to hear your voice for a minute."

"What time is it?" Annie felt disoriented, confused that it wasn't completely dark outside.

Kaden thought she sounded muddled, even for just having been woken up. "It's five thirty there, love. I figured you'd be getting up soon anyway. Are you okay?"

"Yeah." She cleared her throat, looked around. "I just got confused for a minute. I must've fallen asleep on my couch in the middle of reviewing a report. I'm glad you called, because I doubt I would've woken in time."

Kaden bit back the comment on the tip of his tongue and instead said, "How is it going?" He knew about all the screwed-up projects.

"I'm getting through it. The report I was trying to review last night is a real sleeper, obviously." She snorted. "But I'm almost finished with it. It's the last of the super-critical projects that got delayed." She picked up the scattered papers as she talked and flipped through them. "It looks like I got most of the way through it before I fell asleep, and it was on track technically, so I should be able to make the final changes this morning. I promised it to the client by the end of day, ah, today I guess," she said wearily while looking out at the dawn.

"Annie." Kaden's voice was tentative. "Please promise me you'll get some rest this weekend." He knew he sounded like a mother hen, but she was putting in way too many hours and it wasn't even her busy season. Falling asleep on her couch while working was just a little better than falling asleep at her desk.

She took a deep breath then let it out with a long sigh. "I will, I promise. I could use a day off to sleep and do laundry. I'm running out of clothes to wear." She laughed, then quickly frowned and asked, "Why did you call?"

"Just to hear your voice," he said quickly. Maybe too quickly. "But I also wanted to tell you that I've finalized my plans to come to San Francisco."

"Oh!"

Kaden grimaced. "Oh, as in, 'Oh, that's great,' or oh, as in, 'Uh-oh'?" His voice sounded a little strained.

"What? Don't be silly. Of course I want to see you. Sorry, I'm just a little out of it. You did just wake me up, you know." But her voice was soft, and he relaxed a bit. "When are you coming?"

"Mid-July, in about a month. I'm planning on staying for a week, if that's okay with you. I'll fly in Saturday, but I have plenty of appointments set up during the week. I promise I won't be a nuisance." *Jesus, what's wrong with you?* He sounded like a tentative schoolgirl.

"That sounds perfect," she replied, and this time Kaden heard the smile in her voice. He closed his eyes, pictured her leaning back on her couch still mussed up with sleep. And his heart swelled.

"I love you, Annie. I know you need to get moving, so I'll let you go." He paused, hoping beyond hope that she would return the words. When she didn't, he added, "Send me a quick email tonight, okay? Even if it's just to tell me you're home safe."

Annie closed her eyes against her feelings of guilt. He was so damn sweet, she felt like a jerk. "I will, and I'm sorry I missed last night. I meant to finish reviewing the paper then log on, but … well, I didn't quite make it."

"It's okay, I understand. Please just take care of yourself."

"I will. Thank you for calling. I needed to hear your voice, too. Bye."

After she hung up, Annie sat for a minute on the couch, staring out at the daylight that had materialized during the conversation. *God, what is wrong with me?* The past two weeks had been brutal, but they weren't anything she hadn't dealt with before. She needed to get a grip, and she needed to be more sensitive to Kaden. She had given him the keys to her apartment for God's sake, what did she expect? She had invited him to San Francisco under no uncertain terms. And now he was coming. Why was she feeling so defensive? She was just tired, she told herself. She needed to take the weekend off, get some rest, and allow her brain to recuperate.

Kaden leaned back in his chair, frowning at the phone. He didn't like what he had heard. She was exhausted, and it didn't seem like there was any end in sight. He knew this sort of schedule was nothing new to her, but for some reason, he got the feeling the pressure was more intense, and he wondered what was going on. He briefly considered postponing his trip. It wasn't that big of a deal, and it could wait. Although if he didn't go now, he wouldn't be able to get away until late October, and that wasn't a great time to be pushing new product at restaurants gearing up for the holidays.

Besides, he really wanted to see Annie again, and he wasn't sure he could wait any longer. Maybe when he got there, she could ease back on her schedule, and he'd make sure she got some sleep. Well, maybe not *that* much sleep.

As Kaden sat at his desk doing paperwork, trying to focus on something other than his concerns about Annie, he had the odd feeling that someone had been through his desk. Possibly it was just paranoia on his part, but certain things were slightly off—not out of order, and nothing was missing, but the few files he kept looked like they'd been shuffled through.

He pulled open the center drawer where he kept pencils, pens, and other supplies, letting his fingers skim up under the desktop inside the drawer. He frowned, felt to the sides, then forward and back. He felt a moment of panic but forced himself to think as he rolled his chair back from the desk, got up and walked to the door, glanced down the hall to ensure he was alone, then quietly closed and locked it

He then yanked the drawer all the way out and got on his hands and knees to peer up under the desk. *Damn it to bloody hell.* The small slip of paper that he kept taped there—the one with the combination to his safe written on it—was missing.

He shifted the bookcase that rested on the corner of the carpet, rolled the rug back, and pulled up the false floorboards that hid his safe. He twisted the combination lock until the tumblers clicked into place, turned the handle, and tugged the lid open. He breathed a sigh of relief when he saw that nothing had been disturbed; he had a way of placing the top files in a specific but random pattern that no one would notice or consider duplicating. Whoever had taken the combination had not yet located the safe.

He relocked it, rolled the rug back into place, and moved the bookcase back to its proper place. Sitting down in his chair, he leaned back and considered who might have been looking through his stuff, and who the hell had taken the slip of paper. He was careful not to keep any financial documents in the drawers; he barely kept any paper documents anywhere, preferring to keep all records in encrypted files on his computer, which he then backed up online to a data storage facility in Bordeaux. Nothing in the desk had any account numbers, but someone had been looking for something, and now he felt exposed. He briefly considered if Sophia would have tried to clean the drawers, then rejected that idea as his mind shifted to Monique. His eyes narrowed. *That little bitch.* Was it possible she was behind this? He hadn't seen her since he'd kicked her out the month before, but that didn't mean she hadn't snuck back in—it wasn't like the house was locked and guarded. He wondered what had happened to her companion from the market.

Kaden spent the next hour on the phone with his bankers and brokers, confirming there'd been no unauthorized activity and establishing new protocols for his accounts. With the amount of funds he controlled, his instructions were followed without question. "Do not send anything to this address," he told each contact. "I'll also reset all my passwords—it's time for that, in any case—but I need you to disable the online transfer option for anything connected to me. Also, effective immediately, the new protocol for these accounts is that any faxed or emailed instructions must be backed up by my verbal authorization."

"Do you have specific fraudulent activity to report?" The question was a fair one, but Kaden had no idea what to tell them.

"This is precautionary only. Can you establish some sort of alert on these accounts?"

His last call was to the manufacturer of his safe to find out how to reset the combination for the lock. This wasn't so easy, he learned, and required a technician to come to the house. It may be impossible to keep the secret any longer from Henri, but he was far more willing to share the knowledge of the safe's existence with his uncle than to risk losing its contents.

He'd only recently purchased a new computer featuring the latest security protocols and had painstakingly set up password-protected files within files to safeguard his financial data and banking access, but he resolved to be doubly careful with his equipment when he was away from the house, by not just unplugging it all but also removing the cords to a secure location. It would be a nuisance and wouldn't stop determined thieves, but it would certainly slow them down.

Thirty-Five

Kaden's visit to San Francisco was a disaster before it even began.

His flight was scheduled to arrive at noon on Saturday, and Annie had every intention of being at the gate with a big bunch of flowers. But Thursday afternoon, just after the markets closed in New York, she got a call. Her biggest client, Western Properties, a large regional real estate development firm, was being purchased by an even larger national company, Allied Development. Allied had a different auditing firm. She was going to lose the client. But that wasn't the worst news.

Bob Wolverton, the president of Western, called Annie personally to tell her before it hit the newswires. He did this not out of any courtesy but to let her know the key members of Allied's financial team, including their outside audit and tax professionals, would be arriving the next day from Chicago to start the process of due diligence on Saturday morning. Annie was expected to have all the company's tax documents organized for them, and Wolverton was counting on her to make sure the new team understood everything. Time was of the essence, he told her. The deal needed to be approved without delay.

"Bob, this is … incredible news. Congratulations." Annie knew he had significant stock holdings plus stock options. He was going to make a killing.

"But I have a problem with this weekend," Annie continued. "I have another commitment that I cannot change. I'll get all the paperwork ready, of course, and I can meet with the team for a couple of hours first thing Saturday, but then I'm unavailable for the rest of the weekend."

Bob didn't hesitate. "I know this is short notice, Annie, but you have to find a way to be there on Saturday. This deal has to be done, and it has to be done fast. Frankly, all those fancy partnerships you set up make this a tricky deal, and I need you there to reassure the new team that it's all aboveboard."

Annie bristled at the implication that anything she had done was questionable, and her voice gave her away. "Of course everything is aboveboard, Bob. It's complicated because you wanted it that way. We utilized cutting-edge techniques for setting up your deals to maximize book income and value, and we've achieved exactly what you wanted, but it's all within the parameters of the accounting and tax rules. There's nothing questionable about any of it."

"Calm down, now, I didn't mean to imply that. I'm just saying that no one understands it here like you do, and we're relying on you to make sure the new team not only understands it but also accepts it as a value add, not otherwise."

"Thank you for your confidence. You should also be confident enough to know that I can handle all the discussions and explanations necessary, but I can do it next week, starting first thing Monday morning. I'm sorry, but I cannot change my plans for the weekend."

"Well, Annie, I'm very disappointed to hear that." Bob's tone was stiff and formal. "I would hate to think that your absence from the initial due diligence planning might put this deal in jeopardy."

Was that a threat? "That's a little dramatic, don't you think, Bob?" Annie said, trying her best not to scream at him. "I told you I can be there in the morning for a couple of hours—more if you start early. I have an irrevocable commitment and will need to leave by eleven thirty, but if your people can start at eight, that will give me three hours to brief the new team on the basics of the structure. They'll need some time alone with the documents and spreadsheets after an initial explanation anyway, and I certainly don't need to babysit them while they review it all."

"I don't know Annie; I think you need to be there in case there are questions. These are the big boys, and—"

She cut him off, not wanting to hear the rest of that stupid comment. "Bob, do you really want to pay five hundred dollars an hour for me to sit around in a room waiting for someone to ask a question about a document? If these people have any clue what they're about, they'll know how to interpret basic legal structures. I think it would be much more cost effective if I explained it, let them digest the explanation as they reviewed the details, then met with them again to answer questions all at once."

"Five hundred dollars an hour! You're kidding me! That's outrageous."

Annie held her voice steady and even managed to laugh, making it sound like they were ribbing each other. "You know what the firm charges you for my time, Bob. That's what it costs to get the best in the business. Yours are the most complicated deal structures around, and they were set up that way *at your request* in order to accomplish your specific financial accounting goals and to meet the needs of your partners in each deal. If I have to hold someone's hand to understand it, to teach them what I have spent years learning, I'm certainly not going to discount my fee to do so."

"All right, all right, simmer down, young lady." Bob was in his sixties, and he had an annoying habit of talking down to her like she was a child. She gritted her teeth but let him continue. "I know you're damn good at what you do, and I suppose we've been fortunate to have you working on our deals—God knows you've spent enough time on them all. I just need you to understand how important this is."

"Of course I do. I never said otherwise. I already told you I'd change my plans for Saturday morning, but I cannot make any other changes. I promise you I will work around the clock next week, and I will not let you down." She held her breath waiting for his reply.

"Well if that's the way it's got to be, I guess I'll have to live with it. But I need you to have all the documents and schedules and anything else you have on every deal organized and in our conference room by the end of tomorrow. We'll start at eight sharp on Saturday."

Annie hung up the phone, put her face in her hands, and tried her best not to cry. She had worked so hard to clear her desk so she could spend time with Kaden. She hadn't had a day off since the weekend a month before, when he had insisted she take a day and sleep. She had done so but then threw herself back into it, making sure she had everything under control for his visit.

God, she missed John Franklin. He would have known how to handle this. But John wasn't there anymore. One of the little surprises that had been waiting for her when she returned from France was the announcement that John was retiring at the end of the firm's fiscal year, which was two weeks ago on June 30th. And now he was gone. She'd been so busy, and the few times they'd talked, she could tell he'd already mentally checked out. She didn't blame him. His heart attack had been a serious wake-up call. But now she felt very alone.

In most cases, she would have only needed to gather the working papers from all the files related to the company, get them duplicated, and hand them over. But this client was different. In addition to the various corporate entities, such as the management company and leasing companies, every property they owned was held by a different partnership. And each partnership had different ownership, with different profit allocations within each partnership. She knew how complex it was since she had set most of it up. She groaned at the level of detail she'd have to get into with the new team. It could take weeks. And they didn't have weeks. They had to cram it all into the one week that Kaden was going to be here. *Shit.*

At least she could still pick him up at the airport. She shuddered at how hard it had been to win that point. She had never dug her heels in so firmly with any client before, and certainly not Bob Wolverton. She normally bent over backward to make herself available to him. No wonder he was surprised she didn't cave. Of course, her billings with his company alone exceeded a million dollars annually. What the hell was she going to do once this was over? She shoved that thought out of her head. *First thing's first.*

Annie clenched her jaw to keep from interrupting the asinine punk across the table. She stole a glance at her watch. *Shit.* Eleven o'clock. If she had any hope of meeting Kaden's flight on time, she needed to leave soon. So far, the morning had been a complete waste of her time.

The cocky jerk from Allied's accounting firm was challenging everything she was telling him. He wasn't listening to her, and it was clear he had very little knowledge of the subject. Not only had he shown up an hour late to this meeting, but he'd also wasted valuable time telling her all about Allied. Like she cared.

She finally interrupted him to say that she had limited time and needed to give him a basic outline of the structures they'd set up for all the real estate partnerships, show him where the allocation and basis calculations were for each entity, then let him review it all on his own. He had deigned to allow her to start her explanation but then kept interrupting her with questions or, in most cases, nervous outbursts, claiming that what she said made no sense.

"Look," she finally said. "I understand that these structures are complex. But I think your time would be much better spent if you just let me explain it to you without interruption. Once you have the full picture, you can review all the legal documents, the relevant regulations, and the allocations. There's a binder for each entity with a detailed road map of the allocation formulas plus the schedules themselves. For those entities that have had transfers of interests, the basis calculations are at the back of each binder along with the reconciliations for book and tax values."

His eyes glazed over as she spoke, glancing at the thick sheaf of paper she had handed him—the index to the binders and summary of the basic deal structures—and then at the neat stacks of binders lining the wall behind her. *This is impossible,* Annie thought as she inwardly grimaced.

She reached over and plucked the index from his hands, folded it over to the last pages, and pointed. "Here's the fundamental structure that each deal is based on." She flipped another page. "This tells you the modifications made to each deal based on the asset type—you know, office building, apartments, shopping centers, that sort of thing." She flipped to another page then pointed. "This is the index of deals that have special allocations outside the normal structure." She flipped to the last page. "And this one tells you which ones have had basis adjustments."

She leaned back in her chair. "I suggest you start with the deals that have the most basic structure, as indicated on that list, and review at least one of them thoroughly. The good news is that once you understand the first type of deal, the modifications on the others are easier to understand." She pointedly looked at her watch as she stood. "Now, I have to go. I'll be here first thing

Monday morning to go over your questions and take you down to the next level of detail."

As she leaned over to shake his hand, he stared at her in horror. "What do you mean? You can't leave! You need to walk me through it all."

"I just did. It's all organized, and that report"—she nodded to the sheaf of papers she had left in front of him—"has everything outlined."

"But I need more time! You can't just leave when we've just started."

Annie's patience snapped. "You were an hour late for this meeting, and then you wasted another thirty minutes rambling about bullshit. You haven't listened to a word I've said up until the last five minutes. I told Bob Wolverton that I had limited time this morning. It's not my fault that you didn't take that seriously."

At his panicked look, she cocked her head. "Surely none of this is unfamiliar to you." An unattractive flush crept up his neck. She narrowed her eyes at him. "I can't believe Allied sent someone without at least an idea of how it all works."

He just stared at her, and that's when she realized they'd sent a lamb to the slaughter. She sighed. "Look, just trust me. Review the outline and start with the first deal." She sighed again, pulled out a business card, and scribbled her home number on the back. "If you get completely stuck, call me. I won't be back at this number until late tonight, but I can call you back after, say, nine o'clock."

"What about tomorrow?" The poor guy looked petrified, like he suddenly realized he was in way over his head and couldn't bluff his way out of it.

Annie closed her eyes. *This can't be happening.* "Just get through what you can, and we can start again on Monday. I'm not available tomorrow, which is Sunday, by the way. Do your people usually work on Sunday? I don't." *Unless I have no choice.*

She raced down the freeway, praying she didn't hit traffic, praying Kaden's flight was delayed. She had wanted to meet him at the gate. Now she'd be lucky to catch him at baggage claim. Would he even check his bag? *Shit, shit, shit.* That dumbass had wasted her time, insulted her, then inexplicably drew her pity. But worst of all, he'd made her late. She checked her watch.

The airport was still twenty minutes away, but the plane was presumably just landing now. *Shit.*

When she finally arrived at the terminal, she careered into the parking lot, jerked her car into the first spot she saw, jumped out of the car, and ran.

Kaden settled into his first-class seat and accepted a glass of Champagne. He was anxious about seeing Annie, and worse, he was nervous. Which was absurd, but he had a lingering concern that this trip was a mistake, that he was pressing her, invading her space somehow. *Don't be a stupid sod,* he told himself. He *wanted* to press her, but he didn't want her to *feel* pressed. He shook his head at that nonsensical logic.

With nothing to do on the long flight but watch a movie or think, Kaden chose to think. He closed his eyes and let his mind wander to Annie. Tried to put himself in her shoes, tried to understand her perspective. He was in a unique position to do so, given his past life, and while he had never been an accountant, he had worked with enough of them to know their role in deals. Especially the good ones. After his experience with Annie in Washington, DC, he knew she batted with the big boys. Her petite stature was deceptive; she was a major player in her field.

It had been the same for him, once upon a time in London. She was in demand, could pick her projects, but at this stage in her career, she was taking on everything, proving herself, making a name for herself. It was natural—intoxicating and ego boosting, but brutally exhausting. He'd been there, but he'd crashed and burned, he reminded himself. But not from overwork. His problem had been different than Annie's. An unhappy spouse whining for time he didn't have, who ultimately turned deceitful and vindictive. He snapped open his eyes. *Bloody hell,* he never wanted to do that to Annie.

He thought back to when they first met, in La Roque Gageac. She'd been so very closed in, with thick barriers keeping everyone out. And some-how, he'd managed to get through. But was he any different? Hadn't he had barriers, too? After his divorce he'd played around occasionally, but nothing serious. Women hit on him all the time, and he'd become deft at deflecting them. No woman had piqued his interest for anything beyond a casual romp until he saw Annie. And initially, she hadn't been interested in him at all. *Because she's just like you,* he realized.

It was an uncomfortable parallel and perhaps the root cause of his angst. None of what he admitted to himself during this flight was a revelation, but it was the first time he'd examined it all together and acknowledged the striking similarities between their personalities. They were very much alike. No wonder they connected on so many levels. Kaden thought of her as his soul mate, a pretty term he had discounted until experiencing it firsthand. But he had an uncomfortable feeling that finding his soul mate wasn't quite as lovely as it sounded. He had a feeling that, if he wasn't careful, a union this intense could result in heartache, the magnitude of which he couldn't fathom.

Sleep eventually claimed him. Before they landed he brushed his teeth, wet and combed his unruly hair, and changed his shirt. As the plane touched down, his heart was hammering. He had an awful feeling but could only hope his premonition was false.

He paused for a few moments after going through immigration, holding back the crushing disappointment he felt when he didn't immediately see Annie. *Maybe she got stuck in traffic.* Then he looked around more carefully, realizing that nobody was being greeted. *Moron,* he scolded himself. She couldn't be here if she wanted to. He merged with the other deplaning passengers and made his way to baggage claim.

His bag arrived on the carrousel, he grabbed it, then joined the queue at the exit. Outside the baggage claim area, Kaden looked around. No Annie. *She's just running late, probably got stuck in traffic,* he told himself again as he did his best to bury the disappointment. He checked his watch as he scanned the milling crowd. He'd landed thirty minutes ago, on schedule. *Where is she?*

Annie sprinted up to the international arrivals bay and spied Kaden standing off to the side, waiting. *Damn it,* she swore to herself. She'd hoped to get here before he came out. He looked adorable to her, dressed in jeans, a black turtleneck, and a tweed sport coat. Professorial but not nerdy, just … adorable.

"Kaden!" she shouted, perhaps a bit too loudly.

The enthusiasm in her voice released the iron lock around his heart. He looked toward the sound of her voice and stood in place as she ran up to him and threw herself into his arms. Instantly, his tension eased as he breathed in her sweet scent and felt her limbs wrap around him.

"Hi." He sighed, relieved.

"Hi," she said, closing her eyes and burying her face into his chest, holding on to him like she would lose him if she let go. "I'm so sorry I'm late." She didn't want to go into the reason just then. She just wanted to hold him. And he returned the sentiment, squeezing the breath out of her.

She gasped and pushed back, laughing. "You're squishing me!"

"Sorry, love. Just can't seem to get close enough." He tipped up her chin and gave her a tender kiss. Then he looked closely at her face. *She looks exhausted. Damn.*

They walked hand in hand as she led him to the parking lot, and he laughed when he saw her car. It was a well-worn Jeep Grand Cherokee. "What?"

He just shook his head. "You are full of surprises, *chérie*. Somehow I pictured you driving a sporty BMW, not a clunky Jeep. And it is a pleasant surprise, believe me." He kissed her nose and tossed his bag in the backseat.

"Driving a fancy car around the city is just dumb," she said. "I've had this car since I graduated from college. Back when I used to go camping, it was very convenient."

"Well perhaps we can make use of it in that way soon. What's your schedule like this week?" He asked the question casually as she drove them out of the parking lot, but he was nervous about the answer. The dark circles under her eyes did not bode well.

Annie didn't answer right away, instead busied herself with paying the parking attendant, and then concentrated on getting them onto the right freeway as she exited the airport. Kaden waited, not liking the silence.

She finally stole a look at him and saw that he was watching her intently. "I have bad news about that." As they drove toward the city, she explained the situation, leaving nothing out, including her disastrous meeting that morning.

"I'm afraid it's going to get worse before it gets better. The downside to being the only one who understands the technical aspects of these complicated deals is just that, I'm the only one who understands. And when explanations are needed, it's my job."

Tears pooled in her eyes and threatened to spill. "I'm so sorry, Kaden. I tried so hard to get all my work done, and I did. I was completely caught up by Thursday afternoon, but now I'm more buried than ever, and these people expect me to work side-by-side with them around the clock. I got out of this afternoon by sheer force of will, and my client was not happy about it."

She looked so anguished, Kaden forgot his own disappointment. "Annie," he gently caressed the back of her neck as she drove. "I won't pretend that I'm not disappointed, but I understand. I suspected something like this might happen."

He sighed, leaned back in his seat, and watched the passing scenery. "I have plenty to do here anyway. And you won't be sleeping in the war room. At least I'll have that."

She gave him a watery smile. "I'm afraid if we go back to my place, the phone will be ringing constantly. I don't want to check back in until later tonight, and I don't want to be reminded about it."

"Whatever you want, *chérie*. As long as I can be with you, I'm happy."

His words lifted a weight off her chest. *Thank God he understands.* She was afraid she'd crack under any more pressure, especially if it came from him. "I've got the perfect place to start your San Francisco tour."

Thirty-Six

The bluff above Fort Point was chilly, even on a sunny July day. Kaden stood with his arms wrapped around Annie from behind, his chin resting on her head. Her curls tickled his nose as they bounced in the breeze. The view was magnificent, the majesty of the Golden Gate Bridge rising above the frothing waves at the bay's entrance, with the Marin headlands in the distance and Alcatraz Island looking cold and forbidding in the middle of the bay. They lingered there for a while in silence, enjoying the scenery and the comfort of being together.

Next she drove them down through Golden Gate Park, then along the wharf, and up and around Telegraph Hill. She parked at the base of Coit Tower and, grasping his hand, led him through the small park that overlooked the Financial District. The view from here took in the entire span of the Bay Bridge, with Berkeley and Oakland on the far shore and the whole of the financial district at their feet. She pointed out her office and showed him the general direction of her neighborhood.

Back in the car, she warned him about what to expect. "Okay, now, don't freak out … keep an open mind and imagine what this next area *could potentially* be."

As she crossed Market and headed into her neighborhood, she watched Kaden from the corner of her eye. If he was alarmed, he kept it to himself, even when they passed a small huddle of people hunkering down in ragged blankets and cardboard boxes under an overpass.

He remained silent as Annie turned a corner, hit the remote on her visor, and waited while the gate to her garage opened. She pulled in, the gate closing swiftly behind her as she steered to her spot and parked. She turned to look at him expectantly.

"The garage seems secure enough." Kaden had noticed how quickly the gate had shut, the bright lights illuminating the entire space, and the thick iron grids at street level. He also noticed the security cameras trained on the entrance and elsewhere.

At the elevator, she hesitated, not pushing the call button. "This goes up to my floor, but I usually walk up the stairs to the lobby first to get my mail." She glanced at his suitcase. "Do you mind? I'd like to introduce you to the security guard and let him know you have a key. You did bring your keys, didn't you?"

He smiled and pulled them from his jacket pocket, dangling them between two fingers.

In the lobby, she waved to the big, burly man wearing a uniform. "Hi, Sam."

"Afternoon, Ms. Shaw." Sam nodded at her politely and then discreetly looked at Kaden.

"Sam, this is Kaden Macallister. He'll be staying with me for a while. I gave him a key to the building and my apartment. I just wanted you to know."

"Pleased to meet you, sir," Sam said as he held out his hand.

Kaden nodded and shook his hand. "Likewise." Kaden studied the man, liking what he saw. He was big, looked fit and strong, and his attitude was respectful but with the potential to be intimidating. Sam seemed to understand the scrutiny, and he nodded like he was expecting the question when Kaden asked, "Is there a guard here twenty-four-seven?"

"Yes, sir. There are four of us. I'll inform the others of your visit. We like to keep track of who comes and goes here."

"Thanks, Sam," Annie said. She was glad that Kaden seemed to approve.

Before they moved off, Sam spoke again to Kaden. "The building is wired with security cameras, inside and out." He indicated the corners of the lobby, and then gestured to the console in front of him. "They're all on motion sensors, and the system gives off a beep when they become activated. It helps us pay attention."

"I'm glad to hear it. I noticed the cameras in the garage." Kaden nodded again then followed Annie to the elevator.

As the door slid closed behind them, Kaden snaked his arm around Annie's waist and pulled her close, lowering his head to capture her lips in a tender kiss. Annie's hands found their way up and around his neck. They stayed that way until the elevator stopped at the third floor.

Down in the lobby, Sam watched the image on his screen. He'd been head of security for the building since it opened, and Annie Shaw was one of his favorite residents. Friendly and polite, she treated him like an equal rather than a servant. He didn't know much about her except that she worked long hours and almost never had visitors.

Sam watched the screen as the door opened and the couple left the elevator. He had not missed the British accent, and he wondered if Mr. Macallister had anything to do with Annie's recent vacation. *Hadn't she been somewhere overseas?* And she had come back looking rested and happy. He told himself he should remind Ms. Shaw that there was a camera in the elevator.

Annie's apartment was just one step away from industrial, but as Kaden stood in the middle of the space and looked around, he conceded that it fit her. Clean lines. Efficient. Cold. He frowned but remembered that was how she'd been when he first met her. He was in her world now, and he needed to experience it without judgment. Her place felt cold because she'd done nothing to decorate, he told himself, most likely because she had no *time* to do it. Or inclination, he guessed. He doubted she spent much time here except to sleep.

The ringing of the phone interrupted his thoughts, and he looked at Annie as she grimaced.

"I'm not answering that." She sighed as she glanced at the answering machine on her desk. "Christ, already four messages. I told him I wouldn't be back until late."

She held out her hand to him. "Let's get you settled upstairs. My closet space is pretty limited, but I managed to squeeze out a few inches for you."

He was relieved to see the loft bedroom was a warmer space than the rest of the apartment. Up here, the walls were a soft gray green. A thick comforter and pillows in warm earth tones covered the bed, and she had a few nice pieces of art on the walls. As if reading his mind, she said, "My decorating energy ended at the top of the stairs, I'm afraid. I keep meaning to find some big dramatic pieces to hang downstairs, but I've never managed to find the time to look."

Still holding her hand, Kaden pulled her to him and enveloped her in a hug. He kissed her hair, sprinkling little kisses down to her ear, then licked and nibbled her lobe and blew softly on her wet skin, making her shiver. He whispered in her ear. "Will you let me make love to you, *chérie?*" Annie smiled against his lips as she walked them backward toward the bed, pushing his jacket off his shoulders along the way.

———————————————

Annie lay curled up in the crook of his arm, her fingers lazily skimming his chest hair, her brain hazy from pleasure. Kaden was just drifting off to sleep when the phone rang, startling them both.

"Damn it," she cursed softly, not moving from her position.

Kaden tipped her chin up to look into her eyes. "Aren't you going to answer it?"

She shook her head. "Not yet. This may be my last stretch of freedom for a while. As soon as I talk to them, I'll be stuck." She glanced toward the far wall of windows. "It's still light out. If I call them back now, they'll probably try to get me to come in. Tomorrow will be soon enough."

"Tomorrow's Sunday, Annie." His tone was a little stiff.

Cheek resting on his chest, he didn't see her cringe. "I know, but I don't think that's going to matter." She looked up at him, eyes pleading. "Kaden, I honestly don't think I have a choice."

He snorted, expressing a sentiment that came dangerously close to disgust, then lifted her off of him, rolled out of bed, and sauntered naked toward the bathroom. "There's always a choice, Annie." The door closed with a bang.

She rolled onto her back and covered her eyes with the back of her hand. "Great," she mumbled. "So much for understanding." She was frustrated, and now she felt trapped. The shower came on. *Guess that's the end of that conversation,* she thought sadly.

Kaden worked off some of his frustration shampooing his hair, vigorously rubbing his scalp as he talked himself down. He knew he was being unfair, but come on. Sunday? What was wrong with these bloody Americans? He thought he would at least have the weekend with her. God knew she'd be putting in long hours next week. He sighed, rinsed off. If he got angry, it would just make things worse.

Annie was dressed and sitting on a barstool at her kitchen counter, sipping a glass of water and looking tired when Kaden came down. He walked over, kissed her nose, and caressed her cheek. He wasn't going to apologize for his comment, but neither was he going to belabor it. Instead, he asked about dinner.

She brightened, relieved that he wasn't going to push her any more for now. "If you don't mind a bit of a walk, I'd like to take you into Chinatown. It's a unique experience. There's a dim sum restaurant there I think you'll like."

He smiled. "I haven't had dim sum since I was in Hong Kong ten years ago."

Thirty minutes later, standing at the corner of Grant and Clay, Kaden laughed and admitted that the atmosphere did feel authentic. The buildings were close together, all the signs were in Chinese characters, and but for a few token Caucasians, the throng of people pushing around them were all Asian. There were even plucked chickens hanging upside-down from a butcher window with feet and heads still attached.

Annie led him a few more blocks to the dark door of a dingy-looking restaurant and shook her head at the wary expression on his face. "Uh-uh, don't judge this place by how it looks on the outside."

He opened the door for her. "Yes, ma'am." The interior was dimly lit, but the space was bigger than it had appeared from the outside, and it was packed. They didn't have to wait long, though, and once they were seated and the carts laden with assorted delicacies started rolling past, Kaden admitted that Annie was right. The food was superb.

The phone was ringing as they arrived back at her apartment later that evening. She closed her eyes and swore, letting it roll over to the answering machine. When the machine beeped to indicate that a message had been left, she turned to Kaden with a resigned sigh.

"I can't put this off any longer. I need to listen to the messages and start calling everyone back." She glanced at the machine. There were now eight messages, and she could only guess how desperate they were.

She was dismayed that the messages were bordering on hysterical. The first three were from the clueless idiot she'd left on his own that morning. He had been so far over his head, it was a lost cause.

The next two were from Western's CFO, telling her that she *really* needed to come back today. *Too bad,* she thought. Wolverton knew her plan. And she had promised Mr. Clueless that she would get back to him this evening. It was now eight thirty. That qualified as this evening.

The next message was from Wolverton himself. He was calmer than his CFO, but his tone was terse. "Annie, I know you said you weren't available this weekend, but I need you to call in. I heard what happened this morning, and I'm sorry your time was wasted. Allied's team obviously did not understand the complexity of our structure. But they've called in their big guns now. Someone from their DC office is flying in tomorrow morning, and I need you to meet with him as soon as possible."

Sigh. The last two messages were from her own partner, Joe Miller, head of the audit team for the client. He was direct. "Where the hell are you, Annie? Why weren't you in the war room today?"

"Oh for God's sake," she muttered and called him back first. It was in her best interest to make sure he understood her position before she battled the client. She made the call using the speakerphone because she wanted Kaden to hear the kind of pressure she was under.

She talked to Joe for a few minutes, calmed him down, explained why she hadn't been there this afternoon, and pointed out that she had wasted almost four hours this morning with an incompetent idiot who hadn't the first clue about real estate structures. She made sure he understood everything she *had* done, with one day notice, in order to prepare for the due diligence review. It wasn't her fault that Allied had sent a rookie.

With Joe mollified and back in her corner, Annie called Bob, also on speakerphone. To his credit, he was apologetic about the screwup. "God knows why they sent such a greenhorn. I don't blame you for being frustrated. I talked to the Allied's CEO myself early this afternoon to let him know their auditors had goofed. They promised a qualified person would be here tomorrow."

"What time?"

"First thing in the morning."

Annie knew he was hedging. "What time, *exactly,* Bob? I'm not going to show up until I know someone is there and ready to work."

Kaden was sitting at the kitchen bar listening, and even he was surprised at her bossy tone. *Good for her,* he thought. She'd already conceded the day, but at least she wasn't letting them push her around.

"I don't know, Annie, they told me he would be on the early flight out of DC." He sighed. "But you make a fair point, and I appreciate you changing your plans to help us. How about if they call you when he's ready to start? How long will it take you to get to the office?"

It was a concession, and she decided not to push any further. With luck, the new guy would know something about their business structures, and he'd need time to review everything after her initial explanation, so she held out hope she'd only be there for a few hours tomorrow. Bob also agreed to call his CFO to make sure the man had his facts straight.

As she hung up the phone, she glanced at Kaden, who was watching her intently. "All I can say is, thank God I dug in my heels about today. What a waste of time that would've been." She shook her head, defeated. "There aren't any flights leaving Dulles before six in the morning. By the time their guy arrives and gets settled, I wouldn't be surprised if it was almost noon."

When Kaden didn't say anything, she continued. "I guess I should be flattered that they're getting someone from the national office. At least now there's a chance I won't have to hold his hand all week." She looked at him again and sadly shook her head. "I'm sorry, Kaden. You heard them. I know you think I have a choice, and of course I do—I could just tell them all to fuck off. But I don't think that's the right thing to do here. At least they're being nice about it—actually acknowledging the concession I'm making."

Kaden had to admit she'd handled her partner and her client well. And he knew he was being selfish. *Enjoy what time you have,* he reminded himself.

Thirty-Seven

Rather than spend their time lounging in bed, Annie roused her sleepy traveler at the crack of dawn and dragged him out to her favorite coffee shop. With their coffee in to-go cups, they crossed the wide avenue to the waterfront and walked south along the deserted sidewalk in the still morning air, past the working piers, all the way down to China Basin. She explained the planned development of the new ballpark there, and then they turned up Third Street, where she showed him the other major projects underway near the convention center.

"Once the park and museum are completed," Annie said, "it won't take long for the neighborhood to really start hopping, and this is just the beginning. Developers are eyeing the whole area over here." She waved at the tired but classic buildings around them. "It's ripe for redevelopment, and the new tax credits make these projects that much more promising as an investment."

"It worries me that you live in such a dubious neighborhood, but I can see you've made a very good investment." He squeezed the hand he held in his as he looked around. "I hope Sam and his crew take their jobs seriously."

She smiled at him. "They do. And trust me, I'm careful, too. I never walk around after dark, and I stay alert and aware in daylight. This is my favorite time of day—hardly anyone else is out and about, and it's very peaceful."

They returned to her apartment by eleven. Annie didn't want to push her luck and miss the call she was expecting.

Showered and dressed, she was eating an apple when the phone rang. The clock above the stove showed the time: a quarter to twelve. Grimacing, she answered it. The new guy had arrived, and it was time for her to go.

Kaden dropped her at a downtown high-rise, leaning over for a kiss as she opened the door. "I should be back by five," he told her. "If you aren't home by then, call me, okay?" He'd commandeered her Jeep for the day, intending to visit the bonded warehouse that would house his wine for West Coast distribution. The building was across the bay in Vallejo and served as a convenient wine storage facility for the nearby Napa Valley vintners. His original plan to take Annie to Napa Valley—he'd wanted to see it himself and had envisioned a romantic afternoon in the wine country—had necessarily been aborted. Instead, he resigned himself to taking care of his business.

"I will. Bye." She kissed him again and jumped out.

He saw her square her shoulders before heading into the building. She was tenacious, he'd give her that. And brave. His personal opinion was that her client and the team of advisors were a bunch of self-important pricks trying to push their weight around with her. But it was Annie's world, and he had to let her do her thing.

This time Annie was not dissatisfied by the caliber of professional who had been sent to review her work. She realized, as she stepped into the war room, that she knew him. Knew *of* him, she corrected herself. They'd never actually met, but she'd seen him at conferences and had heard him speak. He had authored several insightful articles about the regulations that had been issued the prior year, the same ones that she'd been working with, and he'd been on the speaking circuit talking about them, as had she.

She guessed that he was in his midforties and had been in Washington for most of his career. Like most people in the business there, he'd spent time at the IRS before moving to private practice where the pay was significantly better, as was the respect, if not the power. There was a slightly rumpled look about him that proved he'd just spent the morning on an airplane.

Recognition dawned in his eyes at the same time, along with something akin to respect. *Good,* Annie thought. Now we know where we stand. Her performance at the conference the previous fall had made her a minor celebrity in their small world of real estate tax experts.

She held out her hand. "Annie Shaw."

"It's a pleasure to meet you, Ms. Shaw. I'm Kurt Banning." He stood, accepting her hand. She could tell he wasn't thrilled to be here, but then, neither was she.

"Annie, please, and it's a pleasure to meet you, too. Sorry you had to be dragged out here at a moment's notice. The first batter up couldn't find the bat, much less hit the ball." Even with the silly baseball analogy, but she couldn't keep the resentment out of her voice.

"So I was told," he sighed. "At least it gets me out of DC for a few days. The weather is unbearable there right now." He gestured to the chair across the table.

She glanced at the papers spread out on the table in front of him, pleased to see he was already halfway through her deal index and outline.

"Where would you like to start?" Annie decided to let Kurt dictate how he wanted to approach the project.

He looked at her, pushed his glasses up his nose a bit, and smiled for the first time since she'd walked in. "Actually, I'd like to start by telling you how much I enjoyed your presentation last year in DC. It was outstanding, and I confess I've shamelessly used some of your analogies in my dealing with clients." He laughed at her surprised expression. "Don't worry, I haven't used them in my talks—or at least when I have, I've given you credit."

She nodded her thanks at the compliment.

Then he was all business, summarizing what he'd surmised so far from his quick but incomplete reading of the index. He'd made it through the first couple of deal summaries, and now he flipped back through the document asking cogent questions about the basic structure and how she determined which variations to use.

He listened intently as she explained the reasons for the basic, albeit complex structure, what financial accounting goals they had sought to achieve with the basic deals, and more importantly, what financial treatment they wanted to achieve at the exit strategy for each property. He stopped her often, probed for details until he was satisfied, then moved on.

Over the course of the afternoon, Annie walked him through each deal, variation by variation, explaining the reasons for how they'd been set up, the properties that were involved, and where the projects were in terms of completion. He guided her explanations to meet his needs, which was fine with Annie, and he took copious notes. Rather than relying on her diagrams, he drew his own, making sure he understood each detail.

When she leaned back in her chair to stretch her back, he eyed her thoughtfully. "Do you need to take a break?"

She looked at her watch. *Shit!* It was almost six o'clock. They'd been concentrating without more than a toilet break for almost six hours.

"I need to make a phone call," she said, standing. *Ouch,* her back hurt. And she had a headache. Her temples were throbbing. "How much longer do you need me tonight?"

He glanced at the outline. "It looks like there's one more variation to cover still. Maybe another hour? If we can get through this last one, I can spend the bulk of tomorrow reading the documents, and we can reconvene in the afternoon for another round of questions."

She groaned. Kaden wasn't going to be happy. "I'll stay until seven, but then I really need to go. You have a clear grasp of this stuff, and the last one isn't much different … just a little trickier due to the fact that it was a rollover property."

He turned back to his notes. She looked at him and frowned. There was a phone in the conference room, but she didn't want to have this conversation with an audience. "Is there a private phone somewhere?"

He took the hint. "Oh, ah, hmm … I'm not sure. Let me just step out and stretch my legs."

"Thanks."

Kaden picked up the phone on the first ring. As expected, he was less than thrilled about the extra hour. Annie promised that she would leave not one minute past seven and that she would take a cab, but she could tell he was practically gritting his teeth to keep from saying any more about it.

"What would you like to do for dinner?" He asked instead. "We can go out, or I can order something to be delivered."

"Something delivered would be nice. I'd rather not go out, if that's okay with you. I have a splitting headache and just want to put my feet up, maybe have a glass of wine."

His anger melted, realizing how grueling her day must have been. When he asked about it, she admitted that it could have been much worse and explained who was here and the gist of their marathon session. "At least he gets it and is asking good questions. I'm not teaching him the rules, only showing how I've applied them to the deals."

Her apartment smelled wonderful when she finally arrived home. Annie was exhausted, feeling like she'd been interrogated, which wasn't much of an exaggeration. Kaden kissed her forehead and led her to the couch. "Sit," he commanded. She did. He knelt down, pulled off her shoes and socks, picked up her legs, and swung them up onto the coffee table. She laughed and snuggled back into the cushions.

Next he poured them both a glass of wine and sat down next to her, touching the edge of his glass to hers.

"Thank you," she said softly before taking a sip.

He had discovered an Italian restaurant not too far from her apartment that delivered both the delicious food and the wine. They relaxed on the couch while they ate, shared the details of their day, and then went to bed early. Annie wasn't sure how late she'd be the next couple of nights, but she had a sinking suspicion that Kurt would summon her in the late afternoon and would require her to spend the evening hours going over what he'd reviewed. She hoped she was wrong.

Thirty-Eight

Annie spent Monday morning in her own office, making sure anything new was handled. She wanted to have lunch with Kaden, but he had appointments in Berkeley. He promised to call her by midafternoon, before she went back to Western's office.

Kaden had the same concern about Kurt's work plan that Annie did, but he kept his mouth shut and let things take their course. It turned out to be worse than he imagined.

At four in the afternoon, Annie was summoned for another long work session. She finally called the apartment at eight, telling him to go ahead and eat without her. She got home just before midnight, exhausted. He was sitting on the couch, his laptop hooked up to her phone jack with a long cable when she let herself in. He'd been studying financial reports to keep his mind off his frustration.

When she begged him to take her to bed, she fell asleep the minute her head hit the pillow. He watched her sleep, lightly tracing her jaw with his fingers. Then he kissed her temple, rolled over, and tried to fall asleep, too.

This pattern repeated itself for the next two days. Kaden had his import business to take care of during the day, and he was making decent headway with it, meeting with many restaurants in the Bay Area and arranging for samples to be delivered. In the evening, however, he found himself stewing alone in Annie's apartment. The great Kurt Banning couldn't bring himself to flip his schedule, where he would take the eight or more hours of Annie's day *during* the day—no, he had to have the daylight hours for his own business, then meet with her in the evening.

After the second night of Annie crawling home just before midnight, Kaden tried to reason with her. "Why can't he meet with you in the morning, then stay up all night reviewing what you've gone over? Why do you have to be with him until midnight?" Kaden understood deal timetables better than most people, but this was nonsensical.

"Put your foot down, Annie," he demanded. "This is ridiculous. It isn't like this is your deal."

"That's exactly why I can't do anything," she argued wearily. "It's not my deal, and I'm not calling the shots."

"Have you even *suggested* to him that it might be more efficient for *you* if he adjusted his schedule?"

She glared at him in response.

"Or perhaps you're enjoying spending your evenings with him," he added quietly. Kaden winced as he said it, wishing it back. But damn it, the man was using her. It was completely stupid to put her through midnight sessions that could easily have taken place during regular business hours.

"Yes, Oh Deal Guru, for your information, I did suggest that. Unfortunately, his other commitments require him to be available to people on the East Coast during the morning; then he needs to get through the next batch of documents before we meet. I don't like it any more than you do, but I don't see a way around it."

She was tired and frustrated. "Look, I'm sorry. I'll try to get away earlier tomorrow."

But she didn't. Or the next night, the fourth in a row of her working until midnight, at which point Kaden finally lost it.

He was standing at the windows, still dressed in his business attire, looking out at the dark street, when he heard her key in the lock. He looked at his watch. It was almost twelve thirty. Closing his eyes, he struggled to get his emotions under control, but it was impossible. He'd tried to be reasonable, tried to put himself in her shoes, and tried to talk himself out of being angry for the past week, but now he was done.

The way he saw it, Annie was letting herself be used. She wasn't fighting back, and nothing he said to her seemed to sink in. She wasn't getting enough sleep, wasn't eating enough, there were dark circles under her eyes, and damn it, she was being short and unresponsive to him. Part of him was jealous of the man who was monopolizing her time—*unfairly* monopolizing her time, he reminded himself. And the jealousy just stoked his anger.

"What?" Annie said defensively when he just stared at her with a stony expression. Worn thin, she was almost to the breaking point. She felt bedraggled and unattractive at that moment but was too tired to care. She was also too tired to catch the dangerous look in Kaden's eyes.

"I was hoping you might be able to break away before midnight, at least once while I'm here, to have dinner with me," he said tightly. "Or even to have a conversation without you falling asleep in the middle of it. I've barely set eyes on you in the last four days."

"Oh for God's sake," Annie muttered, squeezing her eyes shut and rubbing her temples. "I can't have this conversation now."

"When would you like to have it?" Kaden snapped back.

Annie threw her hands in the air. "I don't know! I just don't know! Can't you see I'm exhausted? God, Kaden, *you* of all people should understand this. I don't like it any more than you do, *but I don't control it!* I know this isn't what you expected, but guess what? Neither did I. There's nothing I can do about it. I didn't ask for this to happen now. I didn't ask for you to be here now." She spat the words at him, unleashing her own frustration. She couldn't understand why he wasn't helping her cope with the situation.

Kaden stood very still, studying her. When he finally spoke, his calm voice belied the turmoil ripping open his heart. "No, you didn't ask me to be here, did you, Annie? You've never asked me to come. But you gave me the keys to your apartment, so I assumed that I was invited. Forgive my error. It won't happen again." And then he turned on his heels and walked to the stairs, climbing them two at a time until he disappeared into the loft.

"Wait!" Annie cried. "Kaden, Jesus Christ, that's not what I meant. Of course I want you here … just … just not like this!" She chased after him up the stairs, totally frustrated. *Why doesn't he understand?* "Do you think I'm *happy* spending all night with a client instead of being with you?"

She stopped at the top of the stairs. Kaden was packing. *He's packing! Shit, shit, shit.* "Kaden," she pleaded, bone weary. "Please, wait. Don't do this."

"Why not? You said yourself you don't want me here."

"God damn it, that's not what I meant!"

"I think it is," he said, willing his voice to hold steady. He hoped she couldn't hear the pounding of his heart, which thumped so loud in his ears that he could barely hear her voice. He took a deep breath, not daring to look at her. He had to get out of there before he said something he might regret.

Annie was stunned. Then, in her bleary state, she lost it, too. "No, it isn't, and you know it, but you're too pigheaded to admit it. I'm sorry I ruined your trip because I wasn't available, Kaden. I'm really sorry to have been such an inconvenience to you. Did you honestly expect me to blow off my biggest client? What would you have done in my place?"

He stopped shoving clothes into his suitcase and stood still, his back to her, shoulders rigid. Then he turned around and regarded her with a look that could have been amusement, except that his eyes were hard as nails. "You mean your biggest client that is no longer your client despite this circus you're dancing to? You're killing yourself for nothing, Annie. *Nothing.* They don't care about you. None of this means anything. Don't you see? If you told them no, you can't stay until midnight, they would deal with it. They probably wonder why you push yourself so much. Are they there working alongside of you? Or are they at home with their families, letting you do it all?

"You want to know what I would've done in your place?" He sneered. "I would have told them to bugger off and let their new auditors do the work. This guy Banning is smart. He doesn't need you. I think he just likes the mental gymnastics. I know I would, particularly if I had you to dance to my tune. You gave them everything they needed. Your part is done. No one cares. At the end of the day, none of it matters. I'll be surprised if they even pay your bill for all this—it's got to be exorbitant at this point for all the hours you're putting in. I got out of this life-sucking rat race for precisely that reason."

"Right, that and the fact that you were a drunken mess," Annie hissed at him, then immediately regretted it. But he had cut her to the bone with his too-close-to-the-truth assessment of her worthless efforts, and she couldn't stop herself. Refusing to admit to her cheap shot, she stood with hands on hips and glared at him.

Kaden stared at her, expressionless. The twitching jaw muscle was the only evidence that her words had affected him. "Right, that too," he mumbled. Shoving the last item into his bag, he zipped it, then picked it up and turned around. He looked her straight in the eye, so close to breaking that he had to get out of there *now*. He couldn't take her stunned, hurt expression one minute longer, like this was somehow all *his* fault. The pain in his chest made it hard for him to breathe, but he wouldn't let her know how much it hurt. "Goodbye, Annie. Good luck with all this."

Then he walked past her and down the stairs. She just stared at his back, couldn't even muster the strength to say a word. Annie heard a metallic clink, like he dropped something on the table, then the door opening, footsteps receding, and finally the door shutting on its spring-loaded hinge.

She stared down the empty stairs, unable to process what had just happened. Then she sank down into the carpet, curled her hands around her stomach, and burst into tears. *What have I done?* She loved him so much, it hurt, and she had just let him walk away. *No,* she corrected, *I pushed him away.* She sobbed harder.

Thirty-Nine

Kaden stepped out of the elevator at the lobby, praying the neutral expression plastered on his face would hold for a few more minutes. He asked the security guard to call a cab and waited just inside the door until it pulled up.

"Have a good evening, Mr. Macallister," the guard said politely as Kaden opened the door to leave.

He nodded and walked out, tossed his bag in the trunk of the cab, got in, and directed the driver to the airport. He had no plan, had not planned on leaving, he only knew he couldn't stay there any longer, watching Annie destroy herself while she ignored him. Actually, it was more than that. The ugly truth of it was that he had allowed himself to be blinded by raging jealousy. Not directed at the man she'd been holed up with, per se; it was her priorities. Priorities that didn't place him close enough to the top. She'd proved that he wasn't important enough to her to try to get home before midnight. Four nights in a row.

He closed his eyes and sat back against the seat. *What a bloody mess.* He'd done exactly what he had warned himself *not* to do. He'd become petty and demanding. Rather than hold and support her, and help her get through it, he'd lashed out. Made it about him and his needs. Criticized her and questioned her motives. Told her that her work didn't mean anything and that nobody cared. God, did he really say that to her? *Bloody hell.* How could he have been so stupid to lose control like that?

Of course I want you here ... just not like this. Those words had sliced right through his heart. *How else?* His chest ached, as if his heart was bleeding out in his chest. She had become so important to him, she was his heart, his life. His soul mate. They belonged together. Didn't she see it? Was it possible that she didn't love him? She'd never actually said the words—he'd been listening for them—but she'd showed him. Of course she loved him. Didn't she? *Oh God, Annie. What have I done?*

Annie remained where she was, crumpled on the floor of her bedroom, sobbing. She must have cried herself to sleep, because when she woke in the still-dark hours of morning, she was curled up on the floor. Her eyes were swollen and stinging, her nose was running, and her throat was so dry it burned. She dragged herself up and stripped out of her clothes, gulped down some water, washed her face without looking in the mirror, then crawled into bed.

She woke again three hours later. When she summoned the courage to look in the mirror, she burst into tears again. Her puffy eyes and blotchy cheeks looked monstrous. There was no way she could go to the office today—she'd be unable to hide her misery, and she looked like hell. Annie called her secretary's line and left a message, saying she was ill and wouldn't be in. Four straight sixteen-hour days would just have to be her limit. How ironic that it took Kaden leaving for her to finally take his advice.

He's gone. He left me. She fingered the silver heart around her neck, thinking about how cold he had looked when he said goodbye. More tears sprang from a seemingly endless well of them. She deserved it. She'd been unfeeling, and unrelenting. She had assumed—had hoped—he would understand, without being hurt. But of course he was hurt. She had practically ignored him, and then, to make things worse, she'd said things she ... shouldn't have. *Oh, God.* She closed her eyes against the memory as her guilt continued to well up. He did nothing but care for her, was concerned about her, and had only wanted to spend a little bit of time with her. But she had thrown his concern right back in his face. She loved him, and she'd driven him away.

She needed air. If she was going to blow off the day, at least she could try to clear her head and get some exercise. Dressed in sweats, she found the biggest pair of sunglasses she owned to cover her swollen face and yanked a ball cap down on her head. As she headed for the door, she stopped cold. The campy Golden Gate Bridge keychain she'd given Kaden was sitting on the table by the door. *He left his keys. He really isn't planning on coming back.* Her heart wrenched, and fresh tears spilled down her face.

When Kaden arrived in Paris early Saturday morning, he called Henri to let him know that he was going to Les Eyzies but would be back in Rasteau by the end of August for harvest.

"Why are you back early? I thought you weren't coming home until next week." When Kaden didn't respond, Henri guessed. "You had a fight."

No response.

"You had a fight, and then you left without resolving it."

Kaden closed his eyes and leaned his forehead against the glass of the phone booth. He felt like a fool. After sitting at the airport for a few hours, he'd calmed down and thought about going back and apologizing, but he'd been such an unforgivable ass, he didn't think she'd let him back in. Better to let a little time pass for both of them.

"She was so busy, so wrapped up in this big project. I got possessive and juvenile, and it got ugly. She didn't appreciate me telling her that she was being used and her work was meaningless." He cringed even as he said it. "We both said hurtful things."

His uncle hesitated, hearing the pain, and waited for him to say more. When he didn't, Henri said, *"Mon fils,* I'm sure she shares your pain and has her own regrets. Life is not always easy, as you know, and it doesn't always go the way you want. She is very much like you, you know. Smart. Stubborn. Tough. Proud. You can't just tell her something like that and expect her to listen. She has to figure it out on her own."

"I know that, but ..."

"You are older, and you have been down that road before. Don't forget how difficult that path was. But she bonded with you, and she bonded with this land. She felt the pull of this life the same way you did. And this is why you are at peace with your decision."

Kaden didn't say anything. He knew Henri's words were true, but he was afraid that bond wasn't strong enough for Annie.

Henri sighed, overcome with compassion for his beloved nephew. Kaden and Annie shared a special love, but Annie had to make her own decision, in her own time. And it appeared that she was not yet ready. If Kaden wanted to spend the rest of his life with her, he had to give her the space she needed to find her way to him. He had pushed her, and she had resisted. It was that simple.

"Get yourself down to the river and ground yourself there as you always do. You will feel better, and then you can call her. But don't do it until you can apologize and tell her you understand."

Kaden took the TGV to Bordeaux, then caught the local line to Les Eyzies, getting there in the early afternoon. He called Jean Claude, who came to fetch him from the station.

"You screwed it up, didn't you?"

"Bloody hell, is it that obvious?" Kaden asked as he leaned back and closed his eyes. "Henri said the same thing." He paused, massaging his temples in a futile attempt to get some relief. "And yes, I did. I don't want to talk about it. I need some hard labor. Please tell me something needs to be fixed. I need to pound the hell out of something, or tear something apart."

Jean Claude threw back his head and laughed. "Nicole will be thrilled! She wants the stable finished."

"Perfect," Kaden said dryly. "I'll even have Belle to keep me company. The ideal lady—easy to look at and doesn't talk back." Jean Claude laughed again as he parked in front of the house.

Kaden opened the barn doors wide and stowed his suitcase in the closet without unpacking. He took a quick shower, put on a tee shirt and faded cargo shorts, slipped his feet into his worn river sandals, and headed back over to the main house.

Nicole greeted him at the door, kissed his cheeks then made a mock show of slapping his face. "*Mon Dieu,* Kaden, what have you done now?"

"Please, *petite,* not you, too." He shook his head in resignation, broad shoulders slumping. "Let me just admit that I'm a stupid sod and we'll leave it at that. I don't want to talk about it." Then he attempted a half smile for her. "By the way, you are looking lovely as always. Where are the plans for the stable?"

Nicole smirked but said nothing. Jean Claude already had the plans spread out on the kitchen table, but before Kaden could get there, he heard a racket behind him. At that moment, the boys, Michel and Alex, raced into the room. "Uncle Kaden. Uncle Kaden!"

He grinned and knelt down, bracing himself for the impact of two small bodies. He hugged them until they squirmed out of his embrace, and then laughed as he watched them dance around making all kinds of noise. A sharp stab hit in the vicinity of his heart. He'd allowed himself to hope that someday he and Annie might have children of their own. Now … he just didn't know.

He shook the thought away as Nicole corralled the boys and managed to distract them. Turning back to the plans, he reacquainted himself with the design he'd created the previous summer, thought about how to get it started, what lumber and other materials he'd need, but for now …

"I'll get the junk cleared out this afternoon, then start pulling the roof down tomorrow," he told his cousin, who nodded his agreement. "Make sure the boys are clear from the area when I start the demo. I don't want them anywhere near the falling debris."

He turned to leave the house, but Jean Claude stopped him with a hand on his arm. Kaden turned to see concern in the other man's eyes. "Have a care, my friend. That structure is not terribly sound, and you are distracted. I don't want to have to haul you off to the hospital."

"Don't worry," Kaden said with a derisive snort. "I may be an idiot, but I'm not stupid."

Kaden rigged a wagon cart to a small tractor and brought it around to the stable. He led Belle out to a hitching post under a tree to get her out of the way. She watched him with big brown eyes as he loaded up the wagon. When it was full, he drove it to one of the stone huts down the hill and neatly stacked the stuff in there. Why Jean Claude didn't just toss some of this old junk, he didn't know, but then, what did he care? He'd asked for labor. It didn't matter to him what it was.

He finished with the last load around eight o'clock, then led Belle back into her stall, forked in some alfalfa, scratched her behind the ears, and closed up the doors. Jean Claude and Nicole were working, and he didn't have the mental energy to spend the evening with the boys and their nanny, so he commandeered the old truck and drove into town.

As he sat brooding over a beer at the bistro in town, waiting for his *steak frites,* he couldn't keep his thoughts from that last night in San Francisco. Would Annie ever forgive him? Would she eventually see through his anger and understand his pain? Would it matter if she did?

His labors that afternoon had resulted in no mental relief—just a few blisters and a stiff back. But at least it gave him something to do, and if he stayed focused, he might just get the project finished by the time he needed to head back to Rasteau.

The waiter delivered his meal, but it tasted flat to him, as did the beer he wasn't enjoying. Everything just seemed off. He couldn't clear the bitter taste from his mouth, a bitterness his own words and actions had created. He forced himself to eat, then paid his bill and went home.

Forty

Annie didn't go to the war room Friday afternoon, but she did talk to Kurt on the phone from her apartment. She claimed a nasty sinus infection, which was plausible from the sound of her voice, pinched and strained and stuffed up from so much crying. As it turned out, he had completed his review and only had a few last questions, so they were able to finish up over the phone.

It was a hollow victory. Her work had withstood the scrutiny of one of the most respected professionals in her field, and he had admired her creativity in the setup. But now she was finished with the client. Unless something completely unexpected happened, the deal would go through. Western represented about two-thirds of her billings. It was her biggest client—one of the firm's biggest clients. She had no idea how she would make it up.

At midnight on Friday, Annie still hadn't tried to sleep, even though she was drained. She thought about trying to eat something but couldn't muster the energy to open the refrigerator door. Instead she just lay on her couch and channel surfed with little focus. She kept glancing at her computer, wondering if she should send Kaden a message. *And say what?*

She assumed he was home by now—probably just arrived. If he caught an early flight out Friday morning, he would have arrived early Saturday morning, Paris time. She tried to imagine what he was doing, if he'd go to Rasteau or Les Eyzies. Was he thinking of her? Did he regret his angry outburst? *He's not the only one who threw out angry words,* she reminded herself. *Yeah, but he started it.* Did he? *You don't think you provoked him just a little? Maybe a little. Okay, maybe more than a little.* She sighed. This was getting her nowhere.

Annie had a sudden and horrifying thought: did Kaden know that she loved him? She couldn't recall if she'd ever actually said the words. She'd shown him time and again, and she had definitely expressed her adoration, even calling him, *mon amour.* Surely he understood her feelings. But Kaden had a vulnerable side, and perhaps, because she'd never said the words, he was insecure about how she really felt. That would certainly explain his anger. Men like Kaden didn't cry; instead, they released their emotions by getting angry.

She looked again at her computer. What could it hurt? Her heart was already ripped to shreds. If he chose to ignore her, a little lost dignity could hardly make things worse. No matter how unfair she thought his behavior had been, she still loved him. Angry words couldn't change that. If he was hurting, too, would it help him to finally hear the truth from her? Better yet, in her own voice? Was she brave enough to call him? She wasn't even sure where he was.

Before she lost her nerve, she fired up her computer and waited while the modem connected. She logged on to her email, half hoping there might be a message from him. There wasn't. Disappointing, but not surprising.

Her message was simple and to the point.

> Dear Kaden,
> I'm so sorry. I love you with all my heart, even while it's breaking.
> Can you forgive me?
> Annie

Unfortunately, Kaden didn't get the message. He never even thought to turn on the laptop he had with him. Whether it would have changed what happened that day, they would never know.

After a fitful night's sleep, he got up early. He pulled on a tee shirt and jeans, shoved his feet into a pair of worn boots, and grabbed a pair of leather work gloves to protect against splinters. He helped himself to a cup of coffee from his cousin's kitchen then headed down to get started on the demo.

The boys were unhappy that they couldn't help him, but he was firm. "It's too dangerous, *mes petits hommes.* But I'll make a deal with you. If you are good and stay here in the house with your *maman,* then I'll take you fishing this afternoon when I'm finished. *D'accorde?*"

The boys cheered and did as they were asked.

Kaden thought about erecting scaffolding inside the structure while he pulled off the roof, but he decided against it, thinking it would be easier to work from above than from below. He'd just be careful.

Belle rambled behind him as he led her out to her post beneath the tree, and he spent a few minutes scratching behind her ears and talking to her before feeding her a handful of oats and leaving her on her own.

He started by inspecting the roof from the inside. Jean Claude had a ladder that was tall enough for him to get up close to the roof to see how it was made. As he studied it, he realized that the original roof structure had been designed for a thatched roof, but at some point, the thatching had rotted out, replaced by plywood and some cheap roofing material.

The design was simple, with rounded wood beams extending from each of the four corners of the structure up to a center ridgepole that ran the length of it. There were smaller crossbeams extending from each corner beam, roughly half a meter apart. These would have been the supports for the thatching, but now the plywood was attached to them. That meant he'd have to climb up on the roof to pull off the plywood before he could disassemble the crossbeams.

He tested the stability of the crossbeams by grabbing on to them and shaking, then hung from a few to test their strength. From his position, he couldn't see any immediate problems with rot.

Satisfied, he carried the ladder out and leaned it against the side of the building, buckled on his tool belt, and climbed up. He was able to get most of the plywood off without actually climbing on the roof, but it was more rotten than it had initially appeared, and some pieces clung to the beams up at the top near the center ridgepole. There was also quite a bit of the original thatching material, rotted but still clinging to the supports.

The day was hot and the work was hard, and sweat kept trickling into his eyes. Coupled with the swirling dust kicked up from disturbing a century-old thatched roof, he was having a hard time keeping his eyes clear. He climbed down the ladder, removed his shirt and wiped his face with it, then rolled up the bandana he had in his pocket and tied it around his head.

He tossed his shirt over a fence rail and climbed back up the ladder. Surveying the roof, he realized he would need to climb up onto it to loosen the crossbeams from the corner beams, then disassemble the corner beams and the ridgepole. That part could probably be done from down below, but the crossbeams needed to come off from the top.

Gingerly testing the strength of each beam before letting it take his weight, he crawled up to one end of the ridgepole, straddled it, and began swinging a heavy mallet to remove the top cross members. Starting from the top, he hoped to maintain the integrity of the structure, braced from below by the lower crossbeams.

As he worked, he thought about Annie. What she was doing? Was she still spending her time with Banning? A burst of anger surged through him. Or was it jealousy? He shook his head and reminded himself that he had no right to feel either. She had been doing her job—doing it the way she had felt it needed to be done. Who was he to tell her otherwise? *I'm so sorry, Annie. I had no right to get angry.*

The crossbeams turned out to be rotten, too, and as he pried them up and yanked them off, they splintered apart in his hands. He let the pieces drop to the floor below, glancing down at the growing pile. It would all need to be hauled out before he could set the ladder back up in there for the final disassembly of the roof structure.

He needed to call her. His pride had caused this, and he needed to suck it up, admit he was wrong, and beg her to forgive him. She might—just might—understand that he had been insecure and hurting, that he hadn't really meant what he had said about her job. *Well, that's not entirely true, is it?* He did think it was all worthless, but his perspective was unique on that score. And anyway, that was beside the point. If he had to get on his knees and beg, he would.

Hell, he'd move to San Francisco if that's what it took, but he cringed at that notion. If he hadn't left the damn keys, he'd go back there and wait in her apartment until she showed up. Grab her, tear off her clothes, and make love to her until she forgave him.

Distracted by that last thought, Kaden leaned down to yank hard at a stuck beam, and he lost his balance. He was straddling the ridgepole, about a third of the way down from the end. As he began to fall toward the stuck beam, he dropped the mallet and put both hands out to catch himself on the beam. The impact of Kaden's 190-pound body against the stubborn beam broke it loose, and he pushed right through it. He reacted quickly, reaching out farther to grab the next beam as momentum carried him down. And he would have caught it, but his pant leg snagged on a nail that stuck out from the other side of the ridgepole where a plywood plank had been attached. The nail caught the fabric just below his knee as his body tilted, arresting his outward reach and scraping deep into his calf as gravity pulled him down. *Bloody fucking hell!*

With nothing else to stop the fall, Kaden crashed down three meters, face first onto the pile of rotten timbers. Although the instinct to put out his hands possibly kept his neck from snapping before his skull smacked against the mallet that he'd dropped seconds before, it broke both his wrists. He turned his face to the side at the last second. The bandana kept the corner of the mallet from punching a hole in his temple, but it did nothing to blunt the force of the impact.

The pain exploding in his head and in his chest eclipsed the unbearable pain in his wrists, right before he lost consciousness.

Forty-One

The piercing ring of a telephone brought Annie out of her sleepy reverie. It was Sunday morning, and she was in bed, drifting in and out of sleep, trying to summon the energy—or the courage—to get up. She had finally crawled into bed around midnight, disappointed to her soul that after twenty-four hours there'd still been no reply to her email.

She frowned at the phone, reaching for it, her pulse quickening. Could it possibly be Kaden? She glanced at the clock as she picked up the receiver. "Hello?"

"Annie?" a heavily accented French voice asked.

She jolted up in bed. "Yes, who's this?"

"Annie, its Henri Bouvier."

"Henri!" An alarm sounded in her heart. "Oh, God, what's wrong? Has something happened?" There was hysteria in her voice.

"Yes, *ma petite,* but please stay calm and let me tell you. I don't know how else to say this, so I will be direct. There has been an accident. Kaden fell through a roof in Les Eyzies and was seriously injured. He's currently in intensive care at a hospital in Bordeaux."

"*What?*" Annie fought down the panic. *Seriously injured.* "He fell through a roof? Why did they take him so far? What are his injuries?" Annie was no stranger to the ICU, or brutal injuries. Her mind raced at the horrible possibilities, even as she prayed. People recovered from serious injuries all the time, and Kaden was fit and strong.

"They airlifted him to Bordeaux because he has a punctured lung, and … Annie, he is still unconscious."

"*No!*" She felt the tears come and heard a strange keening noise—from her, she realized. Her heart was strangling the breath in her chest.

"Annie, please, I need you to listen to me. Annie, can you come to France? Can you meet me in Bordeaux? I don't know about trauma patients or comas, but I know he would want you here."

She closed her eyes. *I'm not so sure about that.* "Uh, Henri." Sniff. "I don't know what Kaden told you, but we didn't part on good terms. I'm not sure he would want me to come." Her voice was small, and she hiccupped as she tried to control her emotions.

"I know that he left in anger, *petite,* and I also know he feels very bad. He fears he hurt you terribly. He regrets the things he said." Henri waited but heard only sniffling.

"*Chérie,* for all his strength and confidence, my nephew is a sensitive, vulnerable man. He loves you deeply. Whatever happened in San Francisco hurt you both, but he knows he overreacted. Trust me, he needs you. I need you, too, *petite.* I don't know what I would do if I lost him."

Annie heard the despair in Henri's voice. She wiped her eyes. "Are you sure?" Her voice was small. "I want to come, but I'm afraid, Henri."

"Don't be afraid. Please say you'll come."

She called Air France and booked herself on the next flight out. With just three hours before the flight left, she packed in a scramble, jumped in and out of the shower, and called Sam to hail her a cab. She had no idea how long she'd be gone, and she didn't care. Nothing was more important at that moment than getting to Kaden.

As the hours of the long flight ticked by, Annie felt helpless, agonizing over her foolishness. How could she have not told Kaden her true feelings? How could she have just assumed he knew? This was exactly what she had feared. Overwhelming guilt battled despair. Was he lying alone, hurting, thinking he was unloved? How could she survive this again? She couldn't. And if she lost him before he knew how much she loved him … She simply couldn't lose him. He was her life. In startling clarity, she recognized it and understood that nothing else mattered. She felt the tears on her cheeks but couldn't find the strength to wipe them away.

Twenty-two excruciating hours after taking Henri's phone call, she was sitting at Kaden's bedside. She had flown straight to Paris then caught the high-speed train to Bordeaux. Henri met her train and took her to the hospital, and then smoothed the way for her to enter the ICU.

Annie squeezed her eyes shut when she saw him, and fresh tears began to fall. His face was cut, scraped, bruised, and swollen; both eyes were black; and several days of stubble covered his jaw. He had a ventilator tube sticking out of his mouth, and both of his wrists were wrapped in thick gauze. Henri hadn't mentioned his wrists. She studied the unconscious man laid out before her. The thin bed sheet was pulled up just over his hips, revealing a torso that was wrapped in gauze as well.

The array of bedside monitors indicated a steady heart rate and blood pressure in the normal range. There was one scary-looking monitor connected to nodes at his temples, the screen showing a wavy, warbled image that did not give her any comfort at all. She sat on a chair beside the bed and tentatively reached out to touch his hand. The protocol at this hospital was unclear, but they'd allowed her in the room, she reasoned, so surely she could at least touch him.

She tried to say his name, but her voice was a croak. She cleared her throat, slipped her fingers under his as they lay still by his side, and gently wrapped her thumb around them. "Kaden," she whispered. "It's me, Annie. I'm here. I don't know if you can hear me or not, but I'm so sorry. I'm sorry about everything, but mostly I'm sorry that you're hurt. I love you so much. Please don't leave me. Please come back to me." She choked on her tears and leaned her head down so her forehead was just touching the tips of his fingers.

It may have been her imagination, or the trembling of her own fingers that touched his, but she thought she felt one of his fingers twitch. She jerked up to look at him, but his face was passive in his unconsciousness.

She stroked his fingers with hers, whispering his name again. Not sure what to do, she looked around. Henri was watching her from the doorway. He must have read the anguish in her eyes, because he came toward her and put a hand gently on her shoulder.

"Can you tell me what happened?" she asked weakly.

It was Alex who found him. When Kaden didn't come to fetch them for their fishing excursion, the boys became impatient and snuck out of the house to go investigate. They stopped at the top of the hill, torn between their promise not to go near the stable and their curiosity about where he could be. They called his name when they didn't see him. After several minutes with no answer, curiosity finally won out, and Michel stood guard while Alex snuck down and peeked his head in through the door.

At first Alex didn't see him, camouflaged by all the dust and debris. Then he saw a boot poking out from the pile. He went running back to his brother, and they both raced for the house, yelling for their *maman.* Poor little Alex had tears streaming from his terrified eyes as he tried to explain that his uncle Kaden was dead.

Nicole called for an ambulance before taking both boys' hands and going down to the stable to see for herself. While they waited for the EMTs to arrive, she was able to ascertain that Kaden still had a pulse, and she did her best to reassure her distraught little boys that he was alive. But it was not good—not good at all.

Kaden had pink foam bubbling out of his mouth—a sure sign of lung damage, and the small hospital in Sarlat was not equipped to handle this level of trauma. He also had a nasty gash on his head where he'd slammed into the iron mallet, and his blood-soaked bandana had fused itself to the wound. His unconscious state, unaffected by the minor jostling around as they collared him and rolled him onto a board to carry him out, made them even more leery. It was the EMTs' decision that the safest course was to airlift him to Bordeaux.

Nicole had then called Henri, who had called Annie. As soon as Henri knew Annie's travel plans, he made the six-hour drive to pick her up himself.

It was a grave prognosis. Coma patients are always tricky, and there was much that remained unknown when it came to brain trauma.

"But there is good news, *petite,*" Henri said. "It appears there is no spinal cord damage. His muscles respond as normal to stimulus. The doctor thinks he put out his hands to break his fall. His wrists took the brunt of the impact instead of his head."

"He broke both wrists?" Annie looked again at the fat gauze wrappings.

"One is apparently worse than the other, but both will heal in time. He also cracked two ribs, and one of them may have punctured a lung. We're not sure how long he lay unconscious. The blood on his head wound was dried, so it had to have been at least an hour. Were it not for the boys, who knows how long he would have been there?"

Annie had been holding Kaden's fingers as they spoke, softly caressing his knuckles. She told Henri what little she remembered about brain injuries.

"If there was no fracture to the skull, it is possible that his brain is simply resting in order to avoid the pain of the blow. Tissues are usually ripped inside the skull, and they swell, which impairs brain function for a time." She paused. "That's what happened to me."

"He told me of your accident. How long were you in this condition, *ma petite?*"

She closed her eyes and took a deep breath, then opened them and looked directly at Henri. "Ten days."

Henri just stared at her for a moment. "Let us pray it does not take him that long."

Annie could only nod in agreement. She didn't think she could bear ten days of this torture. She wasn't sure she could bear ten more hours. It had already been more than twenty-four hours since he'd lost consciousness.

The nurse came in to take vital signs and check his lungs. She allowed Annie and Henri to remain in the room, and she relayed her findings to Henri. Annie wanted to know about the monitor connected to the nodes at his temples, and she waited impatiently while Henri conversed with the nurse about it. Eventually Henri seemed satisfied, and the nurse left.

"It's some sort of measuring device that monitors swelling and fluid movement in his cranial cavity. I don't understand all of what she said, but they are worried about an alteration in cerebral blood flow and pressure within the skull, which could ..." Henri looked away and cleared his throat. "Which could cause even more damage to his brain that the initial impact."

Annie stared at him a moment before shifting her gaze to Kaden's relaxed features, then to the image on the monitor. "Did she say, ah … did she say what …" she nodded at the monitor. "What does it indicate?"

Henri reached for Annie's hand and squeezed it. "She said there is nothing to indicate a dangerous level of fluid yet … but they will keep watching it carefully."

Annie felt her whole body go numb. *Was this what my brother went through when I was in a coma?* It was beyond unbearable to think her beautiful, intelligent, and sensitive man wouldn't come back to her whole.

Henri cleared his throat again. "There is some good news, though, *petite.* His lung function is not impaired as they initially feared, and they will take him off the ventilator. The organ apparently sealed itself."

The nurse returned at that moment with a doctor, and they swiftly extracted the tube from Kaden's throat. He gagged slightly as it came out—a good sign according to the doctor, who explained that the presence of the body's natural reflexes were positive events in brain injury victims. He lifted Kaden's eyelids and flashed a penlight across each one, seemingly satisfied with whatever he saw. As he scribbled a note on the chart hanging from the wall, the nurse set a cannula under his nose, looped it behind his ears, and adjusted a dial on a console next to the bed. When she finished, she said something to Henri before nodding to them both and leaving with the doctor.

Annie sat back down in the chair beside the bed and took Kaden's hand in hers again. He looked much better without the big breathing tube, and it gave Annie a small amount of hope. She ventured her other hand up to touch his jaw. He was warm but not hot, and his breathing seemed steady. She closed her eyes and prayed to a God she had never thought much of.

Forty-Two

Henri left Annie at Kaden's bedside later that evening. There was no sense in both of them being there, and since Annie refused to leave, Henri figured he might as well go find a place to stay. He brought her something to eat before kissing her cheeks, hugging her tight, and bidding her *bonne nuit*.

After staring for what seemed like hours at the unchanging amoeba-like image of the brain fluid monitor, Annie finally fell asleep against the side of the bed, her face on her arms and Kaden's fingers clutched in her own. She dreamed about him, but the dream was disjointed. At first they were on the river in a canoe; then they were on top of the Empire State Building; then they were making love in a Jacuzzi. He was whispering something to her that she couldn't quite make out.

The foggy haze of her dream started to lift, but the whispering persisted. She squeezed her eyes shut to keep from waking, wanting to understand his words, but they were just beyond the periphery of her awareness. Then she felt the slightest pressure on her hand. She stilled, suddenly wide awake.

"Annie." A faint, hoarse whisper, but she heard it, and she felt the pressure again.

Her heart leaped in her chest as she lifted her head and looked up at Kaden's face. His eyes were open, barely, and he was struggling to swallow, like his throat was bone dry, but he was staring at her. The gaze that met hers was not clouded with confusion as she had feared, but it was filled with the intensity of focus that was uniquely his.

"Oh!" was all she could muster, as she dragged herself up. "You're awake!"

Kaden felt like he was floating in some weird fog, unsure whether he was dreaming or conscious. He had sensed Annie's presence, and it was that magnetic draw of her soul to his that had pulled him from some misty abyss—an abyss that threatened to pull him back down. His throat was raw, on fire, and his head pounded as he struggled to maintain the connection with her. His eyes darted to the pitcher on the table near the bed, then back to her. "*Water,*" he whispered.

"Oh! Of course!" She jumped up, but before she could remove her hand from his, he pressed hers with surprising strength. She looked back at him and reeled at what she saw in his eyes.

"*Love you,*" he whispered, struggling to get the sound out.

Tears filled her eyes and spilled over the rims. She gave him a watery smile, and gently caressed his fingers. "I love you, too. I'm so sorry I never told you before. I was so scared I would lose you before I'd get another chance."

He lifted the corners of his lips as much as he could. Then his eyes darted to the water again, and he released her hand.

"Right." She jumped up and swiped at her tears, then with shaky hands, poured water into a plastic cup. She held it to his lips and tipped the cup. Most of it ended up running down his chin, but she managed to get some in. He blinked his eyes, swallowed, winced, then opened his mouth for more. After finishing most of the small cup, he cleared his throat and swallowed again.

"Thank you," he said softly, his voice no longer as hoarse.

She gently wiped the water from his chin and cheeks. His eyes never left hers.

"What are you doing here, Annie?" His voice was so soft, like he had no volume control. She was sitting with one hip on the edge of the bed facing him, and she felt him shift his hand to touch her.

She hesitated, bit her lower lip, and lowered her eyes, clutching the little cup in her hands. "I … Henri called me …"

"Annie," Kaden whispered, his fingers lightly stroking her hip where his hand could reach her from its prone position on the mattress.

She looked up at him through damp lashes.

"Thank you for coming." He swallowed again. "Could I have more water?"

Annie refilled the cup and brought it to his lips again. She carefully poured in small sips, let him swallow, and then gave him more, repeating until he had finished the cup.

He swallowed the last bit, then licked his lips and cleared his throat again. His foggy brain cleared a little more as Annie sat watching him. She shifted the cup to her other hand, then gently touched his lips with her fingers, softly running them across his lower lip. Kaden closed his eyes to savor the sensation.

She pulled her hand away tentatively, still clutching the cup, and looked at her hands because she couldn't look into his eyes. "Kaden," she spoke softly, the anguish evident in her shaky voice. "I'm so sorry. I don't know what happened last week. I ... it was my fault and ... please say you'll forgive me. I love you so much, it ... it scares me." She finished in a whisper. She had so much she wanted to say, but she didn't know where to begin. And now wasn't the time. She just wanted him to know how she felt, and if he could accept her with her faults, she would find a way to make everything else work.

"Annie, look at me." His voice was so gentle.

She swallowed and looked up. There it was again—that incredible love shining from his battered and swollen eyes.

"It wasn't your fault. It was mine," he said. "I was out of my mind with jealously." At her confused looked, he closed his eyes briefly, then opened them again and said, "I'm ashamed that I let my insecurities take over. I love you, my beautiful, brave Annie, and I want to be with you always."

Her tears unchecked, she managed a small smile. "I want that, too."

"Can you forgive me? I said some awful things. I'm so sorry that I hurt you."

"You didn't say anything worse than I did."

"Will you kiss me?" He sounded so tentative that her smile widened. She leaned down and brushed her lips against his, gently smoothed back the hair from his brow, and kissed him again.

"Nice shiners," she said, lightly touching the side of his face.

He winced. "I wish that was the worst of it. I'm going to be paying for this one for a while. What day is it? Where am I?"

She looked at her watch. "Early Tuesday morning, at a hospital in Bordeaux. You were airlifted here on Sunday afternoon. What happened?"

"I was taking the roof off the stable, made a stupid move, and lost my balance."

She closed her eyes and shook her head. "You wouldn't have even been there if it weren't for me."

"Annie, don't. It's not your fault. If anyone is to blame, it's me. I shouldn't have left." He closed his eyes.

"Let's argue about that later." She brushed her fingers along his brow again. "You need to sleep now, love. You need to let your body recover."

He tried to lift his eyelids but couldn't. In a moment, his breathing was even in what appeared to be an untroubled sleep.

Annie held his hand, stroking it softly, watching him rest. The night nurse came in, and Annie told her in all the French she could muster that he had awakened and she'd helped him to take some water. The nurse asked a few questions that Annie didn't understand, shrugged, made a note on the chart, and left.

Kaden slept until the doctor poked him awake the next morning. The nurse who accompanied him raised the bed so Kaden was in more of a reclined sitting position, and the doctor did a series of exercises to test his patient's eyesight and peripheral vision, then checked the dilation of his pupils and their reaction to his penlight. He checked the reflexes of other muscles and other motor skills, palpated the knot on Kaden's temple, and tested the strength of his lungs. Then he pulled back the bed sheet to expose the angry, jagged gash on the inside of Kaden's calf, and Annie gasped.

"Don't worry, *chérie*," Kaden chuckled and immediately winced. "I don't even feel it over the throbbing in my head." As far as Annie was concerned, the fact that he could laugh even a little was as good a sign as any. The doctor examined it for infection, apparently satisfied that it was healing without incident.

Henri arrived shortly thereafter with coffee and croissants, and Annie filled him in. The nurse and an orderly shooed them out so they could wash the patient and change the bed sheets. Annie used the ladies room to wash her face and comb out her hair. She felt like moldy scum and desperately needed a shower.

Kaden slept the rest of the morning, and Annie stayed beside him. Later that day he was moved to a large private room out of the ICU, his doctor having declared that he was no longer in imminent danger but would require at least one more day's monitoring. The ominous brain fluid monitor stayed with him, but to Annie's eye, the image had not changed.

After he had been settled into his private room, he insisted Annie go with Henri for a shower and some rest. "No arguments, *chérie*. You're beginning to smell worse than me." He managed a smile at her horrified expression, but the jest worked.

Nicole and Jean Claude showed up Tuesday evening with dinner for everyone and the boys in tow. The nurses on duty protested at first but then gave in and allowed it, even helping to find more chairs for the spacious room. For the first time in more than a week, Annie laughed as she watched the chef take command of the hospital staff. She didn't miss the food containers that made their way out to the nurse station, but whatever he did, it worked, and Kaden's room shortly resembled a dining room.

Michel and Alex were hailed as *les petit héros* since they were the ones who had "rescued" their uncle from the stable. They told the story over and over at increasingly louder volumes until one of the nurses came back to shush them.

Henri distracted them with a game Nicole had brought along, but Annie noticed that Alex paid only partial attention to it, his gaze shifting regularly toward Kaden. She nudged Kaden and tipped her chin toward the boy. Kaden reached his hand out and softly said, "*Alex, viens ici pour une minute.*"

Alex abandoned the game and shuffled toward Kaden's bed, his small hand reaching for his cousin's large one with eyes wide in concern. "Does it hurt?" he asked in a shaky voice.

Annie's heart clenched at the soulful sincerity in the little boy's voice. At six years old, Alex demonstrated the empathy of a much older child.

Kaden wrapped his fingers around the tiny hand and, when Alex hesitated, gently towed the boy toward him. "*Oui, mon petit bonhomme courageux.*

It hurts. But I will heal, thanks to you. Come give me a hug, but be gentle. *Je t'aime.*"

Alex wrapped a thin arm around Kaden's upper chest, mindful of the bindings around his ribs, and buried his face in his shoulder, sniffling back tears. "*Je t'aime aussi,*" he whispered.

They stayed that way for only a brief moment, Alex being a squirmy six-year-old after all, but it was not missed by Nicole. Annie witnessed the other woman's reaction, a subtle but unmistakable surge of affection for both the boy and the man, before Nicole trained her motherly gaze on Annie. *Family is everything, and we stand by each other,* is how Annie interpreted the unspoken message.

Once Alex went back to his game, looking more relaxed as if the interlude had reinforced Kaden's presence in his life, Annie positioned her chair close to the bed, her fingers wrapped around Kaden's. His strength was already returning and she prayed he wouldn't relapse, but the brain monitor continued to worry her. His speech had been slurred the night before when he'd first come back to consciousness, but she hadn't noticed it since. He had slept most of the day, and while his face still looked terrible, his eyes were bright and his smile was quick. She wasn't fooled, though—he had suffered major trauma and would require weeks of convalescence. But his resilience surprised her, and she said so.

"The love of a good woman" was Kaden's quick response, pressing her fingers. "I doubt I'd be feeling nearly so motivated if you weren't here." He slowly lifted her hand to his lips and kissed the tip of each finger. "Thank you again for coming to me."

She leaned forward to kiss him, and Jean Claude chose that moment to look over.

"All right, all right, enough of the quiet whispering, you two." He laughed when Annie blushed. "Now that we know you aren't going to die, tell us what happened."

Kaden shook his head and immediately regretted it, pausing a moment to let a wave of pain and nausea recede, his features forming into a grimace of disgust. He didn't want to talk about it. "An unfortunate lapse in judgment," he said. "A mistake I won't make again. I'm sorry your contractor won't be able to finish the job this season, Nicole."

"*Pas de problème, chér.* We'll just put Belle in the barn for the winter." Everyone laughed, and Kaden couldn't help but smile.

"I'll hire a couple of boys at the river—there are always a few looking for a job. I'll play foreman, but I won't be swinging a hammer anytime soon."

"Better your wrists than your neck, *mon vieux,*" Jean Claude chimed in.

There was a double knock on the door before it swung open to reveal a large, older man who resembled Henri. As he stepped into the room, Annie saw another tall lanky figure behind him.

Henri was the first to react. "*Maurice! Bienvenue, mon frère. Nous faisons une petite fête de famille! Et Fernand!*" he added, noticing the man trailing behind him.

The boys jumped up. "*Papy!*" they chorused as they rushed to him.

"*Bonsoir, mes petits-fils,*" Maurice said, kissing them each in turn before swatting them affectionately on their bottoms.

Maurice didn't spare anyone at the table a second glance, including his son and daughter-in-law. Instead, he turned to Kaden with a frown. "*Comment ça va?*" He glanced at Annie and noted their locked hands before refocusing on Kaden.

In English, Kaden introduced his uncle and older cousin to Annie, then answered his question, also in English. Maurice told him he was happy he wasn't dead, in English, and joined the group at the table.

Kaden glanced at Annie and winked.

After greeting the rest of the group, Maurice and Fernand pulled their chairs up to the opposite side of the bed from Annie. Kaden filled them in on the accident, giving as few details and making as little a matter of it as he could, then turned the conversation to the progress of the import business and the upcoming harvest.

The party atmosphere continued for another hour, but despite the front he put up, Kaden was tiring. Annie caught Nicole's eye and tilted her head slightly in his direction. Bless her, Nicole got the message.

"*Maintenant nous devons quitter.* We need to let uncle Kaden get some rest."

Forty-Three

With a bag of meds and a don't-even-think-it list of orders, along with some last-minute harping in French from his bossy nurse, Kaden was released into Annie's care.

"*Alors*," the nurse finished, "*au revoir*." And with that, she turned away and left them at the front entrance to the hospital. Kaden started to stand up from the wheelchair they had insisted on using, but both Annie and Henri stopped him.

"No way, you stay put," Annie said. "Henri will bring the car around."

Kaden groaned, looking to Henri for support, but he simply smiled his sparkly smile and shook his head.

Henri drove them back to Les Eyzies and helped Annie install Kaden in a rented hospital bed that, thanks to a quick phone call between Annie and Nicole, had been set up in the downstairs area of the barn, with the couch shoved up against the fireplace. Kaden protested loudly about the absurdity of it, claiming he could easily walk up and down the stairs to his own bed, but again, Annie insisted, and Henri kept his mouth shut.

Henri announced that he would stay for a few days to take his great-nephews fishing, kissed Annie on both cheeks and left them alone.

"Annie, this is ridiculous." Kaden waited until Henri left, but enough was enough.

She turned to him with innocent, wide eyes. "What do you mean?"

"I don't need to be confined to a bed like an invalid."

Annie had anticipated this and smiled at how quickly the protest had come. But she was prepared. Turning to him, she arched a brow and gave him a sultry look. "You were ordered to stay in bed until the end of the week, and your lung is still weak. You shouldn't be climbing stairs." She held up her hand when he opened his mouth to protest. "Before you protest overmuch, perhaps you should reconsider your surroundings."

Kaden noticed the heat in her eyes but was still confused. "What do you mean, exactly?"

"I mean exactly what I said." She walked to the front door, flipped the latch to lock it, and then sauntered slowly to the rolling doors, making sure they were latched but leaving the glass sliders open to let the breeze flow through the cracks in the wood slats.

Purposely keeping her back to Kaden, she walked through his kitchen, leaned over the sink to open the window there, then opened the window at the base of the stairs, letting in as much of the late afternoon breeze as was possible while securing their privacy.

Then she turned to him. "Have you figured it out yet?"

He was prone on the bed with the back canted up, reclined on top of the sheets where they had positioned him just a few minutes ago, wearing loose khaki shorts and an unbuttoned short-sleeved shirt. The bandages around his torso moved up and down with the rhythm of his breathing. It was warm, but the breeze that wafted in through the gaps in the barn door and the open windows left it cool enough. He had no use of his hands—his bound wrists gave him only slight mobility with his fingers—and they lay useless at his sides. The ugly gash on his calf was scabbing over.

He didn't answer, just watched her as she moved toward him. They hadn't had much time alone, despite Annie's vigilance at his bedside. For most of her stay thus far, he'd been sleeping, being poked and prodded by the medical staff, or surrounded by others in the room with them. Kaden's mind flashed to how quickly Henri had departed once they got him settled.

They hadn't talked about what happened in San Francisco beyond the few moments when Kaden had first regained consciousness. He still wasn't sure where they stood, although Annie seemed to have forgiven him and had been a loving, concerned, and doting companion for the last several days. He didn't even know how long she was planning to stay.

"What are you about, Annie?" he asked warily.

He was answered with wide, innocent eyes. "Nothing," she breathed. Then smiled. "Well, maybe just this."

She moved toward him then, slow and sensual. As she came forward, she started unbuttoning the placket on her button-up blouse.

He swallowed hard, keeping his gaze riveted on what she was about to reveal. He would not admit how horny he'd been in the hospital. Thank God for loose sheets. He'd been aroused on several occasions just from looking down her blouse as she'd leaned over the bed.

Once she had the buttons undone, she slowly pulled the tails out of her jeans and then shrugged the shirt off her shoulders. She was wearing that lacey pink bra she'd worn on his birthday. Kaden swallowed again and then licked his lips. He didn't need to look down to know what was going on in his shorts. Annie caught the movement and grinned like she'd won a victory.

She stood a few feet from the bed where he had an unencumbered view. Slowly, she unbuttoned her jeans, let down the zipper and shimmied out of them. Her panties matched the bra—equally skimpy, equally mouthwatering.

Kaden wondered how the hell she was planning on accomplishing anything in a hospital bed, when it hit him. He pulled his gaze away from Annie and noticed the bed for the first time. It was huge. Well, not huge, exactly, but not a skinny single mattress like the one he'd had at the hospital. Then he looked back at her and mirrored her seductive smile. *She rented a double bed.*

"Have you figured it out?" Annie saw the understanding dawn in his eyes, followed by a hungry look.

"Promise me you won't let me puncture my lung again," he said hoarsely. He was already breathing heavily, his bindings tightening across his chest, and he could feel the scraping stiffness in his lung.

She crawled up onto the bed toward him, curls dangling around her face, like a silky lioness about to devour her prey.

"Guess you'll just have to give in and not fight it."

Although it went against everything Kaden felt as a man, he knew she was right. He could just sit back and let her give him mind-blowing pleasure that wouldn't last long, or he could blow out his lung trying to ensure her pleasure.

"Don't hold it against me if I don't last long," he warned.

She laughed throatily. "Not a chance. And payback is hell, you know."

"Count on it," he whispered as she straddled him.

Forty-Four

Despite his bravado, Kaden needed plenty of sleep. Annie worried their playtime may have been a mistake, because afterward he slept like he'd slipped back into a coma, and his chest seemed warm and flushed. The only thing that kept her from calling the emergency number was that he kept her pinned to his side while he slept. Beside the fact she couldn't have wriggled free to make the call, no comatose man would do that.

As she rested against his warm body, careful not to poke an elbow in his ribs, she let a little bit of reality slip into her brain. She needed to call her office. She'd left a cryptic message with her secretary—*traumatic accident in the family, flying out of town immediately, will call you when I can*—but she knew that would only be good for so long. And on top of her "I'm sick" stunt on Friday, she wasn't sure what her new boss would think. If John Franklin had still been there, she wouldn't have worried, but she wasn't so confident in his replacement.

Kaden was still sleeping as dawn lit the sky the next morning. Annie managed to pry herself out of his grasp without waking him. She went upstairs to take a shower, pausing to look around when she reached the top step. She'd never actually been up here, but the design was similar to her own loft bedroom. She liked it.

When she came back down, Kaden was still asleep. She frowned and went over to check on him, but his breathing was even and his pulse seemed strong, so she left him alone. It took her awhile to find all the coffee paraphernalia and get a pot going, and by the time she had it gurgling and was searching for a coffee mug, she felt eyes on her. She spun around and saw that Kaden was watching her.

She smiled. "*Bonjour, mon chér.*"

He smiled back lazily and burrowed down a little in the covers. "*Bonjour, ma chérie.* I missed your warmth."

She laughed. "You are an incorrigible patient. And don't even think about it. I thought I'd thrown you into another coma yesterday, or popped your lung again."

He grinned wickedly. "It would have been worth it."

The beep of the coffee machine saved her. She turned back to it and busied herself with pouring herself a cup and searching for cream. "Do you have any milk or cream?" she asked with her head buried in the fridge.

"No, sorry. But Nicole will. She won't mind you taking some. Just go in the back door, but will you pour me a cup first?"

"Sure, but ... how do you plan to, uh ..." She mimicked bringing a cup to her mouth.

He frowned. After a moment's consideration, he shifted the sheet and swung his legs over the side of the bed, wincing at the pain in his chest from the sharp movement. "Just put it there on the counter. I'll figure it out."

After their coffee—an undertaking for Kaden, who had to brace the cup with the fingers of both hands to take a sip—she eased him up the stairs and into the shower. She removed his chest bindings and secured plastic bags around his wrists with rubber bands to keep the bindings from getting wet, essentially rendering him helpless. She ended up stripping back out of her clothes so she could get in the shower with him to wash his body and his hair. It was amusing but serious at the same time. How was he going to do *anything?*

She took delight in making him kneel in front of her as she scrubbed his hair with shampoo and conditioner, massaging his scalp with her fingernails and making him groan against her belly, only to gently smack him away when he started to kiss and nibble on her skin. Then she knelt down with him and spread the shampoo over his chest and shoulders, being careful of his ribs but playfully scrubbing under his arms and his groin. He sucked in a breath, but she just shushed him. "Think of me as that bossy nurse in Bordeaux."

"Impossible, *chérie*."

"Keep your hands up!" She admonished, albeit playfully. An unbidden thought popped into her head. *If she hadn't been here to do this for him, who would have?* She definitely needed to figure out a way to stay longer, because she was damned sure no one else was going to get in the shower with him.

She dried him off, rebound his chest, and helped him into clean clothes, laughing at the selection in his closet. How many pairs of faded khaki cargo shorts can one man own? He was clearly enjoying her ministrations, and he tried everything he could to prolong it. She let him, cherishing the light, playful moments.

He protested when she tried to force him back into the hospital bed. "Annie, be reasonable. I can walk, and I can climb the stairs. I can't breathe well, I can't use my hands, and I have a splitting headache, but I'm not a complete invalid. As much as I enjoyed this bed last night, we don't need it and it's in the way. I promise I'll stay down, but I can do that on the couch."

"You have a headache?" she asked, immediately concerned.

He rolled his eyes. "Yes, right here." He pointed. "Where there is a big lump and a nasty gash."

"Okay, okay, don't be a smart ass. Just promise me you'll tell me when your vision goes double."

The rental company picked up the bed later that morning. Henri helped Annie move the couch back into position when he brought over lunch, and Kaden lay down on it to rest. However, Annie had an idea and whispered it to Henri. In the late afternoon, when the sun was spilling in through the barn door enough to heat the place up but a portion of the patio was shaded by a large tree, Annie coaxed him out of his nap.

"Come with me, love. I have a little surprise for you."

Groggy from sleep, his skin sweaty and heated from the stifling air inside, Kaden allowed her to help him up and lead him out to the patio. Henri was there, smiling widely, standing in front of a brand-new, very cushy chaise lounge set up in the shade.

"You're the best." Kaden mumbled with a smile as he stumbled to the chaise, settled in, and immediately went back to sleep.

Annie gave Henri a grateful look. *"Merci beaucoup, Henri, c'est parfait."*

"J'ai le plaisir, ma petite."

While Kaden napped, Annie used his laptop to access her business email account, finding only a few messages that were important enough to respond to. It was still too early to call the office, but she needed to find time to do so later that evening.

They had not talked about how long she would stay … he hadn't asked and she didn't know herself. But after the shower experience, she felt a rush of protective need to stand by her man. *My man.* He was definitely that. She had almost lost him, but now she would fight like a she-cat to keep him.

She poked around his kitchen to see if she could figure out something to make for dinner. They'd skipped it the previous night, this morning they'd pilfered milk and croissants from Nicole, and then Henri had brought sandwiches for lunch. She needed to get with the domestic program here, but despite her determination, she acknowledged her limitations. While Kaden napped, she marched back across the lawn to the main house for a consult with Henri.

Kaden slept like the dead on his outdoor lounger, not waking until almost eight o'clock, which was fine with Annie because it had taken her that long to get organized in the kitchen. With Henri's help, she had a succulent chicken in the oven and a salad tossed and ready to go with it. She even had a dish of cured olives set out for aperitif to enjoy with rosé, the only useful thing she'd found in Kaden's tiny refrigerator. She'd drawn the line at dessert, settling for cheese and bread.

To her delight, it was the smell of the roasting chicken that eventually woke Kaden. In exchange for Henri's help, and because the Bouviers were working, she invited him to dinner. That was no hardship; he was family and she loved him. Plus, she wasn't ready for any heavy conversations yet, and having Henri around was a good diversion. She just wanted to play house and take care of her man.

Kaden fumbled a bit with the flatware but eventually found a way to brace a fork between the fingers of his left hand and scoop his food onto it with a knife braced in his right. He couldn't cut anything so Henri leaned over his plate and sliced up his food like he would have done for Alex. Kaden quickly became frustrated by his limitations, but Henri and Annie kept him light-hearted about it. Annie bit her lip and watched him from under her lashes. He was so independent; this was going to be a sore trial for him—for them all.

Over the cheese course, Henri forced the issue Annie had been reluctant to bring up. "So, *petite,* how long can you stay to nurse our patient?"

She glanced at Kaden, who was studying the cheese on his plate like it might get up and walk away. "Well, actually …" she hesitated, taking a sip of wine while waiting for some sign from Kaden. She didn't get one. Or maybe, his inability to make eye contact was the message. *Does he want me to stay or doesn't he?* She shrugged. "Actually, that depends on the patient."

That got his attention. "Meaning what, exactly?" How was it that his eyes were every bit as intense and compelling despite the fact that they were ringed with purple-green bruises?

She looked down at her plate. "Meaning I can stay awhile longer if you want me to, and if not, I'll understand, and go home."

"I want you to stay." He didn't even hesitate.

"I'll need to do some laundry."

"I have a machine here."

"Are you sure?"

"I hit my head pretty hard, but I wouldn't forget the washing machine."

She rolled her eyes. "You're such a dolt."

"Please stay, Annie." He reached out and touched her hand with the tips of his fingers. "I need you. And not as my nurse."

Annie's chest tightened, but she was suddenly conscious that Henri was now studying his cheese plate. She laughed. "Henri, don't pretend you're not here. You started this."

Henri looked up in childlike innocence, but his gray eyes were sparkling. "*Ma petite,* whatever do you mean? I just asked a simple question."

She shook her head. "You are as bad as he is; it clearly runs in the family."

Forty-Five

Kaden gained strength and lung capacity every day, and his headaches became less acute, much to Annie's relief. She was terrified about long-term effects of his head injury, but so far, a week since the accident, there was no sign of any problems—at least, none that he admitted. They'd been to the clinic in Sarlat to have his wrists checked and rebound. Now that the swelling had subsided, they could apply permanent casts that he would have to endure for another seven weeks. But there was very little he could do with his hands until the bones in his wrists knitted back together. And because of that, he was helpless as a babe in many things.

They did give him shower mitts to pull over his casts so he could wash himself. "If I can learn to hold a bar of soap with the tips of my fingers." He snorted as he took them.

Satisfied that Kaden was in good and loving hands, Henri took himself back to Rasteau, telling him they would handle the harvest without him, whether he decided to stay in the southwest or come home. He would have teased him more, but Henri sensed how disappointed his nephew was, so he simply assured him that all would be well.

By the evening of the third day out of the hospital, Kaden was feeling restless, tired of napping, and he turned on his computer for the first time since coming home. Annie was puttering in the kitchen, working on something that smelled surprisingly good, humming and looking like she was thoroughly enjoying herself.

She was taking her role as caretaker seriously. It had amused Kaden that his high-powered tax pro toiled in the kitchen for him, but he found it incredibly endearing, too, and didn't want to spoil it by teasing her. Kaden watched her out of the corner of his eye as he logged on to his email account. From the delicious aroma, he guessed she was making some sort of tomato-based sauce, presumably for pasta. He knew Henri had helped her organize some meals and written out a few recipes for her, and if he was not mistaken, it smelled like Henri's marinara sauce.

As his email messages from the last week poured into his inbox, he looked toward his wine rack under the stairs, trying to remember what wine he had at the barn that would go with the pasta. He turned back to the computer screen when he heard the *beep* indicating all messages had been received, then methodically started deleting all the junk. *Christ, there are suddenly so many junk emails coming through.* He made a mental note to look for software to filter out some of it out.

The newest messages were displayed first, those that had come in just after he left San Francisco showed up last. He was almost all the way through them when he noticed one from Annie. He glanced at her then back at the date the email was sent. It was dated Saturday morning before he arrived back home. She'd sent it that Friday night, less than twenty-four hours after he had stormed out of her apartment.

Bloody hell, he thought, not knowing what would be worse: if she had told him to bugger off or if she was sorry. *Like she had anything to be sorry about.* He stared at the address line for a moment. There was nothing in the subject line. He'd have to open the message to know what it was about. He glanced at her again. Her hair was slightly mussed up, cheeks flushed from the heat of the stove, one of his ratty aprons tied around her waist. *God, I love her.* He still couldn't believe she was here. That she had actually left her precious work and flown out to be with him when she heard he was injured. *Especially after what you did to her, you stupid sod.* He felt like a moron. Lower than low.

He took a deep breath, felt the pinch of his ribs, and was glad for the pain, knowing he deserved it. He glanced again at Annie, then clicked on the message, read it. *Bloody, bloody, fucking hell.* She had apologized when it had been completely his damn fault. And her heart was breaking. *Mine was, too,* not that it mattered. He looked at the time stamp on the message again and thought back. He hadn't even thought about checking email when he'd arrived home—he'd been too upset. Would his day have turned out differently if he had seen her message? They'd never know.

He deleted the message, accessed some databases, and did whatever he could to take his mind off her email. She had reached out to him, despite his horrid behavior. She loved him. She said it in the email, she said it at the hospital, and she'd told him more times than he could count since then. And even though he knew he didn't deserve it, he could never hear those words too many times.

The next day, Annie drove Kaden down to La Roque Gageac, his intention to hire some local guys to finish the stables. It was a reunion of sorts with Juliette, who welcomed Annie like family with triple kisses on the cheeks then insisted on hearing all the details of Kaden's accident. The news had made the rounds, and there were crazy exaggerations about the actual facts.

As they sat at the bar nursing a beer, people gravitated to Kaden. It seemed that all the locals knew him. He was friendly to everyone, in a distantly polite way to some and with more outward warmth to others, and as they came and went, he casually inquired of a few of them about their availability. Before long, he had a crew.

"That was an interesting spectacle to watch," Annie commented as she steered the old pickup truck away from La Roque Gageac.

"How so?"

She thought for a minute, digesting her impressions of what she'd witnessed. "You're very politic."

He arched his brows. "Politic?"

"Mhmm. You got the men you wanted, without offending the ones you didn't."

"You noticed that?" He sounded genuinely surprised.

"Of course. That's why I called it politic. You were the consummate politician."

"Humph. And here I thought I was being subtle."

Annie arched a brow, stole a glance at him. "You couldn't have *been* more subtle and still accomplished your goal. All I'm saying is, you were good. I was impressed."

He smiled smugly, reached for her hand and awkwardly held it between his fingers. "Thank you. Coming from a master, that's quite a compliment."

"Charmer," she laughed, focusing on the road.

They were just passing through Beynac when Kaden suddenly said, "Turn here," and pointed to the road that bisected the village. She did so but gave him a curious look as she navigated the narrow lane and continued on up the hill.

"There's a view I want you to see." He smiled at her, lifted her right hand, and brought her fingers to his lips. He might not have had any dexterity in his fingers, and he couldn't put any weight on his wrists, but he could touch things and lift his arms. It was the only thing keeping him sane, especially around Annie.

He directed her into the parking lot at the top, and they got out and walked toward the imposing castle. But rather than going into the main keep or the upper village, Kaden steered her to the left along the cliff's edge. They walked a short distance before the path ended at a lookout point with a bench. Although it was the middle of the afternoon in summer, they were alone for the moment.

It was a spectacular view, straight up the river, with the cliffs of La Roque Gageac and the bastide village of Domme in the distance, and Castelnaud all but hidden in the forest across the river to the right. They stood admiring the view for a moment, watching the never-ending line of canoes floating downriver, before Kaden gently steered her to the bench.

He sat and tried to pull her onto his lap, but she resisted. "Your ribs," she scolded.

"You won't be sitting on my ribs," he said, tugging her down and wrapping his arms around her the best he could. "Just don't lean into me too hard."

She shifted so she was facing him, draping her arms around his neck and studying his face. The swelling was gone and the bruising around his eyes had faded to a mottled olive yellow. Even in his damaged state, he was handsome.

A little rugged looking, perhaps, with the bruises, the unshaven stubble on his jaws, and his shaggy hair. But she couldn't find any little part of him that she didn't love.

Forearm pressed to her back, he tilted her forward and kissed her, gently at first, but then he deepened the kiss and held her tighter. With one arm wrapped around her waist, he moved the other to cradle her head as best he could, wrapping a curl around his useless fingers. When he finally broke the kiss, they were both breathing harder. He leaned his forehead against hers and closed his eyes.

They needed to talk, but he wasn't certain how to proceed. He knew she couldn't stay much longer, but he didn't want to let her go; he needed her in his life. Seeing her when he woke up in the hospital had made it crystal clear to him. She *was* his life. It was an uncomfortably vulnerable place to be, but he wouldn't want it any other way. She had said something similar … her love for him scared her. Well, it scared the hell out of him, too. But that didn't mean he could do without it.

So he had to do something about it. "Annie," he said softly, kissing her cheek.

"Hmm?" Annie was content to stay wrapped in his embrace, letting him brush light kisses on her face.

"Look at me, love." She opened her eyes and looked into his.

"What are you going to do?" His voice was soft and gentle; it held no judgment, no pressure.

She thought about answering with some flip remark, pretending she didn't understand the question, but she sensed he was serious. "I'm not sure." It was an honest answer. She'd been thinking about it all week. Maybe it was time to tell him everything and listen to his perspective. She knew he wanted her here, and she wanted to be here—no doubt about it—but she couldn't reconcile how that would work with her career. She needed his help to her weigh her options.

Moving off his lap, she settled on the bench facing him and took both his bandaged hands in hers, cradling them in her lap. Then she cleared her throat.

"You know what they say about the Chinese character for 'crisis'—that it is a combination of the symbols for 'danger' and 'opportunity.' That may be true, or not, but I find myself at that same sort of crossroads now with my career.

"I've been a partner at Smith Cole for two years, and I've had reasonable success. I have a good team working for me that I've had the satisfaction of training over the years. I've had a good client base that kept me busy and my billings more than respectable. I've made a national name for myself, and I've had the opportunity to put my technical expertise to work in some interesting and creative ways. It's been gratifying and … well, satisfying."

She gazed out over the vista as she spoke, but now she turned to look at him, to gauge his reaction. He watched her intently, focused on her in that way he had, and she knew he was listening, really hearing every word.

She took a deep breath. "But now with Western all but gone, I'm not sure where I stand anymore. It represents—*represented* two-thirds of my work. Western was the reason I made partner. I'll be expected to make up the lost billings, and I'm not sure where that work will come from, or when." With a shake of her head, she looked back at the view. "But frankly, I find myself … uninterested in chasing it."

She paused and looked directly at him. "Kurt Banning offered me a job in Washington."

That sent Kaden's pulse racing, but he controlled his reaction and merely lifted his eyebrows. "Did he, now? Doing what?"

"Working in his firm's national tax office, assisting with their clients all over the country, writing articles, teaching internally, and becoming active on the speaking circuit. I wouldn't have to worry about billable hours or any of that—the local offices would handle it when I assisted, and I'd otherwise be free to … do what I do best. I'd monitor all the regulations and pronouncements and court decisions in my field—part of what I do now anyway—teach and write, and work with the firm's clients when needed."

"It sounds like the perfect job for you." His tone was neutral, even encouraging. She searched his face, trying to figure out what he was really thinking.

"It is. Of course, I'd have to move to DC. But it would encompass all the stuff that I love to do, learning and being creative and all that, and I wouldn't have to worry about the stuff I don't like. The national tax team in any firm is a revered group of professionals. They're generally very well taken care of, allowed leeway to do things that others are not. I know the people in our national office are."

"Why haven't your own people offered you this opportunity? I imagine it would be quite a blow for Smith Cole to lose you to another firm, particularly in that capacity."

She nodded, agreeing with his assessment. "You're right, it would be. They haven't offered because it hasn't occurred to them. Not that they would anyway, but even so, I doubt the partners in our national office knows that we're about to lose Western. Or, if they do, they haven't connected the dots to realize that I'm suddenly very available. Kurt just happened to be in the right place at the right time. He understands exactly what I'm about to face in my practice. To be honest, I think he offered me the job because when Allied takes over all those entities, he'll be the one stuck working on them. It was a self-serving offer, regardless of how flattering it was."

Kaden chuckled at that, thinking her analysis was most likely spot on. "It's what I would have done," he admitted.

When she didn't continue, he asked, "What's the timeframe of the offer?"

She shrugged. "I need to make a decision fairly soon. If I take it, I'd need to make the move in the next couple of months, get settled there by fall."

They said nothing for a time, just sat holding hands, looking at the view.

"You know, Kaden, we had pretty much finished the night you left." She looked at their intertwined hands. "It was why I was so late. You never gave me the chance to explain."

He closed his eyes as he felt his chest constrict, knowing where this was going.

"I ended up taking the next day off, partly because I was exhausted, but mainly because I spent the rest of the night crying." She didn't look at him, but he didn't miss the little catch in her voice. "Your attitude hurt, and your words hurt even more. I know I could have handled the situation better, but I was under more pressure than I've ever been. I needed your understanding and support that week, not your criticism."

Finally she looked at him. "I can't go through that again."

The pain in his eyes when she met his gaze almost made her wish she hadn't said anything.

He swallowed, looked down at their hands, then back at her. "I saw your email yesterday."

Her brows furrowed for a moment, and then he could tell she remembered it. She just nodded.

"You had no reason to apologize to me, Annie. It was my fault, and I have no excuse for how I behaved, or for what I said," he said quietly. "I'm so sorry to have hurt you. I didn't want to, didn't set out to. I didn't intend to leave, but … I just couldn't stay and …"

She waited for him to continue, knowing there was more.

"I have never felt so insecure and vulnerable in my life. I know it's irrational, but it was how I felt at the time. It was selfish and petty of me, and I'm ashamed, but it's the truth."

He extracted one hand from her lap, tipped her chin up with his fingers, and made her look at him. "I love you more than life, Annie, and it scared me. It's the only explanation that I have. I'm so sorry that I hurt you. I wish I could promise that it won't happen again, but I can't. The only thing I can promise is that I won't put myself in that position ever again."

Annie closed her eyes for a moment and sighed softly. "I'm sorry, too, for not making it any easier for you." She lightly caressed his cheek. "I love you more than I ever thought it was possible to love another person. And believe me, it scares me, too. I know you didn't intend to hurt me. But I needed you to know how it felt."

"The pain in my chest from cracked ribs was nothing compared to the pain I felt in my heart as I sat at the airport waiting for my flight home. I was in agony, and knowing that it had been my own doing only made it worse.

"I was thinking about you when I was working on the roof. I was cursing myself for leaving the keys, thinking that if I still had them, I would fly back to San Francisco and wait for you in your apartment. When you came home, I'd rip your clothes off and make love to you until you forgave me. It was the last thought I had before I lost my balance and fell."

She closed her eyes again, feeling his pain.

"When I woke up in the hospital and saw you there, I thought I was dreaming. The fog was pulling me back down, but I had to know if you were real." His voice was so soft, she barely heard him. "You saved me, Annie. Your love saved me. Just like Henri did all those years ago."

"When Henri called, I panicked. I'd been lying in bed thinking that if only I'd told you how much I loved you, maybe you wouldn't have left. When he told me how critical you were, I was so scared that you'd never know, that you'd …" Her voice broke as she hiccupped back a sob.

Kaden gently wiped at the tears that trickled down her cheeks. "Thank you, my beautiful, brave love, for coming to me. I don't deserve you." Her tentative, watery smile was like sunshine to him.

Kaden cleared his throat. "There's another career option you might consider." His tone was cautious.

She shook her head to get her emotions under control. *Get a grip,* she scolded herself, wiping her eyes with the back of her hand. "Which is?"

He hesitated a moment. Shifting a little to face her, he held her hands the best he could. "Will you marry me, Annie?"

She felt her heart thud in her chest. "That's a career option?"

He smiled, but he was serious. "It could be. I want you to be my wife, first and foremost, and live with me here in France. But I also need someone to run the import company, someone who understands how business is conducted in America. I would stay involved and work with you on strategic direction and marketing, but it would be your show to run."

"But I don't know anything about running a company." Although the idea of trying to figure it out was suddenly very appealing to her.

"Of course you do, *chérie.* You essentially run your own company within Smith Cole now. You have staff, a budget, resources to access, and customers. You are responsible for selling business, quoting prices, managing the projects, seeing them to completion, and billing for them. You may not handle all the day-to-day operations, but you manage those that pertain to your part of the business."

"I don't know anything about wine, either."

He could see the wheels turning in her head. She would rise to the challenge if she decided to accept it. And she'd make a brilliant CEO of his fledgling company. It was risky putting his offer of marriage and his offer of a job in the same sentence, but he wasn't sure she would accept one without the other.

"As to the wine, well, you've said you wanted to learn more, and this would be your chance. You can do as much or as little as you want. Grow the company, or keep it small. Or do something entirely different with it. I only started it to have an excuse to come to America to see you."

He gave her another moment, then said, "Annie, I want to marry you whether you take over the company or not. I can always hire someone else for that. You don't have to do anything here if you don't want to. You never have to work another day in your life if you marry me."

She sat up straighter and opened her mouth to protest.

"But …" he held up his hand to silence her. "I know how important it is for you to have something to do, to contribute. I understand, because I feel the same way. I would never have come to live with Henri as his dependent. It doesn't matter that he doesn't see it that way, and I don't see it that way with you either, but I get it."

Watching her, he felt a surge of affection. She was so adorable in her hesitancy. He could tell she was wondering if she'd be able to do it. If she was brave enough to take the leap.

Annie turned toward the stunning vista below them, her mind churning. *What an interesting turn of events.* Six months ago, the thought of leaving Smith Cole had made her anxious and uncertain. She'd known the only way she could ever be with Kaden permanently would be to leave her job, and it had torn her apart. So much of her self-esteem—her sense of self-worth—was wrapped up in her career. It was unthinkable to toss her career out the window for him. She would be insecure and vulnerable, and that would make them both miserable. *Kaden said he felt insecure and vulnerable, and look how he reacted.* It would be no different for her.

As she thought about it, she recognized that it was the impossibility of her situation, coupled with the fear of that overwhelming vulnerability, that had stressed her out so much while Kaden was in San Francisco. She had felt like she'd had to choose between him or her career, that she couldn't have both, and she had resented it. Resented him, resented the firm, and resented the hell out of her demanding client. It was the first time since she'd joined the firm in nearly fourteen years that she'd been angry about the sacrifices her job required.

But now he presented her with an intriguing compromise. She had spent her entire career at Smith Cole, and it was all she knew. But that wasn't entirely true, was it? He was right in that she did, in fact, run her own business within the larger firm. Of course, she relied on a tremendous array of resources, but it wasn't like she didn't know what went on behind the scenes, even when others performed the functions. There was probably quite a lot that she didn't realize she knew. And he would help her—he would never let her fail.

She pictured it in her mind and realized she could approach it like any other new-client situation. Learning about the structure he'd set up and understanding the channels of distribution, understanding who was buying and why, working on the accounts and the financial arrangements, plotting strategies for growth. It didn't have to be a full-time job, either, but would give her purpose and something to take pride in, including earning her keep. Meanwhile, she could work with him in the vineyards, see the full cycle of the seasons, and rejoice in the simple and honest pleasures of working the land and reaping the rewards of harvest. And she could learn French, a necessity if she was going to live in France. Was she really considering this? She was, she realized. And it felt … right.

She turned back to Kaden, who was watching her intently, as if reading her thoughts and uncertainties. "Are you sure?" she asked.

"I've never been so certain of anything in my life. I love you. I want you to be my wife and have my children. I want you to be my partner in life and in business, and I want to keep learning about new things with you until we're old and gray."

Her eyes got misty as she absorbed his words, and a lump formed in her throat. She wanted his children, too. She wanted to spend the rest of her life with him. As tenuous and unpredictable as life was, she wanted what happiness she could have with him for as long as she could have it. His accident had emphatically underscored how precious a gift their love was.

She looked into his eyes and saw the truth of everything he said. The love she had seen shining in his eyes at the hospital was there now, and had always been there, she realized. "Yes, I'll marry you."

The smile that lit up his bruised face was one she would never forget. She laughed as he tried to wrap his cast limbs around her. Climbing back onto his lap, she wrapped her arms around his neck and kissed him with all the love and passion in her heart.

Forty-Six

"Congratulations, *mon fils*. I told you it would work out," Henri said. "Now let me talk to her." Kaden smiled and handed over the phone.

"*Ma petite,* I'm so glad you will join the family. I've never seen my boy as happy as he is with you. Please take care of his heart. It is more fragile than you know."

"I'm beginning to realize that," Annie said seriously. "I promise I'll love him so much, you will never have to worry." She winked at Kaden, then told Henri she wasn't sure when she would be coming back for good but promised it would be soon.

As Kaden called Nicole at the restaurant to book a table for them that night, Annie watched him and marveled at the incredible amount of love he had in him. Love for his family, love for the land, and love for her. Just two years before, she hadn't even considered letting someone into her life, much less into her heart. Meeting Kaden had changed her life, and now she would be his wife.

The decision had been surprisingly easy. His proposal of marriage had not been completely unexpected—she knew all too well what a near-death experience can do for one's resolve. But his proposal for her to take over his company had been brilliant; it was just the sort of challenge she lived for. And he had found a way to tie the one thing that addressed her biggest concern in to his marriage proposal.

"Are you serious?" Annie's brother was dumbfounded as she broke the news to him the next day.

"Adam, of course I'm serious." Annie tried to keep the defensiveness out of her voice.

"Wow, okay. I didn't mean to sound negative—I'm just surprised is all. How long have you known him?"

Annie sighed. She loved her brother dearly, but he didn't exactly keep track of the details of her life. "We met two years ago, and since then we've communicated almost every day in one form or another. I think I know him better than anyone I've ever met. I certainly know him better than I knew Jack when I married him. I've met his family, Adam, really spent time with them, and I feel welcomed and accepted by them."

Adam understood what she was saying, since Jack's family had been exactly the opposite. He was still outraged at the behavior of Annie's former mother-in-law. "But what will you do for work?" He also knew how fiercely independent his sister was. "Don't sell yourself short, Annie. Good work isn't going to be easy to get for someone who doesn't speak the language."

She laughed at that. "You're right, of course, but in my case, that's not an issue." Then she explained about the import company and her new job responsibilities, and laughed again as his attitude swung from skeptical to awe.

"Who is this guy, Annie? I mean, I knew he was rich, but this sounds like another league entirely."

"He's been very successful, no question, and money is certainly no concern here, but that's not the point, and it has nothing to do with why I'm marrying him. He's the most amazing, intelligent, caring man I've ever met. And he loves me like I thought I would never be loved again. This is right for me, Adam, I know it is. *He's* right for me."

After extracting a promise that he would come to France for her wedding, she bade him goodbye.

Her next call was a little more to her liking.

"Oh, Annie, I'm so happy for you." Marie sounded like she was going to cry. Annie had given her the romantic version, including a short recount of Kaden's San Francisco visit and all that had transpired since.

"Will you promise to come to our wedding? It'll be here in France, probably in Rasteau around the end of the year. We haven't made any plans yet."

"We wouldn't miss it. We'll use it as an excuse to take an extended trip to Europe. John promised he'd take me back to Paris."

The friends chatted some more, Marie filling her in on the happenings with her boys and how much John was enjoying his retirement. She promised to have John call her when he came home.

Her last call, to her only other real friend, wasn't as bad as she had feared, but it made her consider something she'd rather not think about.

"Wow! Congratulations," Lori Sheridan said, the words inconsistent with the disappointment coloring her voice.

Annie picked up on it. "Before you think I've thrown in the towel, there are a few details you need to know." She explained about her lost client, the job offer in DC, Kaden's accident, and finally, the import company.

"He wants you to become president of his wine import company? Actually run the business?" This time, Lori's voice held astonishment. "Do you know anything at all about wine?"

"Not much," Annie conceded. "But you know me, I'm a quick study. I wasn't sure about it either, until Kaden pointed out that I already run my own company-within-a-company at Smith Cole. If you think about it, he's right."

"I suppose that's true—I've never thought about it that way. It does sound like a fantastic challenge for you, and one you can put your whole heart into. A perfect solution, really, and I'm happy for you, but Annie …"

Annie heard the hesitation and concern, and waited to hear what her friend would say.

"Tell me more about Kaden's head injury."

She explained all they knew, that the scans had shown a bit of swelling, accounting for his continued headaches and sensitivity to bright light, but nothing weird in brain wave patterns. Not that a machine would necessarily pick up on that sort of thing …

"How sure are you that he'll make a complete recovery? That he'll, you know, be the same?"

Annie frowned. Kaden seemed fine, no different than before, but that didn't mean something couldn't still go wrong. "I don't know, not absolutely. But I have to believe he will."

"But what if he doesn't? I know you love him now, but are you prepared to deal with a possible long-term brain injury?"

"God, Lori, I can't think like that. I have to believe … I have to believe that whatever happens, our love will never falter. Isn't that what wedding vows are all about? For better or worse? Would you be asking me that question if his accident happened after we were already married? As if my feelings would change if he slurred his words or couldn't add up a column of numbers? Inside, he's still the same man."

Rather than belabor the point, Lori accepted Annie's resolve, and with a promise to come for the wedding, they ended the call. But Annie leaned back in her chair for long minutes afterward, thinking about what her friend had said.

In an effort to shake the chilly fear from her heart that Lori's blunt words had left there, she looked at the computer, all the wires connecting it with the printer and modem and other devices she had no idea about, idly tracing the cords with her eyes until they ended at the wall socket. She frowned. Would she be able to use her own computer here? Was it as simple as using a power converter, or was there some other limitation? That possibility hadn't occurred to her. She reached for her pad of notes and added it to the *Questions for Kaden* sheet, and forced her mind back to those things she could control.

───────◆◆───────

Annie was out of culinary tricks. Over a dinner of *steak frites* in the village, she and Kaden talked through the items on her list. The reality of what she faced became more daunting as they addressed the practical details. Kaden assured her that obtaining a temporary resident permit would not be a problem, and as soon as they were married, she would apply for a permanent one. As a French citizen himself—he held dual citizenship with the UK—it would be just a matter of administrative nuisance. Same with health insurance, bank accounts, and so forth. He promised to get the process rolling while she was gone.

As for her apartment, they agreed it was a good idea to keep it as an investment. The jeep was another story. "I know you're attached to it," he said, "but the cost of shipping it would well exceed its value. I'll buy you a new car, or an older one if you prefer, but something that runs on diesel. Regular petrol is three times the price in Europe as it is in America."

"Really? Why?" Annie had no idea about the price of fuel in France. She hadn't paid any attention when she had rented her car two years ago.

Kaden shrugged. "Lots of reasons, demand mostly, plus lots of extra taxes here."

"Well, I guess you have a point. The jeep is pretty old, but it's in decent shape so I shouldn't have trouble selling it. But I'll buy my own car once I get here. You don't need to buy one for me." She said it matter-of-factly as she glanced down at her list.

He watched her for a moment and then put his fork down. Reaching across the table, he rested his bound-up wrist on the table and set his fingers on her paper. She looked at them, and he rolled his wrist over over and motioned with his fingers. She reached to them and looked up at him.

His voice was gentle, and his eyes were soft. "You're going to be my wife, Annie. Everything I have will become yours the day we marry. If I want to buy you a pot of flowers, or a lacy negligee, or a car, you have to let me do it."

She opened her mouth to protest, but instead, she cleared her throat, looked down at their linked hands on the table, and smiled. Meeting his eyes again, she marveled for the hundredth time how warm they were, how much love was there.

She surrendered. "Flowers and lingerie will always be a welcome surprise, but if you insist on buying me a car, will you please at least wait for me so I can pick it out?"

He leaned over the table and lightly nipped at the tips of her fingers that he tugged toward him. "Agreed. But can I select your computer? I know more about them than you do."

"Ah." She laughed. "I guess that answers that question." She drew a line through *computer* on her list. "I take it I shouldn't try to pack mine?"

"No, it's too bulky, and it's already obsolete. Sell it if you can, but make sure you erase your hard drive first. I'll get you all set up."

"Where will I be working?" It was the next item on her list.

"We'll squeeze together in my office for now. Longer term, we'll break through the upstairs hallway and connect the first bedroom to our wing and rearrange it as an office for you. It has good light and a nice view. Henri and I have already talked about it."

"You have? When?"

Kaden gave her a sheepish look. "We talked about it a few months ago, right after you left." She raised her eyebrows, but he just shrugged. "A man can hope, and sometimes his dream comes true."

After dinner, they walked down to the river, enjoying the cool breeze coming off the water. Annie was leaving in a few days, and now that her plans were set, she was anxious to get the wheels in motion. She fretted a little, her mind already buried in the details, but Kaden just pulled her into his arms and told her he would do anything she needed him to, as long as she didn't change her mind.

He stood in the same position with his arms around her again three days later, in the early morning at the Bordeaux train station. "Call me when you get home, *chérie,* no matter the time."

"I will." They were oblivious to the people around them. When the train glided into the station, he kissed her softly, not wanting to let her go.

"I love you," he whispered into her ear before kissing her there.

"I love you, too. Don't fall off any more roofs, okay? At least not until I get back." She stepped onto the train with her bag and smiled at him from the door until the train moved out.

Kaden watched the train disappear down the tracks until it turned around a bend. Outside the station, he hailed a cab and headed for the hospital. He needed to speak with the brain trauma specialist there to clarify the meaning of some lingering symptoms that he'd kept to himself. And he needed to have his medical records transferred to the hospital in Orange, where he would eventually have his casts removed. He wasn't planning on lingering in the southwest any longer than necessary.

He thought about how things had worked out. He and Annie would have eventually repaired their rift; her tentative email to him, reaching out in her pain, was testament to that. If he had seen it that morning, he would have called her immediately, begged for her forgiveness, a second chance, a way back, anything. But how long would it have taken him to ask for her hand? What if she had accepted the job with Banning? There was only one thing he knew for sure—he would never let her regret her decision.

Forty-Seven

Rasteau, France, September 1990

Annie stood beside the scale outside the cellar door, clipboard in hand, waiting for Edouard to position the bin of grapes onto it. He let it down gently, backed up the forklift, waited for her to record the weight, and then scooped the bin back up and wheeled it away to the crushpad. The morning air was chilly, and she was grateful for her snappy red fingerless gloves.

Harvest had just begun—Kaden hadn't missed it after all—and the vineyards were hopping with activity. Everyone who was able was enlisted to assist in some fashion, and Annie wasn't about to be left out. Henri and Kaden had insisted she stay out of the vineyards, which was fine with her since the business of picking the grapes looked like backbreaking work, and there was plenty to do elsewhere.

Kaden had convinced a doctor in Orange to remove his casts, replacing them with smaller braces that allowed him the use of his hands, but he was admonished to stay away from heavy lifting of any kind. As a consequence, instead of being in the vineyards with the picking crew, he commandeered the crushpad, overseeing the work there and organizing the fermentation logs for each tank. Annie's weight records were among the first pieces of information to go into the logs and were used to make all the calculations for monitoring and making any additions.

The plan this year was to avoid all additions, including the inoculation of yeast to start fermentation. Other than a minimal amount of sulfur dioxide, or SO_2, which was essential to prevent the growth of unwanted bacteria, Kaden hoped their vineyard management plans would pay off and allow for natural fermentation to take its course all the way to the end. They would carefully monitor it along the way to ensure everything went the way they wanted.

Once all the bins from the day's harvest were in and weighed, the laborious job of sorting began. Annie thought pruning was hard on her back, but this was worse. The bins were emptied onto one end of a long sorting table, essentially a conveyer belt, set up in front of a ladder conveyer that carried the clusters of grapes up into a destemmer. The berries were pulled from the stems and dropped through rollers that lightly crushed them. The crushed berries and juice were captured beneath and pumped into tanks inside the winery.

The purpose of the sorting table was to allow the crew to inspect the clusters and remove any portion of them that had rot, bird damage, or excessively dry berries. Annie caught on quickly, and she and Kaden worked side-by-side along with Henri, Edouard, and a couple of others that Henri brought on for the harvest. Kaden kept popping grapes in his mouth, but when she teased him about eating up the harvest, he insisted it was the best way to gauge the consistent ripeness of the grapes.

It was controlled chaos on the crushpad, with a lot of activities going on at once, and except for a few minutes' break between bins, there was very little downtime as bin after bin of grapes was dumped out on the sorting table. There was no relief for her back. After a short lunch break, when Annie laid herself over a barrel to stretch it out, Kaden found her a short stool that she positioned under the table to keep one foot propped up on.

Annie was impressed at how everyone seemed to know exactly what needed doing and when. Kaden would disappear from the sorting table each time a tank was filled, to add the SO2, log the calculations, and label each tank. The other workers would systematically take the empty bins and wash them out with a pressure hose, scrubbing them clean and stacking them out of the way. Edouard and Henri took turns keeping the bins positioned with the forklift while they were emptied on the sorting table, then would jump back into the fray as the clusters rolled down the table.

By the end of the first day, Annie was exhausted but exhilarated. She'd never experienced anything like it, never even imagined such a world as this existed, and as much as her body ached, she was anxious to do it all over again tomorrow.

When Kaden and Henri headed back out to the winery after dinner, she followed along to see what they were up to. She learned that for each tank of crushed grapes, or must, several key measurements needed to be taken, including temperature and *baume,* which measures the density of the must and indicates its sugar level. They hadn't yet taken the initial measurements because the must needed to settle and absorb the SO2, but now it had to be done.

Kaden handed her a sheaf of papers and showed her how to read each sheet as it corresponded to a particular tank and where to record the data. She saw that there was already quite a bit of data recorded for each tank, from date of harvest, grape variety, and vineyard location or block, to weight of the grapes prior to crush and SO2 amounts added, and she began to understand the importance of such intense recordkeeping. The men then proceeded to go down the rows of tanks and bins they'd filled—two five-thousand-liter tanks and four one-ton bins of three-hundred-liter capacity from that day alone. No wonder her back was killing her!

They drew samples from each tank from a spout into a long, wide beaker, then took readings with a hydrometer, dumping the samples into one of the nearby bins afterward. Each tank had a thermostat on a panel of other dials, and she recorded the temperature for each as well. For the bins, it was a messier process ... they had to burrow the beaker into the must, holding it down while it filled. Henri did the honors because of Kaden's braces, and he ended up with wet, purple forearms.

Once fermentation began, they would take measurements twice daily, in the morning and in the afternoon, and at Annie's request, Kaden assigned her the job. He showed her how to use the equipment, how to clean it, and where it was stored. He warned her that each day as more tanks were filled, it would become an increasingly bigger job, but she just smiled.

He also explained to her what to expect during fermentation, including the fact that a significant amount of carbon dioxide—CO2—would be produced, cautioning her to keep the doors open and the fans going while working inside the barn.

"I'll be fine," she said dismissively, then was shocked when he took her by the shoulders and looked at her sternly.

"Annie, I didn't finally get you here only to lose you to asphyxiation. You must be careful and aware at all times in here during fermentation. Never underestimate the danger of CO2 accumulation."

Eyes wide with surprise, she could only nod as she stole a glance at the big fans at the end of the barn. "I had no idea."

"Many don't, and that's when accidents occur." He squeezed her shoulders and kissed her forehead before letting her go.

"When will fermentation start?" she asked, curious as to the whole process but also wanting to lighten the mood.

Henri and Kaden exchanged glances. Henri shrugged and said, "Perhaps tomorrow, perhaps in another day or two. We are experimenting this year with native yeast, to see if we can complete fermentation without inoculating the must with cultured yeast from another source. Monitoring the tanks will be very important to know if our experiment is working."

"Remember I told you about some changes we've made this year?" Kaden asked. "This is part of it. If it works, and we believe it will, it should give a level of purity to our wine that we haven't had before."

Annie nodded, intrigued. "And you can tell just from these two data points?"

Henri smiled widely at Kaden and clapped him on the back. "She is just like you, *mon fils*. Curious and not satisfied with short answers." Turning to Annie, he explained there were a few more tests they would do daily, once fermentation started. "I think you may be fighting Kaden for lab time, *petite*. He likes to monitor everything!"

They all laughed, and Kaden acknowledged it was true. Then he took her arm and walked her back to the lab. "I'll make sure you know what we're doing and why. But for now, let's get to bed. We have many more days like today ahead of us. We won't need to do anything more than these two measures for a few more days."

Forty-Eight

It was a very good harvest—the fruit came in steadily, at consistent levels of ripeness, and the days rolled into weeks of the same daily grind of harvest, sorting, getting the must into tanks or bins, then documenting what they'd done and organizing the paperwork. Annie kept neat records of everything she was charged with.

By the end of the first week, fermentation had started in the tanks and bins they'd filled so far, which was about half the cellar. Annie got excited, thinking Kaden's experiment a success, but Kaden reserved judgment.

"Getting it to start is one thing—keeping it going is another. But it looks good so far." As he checked progress, Annie trailed behind him with her clipboard, recording bits of data as they went down the line of tanks and bins. The CO_2 generated during fermentation pushed the berries to the top, creating a cap that rose up like a soufflé.

"In order to maximize the extraction of color, flavor, and tannins," Kaden said, "we want to keep the skins in contact with the juice as much as possible. We do this by either pushing the berries back down into the must—we call it punch down—or by pumping the juice over the cap. For the tanks, we use a pump system. For the bins, we punch down manually."

He grinned as he reached for a tool that looked like a giant potato masher. "Care to give it a go?"

Annie set down her clipboard and followed him over to the chest-high square bins that took up one side of the cellar, across from the large tanks. Laughing, she struggled with the odd tool as she used it to push the stiff berries on top down into the liquid. It was tough going, as the must was dense.

"It gets easier as fermentation progresses," Kaden assured her. Together they punched down all ten bins, a task that took over an hour.

"Wow, that's quite a workout," Annie said, shaking out her arms as she followed Kaden outside, where they carefully washed off the tools before returning them to their rightful place on the rack.

Next Kaden showed her how to work the pump-over machines for each tank and added the schedule she should follow to each log.

The following afternoon, Annie got firsthand experience with the hazards of CO2. She and Kaden went together to the barn, pulling the doors wide open as they walked in. Kaden flipped on the switch for the fans and headed for the lab while Annie grabbed her clipboard.

"I'll get the pumps started and then do the punchdowns," she said.

Kaden smiled at her confidence. "I've got some samples to test, but I'll give you a hand with the bins when I'm finished."

Annie had completed punching down two bins before taking a break to stretch her back and check on the pumps. She climbed up onto the catwalk and carefully leaned over the rail at each tank to see how it was going. When she got to the end of the row, she saw that the last pump had stalled. Instead of bothering Kaden with it, she turned it off, unplugged it from the power source, and then leaned over the opening to see what the problem was. Like she had any clue! But she was determined to at least try to figure it out, so she pulled the lever that brought the mechanism up out of the tank and started fiddling around with it.

It was awkward, because even though the pump was above the tank opening, she still had to stretch out over the railing to reach it. Hooking her foot around a post for balance, she disconnected the long arms one by one, checking the opening of each arm and the opening of the pump where each one fitted. The pumps had four arms, and it was the last one where she found the problem. There was a blockage of some kind, and when she finally wedged it out of the pump fitting, she held up a wine-soaked piece of wood that looked like a broken-off piece of mature vine wood. *Huh. How did this get in there?*

The process had taken her about thirty minutes of hovering over the tank opening, and as she pulled herself back up to reconnect the power, a wave of dizziness hit her. She grasped the rail to keep from pitching forward and sank to her knees. She managed to prop her shoulder against a post before she blacked out.

Finished with his testing, Kaden came out of the lab and immediately felt the sharp sensation of accumulated CO_2. His gaze flew to the doors and saw they were closed at the same time he realized the fans had been shut off. *Fuck!* He looked around frantically for Annie as he rushed to slide the doors open and flip the fans back on.

"Annie!" he called. "Annie, are you in here?"

Nothing. He raced back down the line of tanks, looking in between them and the bins, calling her name. He finally looked up and cursed when he spotted Annie's slumped figure up on the catwalk.

"Annie! Bloody hell." He scrambled up the ladder, grabbed her under her arms and hauled her down. He carried her outside then sank down onto his knees in the grass beyond the crushpad, cradling her with one arm while gently patting her cheeks to wake her up. Her eyelids fluttered as she took in a deep breath, her confusion clearing when she saw the fear in Kaden's eyes.

But that fear quickly turned to anger now that she was out of danger. "God damn it, Annie, I told you to keep the doors open. And why the hell did you turn off the fans? If you can't follow one simple rule, I won't let you back in the barn."

Annie pinched her brows together, stung by his words. "I ... but ... they were ... you ... we opened them." Tears threatened at the uncompromising glare he focused on her. "I didn't close them, I swear it. And I didn't turn off the fans ..." She sounded confused. "Why would I?"

He closed his eyes and held her close, kissed her forehead and rocked her a moment as he pulled himself back from the edge of panic. "Okay, love, I believe you. You're okay now," he said soothingly. He listened to her explanation about the stuck pump and her effort to fix it, but his emotions were raging. Someone had purposely shut off the fans and closed the doors behind them while she was distracted with the pump. There was no other explanation, but that didn't mean it made any sense. Who would do such a thing without first ensuring there was no one inside?

The smaller bins needed to be punched down three times daily, including late at night. For two weeks straight, Annie and Kaden got out of bed in the middle of the night, dragged on warm clothes, and went down to the cellar to spend an hour getting it done. It was normally a mundane exercise, but after that scare with the barn doors—Kaden had confronted Henri and Edouard, but both men denied any knowledge of it—Kaden kept his senses on high alert.

For her part, Annie had the oddest feeling that they were being watched during these nightly excursions. She never saw anything unusual, but the hair on the back of her neck tingled as they walked down the path from the house. Tonight, as she threw her strength into churning up the must in the bin she was working on, she heard a scuffling noise and glanced up at the open door. At that moment, a gust of wind blew in with a swirl of dust, causing it to rock slightly. She glanced over at Kaden who was muscling his own bin into submission farther back in the cellar, undisturbed. She shrugged and went back to her task.

In the woods beyond the barn, Monique cursed her clumsiness as she scurried away. She'd been pressed against the door, spying on the two inside, when something in the night startled her, causing her to jerk and bump the door.

She followed a path through the woods that she knew by heart, even in the faint light of the waning moon, as she had walked it regularly, night and day, for most of her life. Tonight, and every night for the past weeks, she'd watched Kaden and his girlfriend—*fiancé,* she corrected herself bitterly—work in the barn while her anger and jealousy intensified. *Who does that skinny bitch think she is?* Monique grumbled as she made her way to the edge of the trees that bordered her mother's property.

In Monique's wild imagination, Kaden's inattention to her all these years had been nothing more than typical male arrogance. She was sure that he would eventually admit he desired her. She convinced herself that he had brought the snooty American to the house back in the spring to make *her* jealous. That was why she had waltzed into his bedroom that morning after the woman had arrived, to show him she wasn't fazed by his flaunting another woman.

She had been greatly surprised by his vicious verbal attack on her afterward, and she was truly frightened and perplexed by his threat to expose her. It never occurred to Monique that Kaden had no interest in her. With her voluptuous body and smoldering gray eyes, men found her seductive routine irresistible. She had been hurt and upset at the time, but now she was just mad.

"Well?" The croaking hiss was unmistakable.

Monique nearly jumped out of her skin before her heart stuttered in alarm. "Georges! You scared me. What are you doing here?" Another mistake on her part, she had realized way too late, was telling the creepy Georges anything about the neighbors. Impatient with her failures to find him anything useful on the few opportunities she'd had to snoop in Kaden's office—even the numbers she'd found taped inside his drawer had been a dead end—he was getting more abusive, making no effort to be charming to her like he had been in the beginning.

He grabbed her arm in a bruising grip. "What did you find out?"

Monique gasped. "You're hurting me! Let go!" She tried to wrench her arm away, but he squeezed tighter. "Stop it! What do you want?" Tears sprang into her eyes from the biting pain.

"I want to know what you see and hear when you go down and spy on them every night." Even in the moonlight he could see the shock on her face. "You think I don't know what you do? You're obsessed with him."

"I am not," she whined, unconvincing even to herself. "And I haven't learned anything. They don't talk about anything … ah, anything that would interest you."

"I thought we agreed to do this together, *ma petite pute connivance.* What do they talk about?"

Monique winced at the insult, but at least the words didn't leave a bruise, unlike the iron grip he had on her arm. "He explains the wine-making process. They talk about an import company. They talk about …"

"About what?" He jerked her around and put his face so close to hers, she could smell his foul breath. "Tell me."

"About their wedding! Nothing else." She jerked hard on her arm and he let her go, but she had no illusion that she had escaped him.

"Ah," he goaded. *Ma petite pute est jaloux.*

"I am not jealous, I'm pissed off. He is no better than you, and he will regret that he rejected me." She'd initially balked at helping Georges in his scheme to infiltrate the house to gain uninterrupted time at Kaden's computer. But now, after watching the two lovers working side-by-side in mutual bliss for the last two weeks, her simmering anger and frustration boiled over.

"I want to hurt them," she said, almost to herself. "I want to see them both in pain. Even without the payoff."

"Ah," Georges's silky voice penetrated her. "Good, very good, *petite*. And I have a plan."

The next step in the wine-making process, once fermentation was near completion, was the separation of the juice from the skins. This effort required lots of heavy lifting. The free juice could be drained from the tanks easily enough, but that left the juice-laden skins at the bottom of each tank. These had to be shoveled out and transferred to the big press. It was another job that required a strong back, and it was a slow process, since they had only one large press, and each pressing took a couple of hours. Kaden and Henri were on hand during the entire process, tasting the juice at various stages to determine when they'd pressed enough. Annie joined in, tasting along with them and listening to their evaluations.

"Too much extraction from the skins and seeds can make the wine taste bitter," Henri explained when she asked what they were looking for as they tasted. "We want good structure, with the right level of tannins, but not so much that it tastes harsh."

Is there no end to what I need to learn? Annie kept the thought to herself.

Once pressed, the juice flowed underground to the lower section of the cellar, into large wood casks and barrels for further aging. They then had the job of cleaning out the stainless steel tanks to ready them for the bottling process that would take place the following spring.

There was a whole new set of tests and measurements to take once the juice was pressed and in its new vessel, and Annie and Kaden spent a good deal of time in the lab. Overall, Kaden was more than satisfied with the results, and he and Henri spent many hours discussing the potential of this vintage and what it meant for the future.

By the end of October, all the wine was resting in tank, cask, or barrel. The malolactic conversion process was still underway, but they had completed the first racking, which was essentially pumping the juice off the dead yeast cells and other scum that built up on the bottom of the casks and barrels as the solids settled out of the liquid. There was little to do but monitor its progress. They had gone from daily measurements and tests to weekly, and Annie finally had an opportunity to turn her thoughts to her new career as CEO of Macallister Imports.

It was Henri who broached the subject that was foremost in Kaden's mind. The three of them sat in the main parlor of the farmhouse after dinner, in front of a roaring fire as a steady rain drummed on the roof. Annie and Kaden snuggled together on the couch while Henri stoked the fire.

"Now that the work is mostly finished for the winter, my dear, when will you make an honest man of my boy, hmm?" He was as direct as Kaden, and Annie wondered who learned it from whom.

Kaden looked at her with raised eyebrows. "Tomorrow wouldn't be too soon for me, but I think Annie probably wants a little more time to invite her friends."

Annie smiled. "I don't need much time for myself, but I have no idea how to organize a wedding in France."

"The civil ceremony will take place at the local Mairie, what you would call City Hall," Henri said. "It will be performed by the mayor here in Rasteau. There are notice requirements, and you must have all your documents ready before you can make the application. If you want a church wedding, it's purely ceremonial and would take place after the civil ceremony. Do you wish to have a church wedding, *petite?*"

Annie looked at Kaden to judge his reaction. "No, as long as it won't offend either of you. The church has never been a part of my life."

"Mine either," Kaden said. "As long as you say *oui,* nothing else matters. However, there is a matter of a wedding ring. We need to pick one out for you. I would have done it already, but I thought you might want a say in it."

Annie leaned up and kissed his chin. He was learning.

They agreed on a date at the end of November, pending the confirmation that Annie's brother and friends could all make it. Henri took responsibility for making the arrangements at the Mairie and asked to have the celebration afterward at the farmhouse, with Sophia helping with the cooking. It would be a relatively small party of Annie's guests, Jean Claude and the family contingent from the southwest, François and Juliette, perhaps Kaden's brothers—"If they can spare the time," Kaden mumbled under his breath—and a few of the local neighbors.

Later that night as she lay in bed, secure and warm in Kaden's embrace, Annie considered how completely her life had changed. She'd been in France for almost two months, and during that time she'd worked long hours as she normally did, but the difference in how she felt was palpable. She hadn't been to a gym in months but felt healthier, stronger, and more connected to her work than any other time in her life. For the most part, her days were not intellectually challenging, but finesse and attention was required at all stages. And the end product! Not just a bunch of legal concepts on paper, but a real, tangible, quality product that could be sold and consumed. Something real to hold in her hand (or her glass) and take pride in. Something that gave people pleasure.

She loved working alongside Kaden, loved watching him work, watching him think, watching his expressions as he contemplated the wine. And she loved being a part of what he loved. He included her in everything he did, talked to her as he worked so she understood his reasoning, and he trusted her implicitly, handing over many of the complex lab processes. It had been a fascinating education as well as a satisfying and fulfilling experience. She looked forward to many years of more of the same.

Annie thought back to her visit in May—only five months ago—and remembered her impressions of the people. She remembered how content and grounded they all seemed, and her own feelings of envy at the simple pleasure and satisfaction they took from their work on the land. Now she shared that pleasure and satisfaction. It surprised her that she could feel so comfortable—and satisfied—with such manual labor. She didn't miss her corporate world at all. In fact, she had hardly thought about her old life in the frenzy of all the winery work.

Despite the long hours of harvest and wine making, Kaden still managed to find an hour or two each day to keep tabs on his other business interests. Annie looked forward to becoming involved there, to learning the import business and getting started with it, but interestingly, it didn't make her anxious; she wasn't consumed by a desire to get going simply to prove her worth. More accurately, she looked at it as an extension of what they'd been doing for the last two months. Annie wondered if Kaden had known she would feel that way. They had so easily adjusted to working together, thinking through problems and reaching conclusions. But then, she realized, they'd been doing it by email for the past two years.

For so long, Annie's self-esteem, her feeling of self-worth, had been tied to her achievements at Smith Cole Blakely. Now she realized that none of that had really mattered, and as much as her ego had been wrapped up in her career, none of it defined who she was. She had always thought of her work as important, but it paled in comparison to the immovable reality of working the land, producing an honest product, and living with the challenges and consequences of whatever the vagaries of weather threw at you.

It had taken Kaden to shake her from her world. It was what he had tried to tell her in San Francisco that awful night. And it had taken two months of farm work for Annie to finally understand what he meant. She was free. She was free to take each day at a time, free to love her man and take care of him and their family.

That last thought made her smile. She wanted a family—she wanted children with him. Her hand wandered down to her belly, lightly rubbing the tightness she felt there. It was too early to show yet, but Annie was certain she was pregnant. She had gone off the pill the day she left San Francisco for good, and she had missed her last period. They had made love almost every night since she arrived back in France, and although she hadn't had any tests yet, she knew her body. She needed to tell Kaden soon—it was too exciting to keep to herself any longer, but she wanted to wait until the stress of harvest and wine making was done for the year. He would become overbearing in his attempt to ensure her comfort, and she hadn't wanted to distract either him or Henri.

Annie shifted so that the front of her body was pressed against Kaden's side, laid her head on his shoulder, and wrapped her arm around his waist, hugging him. She thought he was asleep until she felt his palm smooth up her arm to her shoulder, then back down. She looked up to find him watching her.

"Why are you awake, *chérie?*" His voice was soft and grainy with sleep.

"Just thinking." She smiled at him, then reached up and smoothed the unruly hair from his forehead. He raised his brow slightly, and she pressed a kiss onto his shoulder to reassure him. "Thinking about how wonderful it is here, how different it is from anything I ever imagined, and how much I love you."

He pulled her close and kissed the top of her head, breathing into her hair. "I love you so much." He kissed her there again. "I love watching you work, watching you think, seeing your pleasure at new discoveries. I've dreamed of having you here. I've longed for it since the first harvest after we met. I knew you would fit in, and I hoped you would come to love it as I do."

"You had more faith in me than I had in myself."

"Perhaps." He shifted so he faced her, their bodies close. He stroked her from knee to shoulder, kissing her forehead, then her nose. "But you forget, *ma chérie,* I know what a passionate woman you are." He kissed her cheek, rubbing his nose against hers. "Not just with me." He planted more kisses on her cheek. "But in everything you do."

Leaning in, he kissed her deeply, pulling her body into his and stroking her back. His sensual touch sent her pulse racing, and their kisses became more heated. She wrapped her leg around his and pulled her hips to his. They loved slowly in the dark of night, touching and caressing and building their passion until they could wait no longer. Joined together in blissful pleasure, they rode out the storm entwined in a lovers' embrace.

Simple lives, very *rich rewards.* It was the last thought in Annie's mind as she drifted off to a sated sleep.

Forty-Nine

"*Où est le camion?*" Kaden asked, surprised to find Henri leaned over a pot at the stove the next evening as he stepped through the kitchen door. He assumed his uncle was out when he didn't see the old battered truck in its usual place behind the house.

"Sophia needed it to deliver her olives to the press. She finished harvesting this afternoon. She'll bring it back in the morning with the croissants."

Kaden chuckled. Henri had a weakness for the croissants from the *boulangerie* in the village, and Sophia knew it. Whenever she needed a favor from him, her payment was a personal delivery of the buttery treats.

As he crossed the room toward the hallway, Henri stopped him. "Dinner will be ready in about an hour. I think Annie is taking a nap. She seemed exhausted this afternoon. I hope there is nothing wrong." His tone was casual, but Kaden recognized the concern in his old eyes and frowned.

"She hasn't said anything to me, but that doesn't mean anything. She never freely admits to any weakness. I'll keep an eye on her," he promised as he headed down the hall.

Kaden found Annie stretched out on the sofa in front of the fireplace in their sitting room, a book open on her stomach, eyes closed and breath steadily. He knelt beside the sofa and studied her face, relaxed in slumber. He saw dark smudges under her eyes and became alarmed. *Merde!* Why hadn't he noticed those before?

Unable to stop himself, Kaden traced her cheek with his fingertips and leaned over to plant a soft kiss at her temple. She stirred and opened sleepy eyes to meet his gaze. He studied her face as he ran his fingers down her cheek and under her jaw.

"Henri said you were napping. Are you okay? You look so tired, *chérie*." He touched his lips to her forehead. "Perhaps you should stay inside tonight and get some sleep. I can handle the lab work on my own. It's not that critical, anyway, just some analysis I want to do."

Annie stretched sleepily and sat up. "I'm fine. I've just been tired lately. It's probably all the exercise and clean air." She needed to tell him the truth, but she wanted it to be special, and she had a plan. Staying inside tonight was not part of it.

Kaden looked unconvinced but didn't argue. He'd watch her more carefully, he told himself. He pulled the cozy throw from the back of the couch and tucked it around her. "Dinner isn't for another hour. Will you stay here until then?"

At the top of the hill above the house, hidden from view by the vineyards, Monique stood beside Henri's truck, arguing with Georges. "You are crazy! This is crazy! Someone could get killed! *I* could get killed. And if I don't, I'll probably go to jail. I won't do it."

Her pleas fell on deaf ears. "Don't be so dramatic—no one will be killed." He had no way of knowing that, nor did he care. "You will cause only enough damage to send them to the hospital. I need them all away from the house without planning. Macallister won't have a chance to disable his equipment, and I need uninterrupted time at his computer. If you cause enough damage, all three of them will be out of the house long enough." He looked at her with a hard expression on his face. "I thought you wanted to hurt them."

"I did ... I mean, I do, but ..." Monique was scared. She had embraced the *idea* of hurting them, causing them pain to match her own pain of rejection, but now that it was time to act, time for *her* to act, she was far less sure. And she couldn't quite see how she would get out of this uninjured.

"Wear the seatbelt and you will be fine." Georges guessed at the reason for her hesitation but remained unrelenting. He was impatient to get on with it and was unhappy that the stupid slut was vacillating now. "Besides, it will be more believable if you have some bruises, too."

Her eyes widened in surprise. "You actually *want* me to get hurt?"

He shrugged impatiently. *"Bien sûr, idiot.* You don't want them to think your little accident was intentional, do you?"

Monique shivered. He had a point. Her excuse for returning the truck at night was believable, as was the reason that she would come the long way around the top of the hill, dropping off new bee boxes at the far end of her mother's orchard on her way. She supposed she could weather a few bruises for the payday they would get if they were successful. She nodded reluctantly. *"D'accord,* I will do it."

Several hours later, in the dark of a moonless night, Monique spied Annie hurrying down the path to the barn with a bag slung over her shoulder. Looking past her, she frowned. *What was she doing alone?* Wondering what was going on, Monique shifted her position slightly to watch Annie slide open the barn door and enter. A moment later the lights went on. Looking back up toward the house, she still didn't see anything else.

Intéressent. This might just be better than the original plan. She had balked at the idea of harming Kaden, but she had no qualms about the woman. Hurting her might hurt Kaden emotionally, but not physically. She smiled to herself. And then he would need consolation, something she was more than prepared to give him.

It took her some minutes to hike back up to the top of the hill where she'd left the truck. She stopped to catch her breath and calm her nerves before getting in to start it up. She guessed Kaden would be heading to the barn soon, but if she could get there first, it would only be the American bitch who got hurt. *And me.*

Inside the barn, Annie set up her little surprise on a workbench in the corner, beside the row of empty tanks. She had begged Kaden to give her a few minutes before he joined her. He protested, but when she stated that he would ruin her surprise, he relented, confused but curious. Annie had done her best to stifle a laugh. *Men are so obtuse,* she thought as she struggled with the cork in the Champagne bottle. She knew that if he had stopped to think about it for half a minute, he would have figured it out, but fortunately, now she would get to see the surprise in his eyes. *And happiness,* she hoped.

Kaden stepped into the barn at the same moment Annie managed to free the cork, and it was only his good reflexes that prevented the cork from smacking him on the forehead. "Oh shit, sorry!" Annie's eyes were wide with astonishment. "I didn't see you!"

Kaden shook his head as he came toward her, curiosity in his hazel eyes. "I thought we agreed I'd be the one opening Champagne bottles."

Annie made a face. "But then it wouldn't be a surprise, and since this will be the last Champagne I enjoy for a while, I wanted to do it."

She poured out two glasses and handed him one, studying his face.

"What's this about, Annie?" Kaden didn't like the implication. *No Champagne for a while? Does she think she's going somewhere?*

Annie couldn't torture him any further. "It's about our future," she said softly, letting all the love in her heart show in her eyes, "and how happy I am to have one with you." She paused. "And our family."

Kaden stilled, his gaze boring into her, so heated that Annie's knees started to feel weak. Not breaking eye contact, Kaden set his glass down on the bench, reached for her with one hand while plucking her glass away with the other.

"Are you trying to tell me you're pregnant?" The hope in his voice and the sparkle in his eyes told her everything she needed to know.

She held his gaze, smiled a private little smile, and nodded. The next instant, she was crushed in his arms, so fierce was his reaction that he squeezed the breath out of her to the point where she squeaked. "*Ma chérie,* my beautiful love." His voice was hoarse with emotion.

He leaned down and captured her mouth in a searing kiss. She felt dampness on her cheeks and was surprised that she was crying, but then she realized she wasn't. The tears were Kaden's. He reluctantly broke the kiss, but held her close, leaning his forehead against hers with closed eyes.

She reached up and gently wiped the tears from his face with her thumbs. "I love you," she whispered, right before the night split open.

Monique was frozen with fear as the truck careered and bumped wildly down the dirt track, heading straight for the barn. Something was wrong!

Why couldn't she slow it down? She frantically pumped the breaks but they did not respond. *That bastard is trying to kill me!*

In a rare flash of insight, beyond the point of no return, Monique saw the truth of her predicament. Georges didn't care what happened to her, had no concern for her safety, and he'd tampered with the brakes to ensure she met his objective. Before she had time to form another thought, the broad side of the barn loomed ahead in her bouncing headlights.

Pumping useless brakes, her hand flew to the horn, honking wildly before she had to use two hands to yank the truck off its speeding course to the barn. It was impossible—she was too close and was going too fast to make the turn. Bracing herself, she closed her eyes and screamed as the truck met the corner of the building.

Inside, Kaden and Annie heard the honking, the squeal of tires and a desperate scream. Before they could react, the front end of Henri's truck came crashing through the wall.

Kaden threw himself against Annie and managed to get them out of its path just seconds before it plowed past where they had been standing. Shattered pieces of beams and siding showered around them, and there was a loud metallic groan. The roar in his ears was so loud, it was disorienting, but Kaden managed to scramble up and shove Annie further away as the last tank at the end of the row began to topple off its damaged mooring. The force of the fishtailing truck bed had smacked into it as it careered through the wall, and as it fell, it pulled a tangle of metal catwalk with it, screeching above them as it twisted from the pressure of gravity pulling it down.

Annie landed hard on her hands and knees, feeling the jolt of the impact ricocheting through her as her jaw snapped shut. *No fucking way,* she screamed inside her head, ignoring the pain and the roaring in her ears as she scrambled to her feet. She turned around just in time to witness the big tank crash down behind Kaden and lurch into him, knocking him flat. She shouted and lunged for him as the tank's motion was arrested, wedged between the second tank in the line, the truck that now rested askew inside the ruined barn, and the floor.

The force of the tank sent Kaden sprawling, but not far enough. The tank had rested momentarily against the second one in line, but that tank was now creaking and listing to the side from the weight pressing into it. If the first tank settled any further it would crush Kaden. "*No!*" Annie howled over the sharp blare of the truck's stuck horn. She didn't spare a glance at the truck but took hold of Kaden's elbows and pulled with all the strength she had.

It was an awkward hold because she didn't want to reinjure his wrists by pulling on them, and every muscle strained, but she didn't give up. She was sweating profusely, her heart pounding so hard, it might burst through her chest, but she was crazed with fear and pumped with adrenaline. With a surge of strength from sheer force of will, she got his inert body in motion and dragged him well away from the wrecked tank before slumping down on the cement floor. As she heaved in huge gulps of air, the second tank shifted and the first tank crashed to the floor, right where Kaden had been lying. Her last thought before she passed out was the frightful realization that Kaden had not even flinched as she dragged him across the floor. Her heart went cold as her mind went blank.

Fifty

A lone figure lurked in the shadows outside, surveying the damage and noting the three bodies. Satisfied, he slithered back into the woods to wait for the fourth player in his little drama to arrive. From what he could make out in the barn, Georges was confident the chaos he'd staged would occupy the household for many hours. He waited for a moment after Henri appeared before quietly making his way toward the house.

The scene that greeted Henri as he rushed into the barn, having heard the crash followed by the ear-piercing howl of the horn, might have been comical if it wasn't so horrifying. His old truck, battered now even more from crashing through the wall, sat innocently in the middle of the room. There was a body slumped over the steering wheel, accounting for the stuck horn. One large steel tank was crumpled on its side, a section of catwalk sticking up from it like a twisted appendage. Beyond the wrecked tank, he could just make out another body slumped on the floor.

He swore as he quickly picked his way through the debris to the truck, wrenched open the door and gently pulled Monique's limp body off the steering wheel. The horn ceased abruptly, plunging the barn into an eerie silence. Her face and hair were covered with blood. He checked her pulse. It was faint, but steady.

Henri left her there, unconscious, held in place by the seatbelt. When he rounded the end of the tank, he realized there were two bodies sprawled out on the floor and neither was moving. His heart lurched, and tears stung his eyes. He knelt beside Annie, smoothed the hair from her face, and felt for a pulse. It was beating rapidly and her skin was damp, sure signs of shock. There were scrapes on her hands and her face was smudged with dirt, but otherwise there was no visible damage.

Turning to Kaden, Henri couldn't stop the sob that tore from his throat. *Mon Dieu, pas encore, not again.* Sprawled out on his stomach, some two meters from the tank, Kaden was covered in dust but with no visible blood or injury. Henri felt for a pulse—it was steady. He surveyed the scene again, unable to fathom a purpose behind the destruction.

Relieved that everyone was alive at least, he allowed himself a few moments to steady his breathing. He went into the undamaged lab at the other end of the building and used the phone there to call the *gendarmerie* and an ambulance. Then he called Sophia.

His neighbor was the first to arrive, rushing in through the door only to stop in her tracks, eyes wide in horror. She let out a low cry as she rushed to Monique, but before she could touch her, Henri called to her to stop. "*Non, ne pas toucher à son.* We don't know how bad she is, and we don't want to make it worse. She is alive. The ambulance is on its way."

Henri turned back to Annie, who he'd been in the process of tending. He covered her with a tarp, and folded another under her head to give her a cushion against the cold floor. Her skin was clammy and gray, and Henri was frightened for her. She remained unconscious, and as he carefully ran his hands along her limbs and torso, trying to determine if anything was broken, she didn't flinch. Frustrated there was nothing more he could do for her, he turned to Kaden.

Sophia stood frozen in place as she watched Henri, torn between standing by her daughter and helping him. She saw the tears wetting his weathered cheeks. Kaden was everything to him, she knew, and the pain in his eyes was unbearable. Her own eyes grew watery as she watched him tenderly touch his nephew, trying to determine the extent of the damage.

The high-pitched *WAH-wah-WAH-wah* of a police siren could be heard on the road below, getting closer as it made its way up to the barn, an ambulance in its wake. The paramedics jumped out to attend the injured while the *gendarmes* stepped more carefully out of their vehicle to secure the scene. Neither Henri nor Sophia could explain what had happened, but they gave what little information they had, speculating on what they did not know for fact. What didn't make any sense to either of them was *why* Monique had been in the truck. The last Sophia knew, it had been parked in her driveway. A quick inspection revealed the brake line had been cut, a deliberate sabotage. The discovery caused further confusion and speculation.

Monique was carefully laid onto a stretcher after a restraining collar was placed around her neck, and transported to the waiting ambulance. She had suffered a blow to her head. In addition to a likely concussion, it was probable that she had damaged the muscles and tissues in her neck, the extent of which they could not determine without better facilities.

Kaden was checked, gently rolled over onto a stretcher and checked again. Henri was concerned about his ribs, having been fractured not four months earlier, but it was hard to tell if there was any damage. As the paramedic attending him palpated the area, he began to stir. Henri immediately knelt down beside him.

"*Kaden, c'est moi, Henri. Tu m'entends?*" *Can you hear me?*

Kaden groaned and started to move, but both the paramedic and Henri held him still.

"*Attende un instant, mon fils,*" Henri cautioned. "Let the man check you first. Can you open your eyes?"

Kaden stilled, took a breath, and forced his eyes open. His vision swam and he blinked hard, which only served to turn five shaky images into two. He shook his head and blinked again, finally seeing only one blurry Henri. "Annie ..." he slurred the word as he tried to sit up, but the two men held him down.

"She's here, calm down."

"The baby!" Kaden sounded panicked. "We ... we need ... we have to keep her safe ..."

As Kaden was stirring and mumbling incoherently, the other paramedic was attending Annie. He checked for injuries as Henri had done earlier, and she also began to stir. Rushing to her side, Henri tried to make sense of Kaden's slurred words.

"Annie, *petite,* it's Henri." He took one of her small, cold hands between both of his and gently stroked it. Her eyelids fluttered, she licked her lips and swallowed, struggling into consciousness.

Henri turned to the paramedic. "Can you fetch some water? The sink is in there, cups in the cupboard." He nodded toward the lab before turning his attention back to Annie. "Hold on, water is coming. Relax, you will be okay." Closing his eyes on a brief prayer, he added, "Kaden will be fine, too."

That got her attention. "Where is he?" She struggled to move, but Henri held her down gently while shushing her.

"Shh, don't get up. He is right here."

The paramedic returned with water and knelt down to hold Annie's head while Henri gently put the cup to her lips. She swallowed a small amount then nodded.

She cleared her throat and looked pleadingly at Henri. "Please, Henri, help me up. I have to see him."

Henri and the paramedic exchanged a concerned glance but helped her to sit up. She started to swoon, but Henri caught her. "I'm okay ... just ... just a little shaky."

Annie knelt beside Kaden, whose eyes had closed again, but when he felt her hands on his face he opened his eyes. "Stay with me," she whispered. "Please ... stay with me."

"*Chérie* ..." he whispered back, and reached for her hand. His grip was weak.

"Shh," she said softly. "I'm okay."

"His pulse is strong, but he's a little disoriented. Can you tell us what happened?" Henri was still kneeling by her side, and by now the other paramedics and the *gendarmes* had gathered around her.

Annie didn't take her eyes or her hands from Kaden as she spoke. "It all happened so fast. We were standing over there in the corner." She gestured to the now-destroyed section of the barn. "We were having a private ... uh, discussion ..." She didn't elaborate, so Henri let it go.

"All of a sudden we heard frantic honking, tires squealing, and then a woman screamed. In the next instant, the truck crashed through the wall. It would have run us over if Kaden hadn't grabbed me and dived out of the way. We landed there." She indicated where the tank was now. "Then the tank started to topple over, and Kaden shoved me out of the way again, but the tank crashed down before he could get out of the way, and it knocked him down." She closed her eyes at the horrid memory but couldn't keep the tears from falling down her cheeks.

Henri squeezed her hand, waiting. He glanced at the paramedics, who where both frowning. When Annie didn't continue, Henri probed gently. "Annie, when I came in, Kaden was not under the tank. He was lying here, where he is now. He was unconscious, but he was clear of the tank."

Annie shuddered, eyes closed, but slowly nodded. "I think … um, I mean, I think I remember …" She took a big gulp of air, struggling to continue.

No one said a word, waiting for her to continue. Annie took a few deep breaths, sucking back her panic at Kaden's slightly unfocused gaze. "I dragged him clear before the tank settled." She could feel many eyes on her, and hesitated. It sounded crazy even to her, and it was her memory. "I … I don't remember exactly, it all happened so fast, but … but, I remember seeing the tank knock him over then the second one started to shift. I remember grabbing his arms so I wouldn't hurt his wrists …" She closed her eyes. "I must have dragged him across the floor."

Henri exchanged glances with the *gendarme* in charge. "You may have saved his life then, *petite*. That tank, even empty, could have crushed him."

Henri hated hospitals, hated his loved ones being stuck there, and couldn't bear to see either Kaden or Annie dragged back into one. He had his own physician, whom he would call immediately, and argued with the paramedics about the benefit, or lack thereof, of hauling Kaden to the ER when there were no visible injuries. He eventually convinced them to let both Kaden and Annie stay, while they took Monique to the hospital. Sophia went with her in the ambulance, and the two *gendarmes* stayed to transport Kaden, conscious but disoriented, back to the house. Annie leaned heavily on Henri all the way up the path.

As they approached the house, Henri frowned and called a halt to the procession. He had been reading in his den when he'd heard the commotion, and he remembered being hindered in his progress to the back door because there were no other lights on in the house. He didn't recall turning them on, yet now a light shone from the kitchen.

"Something is not right," he whispered to the *gendarme* closest to him. "There are lights on that were not on before. There should be no one else in the house."

The *gendarme* nodded, slipping his pistol from its holster. They set the stretcher down in the yard near the door, with Annie and the other *gendarme* to watch over Kaden, while Henri and the first *gendarme* crept silently into the house.

Georges was so caught up in the challenge of breaking through Kaden's initial lines of electronic defense, arrogantly confident that he would remain undetected, that he missed the creaking of the floorboards in the hall as the two men approached. It was not until the office door swung open and hit the wall with a bang that he started and turned around from his position at Kaden's desk. Finding a pistol pointed at his chest, and no other exit from the room, he cursed.

<hr />

Annie stayed beside Kaden as he waivered in and out of consciousness, and to her relief, each time he came awake, he appeared more focused and alert. Henri called his physician––the best in the area––who arrived within the hour.

There was a visible bruise on Kaden's shoulder and another more concerning one on his forehead where he had likely banged his head when he went down. A second blow to his head so soon after his roof accident could mean further damage to his already traumatized gray matter. The doctor checked his pupils, did a few basic response tests and concluded that everything looked normal. His advice, in a word, was to wait.

Henri also insisted that Annie let the physician check her out as well. He suspected the truth but didn't want to pry. She allowed the exam, confiding in the doctor about her condition but swearing him to secrecy. She wanted Kaden to be 100 percent with her when they told Henri together. The doctor agreed, took a blood sample to confirm it, and otherwise allowed that she did, indeed, seem to be fine.

Late the next morning, Kaden jerked from a tortured nightmare of twisted steel and roaring chaos. He lay still as the sounds and scents of his surroundings began to penetrate, then tentatively opened his eyes. To his relief, his vision was clear in the bright morning light, and the pounding in his head was just a dull throb. He heard the sharp tone of Annie's voice downstairs, telling someone off, and he smiled. She sounded angry, which meant she was probably okay.

Annie strode into the room with an armful of sheets and headed straight for the bed. She'd had to practically rip them away from Sophia who, she knew, was only trying to be helpful. But Annie was damned if any woman, no matter how old, would see Kaden naked. She hadn't meant to be so harsh with the older woman, and would apologize later, but right now, stress colored her judgment.

She dropped the sheets when she caught Kaden's piercing gaze. There was nothing vague or disoriented about it. In a heartbeat she was kneeling beside the bed, tentatively reaching out her hand to his face. She gasped as he reached up and snatched it, pulling it the rest of the way so he could kiss her palm and snuggle it against his cheek.

"Hi," he said, his voice sounding rough.

"Hi." Annie smiled and felt the sting of tears in her eyes, but this time, they were tears of joy. *He's come back to me!* She wiped her cheeks and leaned down to tenderly kiss his brow, her heart constricting, pulse racing.

She helped him to sip some water, and he cleared his throat, never letting his eyes waver from hers as he reached for her hand again. The anguish was evident in his expression as he asked the question he dreaded. *"Our baby?"*

Her face lit up in a glowing smile. "Fine. We're both fine."

Five months later, March 1991

Annie stood up from the vine she pruned and stretched backward, hands massaging her lower back. Her fingers were stiff and dirty, but her hands were warm in her well-worn red fingerless gloves. It was winter pruning in the vineyards, the most important work to be done in the fields other than harvesting the grapes, and it was even more taxing and time-consuming than her experience of the previous May. At least the weather was sunny, if not exactly warm. Her belly was round but not huge yet, and she found that, other than a nagging backache, her stamina in the vineyard was good. She still wasn't as fast as the men, but she held her own—a fact she was inordinately proud of.

She looked down the row she'd been working, at the piles of canes in front of each vine, and allowed a self-satisfied smile. She thought about where she had been at this time last year, at her office in San Francisco, frantically pushing papers and filing tax reports. She laughed to herself. *My goodness, but has my life changed. And definitely for the better.*

At that moment, Kaden popped up a few rows away, looked around, and spotted her, then immediately frowned as he saw her rubbing her back. She smiled and shook her head—she was fine, she indicated—and was gifted with his handsome smile in return, before he nodded and knelt at the next plant in his row. He had tried to talk her out of joining the pruning crew, but she'd insisted, and he was wise enough to let her determine for herself what she could, and could not, do. He trusted her not to push herself beyond her limit, but that didn't stop him from worrying, which to her surprise, she found more endearing than annoying.

He had been beyond ecstatic when he learned she was pregnant, and despite the horrible events of that evening, she would never forget the sweet moments they had shared when he learned the news—that initial moment before all hell broke loose, and the second time, when he came back from a frightening bout of disorientation. That their child had been the first thing on his mind had squashed any lingering qualms Annie had had regarding his feelings about parenthood.

When he was able to get up from bed shortly thereafter, they shared their news with his uncle. Sweet, loving Henri had shed shameless tears of joy even as he confessed he had suspected, and Annie wasn't sure if the emotion was due to the prospect of finally having children running around the house or the glow of happiness that suffused Kaden's demeanor as he spoke of becoming a father. Either reason was fine with her. She'd never felt so loved, so welcome, so much an integral part of a family in her whole life.

It had been the same at their wedding, an intimate but surprisingly lively affair. They had not delayed their plans despite the damage caused by the reckless behavior of Georges and Monique. Once Kaden was back on his feet, essentially unharmed but for the nasty bruise on his shoulder, he had orchestrated the cleanup and repair of the barn as well as the replacement of the damaged equipment. Both perpetrators were arrested and charged, and then swiftly convicted. Monique spilled the entire story, admitting her part in it. Georges would be behind bars for some time for attempted murder, and although Monique received a somewhat lighter sentence, she too was incarcerated.

Sophia had been nearly inconsolable, but she accepted what she could not change. Her own guilt over the actions of her daughter would be punishment enough, and Henri, Kaden, and Annie all assured their friend that they did not blame her. In fact, they went out of their way to help her get through the agonizing process of watching her daughter go to jail. There was a grief that settled about the older woman after the incident, and Annie guessed it would be a long time before it lifted.

For their wedding, the entire contingent from the southwest had arrived, including Maurice and Fernand, Jean Claude, Nicole and the boys, and Juliette and François. All of Annie's guests made the trek. Marie was her matron of honor, and Jean Claude served as Kaden's best man. Henri acted as father of both the bride and the groom, beaming with pride and playing the charming host to everyone.

They picked the last Saturday of November to be married, coinciding with the American Thanksgiving holiday, and her new French family indulged Annie with an American-style Thanksgiving meal as her wedding dinner. Sophia, Henri, and Jean Claude did most of the cooking, with Marie, Annie, and Lori helping with authoritative directions on tradition whenever there was a question. It turned out more French than American and was more delicious than any Thanksgiving fare the Americans could ever remember, but the spirit of sharing and being thankful for family and friends was there, and it served as an icebreaker for the people from two cultures.

Kaden's two brothers declined the invitation but sent well wishes and generous gifts instead, which didn't seem to upset Kaden in the least. There was a reason he lived in France rather than England, Annie realized, and it was only partially related to the crash-and-burn story of his first marriage and former career. Kaden felt the pull of the land and the connection of family on French soil much more intensely than any familial connection in England. He had loved his childhood summers in France, and he had always shared a special bond with Henri and his mother's family. They in turn loved him, welcomed him, accepted him for what he was, and stood by him. They didn't have the wealth or position of his English family, but Annie knew how irrelevant that was to Kaden. And they accepted Annie unconditionally, which was the most precious gift of all.

It was quite a celebration. As she sat next to Kaden at the big table in Henri's dining room, being toasted, roasted, and teased, she silently gave thanks for the serendipitous circumstances that had brought them together, his persistence and patience, but mostly, for the man himself. It didn't matter whether she labored in a field, fished in a stream, crafted clever tax structures, or organized shipments of wine for import, as long as she was by his side, embraced in the incredible energy of his life and his love, she was complete.

As she knelt at the next vine in her row, sinking her knee into the stony soil and touching the gnarly old plant with practiced fingers, she smelled the sweet pungency of the earth, felt the morning frost on her fingers and the warm sun on her cheeks, heard the trill of birds in the trees and the soft buzz of insects nearby, and felt bound to the land. It was such a deep-seated feeling of contentment, it made her sigh. She was well and truly home.

Epilogue

Yosemite National Park, six years later, May 1997

"Hurry, Papa! We're almost there!" Five-year-old Henri stood at the top of the rise in the trail, impatient for the rest of his family to catch up.

Kaden and Annie, not twenty paces behind him, struggled not to laugh as Henri's little sister wiggled wildly in her perch above Kaden's shoulders, taking up the cry. "Hurry, Papa, hurry!"

"Wait for us, Henri," Annie cautioned. "You must walk with me on the next stretch." She held out her hand to him as she crested the rise, stopping for a moment to survey the view.

They hiked on the John Muir Trail high above the Merced River, looking down to where the river dropped off the precipice of Vernal Falls. It was a stunning vista, and they stood together, hand in hand, taking it in. The main trail continued up toward Nevada Falls, a beautiful white horsetail of water in the distance, but there was a short downhill spur trail that took them to the top of Vernal Falls. With a five-year-old and a two-year-old, this would be the extent of their trek.

Annie had been concerned about Henri's stamina for the mile-and-a-half uphill hike, but she shouldn't have worried. Little Marie had simply enjoyed the ride in her father's modified backpack, securely strapped in at his shoulder level so she could watch the scenery over the top of his head.

It was late spring, a gorgeous, sunny day in the California High Sierra, and a perfect day for this family outing. They had planned this short side trip as an add-on detour to their annual visit to San Francisco. Annie had wanted Kaden to see the place where she had spent so many happy days in her youth.

She had not been back to Yosemite in the seventeen years since her accident, and she was ready to bring closure to her memories of that fateful day when she had lost so much; ready to replace her last memories of this place with happier thoughts.

It had been her idea to bring the children. Normally, they left them with Henri and Sophia in Rasteau when they traveled for business, but Annie knew she needed her beloved children to be with her here, to ease the pain of the loss she knew she would experience by being in Yosemite again. Their youthful vibrancy, along with the incredible love of their father, was proof that life truly did go on, and that great tragedy did not have to mean the end of living.

"*Allons-y!* Come on!" Henri cried, tugging at her hand.

Annie laughed. With one hand clutched tightly to her son's, and the other laced with her husband's, she felt like a link in a chain.

"You best not keep him waiting, *chérie*. We'll be right behind you." Kaden winked at her as he let go of her hand, giving Henri the opportunity to pull Annie down the trail.

The river was flowing fast and furious, the spray tossed up from the frothy water flashing like diamonds in the sun. The sunny days melted the snow quickly in the high country, causing the river to swell with the runoff. Annie knew how dangerous the river could be and held tight to Henri's small hand as they stood at the railing, mesmerized by the sheer volume and force of the water raging over the lip of the precipice. The noise was deafening, with the cacophony of the dancing rapids above the falls and the crashing of tons and tons of water on the cliff face below, creating a roaring symphony of cymbals.

Kaden caught up with them at the top of the falls, and even little Marie seemed enchanted, reaching her pudgy little hands up as if to catch the glittering water droplets as they rose from the churning mass of water. Even though she was securely strapped in, Kaden held fast to her feet that poked out from under his arms.

After a few more minutes of watching the water crashing over the edge, they eased back away from the falls and found a flat rock farther back to sit on for a short rest. Annie fished juice boxes out of her backpack for Henri and Marie, then took a long swig from a bottle of water before handing it to Kaden. Henri immediately started telling Marie everything he had seen, oblivious to the fact that she'd seen it too.

Annie reached for Kaden with one hand and pointed down river with the other. "That's Sierra Point." She indicated a promontory with a railing, just visible high up on the right. He squeezed her hand and nodded in understanding. She didn't need to explain any more; Kaden knew the whole story, having finally asked her about it right before Henri was born. She had held nothing back, and he had learned of her private memories of her first husband and her deeply buried guilt about the loss of her first baby. She would always have a spot in her heart for them both, and he had come to terms with that. They were her past, a part of what made Annie uniquely her, but he was her present and future.

As Annie sat in the sun in the High Sierra, with Kaden's silent strength supporting her and her children jabbering away nearby, she felt a small knot of sadness loosen in her chest. This pilgrimage was a cleansing of sorts; her hope was that if she faced the place where she had suffered so much, the strength and love of her family would wash away the faded remnants of her pain.

At its most elemental, her life was not so different, really, than what she had dreamed of the last time she had sat on a rock in this beautiful place. She had a husband who adored her, and whom she loved with all her heart, two beautiful children, and a place in the world where she was accepted, respected, and loved. In the irrelevant details of where she lived and what her work entailed, her life could not have been more different, but in the end, those were just details. Her life was simple and good, and she would not change a thing about it.

Sensing her need for solitude, Kaden distracted the children a few yards away while Annie continued to contemplate the vista before her. She watched the light play with the mist above the waterfall, remembering how it had looked from another perspective all those years ago. As the power and the roar of the pounding water reverberated in the air around her, she finally understood that she had nothing to regret. She had loved and lost, and now she loved again. She was unashamed that life had given her a second chance, and for the first time since she awoke from that coma, she felt no guilt.

She turned at the sound of her little girl's squeal, and laughed as she saw a chipmunk scurrying away from Marie's outstretched hand. Annie watched as her handsome husband picked their daughter up and swung her high above his head, causing another squeal and a peal of laughter. In that moment, another revelation came to Annie: life was too precious to indulge in sad thoughts of things that could not be changed. There was barely enough time as it was to enjoy the small pleasures of daily life. If she wasn't careful, she would miss them, and she had no intention of missing a thing.

As she stood up to join her family, that lingering sadness drifted away, and Annie knew she was finally free of it.

Join Annie and Kaden as their love takes root and flourishes, and intrigues entangle their lives in ways more difficult to prune than the grapes of their vineyard.

Louise Marcel crosses the pond with a perfect American smile and a flowing Southern accent to study medieval architecture. What she discovers and rescues from the ruins is the ruins of Alex Bouvier, the next generation of Kaden and Annie's dynasty, who has been beaten and left for dead.

Alex is on to something … but what? And for whom? Louise must decide if he is more trouble than he is worth. And can he be trusted with her own hidden agenda?

Help her decide, in *French Twist* the next in the series *A Foreign Affair* by Nancy Milby, available now on Amazon.

A word about

A Word with You Press
Publishers and Purveyors of Fine Stories

In addition to being a full-service publishing house founded in 2009, *A Word with You Press* is a playful, passionate, and prolific consortium of writers connected by our collective love of the written word. We are, as well, devoted readers drawn to the notion that there is nothing more beautiful or powerful than a well-told story.

We realize that great writers and artists don't just happen. They are created by nurturing, mentoring, and by inspiration. We provide this literary triad through our interactive website, www.awordwithyoupress.com.

Visit us here to enter our writing contests and to become part of a broad but highly personal writing community. Improve your skills with what has become a significant, *de facto* writers' workshop, and approach us with your own publishing dreams and ambitions. We are always looking for new talent. Visit our store to buy from a distinguished list of our books, which include the work of a Pulitzer Prize winner, an award-winning poet, and first-rate literary fiction. Attend our seminars and retreats, and consider joining our growing list of published authors.

A writer is among the lucky few who discovers that art is not a diversion or distraction from everyday life; rather, art is an essential expression of the human spirit.

If you are such a writer, join us on our website, www.awordwithyoupress. com. If you have a project to discuss, we will assess the first thirty pages you send us *pro-bono*. Send your inquiries to the Editor-in-Chief, Thornton Sully, at thorn@awordwithyoupress.com. Be sure to indicate in the subject line *"pro-bono assessment"* and send your submission as a word doc attachment.

A Word with You Press
Publishers and Purveyors of Fine Stories
310 East A Street, Suite B, Moscow, Idaho 83843

Available or coming soon from

A Word with You Press

The Mason Key
Volume One
A John Mason Adventure
by David Folz
A street urchin in England about the time the Colonies declare independence cheats the hangman to begin this historical adventure series. He discovers that his father's death may not have been an accident at all, but part of a broader conspiracy.

The Mason Key II
Aloft and Alow
A John Mason Adventure
by David Folz
The historical saga continues as young Mason becomes
a mid-shipman on the very ship on which he was as
stow-away at the conclusion of *The Mason Key, Volume One.*

The Mason Key III
The Return
A John Mason Adventure
by David Folz
Mason and Marie fend off pirates en route to her father's plantation. John struggles with the Third Principle, Honor, and the Cruelty of Slavery while making his way back home.

Almost Avalon
by Thornton Sully
A young couple struggles with love and life on the island
frontier just twenty-six miles west of Los Angeles.

Angus MacDream and the Roktopus Rogue
by Isabelle Rooney-Freedman
Young adults on a mythical Scottish island save the world. Delightfully illustrated by Teri Rider

The Wanderer
by Derek Thompson
A stranger wakes up on a deserted beach and embarks on a journey of discovery. The first in our *Magical Realism* series.

The Coffee Shop Chronicles, Vol. I,
Oh, the Places I Have Bean!
An anthology of award-winning stories inspired by events that occurred over
a cup of coffee.

The Coffee Shop Chronicles, Vol. II,
A Jolt of Espresso
Stories condensed to exactly 100 words each, inspired by our favorite brew.

Visiting Angels and Home Devils
by Dr. Don Hanley, Ph.D.
A discussion guide for couples.

The Courtesans of God
by Thornton Sully
A novel based on the real life of a temple priestess in the palace of the King
of Malaysia.

Bounce
by Pulitzer Prize winner Jonathan Freedman
A nutty watermelon man, a spurned she-lawyer, a frustrated carioca journal-
ist and a misanthropic parrot set out to Brazil to change the world.

Left Unlatched
in the hopes that you'll come in...

A Book of Poetry
by R.T. Sedgwick
Winner of the 2012 San Diego Book Awards – Poetry.

The Boy with a Torn Hat

by Thornton Sully
Debut novel was a finalist in the 2010 USA
Book Awards for Literary Fiction
"Henry Miller meets Bob Dylan in this coming of age romp played out in
the twisted alleyways and smoky beer halls of Heidelberg. Sully is a cun-
ning wordsmith and master of bringing music to art and art to language.
Excessive, expressive, lusty, and once in a blue metaphor—profound. Here
is what I mean: 'Some women are imprisoned like a tongue in a bell—they
swing violently but unnoticed until the moment of contact with the bronze
perimeter of their existence—and thenthe sound they make astonishes us its
power and pain and beauty, and its immediacy' —Wunderbar"
—Jonathan Freedman, Pulitzer Prize winner

Raw Man
by Pulitzer-Prize nominee Fred Rivera
This lightly-novelized Vietnam memoir, now required reading at major
universities, derives its title from the author's epiphany: "Twenty-seven years
after I got on the flight home, I saw that Nam war was just *raw man* spelled
backwards. I'm pretty raw today."

A Word with You, Vol. I
The best from A Word with You Press

An anthology of select winners from the literary contests of *A Word with You Press* from 2009 to 2015

Falling for France
by Nancy Milby
The first in *A Foreign Affair* series finds Annie Shaw having to choose between a successful career and real romance with a French aristocrat, and wanting both.

French Twist
by Nancy Milby
The saga continues as American archeologist Louise Marcel becomes entangled in nasty business on French soil, as she conceals her own hidden agenda.

Finding France
by Nancy Milby
The third in *A Foreign Affair* series finds Gabrielle Walker lamenting a life unraveling when a letter informs her she is the inheritor of a large estate in France. Then it gets complicated!

Finding Home
by Nancy Milby
Etienne, the recurring enigma in the series *A Foreign Affair,* is brutal to his enemies but a gentle giant to those he loves. Can the secret woman in his past enter his life again? Perhaps, but not with complications—some predictable, but some…

Max and Cheez go to Spain
by Naureen Zaim and David Ulrich
A delightful illustrated children's book finds two cats on the first of many adventures, stowing away in a suitcase to Spain. What other countries will they investigate, now that they have the travel bug? A great way to introduce young children to the cultures of the world.

A Word with You Press˙
Publishers and Purveyors of Fine Stories
310 East A Street, Suite B, Moscow, Idaho 83843

www.awordwithyoupress.com

About the Author

Nancy Milby lives in Laguna Beach, California, with her husband, Steve, and their lovable cats Beckham and Boo. After finding her own way out of the corporate world, Nancy founded the local cooking school, Laguna Culinary Arts, which, for twelve years was synonymous with great fun, great food and wine, and great culinary adventures to destinations around the world. Currently, Nancy runs the breakaway division, LCA Wine, a boutique wine shop and wine education center, where she shares her passion by teaching wine classes and leading small groups of food and wine enthusiasts on overseas adventures.

To check out the fun, go to www.lcawine.com or www.nancymilby.com.

40489174R00207

Made in the USA
Charleston, SC
07 April 2015